Imperial Privateer

Imperial Privateer

Andrew Moriarty

Version 1.00

ISBN 978-1-956556-24-7

Special thanks to my dedicated team of beta readers – A J, Adam G, Aleeta, Barbara M, Bryan, Christopher G, Danny H, Dave M#1, Dave W, David H, Dave M#2, Djuro D, Elizabeth S, Greg D, Haydn H, J Anderson, John E, John S, Jolayne W, Justin H, Keith C, Kent P, Lorna, Michael G, Michael R, Nathan T, Penny L, Peter B, Ralph J, Ryan P, Scott, Skip C, Susan G, Tigui R, Vince P, and to my editor Beth Lynne.

CHAPTER ONE

"I've never robbed a bank before." Scruggs flipped the cylinder of her revolver open, checked the loads, then shoved it into her thigh holster. "Is it hard?"

"There's a knack to it," Senior Centurion Anastasios said, marching beside her. "Takes practice. And keep your weapons hidden. Still people on the street. We stand out enough as it is."

Scruggs scanned the darkened street. The main street from the spaceport didn't run to streetlights, or sidewalks, or sewers. But it had selections of businesses that were open at night. This block contained a tire repair shop with tires spilling into the street and a pawn shop with armored doors and bars on the window. A cluster of three smokey restaurants edged the corner. She surveilled the patrons—they might not shoot her for looking at them, but if she shot first, they'd shoot back.

Most pedestrians wore loose shirts over shorts, some light-weight business suits. Centurion Anastasios wore drab gray ship coveralls over a dark skinsuit, cinched with a dirty creased utility belt. Scruggs's starched uniform, new belt, clean back-pack and shiny pouches gleamed in the store lights. "Sorry, Centurion."

"Don't worry too much. We don't want people connecting three armed wanderers with the upcoming bank robbery. Not the way it's done."

Dena, sauntering a step behind the two, laughed. "Robbed a lot of banks, have you, Old Man?"

Ana counted on his fingers. "Seventeen. Well, sixteen. I robbed one twice."

"Why in the Emperor's name were you robbing banks?"

"Because that's where the money is, of course. Private, next item. Rules of engagement. Confirm those bullets are frangibles?"

"Yes, Senior Centurion. No deaths, like you said."

Dena stepped next to Scruggs and draped her arm over the younger woman's shoulder. "Look at you two hardened killers, worried about hurting somebody."

"Centurion says that the police always work harder if there's violence during a robbery, so only as much violence as necessary."

"Who decides the necessary amount of violence? Is that you, Old Man?"

"Nature Girl." Ana scowled at Dena. "First, this insurance place is supposed to be empty at night, according to our contacts. Second, if it is not, there will be no shooting unless absolutely necessary. We want to get in and get out quickly and quietly. Thus the frangibles. And speaking of deaths, take care with that slingshot of yours. You can break some bones, but not heads, understood?"

"You're not the boss of me, Old Man." Dena removed her arm from Scruggs's shoulder, flipped a metal sphere into the rubber pocket of her slingshot, extended, aimed, and let fly. She shot a wall two hundred feet away, next to a preening raccoon. The animal yowled and fled into the dark.

"Don't hurt him!" Scruggs said.

"Relax, Baby Marine." Dena flexed her rubber band. "I didn't hit him. He's not hurt, only embarrassed."

"Don't hurt the animals."

"I don't hurt animals, only people. Unless I'm in the woods and hungry, then the rules are different."

"Good. I like animals." Scruggs wiped sweat off her face. "Warmer than I expected."

"Midsummer by the lake," Dena said. "Skinny-dipping weather."

The crew turned down a side street. Archan-3c, despite being in a triple star system, was always dark. The triple system was all dwarf stars. They produced only twenty percent of sol's illumination in the visible range, but plenty of infrared heat to make up for the light.

"It's like being in a damp oven," Dena said. "These clothes are sticking to me. They'll be impossible to get off."

"Sorry we're cramping your style, Nature Girl." Ana settled his pack lower on his shoulders. "You'll have to keep your clothes on for once. But I'm sure you can find some other way to misbehave. You always do."

Dena stuck her tongue out at Ana, then peered around in

the gloom. "Not here. Dismal place. Nothing open looks fun. We should have picked somewhere more exciting."

"More excitement means more authorities, more cameras, more notice. Warehouses full of cotton and tobacco don't warrant much security. And carrying all these weapons past the main gate would have been noticed." Their ship was parked at a pad a few miles inside the starport. To avoid scrutiny, they'd loaded up their packs with guns and stooged past shipping warehouses closed for the day. After cutting the perimeter fence, they snuck into the warehouse district.

Dena kicked the ground and dirt puffed up. "You should have at least told me about all the dust. I wouldn't have worn my good boots."

"Those are pretty." Scruggs pointed at Dena's knee-high, fitted black leather boots. "They look good on you."

"You have a pair, why not wear them?"

"They don't go with the outfit."

"Outfit? That's not an outfit. You're wearing a skinsuit and military coveralls, Baby Marine. You look like a skinnier version of the old man there."

"Form follows function, ladies." Ana waved at his own outfit. "Harness, spare ammunition, holster, flashlights, racks for my helmet and air system. Everything the well-dressed bank robber needs."

"She still could have worn the boots. Much more stylish than those clodhoppers she's got on."

Scruggs lifted her foot up. "Good, solid marching boots, and if I have to kick somebody, heavy enough to do damage."

Dena snapped her sling. A light pole a hundred feet away

thwanged as the shot hit it. "I don't let them get close. Old Man, in this light, you're almost invisible in that fashion crime, but I can see her clearly. How come?"

Ana adjusted his pack. "It's the same gear, more or less. Mine is more worn. The gleam's off it—I darkened everything with grease. And it's all soft and saggy. The private still has that shiny new scrubbed look about her, and she's all starchy and straight lines. Straight lines stick out in the twilight."

"Should I go roll around in the dirt, Centurion?" Scruggs asked.

"I'll bet you'd like that, Old Man," Dena said. "Baby Marine here squirming around. Scruggs, open your shirt an extra button and do some squirming."

Scruggs blushed.

Ana laughed. "No need for that. Age and life experience tarnishes everything eventually." Ana produced a pill bottle, then popped the top off and shook one into his mouth. "Age and experience indeed."

Lights gleamed at the corner. A vehicle ground along the street ahead of them, the lights blinding. Conversation stopped. Dena stepped right to clear her sling hand. Scruggs and Ana unsnapped holsters.

The lights illuminated the trio, then the driver switched them off. Gears clashed, and a fourteen-person bright pink bus pulled next to them. Durriken Friedel, Imperial Duke, sometime-fugitive, former lover of the Empress of the known galaxy, and the frequently drunk-driving pilot of their starship, the Heart's Desire, stuck his head out of the passenger window.

"Get in. We're late."

"Navy, what in the name of a tabbo's tail is this?" Ana stepped back from the curb. "It's pink. It's huge. It's loud. And did I mention it was pink? You were supposed to find something discreet that wouldn't be missed."

"It's got plenty of room for all of us. It belongs to the local taxi company. All their cars are pink, and they're all over the city. Now we're another one. We took it out of an unsecured parking lot with dozens of others in there. It won't be missed 'til morning. That's why I took it."

Ana crossed his arms. "You? You stole it?"

"Centurion." The driver, Gavin Crewjacki, their engineer, leaned over. "Technically, it was me that stole it."

"We both did." Dirk nodded.

"No, we didn't. I did the actual stealing, with the tools and all."

"All you did was cross a couple of wires."

"After taking off the key lock, and checking which wires were live with the voltmeter, yes."

Scruggs tapped the car body. "Neat. Can you show me how to steal a car, Engineer?"

"Sure."

Dirk held up his hands. "You saying I didn't help?"

"You did hold the flashlight."

"See?"

"Until you dropped it in the dust and broke it. But that's okay. I didn't need it. I was fine without it." Gavin gunned the engine. "I could have done it myself, but it was nice having you along. For... companionship. You know."

Dirk gritted his teeth. "Fine. I stand corrected, you stole it yourself. But either way, it's stolen, and we're here. Everyone, get in."

Scruggs clambered in first. "I'm going to rob a bank!"

"It's not a bank," Dirk said. "It's a mutualized insurance company."

The others climbed in behind Scruggs.

"Does it have a vault?" Dena asked.

"A locked cabinet. That's where the software will be."

"Will there be money in the vault?"

"It's a cabinet, and not very much, but I suppose some."

"Then it's a bank. Baby Marine, you're going to rob a bank!"

"Yay!" Scruggs said. "Adventure awaits."

***

Mutual of Archan occupied a three-story building, midway between the warehouse district and the commercial center of town. Stretching an entire block, it was standard Imperial colonial construction: metal girder frame, plastic panels as walls, floors, and ceilings. Two doors faced the street, no windows. After a twenty-minute bumpy drive in the Pink Pony, as Ana had christened their ride, they stopped three blocks away and assessed the situation.

"How come no windows?" Dena asked.

"Windows let in sun and heat," Dirk said. "And make it harder to build. This would have been some sort of Imperial offices, in the early days. Might have been a scout or a Navy building, back when they had a base here."

"Dismal place to work, very dismal."

"Neighborhood's not great either." Dirk pointed. "A tattoo parlor, warehouses, what looks like a car-repair shop, and a woodlot."

"A woodlot?"

"People need wood. For repairs, and fireplaces. Odd place for an insurance company, though. You'd think the neighborhood would be nicer."

"I'd like the roads to be better," Gavin said. "Those ruts and bumps were insane. And haven't they ever heard of asphalt? Why dirt roads in the middle of a city?"

"Low-tech cities are like that. Pave what you can afford. Yes, Lee?" Dirk keyed his comm. "Lee? Repeat that, please."

"I said, status update, Pilot." Lee Michaelson, their navigator, doctor, and emergency pilot, was back at their ship, monitoring local police channels. "Everything is clear so far. No warnings on the radio. I took liberty of paying for some passwords—I can get into the police tracking system. One problem—your comms are all broadcasting locations to the city services. If I can pick it up, somebody might hack in. Either way, there will be a record."

"Beacons off, now." Ana fiddled with his comm. "Go dark."

"Outstanding work, Lee. Going dark." Dirk shut his beacon off. "Gavin, pull us up in front of that building and let's get to work."

"Nope." Ana shook his head. "That's not how it's done. Parking any vehicle, especially this pink pony, directly in front of the place we're hitting will draw notice. And five of us exiting at once will draw even more notice. No, we'll deploy scouts down the side streets to observe the situation. Once the scouts have eyes on the target, we'll wait for their report. If all is clear, we'll send in the burglary team."

"Centurion, "Dirk said. "Have you forgotten that I'm in charge?"

"Completely forgotten." Ana nodded. "It's like your leadership never existed at all. Oh wait, it never did. Private?"

"Centurion?" Scruggs said.

"Get out here, scoot across the road into that alley across there." Ana pointed. "Tactically advance down that back alley until you're behind that red building, over there, next to our target. Get up on the comm net, check around the corner and observe. Use whatever sensors you have, check out every inch of the back yard. Nature Girl?"

"I'm not tactically advancing to anything," Dena said. "All this dust is killing my outfit."

"Makes you harder to see. That's good."

"This outfit is designed to make people want to look at me, not hide me. Especially men people."

"Good for you. See that doorway over there?" Ana pointed out a deep recess in a shop that sold sports uniforms.

"Yes. And why?"

"Get in there. Keep your eyes on the street here, the target, and that side street area. Watch for motion, lights, anything. Keep your slingshot handy. If somebody spots Scruggs or me, you'll have to cover our retreat, but quietly."

"Retreat from where?"

"From the bad guys."

"Who are the bad guys?"

"No idea, but they always turn up. Engineer," Ana said. "Do a U-turn, bring us back to that last cross street. Then circle around to that other main street we saw, take us down two streets past that crossroad—no, three streets—there's a park there. No lights in a park, this pink pony can wait there. I'll get out and come at the target from the other side. In fifteen minutes, we'll have Scruggs, Dena, and me watching from three concealed vantage points. If it all looks good, we'll wave you in and you can go to work on the door, and the vault once you're inside. Once you're in, we'll all move in to assist, leaving appropriate rear protection."

"The cabinet is a two-man job, Centurion," Gavin said.

"Ms. Dena here has shown some skills in the past at breaking out of restraints, dealing with handcuffs, that sort of thing. She can be your second. We'll call her in once the coast is clear. That work for you, Nature Girl?"

Dena snapped her slingshot. "Always did enjoy being tied up."

"That's weird," Scruggs said. "Why would you want to be tied up?"

Dena rolled her eyes. "I keep forgetting how young you are."

"I'm nearly the same age as you."

"Chronologically, yes, but... I'll explain it later. After the fight."

"Thanks!" Scruggs grinned. "That will be fun!"

"More fun than you can possibly imagine," Dena said. "So, Centurion, I wait here, watch, and if you clear it, I go and meet Gavin at the front."

"Yes. Scruggs and I will cover you once you two are in."

"If you want me to fiddle with locks, I'll need some tools—"

Gavin pointed over his shoulder. "I've got lock picks like you were playing with on the ship in my bag. I bought a spare set, figured they might come in handy."

"Look at you, Mr. Preparedness," Dena said. "Helping a girl out."

"You forgot something, Centurion," Dirk said.

"What?"

"Me."

"I didn't forget you."

"You didn't give me anything to do."

"That's prudence, not the same thing as forgetting you. Stay in the car and watch."

"Stay in the car?"

"And watch. You might learn something."

"I'll remind you, Senior Centurion, that I'm an Imperial Navy officer."

"And if we discover a dreadnought-class battleship inside, I'll be the first to call you in to drive it. But if there's a spaceship in there, it's well hidden."

"And I also remind you, I'm the pilot of our ship," Dirk said.

The comm crackled as Lee joined the conversation again. "Pilot, we've all agreed that for things like this that the centurion has more experience. We're supposed to follow his lead. It sounds like a good plan to me."

"Me too," Scruggs said.

"Me three," Gavin said.

"Me four," Dena said.

"Fine." Dirk crossed his arms. "I'll stay in the car."

"Ladies, out you go," Ana said. The two women popped out of the doors, into the darkness. Gavin had pulled the fuses. The interior lights didn't come on. The women melted into the dark. Gavin headed toward the second drop-off point. He got Lee up on his comm and had her talk him through some alleys and less bumpy roads. While Gavin was distracted with driving, Dirk twisted back to talk to Ana.

"Centurion, did you discuss the rules of engagement with Ms. Scruggs and Ms. Dena? And check their ammunition?"

"You care what happens to some random security guard, Navy?"

"Somewhat. I'd rather not kill some poor old guy working nights to make a little extra money, especially when we can scare him away. The police will investigate murders more strenuously than burglaries. Then there's the matter of Scruggs and Dena. They're both a little young to be developing the habit of killing everybody they meet right away. It's not good for them. If there's killing to be done, you and I need to do it."

"She's killed people before—"

"In a firefight when somebody's shooting at you and you're shooting back is one thing. Or in Dena's case, trying to push you out of a hovering spaceship. But you know going in counting on gutting everyone you meet isn't conducive to sleeping well at night in the future."

"I've killed lots of people. And I sleep at night."

"So have I. And I sleep at night too, which says something not nice about the both of us. I want to make sure they don't have to face the same dilemma. They're part of my crew. I'm responsible for the two of them. Do you agree?"

"I do, I do." Ana nodded in the darkness. "Understood, Pilot. Already taken care of. I confirm non-lethal rules of engagement in effect."

"Pilot? You haven't called me that in a long time."

"That's because you haven't deserved it in a long time."

"It's not for me, it's for them."

"Understood." The car stopped, and Ana swung the door open. "One thing, Navy."

"Yes?"

"You said you and I have to do any killing. Why is it okay for us to do it?"

"That's easy." Dirk laughed. "We're beyond redemption. Good hunting, Centurion."

***

"Got a visual, Centurion," Scruggs said. Mutual of Archan extended an extra story above the surrounding warehouse-office combinations. With its bland walls and beige-painted logo, Scruggs thought it looked like the sort of place that dispirited office workers trooped into every working day, performing meaningless tasks until they died. She suppressed a shiver. Only running away and joining the crew of the Heart's Desire had kept her from that fate. "Quiet, one security light on my side overlooking a narrow parking lot. Spots for a dozen cars parked behind the building, in covered parking just under the upper floors, all empty. And a recessed loading bay in the warehouse part. No other lights or movement."

"Entrances?" Ana's voice rasped as he panted over the radio.

"Nothing here."

"No back door? Side doors?"

"Don't see any, Centurion."

"Huh. Dena, any movement out front?"

"Nothing, Old Man. Quiet as the woods at midnight in a snowstorm."

"Lights?"

"Some sort of night light visible in the lobby. Other than that, no. No streetlights in front either."

"And nothing at all from my side." Ana coughed. "Not even lights. Engineer, you're up."

"On my way." Gavin's door slamming echoed down the quiet street.

Gavin walked down the street, carrying a toolbox in one hand. Scruggs moved in closer until she was across the street on opposite corners from the building. Dena joined Gavin at the front door. The two burglars fiddled with the lock, then pulled the door open. Lights from inside flashed into the street until Gavin killed them.

"All good. We'll leave it open for you, Old Man," Dena said.

"Meet me at the front, Private." Ana moved down the street, staying in the shadows, until he was across from the entrance. Motion to his front. He tracked it with his revolver, then relaxed as Scruggs materialized out of the gloom. They exchanged hand signals and met at the side of the entrance.

Ana flowed through the unlocked front door, Scruggs directly behind. They took guard positions on the inside.

"Centurion," Scruggs said. "Go to scrambled, please."

Ana switched to a private channel. "What can't you say over the common radio, Private?"

"Robbing a bank will be kind of fun, but that Tribune guy gave us plenty of money. Do we have to take somebody else's?"

"We're not doing this for money, Private. We're doing it to get ship software to trade for a laser."

That was their prize, and the reason for the clandestine work. Their ship lacked weapons. Gavin had found a contact that pointed them to a crooked shipyard willing to install a laser on the Heart's Desire, if they could get a laser. Dirk had found a company that would sell them ship weapons—and run by a former girlfriend of his, no less. But weapons were useless without good software. Lee had been updating their navigation program, and she pointed out that the local insurance company for several big trading lines, Mutual of Archan, also provided software updates as part of its service.

Gavin went back to his contact, and the contact agreed that this insurance company might have what they needed, including honest-to-Jove Imperial software modules. That included aiming, targeting, and the coveted random-walk evade programs. Not for general sale—they wouldn't release them without Imperial Navy permission. But if they could get the software some other way...

Ana had located the company offices and shadowed their workers to a local bar. After observing them for two days, he picked a likely target and sicced Dena on him. Dena used her leather outfit, a drugged drink, and compromising photos. Presto! Now they had the plans for the office, including the combo for the safe where the software modules would be stored.

"Can't we go somewhere else and buy it?"

"Sure, we'll tell the nearest Imperial naval base that we're there to get fitted with offensive weapons, that we're authorized by Tribune Devin, who they are supposed to shoot on sight. You can do the talking since there's an Imperial death warrant out on you as well."

Scruggs giggled. "Good point. Do we need a laser?"

"You can never have too many weapons, Private."

"But we don't know how to use it…"

"What makes you think I don't know how to use it?"

"Sorry, Centurion."

"Having an armed ship means unsavory characters will think twice before pushing us around. What did I tell you?"

"The best way to win a fight is to not get into it from the start. Act tough and people will think you are tough. And only start a fight on your terms, not theirs."

"Outstanding."

Gavin's voice cracked over the radio. "Centurion, are we sure we've got the right address?"

"Yes," Ana said. "I don't make mistakes like that."

"Are we sure this is the right company? Mutual of Archan?"

"I double-checked the address. Triple-checked. And to make it easier for you, Engineer, there's a twenty-foot sign painted outside on the wall that says, 'Mutual of Archan.' How's that for confirmation?"

"It's supposed to be just offices up here."

"That's what the plans we were given said. All offices. One locked cabinet in the biggest office, where they keep the program modules. Why are you asking this?"

"You better come up here."

Ana cursed, turned sentry duty over to Scruggs and stomped up the stairs. Dim night lights lit the corners until he reached the third floor. He pushed the crash door at the top, and stumbled into a brightly lit room.

"What in the Emperor's name?"

Their stolen plans showed the upper floor as wide open, except for a row of glass-fronted offices at the back. The middle office was their target.

Reality was different. Instead of an open concept office area, they were in a brightly lit, constrained hallway. Gray metal doors lined cinderblock walls.

"Where did this come from?"

Dena rapped her hands on the doors. "Steel. Got a torch we can use to cut through with?"

"I've got grenades would do it," Ana dropped his pack. "But I don't want to blow up the building. Did your guy say anything about this?"

"He was a computer guy. He worked downstairs but said he could steal the files. His office is downstairs," Dena said. "Saw the name on the list in the lobby."

"Are those walls concrete? Or can we bash through?"

"Solid as a rock," Dena rapped the wall. "Ouch."

"How are they having this heavy a setup up this high, without collapsing the building?"

"Do I look like an architect?" Dena asked. "Where did all this come from?"

"Don't know."

"Should we abort?" Gavin tried to stuff a screwdriver under a metal plate on the wall. "I can't even pry the locking plate off here to get to the electronics. It's welded tight."

Dirks voice came over the radio. "What's going on?"

"Not now, Pilot. Engineer, what do you think?"

"I think bigger security means bigger reward. Must be something really impressive behind this wall to require all this security."

Dena tapped the wall again. "Didn't expect this from the outside, that's for sure. And we're here now. Might as well give it a try."

"Give heavy steel doors and concrete walls a try?" Ana grunted. "Which we lack the tools to drill through or tunnel through. I think I have a spoon. You can start on the wall, Nature Girl, unless you have a brilliant idea to get us in."

"I do, actually." Dena pointed at the wall. "One small flaw. Door hinges are on this side. If we knock those hinge pins out..."

Ana tapped his comm. "Private?"

"Centurion?"

"You still have that pry bar in your pack?"

"Yes, Centurion."

"Get up here."

It took thirty-three minutes of sweaty work, but they

managed to tap the rods out of the hinges. The first rod took twenty-five minutes, because they had to angle Scruggs's pry bar to tap the rod up and muffle the noise with Gavin's jacket. But once they had that rod out, they used it as a tap to hammer the other hinges free and got the remaining two out in a matter of minutes. A few tugs and they were able to jigger the entire door free of the frame, even with the locking bolt still extended on the handle side.

"And easy," Ana said. "Lean it against the wall."

The four of them manhandled the heavy door away from the entrance.

"Good job, crew," a voice said from the top of the stairs. All four reached for weapons, then relaxed as Dirk stepped into view.

"I told you to stay in the car," Ana said.

"Sounded like you could use some help," Dirk said.

"How long did you stand there, watching us haul this stupid door free?" Dena asked.

"I said you sounded like you needed some help, not that I was going to be the one giving it," Dirk said. "Emperor's ear lobes. That's a lot of computers."

They all crowded into the doorway. Racks and racks of computers connected by arm-thick bands of fiber optic cable filled the room. Lights flashed, fans hummed, and ozone crackled.

Dena shivered. "Cold wind in here. Feels good."

"You need good air conditioning to keep all this power cool. Otherwise, the servers burn up," Scruggs said. "Centurion, why is this here?"

"No idea. Pilot, tell me you didn't leave the car out front?"

"Nope. I heard Scruggs talk about that loading bay. Our bus is parked in that handy-dandy entrance out back, hidden under the building. This is a lot of computers. A big data center."

"Where's our software?" Gavin asked. "I want that laser."

"There must be something more than software here," Dena said.

"And we'll find it how?" Gavin asked. "We're not set up for electronic intrusion. We're here to grab ship cassettes and get out."

"Anyone see any cameras?" Ana asked.

Gavin pointed at the ceilings. "Too much clutter, cable raceways, power outlets, wireless hubs, all sorts of electronics. We wouldn't see a camera if it was there."

Ana drew his revolver. "We may not have much time, then. Scruggs, clear left. I'll clear right. Check every aisle and look for hiding places. Engineer, you and Nature Girl, I see offices on the far side. Check them out. Pilot?"

"Yes, Centurion?"

"Stay in the car."

"No car here, Centurion."

"Pretend. Don't move. Polish your uniform buttons."

Dena loaded her slingshot, and Gavin collected the dropped pry bar, and they moved down the main aisle. Scruggs and Ana called to each other as they disappeared to the sides. Dirk waited until they disappeared, then sauntered past the racked computers to follow the burglary team. The computers were stacked floor to ceiling, with no gap at the top or bottom, and thick bunches of wrapped cables ran in all directions.

Gavin and Dena crouched in front of the door to the biggest office. Dena's pants didn't leave much to the imagination. Dirk took a moment to admire the view, then squeezed past her. She gave him a dirty look but continued messing with the door.

"Office-class lock." Gavin set down the pry bar and fished in his toolkit. He used a pointed screwdriver to pop the lock panel off, and crossed wires. "I'll have us in in a minute."

Dena rattled the handle. "Nope."

Gavin crossed more wires.

"Nope."

More wires.

"Still nope."

Again.

"Nope."

Gavin cursed, dug inside, and fumbled with the lock again. "Try it now."

Dena shook her head.

Gavin picked up the pry bar and swung it with full force at the door handle. The lock snapped off and bounced off the ground.

"What was that?" Ana asked over the radio.

Dena pushed the door in. "All good. Engineer has us in the main office."

"Keep it quiet."

"Bite me," Dena said. She and Gavin high-fived then dived into the office.

Dirk continued down the aisle, rattling door locks.

Dena and Gavin re-appeared.

"Well?" Dirk said.

"No software," Dena said. "Cables, metal stuff, and wires."

"Workroom." Dirk rattled another door. "This one looks as big as that one. Try here."

Dena and Gavin moved over and worked on the panel again.

Dirk continued down the hallway, rattling more doors. One swung open. Dena and Gavin stopped and looked at him.

Dirk shook his head. "Cleaning supplies." He peered into the gloom, flicked the lights on for a better view, then disappeared inside.

Ana and Scruggs returned from clearing the room and took a guard station behind Dena and Gavin.

"Nothing, Centurion," Scruggs said. "Just rows and rows of computers."

Ana nodded. "That's all I saw."

"Big place."

"More than you'd need for insurance."

"These are very powerful computers, Centurion," Scruggs said.

Dena and Gavin hissed at each other while they worked on the door.

"Making any progress?" Ana asked.

Dena stood and put her hands on her hips. "We're fine, Old Man. Go shoot a helpless prisoner or something."

Ana shook his head, then tapped the nearest computer.

"Very powerful computers, you say. And how do you know that, Junior Private Soldier?"

Scruggs pointed at a black wire snaking up the racks. "Power cables. Those are special. Very thick. Lots of amps coming into this place. Much more than regular computers need. More electricity means more processing power."

"So it does. Good observation, Private."

"And no model numbers, or manufacturer's plates. All they have is power lights."

Ana regarded the row of computers. All identical, gray faces, with a single green light. But no words, no model numbers, just racks of devices and wires. "Another good observation, Private."

"What sort of private company doesn't put their name on their products?" Scruggs asked. "Or what sort of private company buys things that don't have a model number?"

"Yet another good observation, Private. You're just full of interesting facts tonight."

"It's important, Centurion. This doesn't look like a regular insurance office."

"No, it doesn't, and you're right, it isn't. This isn't what I expected."

BANG. CLANG.

Ana and Scruggs turned, weapons ready. Dena had hammered the handle off the office door.

Dena brandished the pry bar. "Complaints, Old Man?"

"Nope. We're security. You're entry. We have our own problems. Carry on." Ana turned back to Scruggs. "Something's not right. Get my pack from the door."

Scruggs ran off to retrieve it. Dena and Gavin disappeared into the office. Ana surveyed the room. Wall-to-wall, floor-to-ceiling computers, special computers at that. Extra security on the doors. Reinforced floors. His arm hairs were standing on end. Something bad was going to happen. Very soon.

Dirk yowled, and boxes crashed as they fell over in the closet. Ana swung his revolver to cover the closet. Scruggs dropped Ana's pack and aimed her revolver at the door. Dirk stumbled back into view, green liquid running from his hair.

"Emperor's balls," Dirk said.

Scruggs laughed. "Pilot, you're... dripping."

"What's going on?" Ana asked.

"Pilot's covered in floor polish," Scruggs said.

"You sure?"

"I recognize the brand. You made me polish enough with it."

Dirk rubbed his face, and used his sleeves to clean around his eyes, coughed twice, and spat.

Ana holstered his revolver. "Thank you for securing the cleaning closet, Navy. I was worried about the danger from some over-aggressive mops. It's a relief to know you're on the job."

"Thanks, Centurion." Dirk rubbed his hair. "This place is strange. Extra computers, extra security."

"What's up with it?" Scruggs asked.

Ana smiled. "That's the question, isn't it? Well, we know something is not right. Too much security. Reinforced walls. Secret computers. Piles of software. There is much more to this place than meets the eye. Whatever it is will surprise us. Know what I say about that, Private?"

"No, Centurion," Scruggs said.

BONG. ALERT. BONG. ALERT. Red lights flashed on the walls and the speaker wailed an alarm.

"I hate surprises."

CHAPTER TWO

"That was not done with regular weapons. A warship did that." Subprefect Lionel, second in command of the Imperial Star Ship Pollux, frigate class, pointed to the display. "See there? That's one of the containment magnets. It's cracked. You know how big an explosion you need to crack a ruthenium magnet?"

Tribune Devin, sitting in the command chair in the bridge, shook his head. "No, I don't. How big?"

"What?"

"You asked if I knew how big an explosion you needed to break one of those magnets. I don't."

"You need a big explosion."

"How big?"

Lionel leaned back in his chair. He and Devin sat next to each other in separate command acceleration couches on the Pollux's bridge. The bridge was a two-deck-high ten-meter circle, flattened at the front and back. The main screen occupied the front wall, the navigation and helm stations behind and below it. Sensors, communications, and a spare console faced left, and two weapon stations and a spare console sat to the right. The back wall was a hatch and a station for a Marine guard.

Pollux had received scattered reports of suspicious ships in the Verge. They'd been patrolling some remote verge systems where the Nats might stage a flotilla or pause for refueling. The Pollux was at full action stations while they scanned. Like the rest of the bridge crew, Lionel was in a full military skinsuit, with boots and gloves attached, his helmet racked on his shoulder. "Well, really big."

"How big is really big?"

"It's, like, never mind, Tribune."

"No, no, I'm interested. How big? Biga-big. Super-big? Humongous-extrapolic-big?" Devin spread his arms wide. "Bigga-bigga-big-gong?"

Lionel glared. "The Tribune is pleased to be facetious."

"I don't know what that means."

"You don't know what facetious means? You're educated, from one of the first families of the Empire."

"I had a sheltered upbringing. Is it good?"

"More normal than good, I'd say."

"Helm?" Devin said.

Trevor, the helm officer, looked over his shoulder. "Sir?"

"Am I facetious?"

"Every day sir."

"Indeed. Glad I'm consistent. Well, what can you expect from the Mad Dog of the Verge? Subprefect, any word from our boarding party?"

"The Marines report nobody alive. No heat signatures anywhere. Just in case, they're sweeping the ship. Should we have a naval party go over? They might spot something the Marines miss."

"Never mind," Devin said. "We'll let the Marines handle this."

"Sir," Carroll, the communications officer interrupted. "The Marines report that the safe in the captain's quarters has been cut open, the ship's locker is empty of weapons, and the locks have been cut off the secure cargo boxes in the hold."

"Warship crews stealing things? Pirates?"

"We'll leave the Marines to it," Devin said. "Subprefect, accompany me to my quarters for a drink."

Lionel raised an eyebrow. Devin put a finger to his lips, then pointed aft.

Lionel coughed. "Helm, you know where to find the Tribune and me if you need us."

The two men were silent until they arrived inside the Tribune's quarters.

"Bigga-bigga-big-gong?" Lionel asked.

Devin ran his hand over his bald head. "I needed to draw attention away from your damage assessment."

"And why, Tribune, did you need to do that?"

"I wanted the bridge crew to forget it. I'd already done my own damage assessment."

"Going to share?"

"Nope. Going to show you some pictures, though. Remember that cruiser that we fought at Sand Harbor?"

"The one that nearly killed us all and left our bodies to

freeze in orbit for all eternity? That one? I do have a dim recollection of it, yes."

"Let me show you the damage assessment—that that helmsman guy made."

"That helmsman guy? Which one?"

"The one, you know, the one..." Devin waved his hands.

"You forgot his name. You forgot one of your officer's names."

"I'm an Imperial Tribune. Almost a sector governor. There's a war on. I've got lots of responsibilities."

Lionel crossed his arms and glared. "One of your Sand Harbor veterans? And you forgot his name?"

"It's a big ship."

"No," Lionel said. "No, it's not."

The silence stretched.

"Oh, to Jove with it all." Devin hit his comm. "Imin?"

"Sir?" Imin's voice came over the comm.

"When we're secure from action stations, invite all the junior watch officers in groups of three to dinner for the next week. Each once. Cook something nice. And break out the good wine."

"Yes sir. Good wine would be wasted on some of them sir."

"You think my officers don't deserve good wine?"

"Sir," Imin coughed. "Two don't drink at all, as I'm sure the Tribune knows. Religious reasons. And one drinks only beer. Stout, as I recall. Lieutenant Lukas is allergic. He'll drink, but he turns bright red and gets that horrible rash, and of course Lieutenant Carrol is trying to get pregnant. The doctor doesn't think alcohol's a good idea."

Tribune Devin glared at his comm, then glared at the Subprefect. Lionel glared back.

"Imin, make sure that there is a drink of choice for each of them when they arrive. You can choose anything from my personal supplies."

"Young Lieutenant Trevor has mentioned he wants to taste Amiens brandy someday."

"Give it to him. Send me the schedule. And a seating plan."

"Yes sir. Will the Subprefect be joining you?"

Lionel yelled at the comm. "No, Imin. This is all on the Tribune."

"Very good sir. Um, Tribune, if the Subprefect isn't going to be there, perhaps I should give the Tribune a copy of each officer's service record to study beforehand as well. Just to refresh his memory."

Lionel smiled. "An excellent idea, Imin. Thank you."

"Thank you, Imin." Devin cut the connection. "Um. Which one is Trevor?"

"Nope." Lionel shook his head. "You have to figure that out on your own."

"I hate tests." Devin frowned. "Why does everybody still follow me? I don't even know most of their names, do I."

"You're brave. And honest. And you lead from the front. You've never asked them to do anything you wouldn't do yourself."

"Good way to get killed."

"Everyone says you have a death wish. There's even a betting pool on it."

"What are the odds on me?"

"Not good. Want me to put some of your money in?"

"What would you bet on?"

"Your money? You live through everything, of course."

"Why?"

"Well, if you lose, you're dead, and don't have to pay." Lionel shook his head. "Are you sure you went to Staff College? I thought you had to be bright for that?"

"Loyalty is more important than intelligence."

"Then all the people on your side end up being the stupid ones?"

"I never really looked at it that way. Given the way the noble class acts some days, true though. Well, take a look at the battle damage report from Sand Harbor that Lieutenant TREVOR made up." Devin brought a report up on his screen.

"You're guessing."

"Yes. Did I get it right?"

Lionel laughed. "Surprisingly, yes. What am I looking at here?"

"Damage photos. Of the enemy ships at Sand Harbor. What our cameras saw. And note which ship made the hits."

"Right, damage photos." Lionel swiped the pictures to his screen. "Pollux makes a devastating hit. And another. Great shooting on Pollux's part. Must have a top-notch executive officer. More devastating hits by Pollux on the enemy. Huh! One of the corvettes made a hit. It was the Moose Jaw, I believe. Must have been an accident. Pollux hits again. Pollux. Pollux. That executive officer is on his, or her, toes. Another.

Moose Jaw hits. Another accident of course. And Pollux again..."

Lionel stared at the photo, then swept back one. Then forward. Then back. Then rapidly back another half dozen until he stopped again. "This can't be."

"What can't be, Subprefect?"

Lionel fiddled with his display, and two pictures appeared on the Tribune's screen. "These are the damage shots from Moose Jaw's shooting. Two separate hits on two separate ships. Control lines shot away. Scorching where the lasers tracked along the hull. Some puddling here, melting. Here, that's a burn-through. Do you agree?"

"Of course, Subprefect."

"Here," Lionel said, "are a half dozen of the many hits made by the executive officer of the Pollux, a wizard of targeting."

"Pollux is lucky to have him."

"Don't you know it. And here is the characteristic damage. No puddling. No scorching. Just pieces of the hull missing from explosions. Larger than the frigates, of course."

"Of course," Devin acknowledged. "They look different to me."

Lionel swiped and one of the Moose Jaw's pictures showed next to the Pollux's. "That's because the Moose Jaw is armed with a single laser, military grade, which damages by transferring energy to the target—scorching or burning the surface. It attacks from the outside in."

Devin slow-clapped his hands. "Excellent lecture, Subprefect. And the other damage?"

"The Pollux-class frigate is armed with new model positron beams. They produce a stream of particles that are timed to decay inside the target, annihilating themselves in a matter-anti-matter explosion. This creates the characteristic explosion pattern, without burns or scrapes or melting. Because of where the destruction happens, the damage looks more like it happened from the inside out."

"You should have been a professor."

"One of my objectives, in my younger days."

"You have a love of knowledge?"

"I had a love of young female college students. What a place to meet girls. But no, look at this."

Lionel swiped his screen, and the Moose Jaw's photos disappeared, and a new one appeared.

Devin nodded. "Looks like the same damage pattern."

"It is." Lionel grimaced. "It is. And, as you know, this is a picture of the engine room... The former engine room of that freighter out there. The damage pattern looks the same because it was the same weapon. That freighter was destroyed by a warship—one with a positron beam weapon."

"I concur, Subprefect."

"We're a Pollux-class frigate. We're armed with positron guns."

"We are? What a surprise."

"Without giving up any secrets, Tribune, I was given to understand that this was a new experimental weapon."

"It is, Subprefect, it is."

"Then who has positron guns, other than us?"

Devin grimaced. "Another Pollux-class frigate. Or some

other regular naval ship. There's a warship out here destroying freighters."

CHAPTER THREE

Korvettenkapitan Felix Kruder waited in the rear as the shuttle cleared out. As a naval officer under orders traveling up to the Union of Nation's fifth largest shipyard—the closest to the border with the Accursed Empire—he should have been seated at the front of the shuttle. He should also have been in uniform and have some idea of why he was there. Not very respectful. But service is service, and liquor is liquor. He waited.

The naval officers from the front of the shuttle exited to the salutes of the shuttle crew. Then the senior civilians in their somber suits returned formal greetings as they departed. Kruder waited his turn, put his battered cap on his head, then marched to the front.

"Pardon me, Leutnant," Kruder said. "Could you give me directions to—"

The junior pilot looked at his worn skinsuit and merchant coveralls. "Sorry, Dad, you'll have to look it up on the station board."

Kruder stared. The silence stretched until Kruder shifted his bright blue eyes to the senior pilot.

"I said, Dad, you'll just have to—"

"Shut up, Hans." The more senior pilot's eyes locked onto Kruder's battered cap—much abused, peaked, with a white cover. A War Navy captain's cap. "Where are you going, sir?"

Kruder supplied a ring and spoke number, and the pilot gave detailed directions. Kruder thanked him and the pilot braced to attention and saluted. Kruder didn't return it. He wasn't in uniform, after all.

As he strode away, he heard the junior pilot complaining. "Why so nice to that old man? He's just a washed-up merchant officer."

"With that hat? He's a washed-up merchant officer the same way the old man is just an ex-professor. Keep it up and we'll both be running hydrogen shuttles out on the rim."

Kruder walked up stairs, around rings, down stairs, made brief detours past secured and guarded locks. Secret work going on there. Twenty-five minutes later, he arrived at the office he was supposed to visit. There was no sign, just a numbered, locked door. He pushed the call button and entered when buzzed in.

Another junior leutnant sat behind a desk in front of an inner door. His right hand hid on his lap. He didn't salute. Or even stand. The room consisted of metal walls and floors with pipes and conduits above. Nothing on the walls. No other furniture, not even chairs.

The leutnant nodded. "Good morning, Korvettenkapitan Kruder. You are expected. Please wait a moment." The leutnant brought a pistol from below the desk. Not the standard revolver of a ship's officer, but a much more effective, and expensive, Navy-issue gauss pistol.

"A gauss pistol? Who are you afraid of, Leutnant?"

"Nobody and everybody sir." The leutnant keyed the comm on his desk and waited for the far side to answer. "He's here sir. Case Yellow, sir. Yes sir."

The leutnant typed a code on his console, and the door behind him clicked. "Go right in, please, sir."

"Normally, junior officers stand to attention and salute."

"Not here sir. Not today. Go right in, please."

"Go right in to who? And why?"

"Inside, please, sir."

"What is going on? This is most irregular."

"All your answers are behind that door, sir."

Kruder shook his head. "We'll be speaking more about this when I'm done, Leutnant."

"Sir."

Kruder stepped past the desk and pushed through the door behind. He strode into the inner office—easily twice the size of the outer one. A slight, elderly, balding figure sat behind a desk. The desk was larger than the one outside but had the same standard computer console. He wore thick glasses but still squinted at the screen. Next to the console was a portable computer, of a type that was used to encrypt high-security messages.

"I don't understand what—" Kruder drew himself up to attention. Good God, it's the Old Man himself! He's supposed to be in the capital. What's he doing here? "I mean, Kruder, reporting, Konteradmiral Techand."

Admiral Techand looked up from his console. "Yes. Welcome, Kruder. Out of uniform, I see."

"As requested by my orders, sir!"

"Yes. Good. Casual without being slovenly. Just like a senior merchant officer. How long were you in the merchant service, Kruder?"

"Total, sir? Fifteen years. Longer, since during my reserve Navy service, I was still active—"

"Fifteen years is plenty. This freighter you commanded, how long was she yours?"

"Admiral, I commanded three different freighters over time, including—"

"The Elizabeth Kimball."

"Ole Liz? Twenty months, sir."

"What's the longest voyage you took on her, outside of Union space."

"I was in the Confederation for five months, sir."

"Never refueled? Not in the Confederation?"

"Refueled? Sir, I—"

"It's a simple question, Korvettenkapitan. Did you refuel or not? We all know there are issues with supplies in the Confederation. How long did you go without replenishment? Food? Fuel?"

Kruder slid out of attention, he was so confused. "We couldn't be sure of anything with them sir. We took all our food and supplies with us. For the whole trip."

"And fuel?"

"We processed from gas giants, sir. The whole way. I didn't spend a penny on fuel."

"I'm sure the owners were impressed." Techand pointed up. "There's a merchant ship at docking bay 94. I want you to go and inspect her. The yard crew will be there. Speak to them, ask all the questions you need to ask them, then report back here tomorrow."

"Sir?"

"Did I not make myself clear, Korvettenkapitan?"

"Sir, I…" Kruder squared his shoulders. "No sir, you did not. I am confused. Why am I inspecting this ship? And what am I inspecting it for? Fitness, but for what?"

The admiral glared at him, then leaned back, removed his glasses, and rubbed his forehead. "You are correct. I was not clear. This ship was a freighter. She is being converted, in a special way. You are to assess her modifications."

"Modified how?"

"That will be made clear by the dockyard staff."

"And who will command her, Konteradmiral?"

"You, of course. Now get over there and complete your inspection. Finish it by this time tomorrow. No written report but return here and be prepared to answer questions. Dismissed."

Kruder climbed three levels to the connection corridors and skipped along in the lower gravity. Docking bay 94 was on Ring J, one of the outermost rings. It took almost forty minutes of climbing, walking, and at one point pulling down a low-G ladder to access that part of the shipyard. The naval rating guarding the hatch checked his identification before passing him.

The unnamed freighter attached via its main air lock didn't look special. Big for a tramp freighter, capacity for a hundred containers at least. More, depending on how deep he could stack them. Kruder couldn't get a good count because the trusses were... strange. They were loaded full of containers, which was odd in a shipyard. What cargo master wanted their containers sitting unused in a shipyard for a year?

The ship's air lock was unguarded, like any air lock would be for a merchant ship, so Kruder marched in. The bridge hatches gaped open to his left, so he started his inspection there. Eight consoles with built-in acceleration couches. Two pilot, two navigation, two engineering—if the engineer ever bothered to come up from the drive room—and two general purpose. The standard eight-pack for merchant ships.

Kruder had never been on a merchant ship where all eight were working or needed.

The first surprise was the hab module. It wasn't. It was a second bridge, with no less than sixteen consoles installed, but not powered.

"Who are you?" a voice behind him said.

Kruder turned. A freckled, red-haired man stood with hands on his hips. "Kruder. War Navy. Who are you?"

"Hoss. Yardmaster. I've been waiting for you for two days. Do you have some identification?"

Kruder and Hoss exchanged information. Hoss was a military yard gang boss.

"Right, let's go," Hoss said. "I've got crews out on the

hull working, and I'm not happy that you're late. We've had to hold up some items 'til they're signed off. Get your thumb ready."

"I'm not late, I just got notification. The admiral only saw me today."

"Still later than we were told."

"Bring it up with the admiral."

"Oh, I will, I will. Admirals don't pump no hydrogen here. Let's go."

Kruder pointed at the different consoles. "What are these?"

Hoss sighed. "Another one. Those, Mr. War Navy, are called consoles. They are computers used to control the ship's operations, things like atmosphere, life support—"

"I know what consoles are. I'm not an idiot. I already saw the bridge. What I want to know is why there are sixteen of them here. What do you need them for?"

"For the weapons and sensors."

"Weapons? On a freighter?"

"Well, Mr. War Navy, can't go to war without weapons, right?"

"Freighters don't need weapon consoles. If they had weapons, which they don't, you could run them from the pilot's console. Or any console."

Hoss crossed his arms. "You don't know why they're here?"

"No."

"I'm not sure if you're stupid or ignorant. Or both."

Kruder gritted his teeth and bit back a reply. Yelling at yard workers did not get the work done faster. "Pretend I'm both, Herr Yardmaster. Why so many extra consoles? What weapons? I do not understand."

Hoss uncrossed his arms. "You don't know, do you?"

"No."

"Okay." Hoss powered up one of the consoles. "I'll show you here. Are you at least familiar with this type of freighter?"

"I've commanded three like him. Eighty containers, hundred-fifty containers, and hundred containers."

"Good enough." The console beeped. Hoss typed an authorization code in. "Standard hundred-twenty container freighter. Standard jump and thrusters for this model, nothing special there, but we swapped the power generation for a top-of-the-line model. You'll have three times the power generation that this model normally does."

"Three times the power generation means three times the fuel consumption for power."

"Which is why," Hoss brought up a diagram on the console and highlighted the aft container ring, "this entire container ring here has been replaced by giant fuel tanks. And not one, not two, but four hydrogen cracking plants. Naval models, four times better than civilian. You can refuel sixteen times as fast."

"Fuel tanks? It looked like a regular container ring to me."

"Yes, it does, doesn't it?"

"What am I going to do with all that power?" Kruder asked. Only Military vessels need this much power. Or have they done something special?

"First, run your extra life support modules." Hoss highlighted the second from aft container rings. "We've added eight extra modules for purification, freezing out waste gasses, cracking oxygen if necessary."

"Now I have triple power, and eight times the life support. What do I need that for?"

"To run—" Hoss highlighted all the containers in the second and third rings—"life support for all these crew modules. All these container spaces have been replaced with berths—acceleration couches for the crew, some cabins, and high-density housing. You'll need all that life support. You're rated for five hundred berths."

"Five hundred? These freighters have twenty or thirty crew, and maybe a dozen passengers. What will I do with five hundred?"

"You'll need them to manage your weapons," Hoss said. "Gunners, maintenance, sensor operators, that sort of thing.

"What weapons? I didn't see any weapons."

"Here, here, here, and here. Eight double turrets. Lasers. Plus six slug throwers for short-range actions. And hardpoints for future expansion."

"I told you I didn't see any weapons. There are no turrets on this ship."

"True, no visible turrets." Hoss hit his comm. "Lentz? Where are you? Yes. Stand by to decamouflage number three and number eleven."

"Decamouflage?"

"Watch." Hoss manipulated the console, and the view changed to an external camera pointed at a group of containers. "What do you see, War Navy?"

"I see container rings, with standard containers stacked up, ready for unloading."

"That's what we expect you to see." Hoss tapped his comm. "Decamouflage numbers three and eleven. Go."

Hoss held up his fingers and started counting..

"One, two…" Nothing changed.

"Three…" A panel flipped up on the middle container.

"Four, five." A complete dual-laser battery popped out and commenced traversing and elevating.

"Six, look below—" A second container one-sixth of the circumference from the laser had popped open, and a radar antenna was swiveling out.

"Seven, eight, radar has to cool and focus…"

The laser turret completed its three-sixty spin, and the elevation reached eighty degrees. The turret paused its traverse, and the elevation dropped down.

"Nine, laser would be ready now, and…" The radar steadied. The console in front of Hoss bonged. "And ten. Firing solution anywhere on this quadrant of the ship. Not as much coverage as a naval laser on its turret, of course—you don't get the same angles or altitude. But with eight double turrets spread around the ship, you can always get two of them on target. You need to decamouflage to use active sensors. But the passives, the radar detectors, and radio scanners, they're always on—hidden behind radio-transparent coverings. And the long-range telescopes too, they're hidden as struts. Have to move the ship to point them, but no big deal."

"What is this vessel?" Kruder asked.

"Have you read about a Q-ship, Herr War Navy?"

CHAPTER FOUR

"We're getting out of here," Ana shouted. "Grab that software and get ready to move. Scruggs! Eyes on the door!"

"On it, Centurion." Scruggs shouldered her pack and dashed to the front of the data center, disappearing through the gaping double door entrance.

Ana stuck his head in the main office. "Grab whatever software we need—Emperor's ears."

Gavin, Dirk, and Dena stood in front of an open metal cabinet. Hundreds of square numbered drawers lined shelves. Dena had pulled out one of the drawers. Lined up in each drawer was a row of one hundred colored one-inch square modules. She handed a software cartridge to Dirk. "What about this one?"

"They're just part numbers." Dirk spun the inch square modules between his fingers. "What's an N-300-4523-794? What's it do?"

"You're a pilot, you tell me."

"I just fly the ship, I didn't build it. Gavin?"

Gavin pulled out another drawer. "No idea, Skipper. I didn't expect this many. I thought maybe a dozen. And with a legend."

"Don't you use these cassettes in Engineering?"

"Engineering software comes like these, but it's installed on the drive consoles. It's separate from the ship computer. And it's labeled."

The bonging alarms silenced, and the regular lights died. Emergency lights lit from the corners.

"Centurion?" Scruggs came over the radio in the quiet.

"What's going on out there?"

"Nothing. I found the main power panel at the bottom of the stairs, and I pulled the breaker to kill the alarm. All the lights are out down here as well."

"Outstanding idea. Keep watch. Navigator, are you on this?"

"Yes, Centurion. Local police have dispatched a car to check out a silent alarm, heading to your address."

"That wasn't a silent alarm," Ana said. "But whatever. Navigator, can you see the ship computer from where you're sitting?"

"Yes."

"We've got navigation programs inserted, don't we?"

"Sure?"

"What color are they?"

"Color?"

"Yes. Go check."

Lee was silent for ten seconds, then came back. "All my Nav programs are yellow."

"Outstanding," Ana said. "Engineer, when you get updates, do they come on cartridges?"

"Sure?"

"What color?"

"I don't know. Blue. Green?"

"Not yellow."

"Definitely not."

"Can't restrict by color then. Okay, kids," Ana said. "Load up all the software you can carry. But get a mix of colors. If you see a color you don't know, dump it in a bag. Once you've got something of everything, we'll go with it."

Dena and Gavin yanked out drawers and rummaged for different colors, stuffing their pockets.

"Dirk, come here," Dena said. Dirk stepped up and Dena started stuffing cartridges into his pockets. "Red, green, chartreuse. Burnt orange, regular orange."

"Hey," Dirk said. "Take some yourself."

Dena stepped up, slapped her skintight pants and flipped her jacket open to show a revealing bodice. "What software am I going to hide in here? I've got room for a basic maintenance program and a list of edible plants. A short list. The Old Man and Baby Marine are loaded down with weapons and Gavin has his tools. Take off your belt."

"What? Right now. This is not the time…"

Dena dropped to her knees in front of Dirk.

"Dena, I'm flattered, but really, we don't have any privacy—"

"Shut up, Navy Boy." Dena bent down and tucked his coverall pants into the top of his boots, then pulled the cuffs tight. "Now the belt." Dena grabbed it, yanked it free and threw it aside, then reached up and unzipped his coveralls down his chest.

"Woman, what are you, oh—"

Dena grabbed an entire drawer of multicolored software and upended it onto his chest. The cartridges showered into his coveralls, ran down into his pants until they stuffed up. "Shut up. Gavin, dump as many as you can into your bag. I'll load up Fatty here."

Gavin stuffed his pockets and his carry bag. Dena kept dumping different random drawers down Dirk's pants. Ana collected what fell loose and dumped it into his pack.

Dena popped open a small door inside the locker seeking more drawers, revealing a metal door with a dial. "Look what we have here."

Gavin tapped the dial. "Combination lock. Mechanical. I can't hack into it. I'll have to drill it. That will take time. Time we don't have."

"You don't always need to do it the hard way." Dena examined the office. "Three desks. Senior is probably over there." She marched across the office and lay down on the ground next to the desk and pulled out drawers over her head.

Dirk stuffed more software in his pockets. "Now you're taking a nap?"

"Not here, not here... got it. 36-24-36. Got it." She slid out from under the desk and headed for the safe. Left, right, left and she had it open. "Combination was written on the bottom of one of the drawers. Men have limited imagination." She pulled a tray out from the safe and waved a group of software modules covered in black and white stripes. "These look special. Smaller, heavier, and this funny color. I'll keep them with me for now."

"Uh oh," Dirk said.

"What's uh oh?"

"That's not ship software. I've seen pictures of those. Those are codebooks. One-time codebooks for use with coding machines."

"Why would the Imperial Navy have codebooks in an insurance company's office?"

"Those aren't Imperial codebooks. I think they're Nat. Give a merchant ship a codebook like that, and the Nat government can send them secret messages."

"Meaning, this isn't just an insurance company, it's some sort of spy outfitting place for the Nats?"

"Could be."

"Let's grab them and go." Dena shoveled the rest of the Nat cartridges into Dirk's skinsuit.

"How did you know that the combination would be under the drawer?"

"I saw a combination written on the bottom of a drawer once."

"What were you doing looking up at the bottom of a drawer?"

Dena tapped his cheek and smiled. "How about you use that limited imagination to figure it out?"

"Centurion!" Scruggs said over the radio. "Movement. Two vehicles just pulled up. I see long guns."

"The police—wait, long guns?"

"For sure. Uh oh. Centurion, there's some sort of crew-served weapon on the back of one of those trucks."

"Crew-served weapon?" Ana keyed his comm. "Lee, is that the cops outside?"

"No," Lee said. "Police aren't there. They're reporting they've been delayed by a three-car pileup."

"Outstanding. Private—"

BOOM. The building rocked, and smoke puffed up the stairs and into the data center. They heard the bang of a revolver, and then the rapid tat-tat of automatic weapons.

"Grenade, Centurion. They just blew the doors. I fired out and now they're returning fire. That machine gun—"

"Get out of there," Ana yelled.

"Don't have to tell me twice, Centurion," Scruggs said. The firing paused, then another, softer BOOM rang out and the firing started again.

Ana raced to the front, cursing. He'd expected to only have to deal with police, so he had no rifles or shotguns, only revolvers, some small grenades, and his emergency surprise.

He propped open the rightmost stairwell door and dropped to the floor.

Scruggs's feet echoed as she raced up the first half of the stairs. The solid floor-to-ceiling concrete wall hid her until she turned the corner on the landing. Ana counted. Ten slaps, two stairs at a time. She slid into position next to him, rolled onto her side, and fumbled out shells for her revolver.

"Do you have anything other than frangibles, Private?"

"You told me that's all I was supposed to take, so that's what I took."

"That I did. Completely my fault." The floor shook. Something heavy fired into the building below, smashing glass and knocking down walls. Ana cocked his head and waited until the firing outside lessened. "Soon as that stops, they'll rush the door, and then charge up the stairs. Get ready with some grenades."

Scruggs finished reloading her revolver, and placed it by her side, then dropped her pack, and pulled four grenades out, and lined them up on the ground. "Ready, Centurion. Good thing you brought these."

"You can never have too many grenades. Speaking of." Ana pointed at the door to his left. "If they try to bounce their grenades up at us off the wall behind the landing, they'll hit that door and bounce right back down. You see a grenade coming up, dive left and hide. After the explosion, roll back and start shooting. You hear footsteps on the stairs, count three—that means they're committed to coming up, and too far to turn back, but not far enough to shoot. Then lob your own into the corner down there."

A voice yelled "go-go-go" from outside. Ana snatched one grenade, pulled the pin, but held the handle closed. Scruggs did the same.

"With me." Ana counted steps. "Three, two, one, throw." He and Scruggs tossed their grenades down the stairs, then hid their faces. The voices yelled again, disappeared in the BOOM of the grenades exploding, and dust and smoke roiled up. Scruggs coughed, and Ana lifted a second grenade, but didn't pull the pin. Scruggs copied him. Ana waited, trying to make out the yells from below. Lots of noise, but no motion.

"Did you get a good look at that truck-mounted weapon?"

"Small cannon or heavy machine gun, Centurion?"

"Pintle-mounted?"

"Yes."

"Could it elevate? Or just pivot?"

Scruggs cocked her head. "I think, maybe. Yes? It looked like the pictures you showed me. It can depress, because it was up on the truck, and they raked the front door, so they could change elevation."

"So why aren't they blasting us out of here from across the street? Or at least shooting up the stairs?"

Scruggs shook her head. "I don't—they don't want to hit the data center."

"These are the real security. They're supposed to catch us before the police get here. We beat the clock. Stay here. Fire if you hear any movement up the stairs—and bounce a grenade down. Don't worry about hitting them, just dump lots of fire down there, and get ready to retreat. Understood?"

"Copy that, Centurion."

Ana left the grenades, grabbed his pack and raced back to the data center. "Last call for software, get ready to exit the battle space."

"Old Man, I'm still stuffing Dirk's pants here," Dena said. "I just need a few more—wow. Clearing!"

Dena dove aside, dragging Dirk with her. Ana had produced a foot-long cylinder and was pointing it at them. He slid telescoping cylinders out of the front and rear.

"Centurion, I thought you weren't going to blow the building up," Dirk said.

"Plans change."

"Can we go out front?"

Scruggs fired from the top of the stairs, and seconds later, another grenade boomed. "I can hear four of them down there now, Centurion," she yelled.

"Drop a grenade and get in here. Everybody, clear from that cabinet. Get out of that office and to the side, cover your faces."

Dirk, Dena, and Gavin climbed out and fanned down the hallway.

Another grenade boomed, and Scruggs raced into the data center. "Last grenade out that door, Centurion. I'm nearly out of revolver ammo."

"Feed me."

Scruggs rummaged in Ana's backpack, produced a rocket, and slid it in the back of the tube with a click.

Sporadic firing continued outside and up the stairs.

"Listen up," Ana said. "We can't go out the front. They've got that covered. They're out there in force. There's no back door, we're stuck up here. So, we're going to make a back door, get out, grab the vehicle and run for it. And hide what exactly we stole. Got it?"

"Centurion, "Scruggs said. "That wall is just a few feet away. The explosion—"

"Not now. I've done this before." Ana aimed. "Get ready."

"Centurion," Dirk said. "I think you should know that I…"

"Shut up. Scruggs, 'ware the back-blast. Faces down, everybody. In three, two, one. Fire in the hole."

Ana pulled the trigger, then closed his eyes. The rocket

launcher fired, and heat seared his back. He'd aimed not at the wall, not at the cabinet, but at the plastic floor underneath. As he'd hoped, the unreinforced floor was no barrier to the rocket. It barely slowed as it drilled through the plastic slats, then continued down through the story below, striking the next floor and cutting through that. It slammed into the ground floor wall at the back of the building and exploded. The explosion lifted the floor and shook all the walls. The walls held for a moment, then the back wall crumbled, and the offices above it pancaked, and dropped on top. Ana opened his eyes and coughed. The data center behind him popped and sizzled as electric devices shorted and overheated fires belched smoke.

He waved the smoke away, leaning around the doorway to peer into the office. As the smoke cleared, he could see that the back wall with its cabinet had dropped away. He could see the building across the street through the dust. The back of the building had collapsed into a pile of rubble—they should be able to climb down and get out to the pink taxi.

Ana slid a foot forward. The floor was missing, but he could see the metal frames nearby. A bent pipe ran between the two floors. He grabbed it and shimmied down. The others copied his example. He half slid until his feet hit the next floor, grabbed a scrap of wire hanging loose, stretched to full extension, then dropped onto a giant pile of rubble. Dena was next, dropping the last few feet into his hands.

"This is why I wear these pants," she said. "Men always want to put their hands on me. Comes in handy sometimes."

"I'll remember that the next time we blow up a building."

"Stand clear." Gavin tossed his tool bag, then climbed down hand over hand, sliding the last few feet.

Dirk edged down, placing his feet one at a time.

"What's wrong with you, Navy?" Ana said. "You hurt? Is your belly too big to climb?"

"Happens to all of you men eventually," Dena said. "You get older, your hormones change, and you put on weight."

Dirk slid down the pipe. His legs and waist bulged grotesquely. "Shut up, all of you. I'm stuffed with software cassettes. Get my feet, and don't let my ankle straps open."

Ana and Gavin reached up and grasped his legs and helped him get his feet on the ground. Dirk waddled away from the pipe, cursing. Scruggs was next, sliding down and dropping the last four feet to land hands down in the dust, then sprang up. "Ready, Centurion."

"Right, we just need to get down from this pile, find that car, get out of here—"

"Centurion." Scruggs held her hands up. "My hands are covered in pink paint flecks."

"Glad to hear it, Private, but it's not the time for personal —ah, the Empress's jeweled hairbrush, don't tell me."

They were in the shadows behind the building, but there was some light. Enough to tell him that they were four feet above the ground, standing on something.

Something heavy, something large, something that glowed a faint pink through the dust.

Dirk coughed. "Sorry. But you know how it is."

"How is it, Navy?"

"Had to park somewhere." Dirk coughed again. "This

was the closest place. We're standing on the taxi. Or what's left of it."

CHAPTER FIVE

"The ship was impressive, Herr Konteradmiral. Sensors, lasers, even small slug throwers all hidden behind fake panels that moved up and out of the way. It could go from being an unassuming freighter to a powerful warship in seconds."

Kruder stood at attention in front of the admiral's desk. The sparseness of the office contrasted with the power of the man in front of him. Techand looked like Kruder's doddering, un-employed uncle on his way out to shop at a discount clothing store. Even his dandruff-covered glasses might have been bought secondhand. Nothing here indicated the admiral was head of the Council's counter-espionage department, and commanded dozens of specialized ships and thousands of sailors.

Before the meeting, Kruder had walked his entire ship, marveling at the changes. He had extra power, extra life support, and more storage for supplies. He even had four different small craft. One was a big shuttle, two were tugs with internal cargo space and grapplers for shifting containers, and a spiffy captain's boat with room for a half dozen in luxury for station operations.

"Will anyone suspect that you are a warship?"

"I do not think so—the options for camouflage are extensive. But I will need paint, fabric, thin sheet metal, plastic panels, all in quantity. Container loads of each to change our appearance from time to time. Electronic sensors are all very well, but some people will see us with their eyes, and colors and logos stick in their memory."

"It will be arranged."

"And beacons. Many beacons."

"You can have as many of ours as you like. How many do you need?"

"I will need beacons from the Accursed Empire, and the Confederation, and some of the neutral worlds."

The admiral shook his head. "Out of the question. Besides, we have no such things."

"Herr Konteradmiral, it would be a shame to spend all this time and money on such an excellent fraud and leave out the last few items that would perfect it."

"I believe we have a small collection of beacons from wrecked ships. We can offer you those."

"No sir."

"No?"

"Sir." Kruder yawned. "Forgive me sir. I was up late researching. I have made a list of several dozen freighters of comparable size and shape to our raider. If we add a fake truss or sensor pole, anyone viewing us through a telescope would assume the same ship. We can conduct operations under one disguise, jump to another system, reconfigure, and return whence we came with none the wiser. But our beacons must be for real trading ships. Ships that were destroyed, or declared missing, months or even years ago, their beacons are not sufficient. Our entire mission could be exposed by a single curious captain telling the next warship they see that they saw one of these 'missing' ships."

The admiral frowned. "We have no such things, I tell you."

"Sir." Kruder pulled himself even straighter. "I do not ask for a machine, a coder to make my own beacons, or the necessary software to do so. A selection of three dozen or so, from the Accursed Empire, and the Confederation, would be sufficient. We cannot sneak up on other ships. They see us coming, and they have sensors. All it takes is one eager junior watch officer to run some scans, and we will be lost."

The admiral shook his head. "They are merchant officers. They're too lazy to do that."

"Sir." Kruder shook his head. "Sir, the War Navy often discounts the merchant officers. They say they are like sheep. And they are. But like sheep, they watch for predators. If they sense something wrong, they will act on that sense. Where a warship will attack, or investigate, they will avoid. It makes no sense to send us out on a ship that creates any sort of suspicion. To the other merchant ships, we must look like ships that should be in that sector, which have a reason to trade there. Warships will not notice a neutral freighter too far from its home port, but other merchant ships will. And tell others. If something odd is going on, ships on those routes will switch to others. The beacons are necessary for the disguise to work."

The admiral smiled. "You were in the merchants. You should know."

"I do sir."

"Send me your list. I will do what I can."

"Yes sir."

"You can leave in a week?"

"Three weeks would be better sir. I will need time to drill my crew."

"You will leave in three weeks. Not a day later."

"I have another list."

"Another list? You demand more, Korvettenkapitan?"

"It is a list of the crew members I will need."

"Your crew has already been assigned. They start arriving this week."

"Yes sir. But I will need some special types of crewmen, men and women with merchant experience I have worked with before, if we are to stay undiscovered in our operational area for twelve months."

"Twelve months? Hoss said you are only good for six."

The old bastard has been paying attention to the reports.

"With respect, Herr Admiral, Hoss is an excellent yard dog, but he has never commanded a merchant vessel, far less a warship. A few changes in how things are stowed, some extra supplies, and I anticipate we will be able to operate for up to twelve months. We will need to dock for minor maintenance every few months, but if we maintain our systems, we can stay longer. By eighteen months, our maintenance requirements will be such that we will need a major shipyard to effect repairs—all our systems will run down. Then we will have to leave our operational area. Until then, provided we can find local support for minor repairs every three months, we can continue longer."

"You have been careful not to ask where you will be operating."

"The border between us and the Confederation, and in the neutral spaces between, but mostly in the Accursed Empire, I assume."

"The Accursed Empire, you say?" The admiral leaned back in his chair. "We are not at war with the Accursed Empire now, Korvettenkapitan."

"No. But we will be soon, won't we?"

"What makes you say that?"

"Sir, you have not yet told me what my orders will be. You have asked if others will suspect this is a warship, you have asked how long I can cruise, if I am satisfied with the weapons. But you have not given me orders to attack our enemies. Which means I can't right now. Has war been declared while I was inspecting?"

The admiral grinned. "You will be tasked as a patrolling auxiliary cruiser on customs duties. You will seize ships that are violating our space, seize their cargo and intern their crews, by force if necessary."

"You say 'our space.' Our space as recognized by the Confederation and the Accursed Empire?"

"We recognize none of those claims. Our own counter-claims are broad, as you well know. You will enforce our claims wherever you travel."

"Most of our claims overlap Confederation claims and those of the Accursed Empire."

"Are you afraid of the Accursed Empire, Korvettenkapitan?"

Kruder braced to attention, but his eyes didn't leave the admiral. "I am in the service of the War Navy, and I have fought before. Are you making a specific accusation, Konteradmiral?"

The admiral shook his head. "No. Your patriotism and integrity are well known, which is why I sent for you. Korvettenkapitan, let me explain. Things are tense between the Empires. My people believe that if we increased the friction between the two, one would attack the other, and we can pick up the pieces. A number of neutral states all along the frontier would appreciate protection against a war-mongering Confederation. We could easily overcome the Accursed Empire's operatives there, provided they were distracted. You will provide this distraction. You will capture ships of the Confederation and the Accursed Empire who are trespassing in our space. I know, I know—" The admiral held up his hand. "The other Empires do not see it that way. That is not your concern. You will enforce our customs rules, by seizing such ships as you think proper."

"As I think proper?"

"You will not attack regular forces of our opponents, wherever found. We do not want to give them cause for a real war. In any event, you could not defeat a real warship."

"You may be surprised, Konteradmiral. I can defeat small escorts. Perhaps larger ones if the weapons work as I expect."

"Really?"

"I am willing to try."

"Do not try unless you have no other options."

"May I return fire if attacked?"

"Of course."

"Even if attacked by regular forces?"

"If anyone attacks you first, you may fire back, no matter who they are. But your primary duty is to seek out and capture enemy commerce."

"Locating enemy commerce can be a chancy business."

The admiral pulled several software cassettes from a drawer and shoved them across the desk. "The details need not concern you, but we have many ongoing intelligence operations in the Accursed Empire. We have extensive information on ship movements, including routes, cargoes, and where you are most likely to be able to operate undetected. Here are the details, as well as codes to communicate with our agents."

Kruder pocketed the cassettes. "What of the cargoes?"

"Take what you need. Destroy what you don't. You may return prize ships to this naval base if you feel it is warranted. You have broad discretion in that area."

"And the crews?"

"The crews are a challenge."

Kruder drew himself up to attention. "I will not sanction the murder of innocent spacers."

"You will obey your orders, as given."

"Not that one, if it is given. Never."

The admiral crossed his arms. "This is a war."

"War has not been declared. The crews are innocent, they don't know that. And even if it is a war, we have rules. I will follow the rules."

"Even if they are your enemies? You are squeamish?"

"Even if I was, which I am not, there are practical considerations. We are not the only ones who can capture ships, Konteradmiral. What of our own crews captured if we do this thing?"

"An answer both practical and ethical." The admiral nodded. "It is not the problem you think it is. You have excess life support, you will intern the crews on-board during operations. From time to time, return excess prisoners to co-ordinates we specify. There will be ships to take them from you there. The Confed citizens will be delivered to a place where they can return to the Confederation themselves, or not. We will leave it up to them."

"And the Accursed Empire's people?"

"We have a contact in the Accursed Empire who will receive them on our behalf and deliver them to fringe planets in the Empire's zone of influence. They will have the same option to return to the Accursed Empire's jurisdiction as the Confeds. Deliver them there yourself or put them on one of the captured ships."

"Herr Admiral, given the conditions in the Confederation, I understand why some of the crews would like to delay their returns, but even I admit that is not the case with the Accursed Empire."

"We have contacts with a prominent Imperial who takes

care of such things. Our hands are clean. If necessary, you may send some back on one of your prizes. We will hold them for a while."

"And what will happen to them then?"

"Korvettenkapitan, you must have some trust in your superiors."

"As you say sir. I will operate in the disputed areas, capturing such ships as I feel necessary. After my initial inspection, I may cruise for up to eighteen months if I have sufficient fuel and supplies. What type of support can I expect?"

"We will arrange depot ships at regular intervals, in out-of-the-way systems. We will also give you instructions on neutral ports where you may acquire services for a price. Those codes allow you to communicate with some others who may assist you. For obvious reasons, there will be no regular Navy ships available."

"Even a single cruiser squadron would make a huge difference out here on the Verge."

"All are spoken for. Our core systems must be protected. Say what you like about the Accursed Empire, they make good warships. And many of them. You will receive no naval support. Not directly."

"Very well. What is our goal here?"

"The Confeds will blame us and the Accursed Empire. The Accursed Empire will blame us and the Confeds. The two will argue, bluster, and complain. We will not. They will issue provocations. We will not. If we wait long enough, some incident will set them to war out here, which will spread to the main systems. We will watch and laugh." The admiral shrugged. "It may already have happened. We are not entirely sure."

"Am I the only one?"

"The only one at this time. There have been other... experiments."

"I see."

"Now that you understand better, Korvettenkapitan, will you have any issues executing your orders?"

"I will not." Kruder stamped to attention. "Confusion to our enemies."

"Confusion to our enemies. Whoever they may be."

CHAPTER SIX

"Cheese." Tribune Devin thumped the table. "We need better cheese."

"Cheese?" Subprefect Lionel asked.

"White stuff, creamy, made from milk."

Devin and Lionel were sitting in Devin's office, making a list of officers to come to the secret briefing that afternoon. They discharged a convoy and returned to the Papillon system in two jumps. Lionel had a list of topics he wanted covered, and explained who would be presenting, and what information was needed. Devin was working on the menu.

"I know what cheese is. What does that have to do with Trevor's summary of the tactical situation? Why do we need better cheese?"

"It's a staff meeting. We need snacks. We can't have a meeting without snacks."

"Tribune, if I recall properly, the oath you swore said Devin, the Lord Lyon, master under god of the ISS Pollux, Imperial Tribune, and acting sector governor in the absence of the physical presence of a member of the Imperial Family in the Verge, is charged with the defense of the Empire against all enemies, foreign and domestic, to the best of your ability, sparing not even your life."

"Mouthful of a promise, isn't it, yes? And?"

"There's nothing there about providing your crew with a selection of tasty canapes while you do this."

"Canapes! That's the answer!" Devin tapped his comm. "Imin?"

Imin's voice came over the channel. "Yes, Tribune?"

"Can you do canapes?"

"Of course sir. Canapes for twenty-eight, ready for the start of third shift."

"We don't have any of the good cheese..."

"The creamy stuff will do, sir, especially on the crackers I have."

"Outstanding, Imin. Thank you." Devin cut the channel. "Savory snacks, that's what we need."

"How does he know that?" Lionel asked.

"To make canapes? It seems a reasonable request to ask a steward. I assume he learned it in steward school."

Lionel rubbed his forehead. "How does he know that we're having a super-secret briefing at the start of third shift?"

"He... well... I just." Devin shook his head. "No idea."

"And more important, how does he know how many people will be at the meeting? He didn't even ask."

"Good point. How does he know that?" Devin tapped his comm and waited for Imin to answer. "Imin? How did you know what time the meeting was?"

"Latest corvette jumped in from Sand Harbor system two hours ago, Tribune. Time enough for you to download the latest intelligence from there and decide on what to do next. So, you need a briefing. If it was right now, you'd have asked for lunch. Later, dinner. But you wanted appetizers, so it had to be ship-afternoon, which is start of third shift."

"Right, thank you, Imin." Devin killed the channel. "See? Makes perfect sense."

Lionel raised an eyebrow and waited.

"What... Right." Devin called Imin. Again. "Imin?"

"Captains of all the ships in the system, sir, and their executive officers. Brigadier Santana and his staff, yourself, the Subprefect, plus the bridge and logistic officers you've been dining in."

"Thank you, Imin." Devin killed the channel. "Makes sense."

Lionel was counting on his fingers. "That's twenty-six."

Devin sighed and hit the channel again. "Imin... the Subprefect is asking..."

"Myself and the Bosun as well, sir, for quality control."

"Outstanding. Thank you, Imin." Devin killed the channel. "You'll be running the meeting?"

"Yes. Trevor will present the tactical situation."

"Excellent."

"Santana's people have a plan for defending Sand Harbor in the absence of major naval units. Well, major for us out here. But they have a plan. The logistics people have already reported in. I'll append their info, but the tanker, the

Hydrogen Queen, simplifies things, at least for any ships it travels with."

"And the political issues."

"I'll summarize them for everybody. The missing ships, and the core news blackout. Including the... difficulties... with your family. And summarize the operations we've agreed on."

"Excellent. And then I'll speak."

Lionel nodded. "Out of curiosity, Tribune, since we'll already have covered intelligence, operations, logistics, politics, tactics and strategy, what will be the topic of your presentation?"

"I'll give them my inspired leadership."

"Leadership. Outstanding."

"I thought so."

Lionel raised an eyebrow. "And snacks."

"Of course." Devin smiled. "Leadership and snacks."

Promptly at shift change, the Marine assault ship Valhalla's shuttle docked at the Pollux's main lock, carrying Brigadier Santana and his staff. Since the Brigadier was the senior Marine officer insystem, Devin felt it polite to meet him directly.

Santana gave the crossed chest salute. "The Empire."

"The Empire." Devin returned the salute. "Good to see you, Brigadier. We'll be in the dining room this time. Need the space for everybody."

"Of course." Santana followed Devin as they walked the corridors. "I'm surprised the briefing room isn't bigger than the dining room."

"The briefing room is the dining room, or at least it was,"

Lionel said. "The Tribune had the large briefing room repurposed during construction. He turned it into his dining room."

"I thought it was bigger than I expected," Santana said.

"I like hosting dinners," Devin said. "Speaking of hosting, I don't recognize all your officers. Did you bring more than normal?"

"I wanted to have all of my subordinates present, in case any issues come up. Gives us access to a comprehensive selection of viewpoints and prevents any misunderstandings."

"Indeed."

"We're all excited to be here. It's a great learning opportunity, especially for my younger officers."

Devin cocked an eye at Santana. "Indeed?" He turned to Lionel. "Anything to add, Subprefect?"

Lionel shrugged. "I promised them all canapes."

Devin keyed his comm. "Imin, I'm in the air lock with the Brigadier here, and—"

"Don't worry sir," Imin interrupted. "No problem at all. Brigadier called earlier, and I adjusted accordingly. Plenty for everybody."

"Thank you, Imin." Devin kept walking. After a moment, he turned to Lionel. "What do I do here again?"

"Represent the Empire. Provide inspired leadership."

"Right."

"All that," Santana said. "And snacks."

Lieutenant Trevor gave the Intelligence department's presentation of the current strategic situation, punctuated by the crunching of jaws. There was barely enough room for the seated attendees to place comms on the tables between the plates of crackers and crusty bread. The junior officers had to stand against the wall, but Imin had provided them with small plates pre-loaded with a mixed selection of tasty bites.

Trevor projected a list of all the known or suspected Confederation naval units that had been located in the Verge, and their status. Most read either 'known destroyed' or 'known damaged.'

Trevor highlighted their conclusion at the bottom of the list. "After our defeat of the Kazan, as well as her associated escorts at the second battle of Sand Harbor, we believe that there are only two remaining Confed fleet units in or even near the sector. One fully functioning corvette and one damaged frigate. Both were last seen jumping on paths consistent with returning to the Confed core sectors."

"Can they repair that frigate?" Lionel asked. "Out here in the Verge, I mean?"

"Subprefect, not unless they built a naval shipyard somewhere while we weren't looking. Most of our commercial shipyards out here have only limited military capacity. If it had been the corvette, they can fix that at any civilian shipyard, but not a frigate."

"They could bring major fleet elements in from their core fleets as replacements," Devin said.

"They could, Tribune. But if that was their plan, why didn't they before they planned this attack?"

"We were a target of opportunity, for some reason."

"Yes, Tribune. They launched those attacks with only locally available forces. Our assessment was that if the Pollux wasn't here, then their attack on Sand Harbor would have succeeded. And we would have lacked the forces to retake it. They could have presented the Empire with a fait accompli. Whether the Senate would have chosen to respond is a question above me."

Devin nodded. "And in any event, if they send a battle-cruiser squadron out here, we have no choice but to run. We were lucky to get away against a single cruiser. Anything bigger would just be suicide. Let's assume they decide to bring their big fleets here, how long 'til they get here?"

"Months, Tribune. Even if they send a courier right away, it's a long way to their capital worlds. They may get lucky and intercept some transiting fleets along the way, but it's unlikely."

"We have local superiority, for a time." Devin regarded the screens in silence, then pointed at a nearby star system. "Let's say I want to take the fight to them. Can we pick off some of their edge worlds? Like right there?"

The entire intelligence section shook their heads.

"It's mfffrhp." Trevor swallowed—he'd taken advantage of the break to scarf a cracker. "That sausage is amazing. And that mustard. No sir. We've had reports of older naval units being sent out here. After our encounter with that monitor in the Kewa system, we re-evaluated some of that intelligence. We believe they have been systematically converting older ships into monitors rather than retiring them. Removing jump drives and fuel tankage, and replacing them with armor, weapons, and whatever is at hand. Since they don't have to jump, they can be heavily armored and mount powerful weapons."

"But they're limited to the system they're in?"

"Yes, Tribune. And Pollux can take them, most probably. But our assessment is that it wouldn't be easy. There has been enough time for word to filter around, so they'll be wary. We don't know which systems they're located in. And they only have to get lucky once…"

"All right." Devin sighed. "No running off and attacking the Confeds by myself. I understand. Imin, what is this sauce?"

Imin placed another plate in front of Devin. "Fish dip, sir. A local whitefish, a lot like turbot, with some savory onions."

"Outstanding. All right, if we're not blasting the Confeds out of their home systems, do we have to stay here to protect our bases? Brigadier Santana, I understand you have a plan."

Santana scooped up a slice of fish dip and gestured to one of his officers who replaced Trevor at the presentation side. "Sir. Sirs." She brought up her own display. "In the absence of front-line naval units, which the Pollux efficiently destroyed for us—" She paused while the tables cheered. "The only threats to nearby systems would be naval auxiliary units such as armed freighters. We propose to send a company of Marines to Sand Harbor and quarter them there. The Marines cannot stop a naval force from occupying or interdicting the system, but they can prevent occupation of the station itself. As Lieutenant Trevor pointed out, the only naval forces remaining are armed merchant ships, and even a single corvette should be a match for them."

"You want me to post a corvette there?" Devin asked. "We'd need to assign two or more for crew rotations and supplies and suchlike."

"No sir." The Marine shook her head. "We are going to take advantage of the repair facilities in Sand Harbor. One of the corvettes can escort a freighter with supplies every month. It stays for a maintenance cycle, meets the next convoy coming in, and escorts it back. The supplies will be secured, and there's no issue with jumping into a defended system because the Confeds won't be able to land troops on the station. The station troops know the Navy will be back every six weeks. They can hold on that long."

"And useful maintenance. Very well. And I suppose we can do something similar here in Papillon. Well done."

"Thank you sir." The Marine officer sat.

"Questions or comments?" Devin asked.

Trevor stood. "Sir, we've had several more reports of ships going missing. Freighters. Perhaps pirates taking advantage of the current uncertainty. We're trying to run them down, but there isn't a lot of good information at this time. We're not even sure if the ships are actually missing."

"Keep looking into it through formal channels. As soon as we have actionable intelligence, we'll blast them. Given that we're at a bit of an impasse with the Confederation, this pirate hunt assumes greater importance."

"And," Lionel said, "the Tribune and I are investigating via some other, unofficial avenues."

Devin nodded. Meaning he's got Imin asking questions from his smuggler friends.

Trevor sat.

"Which leaves us with what, Subprefect?"

Lionel grabbed a chunk of sausage and stuffed it into his mouth before taking his own place at the display. "That leaves us with Pollux, the Valhalla, and the Hydrogen Queen. Three ships, all similar speed and jump capability. We'll have to put a few people on the tanker, and trade a few with the corvettes. But that leaves us, the Pollux, as a striking force."

"And what do we strike?" Devin asked.

"Not what, but who."

"Who?" Devin frowned. "We strike at the enemies of the Empire, of course."

"As you say, Tribune. And now, we discuss who, exactly who we mean, when we say, 'enemies of the Empire.' Are you planning on returning to the core?"

The two dozen sets of chomping jaws froze. A half dozen officers with full mouths swallowed. All eyes locked on the Tribune.

"Why do you ask that?"

"We have not had regular communications out here in months."

"Communications here in the Verge is often spotty, you know that."

"Other entities are getting their necessary messages and shipments, and non-naval personnel are coming and going. The only holdup is messages to or from the Pollux, or yourself, and a lack of clear direction from the Emperor or the Empress. We're in a communication blackout here, and that can't be good. And there have been some unofficial attempts to undermine your leadership here. Messages signed by the Chancellor, not the Empress, I might add."

"What would you have me do?" Devin snapped. "Charge into the core, guns blazing, to rescue my sister from some supposed threat? Some unknown threat that we have no knowledge of? The Mad Dog of the Verge charging in like some avenging angel, ready to slaughter the supposed enemies of the Empire?"

Lionel glanced around the briefing room. More than half of the officers present were nodding agreement. The other half reached for more canapes. "That does seem to be the consensus, Tribune."

"I remind you I serve the Empire," Devin said. "Not a particular family, even my own. My duty station is here, in the Verge, and I will stay here until ordered away from here."

"Even if your sister is in danger?"

"We have no proof of that. Remember, I have dispatched a scouting mission coreward. They're a team of trained professional spies and experts in clandestine affairs. They are currently acquiring some special weapons necessary to make their mission a success. I expect great things from them. They are competent and skilled, and I've placed the future of the Empire in their hands. As we speak, I'm sure they are fulfilling my confidence."

CHAPTER SEVEN

"Go, go, go." Ana slapped Dirk's shoulder. "Move it. Run faster."

"I can't run," Dirk said. After clearing the building, they had raced into a side street and dashed into the first alley they found. The other four jogged, but Dirk still was encumbered by pants full of software cassettes. "I can only waddle."

"Waddle faster." Ana slapped him again. "You should have stayed in better shape."

"Better shape wouldn't help me with being a human software storage unit." Dirk gagged. The alley stank of day-old garbage, feces, and dead animals. "Is this an alley or a sewer?"

"Get moving before they track us through the alleys."

"We could stop and tell them it was a big mistake…"

BOOM. Fire flared behind them, casting shadows down the alley. Trash cans and piles of crushed boxes crowded each side. The light gleamed for two seconds, then the alley faded to an undifferentiated black.

Everyone froze. "What was that?" Dena asked.

"Well-thrown grenades meeting something flammable. They're not playing around anymore. Get moving, fast."

"Understood, Centurion. C'mon, Dena." Scruggs and Dena resumed their job.

Ana tripped over a foul-smelling puddle. Night vision's gone now. Gonna be a problem for the others any second.

Scruggs smashed full tilt into a trash can and knocked it over. Dena leaped over the dark cylinder, slipped on landing, but kept moving.

Gavin tripped in the muck. His bag of tools and software went flying and he fell.

"Hold," Ana yelled. He stuck out his hand and Dirk waddled right into it.

"Ooof." Dirk fell back. Ana grabbed his chest and hauled him upright. "Can't run, can't waddle and now can't stand."

"And can't see in the dark either."

Ana keyed his comm. "Navigator? Navigator? Come in." He waited for a beat. "Jamming. Scruggs?"

"Centurion?"

"We need transport. You and Nature Girl go up ahead—carefully—walk fast, but don't run. I see lights up there, probably a crossroad. Find us a vehicle."

"I don't have any ammunition left, Centurion."

"Nature Girl has her slingshot. Threaten somebody with that."

Dena stopped brushing the dirt off her outfit. "Slingshots don't work well as threats, Old Man, at least according to you. Nobody knows what they are."

"Which is why we need guns. Scruggs, if you can't use a

gun, figure something else out. Adapt, improvise, overcome. Engineer, why are you on the ground?"

"I hab shib in my node," Gavin said. "And I hab dropped mib bag."

"You ladies go, we'll deal with this."

Scruggs and Dena darted forward. After the first stumble over a pile of trash, they slowed to a fast shuffle. Both kept their eyes on the ground.

Scruggs grabbed Dena's shoulder. "Listen."

BRRRRUP. BRRRUP. BRRRUP.

"What's that, Baby Marine?"

"Automatic weapon. The crew-served one I saw. They're being systematic about shooting that place up. Which means they don't care if we get shot now."

"How truly good," Dena said. "Keep moving."

"I still can't see."

"Your eyes will adjust. Here, drop low and focus down the alley."

"What?" Scruggs said.

Dena's hand guided her down to a low crouch, then lower. "Stare along the ground, look into the distance. Even if it's dark, you'll see the darker junk on the ground silhouetted against the lighter background."

Scruggs peered into the dark. "Three cans on the left side —dumpsters, the right side is clear, 'til that alley."

"Grab the wall and drag your fingers along. We'll follow 'til the next door, then check again."

Moving from door to door, they followed the line of warehouses down the dark alley. At each opening, they dropped low, glanced forward, and used Dena's technique to search for a clear path, then jogged to the next.

"This is great," Scruggs said. "Where did you learn that?"

"Sneaking through the woods at night when people were chasing me."

"Boyfriends?"

"Not the boyfriends, no. Their wives, on the other hand, were pretty unhappy with me."

"You ran away from wives?"

"I wasn't the only one on Rockhaul who could shoot a slingshot. Or beat somebody's head in with an axe."

"I wish I had your life growing up. It sounds so much fun."

"From all accounts, you're fabulously wealthy. That sounds like fun to me."

"My family is wealthy, not me. And money's only fun if you spend it on what you want, not what other people want. I would rather have run around in the woods. And now the Empire wants to kill me."

"Yeah, about that, why do they want to kill you?"

"Not sure. Don't feel the need to find out."

"Isn't that what we're trying to do? Find out what's going on in the core for that Tribune guy?" Dena slipped on a slimy patch and slammed onto her back. "Ow."

Scruggs helped her up. "Maybe. I'm only along for the ride."

"What, in the Empress's name, is the name of this ride, then? Crawling through crap in an alley? In the dark? With people trying to kill you."

"More fun than sitting in offices or classrooms every day listening to people telling you what to think and what to do."

"The centurion tells you what to think and what to do."

"No, he doesn't. He tells me what he wants done, and I have to figure it out myself. If I get it wrong, he shows me how. He doesn't care how I do things. All he wants is results. And it's things I want to learn anyways. The same with you."

"Same with me? How is it the same?"

"You decide what you want to do, and then you do it. You want to sleep with the pilot, you sleep with him. You want to get off your planet, you find a way to get off. You want to be part of the ship crew, you find a way to be useful. If you don't understand how to do something you want to do, you ask for help. And you don't do anything you don't want to do."

"You think I wanted to be sliding along in mud and shit in the dark while somebody tries to kill me?"

"You're having fun," Scruggs said. "You like action. You hate boredom. You'd be unhappy sitting back on the ship talking on the radio like Lee does."

"This is not fun."

"Sure it is. You're only here because it's fun. You stopped sleeping with the pilot a long time ago. You're learning all this ship stuff—sensors, scans. And the centurion says you're already good with a rifle. And you can hit anything with your slingshot. Why not jump ship? Steal some equipment or weapons. Ask the pilot for cash—he would have given it to you. So why are you here, slogging through crap in the dark, Ms. Nature Girl?"

Dena stopped and dropped, and they checked the next

section of alley. Dim lights came out of one of the side alleys. "That must lead back to the main street," Dena said. "We can stick our heads out there and check."

They waded up to the corner. "Well?" Scruggs said.

"Well what? What happens around that corner? Or why am I here in this alley?"

"Both. Either."

Dena giggled. "You know what, Baby Marine, it's the same answer both times."

"What?"

"Adventure awaits!"

"I'm just saying," Dirk gasped. "That for software, these cassettes are heavy, and if we dropped all this, then I'd be able to walk faster and get us out of here."

"The whole purpose of this raid was to get software. Step up here." Ana helped Dirk to climb up a pile of rocks and down the other side. "We need this software to operate those lasers you keep talking about."

"I'm not the one who said we needed weapons," Dirk said. "There are all sorts of problems with mounting weapons on merchant ships. Power. Targeting. Recoil."

"Lasers don't recoil," Ana said.

"I'm talking theoretically, Centurion. We've got this far and not had to shoot at anything?"

"We may not want to shoot at things, but people surely have been shooting at us, so I'd like to be able to shoot back."

"Fine, but why now?"

"Because, Navy, your buddy, the Tribune, wants you to

find out what's going on in the core. And being able to shoot back would be a good thing. Don't you think?"

"Do we need all of this? I've got hundreds of these cartridges. Imperial fingernails!" Dirk slipped on something squishy. "What is that smell?"

"Smells like freedom," Ana said. "It's disgusting enough back here that we probably won't be followed by those shooters. And trust me, Navy, after the firepower we saw back there, we don't want them following us."

"What was that place?"

"No idea. But whatever it was, it wasn't an insurance company, and it wasn't supposed to be there. When it was compromised, they seemed pretty happy with it being destroyed. But either way, we've got our software, and we have to get back to that shipyard and get our laser installed."

Dirk slipped again, cursed, and crawled to his feet. "Gavin has a bag full of software. I should dump this stuff and move along."

"I wouldn't do that, Navy, if I were you."

"Why is that, O great warrior?"

"Because if you're not carrying that software, and we're depending on Engineer's bag, then I don't need to worry whether you get away or not. And that means I can stop coddling you, or eliminate you from consideration, and move along out of this alley."

"Coddling? I'm not being coddled. I might just dump this software on principle."

"As I said before, I wouldn't do that."

"You going to leave me behind?"

"No."

"Ha. I knew you wouldn't."

"Skipper." Gavin spat more mud out of his mouth and wiped his nose for the seventh time. "Just to be clear. He's not talking about leaving you behind. You're making him choose between getting a shiny new attack laser to play with or shooting you in the head and leaving you here. Given the way Centurion thinks, what do you think he'd choose?"

Dirk took a ragged breath. "Interesting question. Would you shoot me, Centurion?"

"Right now? No, I wouldn't shoot you."

"See?" Dirk said.

"I don't have the ammo to spare, so I can't shoot you. But I could beat you to death by bashing your head in with a brick." Ana ran his hands up a nearby wall. "Lots of bricks close by, Navy. Lots of bricks."

"We go out, point our guns at a car, force the driver out, and take the car," Scruggs said, squinting against the light as she and Dena exited the alley.

"It's a revolver, not a magic wand," Dena said. "Waving them at people won't make them do what you want."

"We need a car so we can get out of here," Scruggs said.

Dena shrugged. "Fine, we'll try it your way."

The two women walked out onto the sidewalk and scanned both directions. They were ten blocks away from the Archan Insurance building. Fire bloomed in the distance—the data center was burning.

"Everybody can see that fire," Dena said. "We need to be quick."

"Here's a car right now," Scruggs said. A ground sedan with a single male driver cruised down the road and slowed as the women came into view. The vehicle glided to the curb, and the driver dropped the passenger side window.

Scruggs hid her revolver behind her back and marched up to the door. "Hello."

"Hey," the man said.

"We need your car," Scruggs said.

"You can have it. Sure. Come on in."

"Come on in?"

"Sure. How much?"

Scruggs furrowed her brow. "What?"

"How much?"

"For what?"

"To get in the car."

Dena laughed behind Scruggs. Scruggs blushed, pulled out the hidden revolver, then pointed it at the man's face. "Get out of the car, now, or—"

The driver floored the car, and the moving door knocked Scruggs down. The revolver bounced down the road.

Dena helped Scruggs to her feet. Scruggs cradled her arm and cursed.

"That went well," Dena said.

"What do I—How?"

Dena patted Scruggs's shoulder. "Watch and learn, little one. Watch and learn."

Scruggs retrieved her revolver and hid it in a pocket, cursed some more, then dusted herself off. She flexed her arm. "Show me, then."

Dena unzipped her jacket, stepped up to the curb, faced the traffic, and put her hands on her hips. A set of headlights slowed.

Dena waited until the car pulled up, then bent into the window. "Hey, handsome, how are you tonight?"

The driver leaned over. "Good, pretty lady. Good. How are things?"

Dena leaned further into the window, making sure to squeeze her shoulders together. "Oh, you know, trying to make a living. It's rough sometimes."

"For sure, it's hard for everyone."

"You want to tell a pretty girl all about it?"

"Well…"

"Don't be shy, handsome."

"Oh, I'm not shy." The man stared at her for a moment. "You're sure pretty. Very pretty, but really…"

"Really what, handsome?"

"Your friend."

"My friend. Which—Her?" Dena cocked her thumb behind her. "Woman back there?"

"She's really nice. That hair. Is she trying to make a living too?"

"You don't want to talk to me? You want to talk to her?"

"Yeah. Please."

"I'm right here."

"Yes, but," the man shrugged, "you're not quite, you know, what I want. But she's…"

Dena stepped back from the door. "Scruggs. Come here."

Scruggs stepped up. "Why? I thought we…"

"Man here wants to talk to you." Dena stepped away from the door.

"Oh." Scruggs put her hands on the window frame and stuck her head in the window. "Hello."

"Hello, girl. You sure are pretty."

"Uh, thank you."

"Very pretty. Let me get a closer look at you." The man leaned over until his face was close. "Whatcha want to do?"

"To do? Oh, you mean, what do I want to do?"

"Yeah."

Scruggs smiled. "I get it. Yeah, I want to do something."

"What?"

Scruggs took her hands off the door frame and slapped both his ears as hard as she could. The man yelled and grabbed his head. She snagged his hair, got a good grip, braced a foot on the door and heaved. The man flew out of his seat and partway out the window. She used her other hand to work the door handle, then dragged the door and man out of the car. She smashed his head on the frame and shoved him to the sidewalk. He collapsed, moaning and holding his ears. She kicked him twice in the ribs, rolled him over, and pulled him up by his hair. Then she clasped her hands and smashed him in the back of the head. He took off down the street, staggering as he left.

Dena watched him run. "Emperor's toenails."

"Thanks, Dena."

"Thanks for what?"

"You were right," Scruggs said. "I should have trusted you. Your way is way better."

CHAPTER EIGHT

"Anything unusual to report, Hans?" Kruder asked his new executive officer, Hans Fusterheim. Fusterheim had arrived two weeks ago and had been pushing the refit ever since. He was a gloomy former merchant colleague of Kruder's. Kruder had him drafted into the crew, so his gloom could have come from being back in the War Navy, under discipline, and at a much-reduced salary. More likely it came from having misgivings about this strange new freighter design. Kruder had not shared any detailed information with him.

"No, Kapitan. Operations reports supplies are en route, and the station says they will deliver the last of our needs tomorrow. The yard says that all equipment is operating within tolerances, and we will be able to depart on schedule with no difficulties. I spoke to personnel today, and they say the last of our crew will be here the day after tomorrow."

Kruder rotated his chair in the combat bridge to face Hans. The front of the ship, with the standard eight merchant consoles, was now referred to as the wheelhouse. The extra stations with their coding and decoding equipment, weapons control, and special operations tasks and small craft control were called the bridge. Kruder had one of the consoles removed and installed extra screens at his station.

"Really? Everything is fine?"

Hans shook his head. "I don't believe a word of it either, Kapitan. The yard has never done a full power test on any of the systems, not even in isolation. Something is bound to fall off or catch fire. I'm not happy with the food and equipment supplies that we have received. They were late delivering it, almost like they hoped we'd be gone before we could check it. At least it's all merchant class, and there's tons of it around here. But the ammunition—the metal slugs for the mass drivers, and the chemical ammunition—I'm suspicious about that. Those are uncommon items, and I don't believe the delivery schedule. We're mostly fine on ship's crew, but none of our small craft maintenance people have arrived."

"None?"

"None. And the ones that are on the way are... suspect. There are some confusing inserts in their service records."

"I trust your judgment on this, Hans." Hans had been his executive officer on two of the freighters Kruder had commanded. "Suggestions?"

"Get out and break something right away. Open some boxes and try to eat what's in them. Practice shooting something. Break things, try to fix them."

"Excellent idea, Hans. We have internal power?"

"We do."

"Any reason that we cannot go for a short cruise?"

"None at all, sir."

"Very well." Kruder tapped his comm. "Let us see what we can do."

Red lights flashed, and a klaxon bonged. A recorded voice blared, "Alarm. Alarm. Set condition three."

Kruder waited for ten minutes, ignoring the red lights on the control board. "Well?" he asked Fusterheim.

"No change for the last-minute sir. Ninety percent are ready, but those compartments have not responded and are not answering comms. I've sent runners, and I'll have a report soon."

"Very well." He tapped the bridge control. "Helm, uncouple us from the dock. Take us out to the nearest gas giant. You choose the course there. Put us in a fueling orbit, and have engineering take in one percent fuel load to test the systems."

The helmsman, Spieler, was a blond-haired young man who had been a midshipman on one of Kruder's freighters four years ago. Kruder thought he'd had the making of a good officer then, and he'd seen nothing since he'd reported aboard to change that opinion. "Yes sir."

Kruder turned to Hans. "What else?"

"Take everyone who isn't at maneuvering stations. Have a third suit up and emergency egress to the hull while we're underway. Have another third report to firefighting stations, and the last third take internal security duties. With live ammunition."

"Live ammunition?"

"Maybe that's too much."

"It is. No live ammunition yet. And remind the helm

about the egress—we can have aspect changes but no acceleration changes."

"Yes, Kapitan. Some of the yard workers onboard want to complain."

"Ignore them. Wait, send them to the galley. Tell the cooks to feed them a complete dinner, whatever they want, while they wait. We can test that too."

"Very well."

"How long 'til things go wrong?"

"Very soon, Kapitan, very soon."

Six hours later, Kruder unstrapped himself from his chair on the bridge, stretched and yawned. The bridge was dark except for emergency lights and the glow from console displays powered by backup systems. "You know, Hans, I've never been towed back to a station before."

"Not me either, Kapitan. It's kind of relaxing. Knowing there is nothing you can do."

"I suppose. We could do more scan training."

"We'd need a working power source for that, Kapitan."

"What's the latest from engineering on that?"

"Main distribution bank totally overwhelmed. Cascading breaker failure. They're manually resetting everything. The engineer has no idea which system triggered the cascade, so she has to check all of them one at a time. She says between five minutes and five hours for power to be restored. And before you ask, she can't do the bridge first. Something to do with how far we are from the reactors—all the systems between us and there have to be powered first."

"That's no way to build a warship. But then again, we're not a warship, we're a freighter."

"Indeed, Kapitan. Oh, I did get a message from the system patrol. They have our tug."

"I'll court-martial the officer in charge of that for not attaching it properly."

"It was attached properly. All the clamps were set correctly, and they're still engaged."

"How can they still be engaged?"

"Because the system patrol says the clamps are still attached to the tug. The whole hull mounting broke off. Faulty workmanship."

"Put it on the list. Any good news?"

"The emergency egress went extremely well. One hundred percent of the crew reported to the right place, with all the necessary equipment, exited air lock three, climbed across the ship, and re-entered into lock five. No issues."

"Excellent."

"The firefighting drill went well. The equipment tested good. Several of the crew took it upon themselves to break the seals and discharge the actual equipment. In theory, their officers should discipline them, but the officers in question reported that they'd wanted to test everything now, rather than finding our pumps didn't work during a fire. I told them there would be no disciplining."

"Very well. Anything else?"

"The yard crew refused to eat the food prepared for them. The trays were defective."

"How do you have defective trays?"

"No salt."

"How do you make trays without salt?"

"It's a mystery."

The lights came on, and the console displays brightened. "Excellent. Are the scanners online?"

The duty sensor operator was typing furiously on his console. "So far, yes, Kapitan. It will take time to check them all, but it looks like engineering powered them first."

"Excellent. Commence sensor test, sweep fourteen. Let's see if we can get some more out of this test."

It was another week and two more failed test cruises before the ship left orbit to start its cruise. Kruder had named her 'Pinguin' after an old-earth flightless bird, but he spelt it in the Germanish way, not 'Penguin' like the Accursed Imperials did. A pinguin was short, feathered, furry, and nonthreatening. It was also able to dive hundreds of feet deep into the water, surprising its prey. After the major problem of the electrical couplings had been fixed, and the tug supports welded back on, the other problems were only minor, except the food.

"Surely your men can handle bland food for a time, Kapitan," the admiral had said.

"The salt is necessary for survival, Admiral. We had that shipment of trays analyzed. The salt is contained in the nutrient powder mix that it is fortified with during processing. The nutrient value is only five percent of what it should be. A crew surviving on these rations for months at a time would develop severe vitamin deficiencies. Including diseases not seen since antiquity. Like scurvy."

"What would be the effect on the crew?"

"It starts with weakness, fatigue, bleeding from the gums and skin, personality changes and death from infection or bleeding."

"Why was this not included?"

"The fortification mix is one of the more expensive parts of the manufacturing process, so I'm told. And it's hidden. You can't tell that it's missing. If some of our crew hadn't missed the salt... the effects would have been catastrophic on a long voyage."

"I see. I shall arrange an appropriate response."

"Appropriate response?"

"Perhaps I shall find who authorized this, and put them in cells for months, eating only their own food. It will be in the nature of a science experiment. You are ready to depart?"

"Next shift, Admiral."

"Good hunting."

Kruder sat relaxed as the Pinguin approached the system jump limit. He had filed her exit course exactly like a regular freighter, travelling into the Empire. His naval crew was curious about the ship's special features and where they were going. Kruder had let it be known that they were being deployed in a special anti-pirate operation.

"We are on target for jump, Kapitan," Hans said.

"Change of plan, Hans." Kruder brought up a system on the display. "We will go here—a red dwarf with no planets. A long jump, but within our capabilities. We will conduct a few exercises and modify the ship. Inform the bridge of our new course."

Hans busied himself with the new order, and an

acceleration warning bonged as the pilots brought the ship onto a new vector. Hans waited until they had stabilized on the new course before unclipping from his station and approaching the Kapitan.

"Yes, Hans?"

"I understand we are to hunt pirates, Kapitan."

"That is our stated goal for now, yes."

"Will there be pirates in this next system?"

"I do not think so, but we can practice decamouflage and other operations while we are there, before we carry on to more promising hunting grounds."

"I note that we are moving a considerable distance with this jump."

"We are, Hans."

"Almost to the border with the Confederation, in fact."

"Yes."

"And close to the Accursed Empire."

"Yes. Very close."

"Are there pirates in the Accursed Empire, Herr Kapitan? Ships disappearing?"

"I'm sure there are, Hans, I'm sure there are. If not." Kruder smiled. "If not, once we are there, there will surely be some."

CHAPTER NINE

"Watch the curb! You drive like a crazy person." Scruggs grabbed the door as Dena careened their stolen car to the right, around the corner, and onto a side street. They banged over the curb and scraped a pole.

Dena over-corrected, and the car spun left, heading for a closed shop.

Scruggs ducked. "Building! Turn!"

"I'm trying! It's the car." Dena jiggered the wheel. "The steering is loose, and the throttle sticks." She wrenched the vehicle sideways, smashed three chairs, part of a table, and then corrected into the alley. The delivery car they'd stolen had five seats, a rear-mounted motor, trunk in front, and the suspension bounced like used rubber bands.

Scruggs got on the radio to call the others to the cross street. She was still jammed. Hopefully, the centurion would be bringing them in. Dena depressed the brakes. Nothing happened. She stamped harder, the vehicle barely slowed. She stomped the brakes, and they finally caught, forcing a sideways skid that slid the car perpendicular to the street. The brakes smoked and sparked, covering them in dark soot.

"Go. Go." Ana stepped out of the alley and waved.

Figures dashed out of the gloom. Gavin yanked the rear driver's side door and dove in, followed by Dirk and Ana.

Ana waved the smoke away from his face. "What's this run on, coal?"

"Could be. Or bad diesel. Or grease."

"Or sunshine and rainbows. Which you'll see from the inside of a cell if we don't get moving, Nature Girl."

Dena revved the engine, and the car shook and inched forward. She cursed, slammed the accelerator down and the car putted along.

"We could use some speed, here, Ms. Dena," Dirk said. "I'd like to get away—Whoa."

The car leaped forward. Dena cursed as the car skidded from side to side. "Everything sticks. Steering, gas, the works."

"Couldn't you have found a bigger vehicle?" Gavin asked. "Or one powered by something that doesn't belch black sludge?"

"Sorry." Dena spun the wheel and counted. "One-two-three and turn. This was what was available, and Scruggs's seduction skills need work."

"She seduced her way into getting a car? I thought that was your thing?"

"She has her own pattern, different than mine, she brings her own unique view to male-female relationships."

"Huh?"

"What I mean, wait one." Dena found a crossroads ahead,

then spun the wheel ninety degrees. She counted to three before the turn kicked in, and she took the corner with only a minor amount of careening. "Three-second delay, got it. What I mean is that I try to handle men with subtlety, and a delicate touch. Scruggs uses a different method."

"Which is?"

"She beats them senseless. Wait one." Dena spun the wheel in advance of a corner, and they slung around it. "Think I got it now."

"Dena," Dirk said. "When did you start saying things like 'wait one' and all this other military talk? Have you been practicing?"

Dena cursed.

Ana laughed. "The rubbing off is going both ways, I see. Nature Girl, where are we going?"

"I'm zigzagging to get away from the area. But I'm lost."

Ana activated his comm. "Let's see if we're outside of the jamming. Lee, where are we?"

Lee's voice came up. "You're back. Good. I've been following the police band. The police are still on the scene of that car crash."

"That'll be fake. A setup to designed to pull the police away from the real action. What else is going on?"

"Fire units are responding to a gas explosion in your area."

"A gas explosion? You mean the gas that exploded when those chowderheads opened up on us with a machine gun?" Ana asked.

"No talk of machine guns on the radio, Centurion. What happened?"

"No time for details. Get us out of here and back to the ship."

"I leave you alone for a few minutes, and then the police —never mind. All your beacons are off. Somebody bring one up."

Ana clicked his. "Try me."

"See you now on the screen. Give me a minute."

A large cross street appeared ahead of them, and Ana tapped Dena's shoulder and gestured at the street. "Nature Girl, start taking us generally north. That will bring us to the spaceport fence, and we can follow along 'til we get to the cut we made."

"Which way is north?" Dirk asked.

Ana, Scruggs, and Gavin all pointed to their right. Dena tilted her head right but didn't take her hands off the wheel.

"How do you all know that?"

"Compass," Scruggs said. "Planet has a magnetic field."

Gavin nodded. "Or just look at your comm. It has a display."

"I didn't know you could do that," Dirk said.

"Does it bother anybody other than me," Dena said, "that our starship pilot has a problem with directions?"

"You're only just noticing that?" Ana said. "I'm surprised at you."

Dirk sniffed. "Directions are relative in space. You say them differently."

"Turning right. Or as you would say, yabba-dabba-do, or some space speak." Dena spun the wheel and started her count.

Lee cracked over the radio. "All the jamming has stopped. Wait! Don't go right!"

"Too late." Dena glided the car past the corner. "What's the problem?"

The dust and smoke from the fire cleared. Ahead, on the right side, sat two trucks, with uniformed figures milling beside. One, a flatbed, had a rear-mounted machine gun, aimed to the side.

"You've gone in a circle—you're in front of the insurance building again."

Dena slammed on the brakes. Nothing happened.

"GO-GO-GO. Forward." Ana pulled his revolver, swapped hands, stuck his arm out the window and fired it left-handed. Bullets tinged off the truck cab.

Dena pumped the brakes once, twice, three times, then gave up and slammed the gas down. She pulled the wheel to the right.

The car wheezed faster. A uniformed woman wearing a red bandanna grabbed the fender of the rear truck and jumped up onto the back. She flinched as a bullet banged off the truck but rolled behind the machine gun. Hiding behind the gun shield, she reached to grasp the triggers. She pivoted, waited for the car to steam directly into her sights, aimed down the bore, led the target, and pulled the trigger.

The car's hydraulics caught up with Dena's actions. It stopped dead, then surged forward and spun right, cutting across the front of the armed truck. The machine gun chewed the ground harmlessly beside her.

Five armed troopers stood beside the next truck. All five

aimed, but hitting a moving car from a standing position is difficult, especially when said car is careening directly at you. They scattered. Dena whipped by, clipped a trooper, side-swiped the truck and bounced off to the left as her frantic wheel motions caught up. She steadied the vehicle, aimed at a cloud of dust from her collision, and shoved them into the middle of the road.

Everyone in the car yelled, ducked, and covered their faces.

Ana pulled his gun inside, shielded his head until the swaying stopped, then popped up "Close one that. Navigator—directions."

"I see you on the screens now," Lee said. "Keep on this road and you'll hit the main gate at the spaceport in about ten minutes."

"Turn us off before then," Ana said. "Get us somewhere quiet on a side street."

"Working on it," Lee said. "Dena, take your next left, then next right."

TING. Everyone in the back seat ducked.

"They're shooting at us," Dirk yelled.

"Try not to soil yourself, Navy," Ana said. "I hate the smell. And of course they're shooting at us. We blew up their super-secret data center. And does anybody know why that place was a super-secret data center? I thought it was an insurance company. Engineer, your friend said they were slightly crooked, but this seems extreme."

"Something I think everybody should know." Dirk related the information about the coding software he and Dena had found.

Ana grunted. "A Nat spy ring. Explains the security. And the cops must have been paid off not to respond. The last thing they would want is police roaming around their secret office. Did you know this, Engineer?"

Gavin coughed. "Well."

Ana leaned forward. "Give it up."

"Well…" Gavin wiped dirt from his forehead. "It's crooked, sure, but my friend said that it might actually be a front for Nat naval intelligence. Maybe doing some listening to Imperial and other communications, and maybe some code breaking."

"We just attacked the Nat Navy?"

"Disavowed, they call it," Gavin said. "No official cover."

"They're going to be unhappy that we blew it up."

"They blew it up themselves," Dirk said.

"I'm fairly certain that's not how it will read in the after-action report. Certainly not how I'd write it. 'Unknown opposing fire caused widespread disruption.' Something like that."

Scruggs turned around from the front seat. "You fake your after-action reports, Centurion?"

"Not all of them," Ana said. "Ammunition expenditure, for example. I was always honest on that."

"You didn't over-report usage and sell the rest?" Gavin asked. "Or at least keep it for practice?"

Ana blinked. "You know, you think you're too old to learn something new, and then it just pops up and bites you on your elbow. Engineer, that's a marvelous idea, I don't know why I didn't think of it before."

TING. Dirk ducked again. "Can we discuss something else, like how to get away safely, without getting shot up. More shot up, that is."

"Calm yourself, Navy," Ana said. "We're exiting the battle space at speed, our enemies are disorganized, and are not pursuing. We're in good shape."

Dena turned left as directed by Lee. The crossroad was narrower, and still not paved. The next turn put them in an alley. Wide, open, but rutted and potholed.

Dena cursed some more, trying to time the delayed steering in advance of the potholes. The car rocked as they dove into a rut and the whole rear seat banged heads on the roof.

"This isn't the best road, if this keeps up, we're—"

WHAM. The front hood snapped fully open. It smashed the windshield into a spiderweb of cracks.

"Shape just got worse," Dena said. "I can't see to avoid—" The vehicle rocketed again as they smashed into another pothole. "Mother of Empresses, that hurt."

"Slow down," Ana said. "We'll take it easier, they won't be able to get behind us in that alley. Lee, how much longer?"

"Six minutes on this road at that speed."

Dirk exhaled. "Good. Only a few minutes, and we can turn off, ditch the car, and get back under that fence. Everything is going our way now."

POOF. The rear-mounted radiator blew in a cloud of steam, and wet smoke poured out of the back. The transmission revved and the car glided to a stop. Everybody bailed out of the doors, rolling away from the steam bath and cursing.

The car blew another blast of wet air. They crawled away from the steaming, spitting engine.

"Or not," Dirk said.

"Ladies, I don't need more help." Dirk squirmed.

Dena ignored him. "Scruggs, just lift him up. We can drag him up."

"I will not be dragged," Dirk said.

"You're porkier than I remember." Dena helped Dirk to his feet. "Maybe spend a little more time in the gym in the future."

"The pilot is not porky," Scruggs said. "He's..."

"Chunky?" Ana loaded the last of his bullets in his revolver. "Portly? Plump? Fleshy?"

"Portly works," Scruggs said. "It sounds kind of dignified."

"Thank you, ladies," Dirk said. "I will be fine now. Let's be on our way." He stumbled along the road. The piles of software had slid farther down his coveralls. His legs now resembled two greasy sausages. He couldn't squeeze them past each other, so he had to adopt a rolling side-to-side motion. After ten feet, he tripped over a pothole and fell again.

"Outstanding," Ana said. "Engineer, can we dump any of that software?"

"Your guess is as good as mine, Centurion." Gavin hefted his bag. "I've got dozens crammed in here, but the only labels are 12-digit part numbers—we can only guess if we have what we need, and I'd hate to throw away something good."

"So, we watch Navy here waddle down the street. And wait for those chowderheads in those trucks to shoot us down as soon as they find us."

"And they've paid off the local police, so no help there."

"No." Ana smirked. "No help there at all. Not if they've paid off the police. Maybe we can use that. Navigator, are you there?"

Lee's voice came over their comms. "I am."

"Where's our pursuers?"

"Not sure, Centurion. There's police activity five blocks away, but the reports of gunfire have gone away."

"Right. Lee, we need a bar."

"A bar? You want to stop for a beer?"

"I don't drink beer. Brandy is what I drink. Neat."

"I'm not sure—"

"Find us something close by that sells alcohol, and track where the police are located."

Ten minutes later, the five of them swarmed out of an alley and into an intersection. All, even Scruggs, had bottles in their hands and clothes that reeked of spilled alcohol. Ana, Gavin, Dena, and Dirk smoked local cigars. Scruggs carried hers. Ana was singing a ribald song called "The Talented Girls of Tango-D." Dirk and Gavin threw in their own verses from time to time. Dena extemporized complaints about the minimal capabilities of the boys of Tango-D, and Scruggs blushed a lot.

Two police cars with flashing lights surrounded two cars crashed in the middle of the intersection. A battered black four-door sedan and a blue panel van were locked together. Other police cars were parked on opposite sides of the crash at the head of adjacent alleys. The two crash victims stood next to the driver's side of the T-boned sedan. Two police officers stood next to them laboriously filling out forms on their comm. A third walked around waving away what little traffic had stopped. Power and light poles lined the street. Overhead lights and Traffic Control lights draped across every corner, barely cutting through the gloom.

The two drivers answered questions. No, they hadn't been drinking. Happy to wait for the alcohol check. Didn't see the other. Not hurt at all, very lucky. Mistakes happen, they were sure their insurance would cover it. No problem, officer, take your time. How do you spell that? It's complicated. Do you need my middle name?

"Hey," Ana yelled. "Over there. Minions of the law. You looking for us?"

The two police officers turned and glared. Then their eyes widened. The two 'accident' drivers' eyes also widened, and they reached for comms and started muttering in them.

"No," one of the officers stuttered. "No. We're not looking for anybody. Traffic duty."

"You sure?" Ana marched closer. The alcohol fumes preceded him. "Not looking for terrorists who bombed an insurance company a few blocks from here?"

"You know about that?" one of the drivers said.

"Know about it? We did it," Ana said. "And proud of it."

The two officers turned white. "We don't know anything about that. I think we're done here. I'm sure this was an accident. No need to file a report."

"We can wait," Ana said. "I'm sure these fine gentlemen want to get everything about their accident squared away. Maybe call somebody, tell them something."

Both drivers stared. One of their comms bonged, and the man answered it. "Yes. Right here. Yes. No, there's five of them. No, we don't, you said don't bring any... Now? Fine." He lowered his comm and muttered to his friend.

The police glanced at the accident victims. The older of the two shook his head.

"Well," the officer said, "I'm sure you didn't mean it. You two can go, and all you folks go away, or we'll arrest you—"

"Outstanding," Ana said. "That's what we're looking for, being arrested. Being taken into custody? Becoming the responsibility of the local police."

"No, no, no, we—"

Ana clenched the cigar in his teeth, stepped forward and slapped the policeman across the face. "There you go. Assaulting an officer. Arrest us."

"No, no—"

Ana slapped the police officer again, knocking him down. "Arrest me. Arrest me."

The police officer jumped back up and reached for his weapon. The other grabbed his arm. "Not our fight, Diib. Remember what we were told. Don't get involved with that office. Call it in. Let them go. The others will take care of it."

A round of applause came from the half dozen or so watchers beyond the traffic lane. "That's it. Give it to the man!" a long-haired man yelled.

The two driver types were muttering into their comms again.

Ana advanced on the police. The second officer dragged the first away, muttering in his ear.

Ana brandished his cigar. "Aren't you going to arrest me?"

The police scuttled away. The accident drivers backed away, chattering into their comms. The remaining four of Heart's Desire's crew drifted apart.

Two trucks gunned into view down the street. Their lights lit the tableau. Ana had chased the police officers across the street and to the corner. The drivers and the crash stood in the middle.

"Arrest me," Ana said again.

"Not our problem anymore, buddy. Our friends will take care of you." The police backed out of the light.

Ana measured the approaching headlights. "Scruggs, with me. Dena, get ready. You're left and back, I'm right and front."

Scruggs jogged across the street to stand next to Ana. "Suck in," Ana yelled.

Dena stuck her cigar into her mouth and drew a big breath. The tip glowed brightly. Dirk and Gavin did the same. Scruggs tried, but she coughed and gagged as the smoke entered her lungs.

Two heavy trucks appeared out of the gloom and slowed as they approached the intersection. With the crash and the police cars, they wouldn't be able to get by, so the two vehicles slowed to a crawl.

Ana waited until they were only two dozen feet away. "Light em up!" He stabbed his cigar into the wick hidden inside his bottle, and the alcohol-infused cloth lit. He flung the bottle at the driver's side of the closest vehicle. It was one-third full of sand for weight, the rest full of a mixture of bought alcohol and stolen hand soap. It smashed and sheeted flame all over the side of the truck. Scruggs's bottle followed a second later, hitting the rear door, and flaming over the top and back part.

Dena, their official low-tech athlete, threw an arcing toss over the first truck. Her bottle smashed onto the hood of the second vehicle. Dirk, beside her, lit his fuse, then handed it to Dena. Nobody believed he would hit anything.

Gavin scooted away from the collision, pausing to toss his bottle into the police car next to the crash. Rifles fired from the burning trucks at random targets. The two police hiding behind the burning car fled to a side street, followed by the two fake crash victims.

Troops dove out of the two burning trucks.

"With me, Private." Ana ran. "Get a weapon."

The passenger of the first truck dove out and rolled, away from the fire, rolling over and over, coming to rest against Ana's waiting boot. Ana stomped on his hand, and grabbed the now free rifle, and stepped back. "Hands up. Both of you. All of you."

The driver dove out of the burning truck and rolled to her knees, hands held high. Ana's capture lay still and lifted his hands. The truck belched a gout of flame. Another body dove out of the back, hitting the ground with a thud. Scruggs scooped up his rifle, stepped back, and helped cover the three.

Ana walked backwards from the burning vehicle. "Scruggs, herd 'em up here. I want to hear what they have to say."

Scruggs yelled and gestured, and the three captives stumbled forward away from the heat and flame, hands held high.

Ana stopped midway between the burning trucks and the police-accident fire. Dena and Dirk's attack had been just as effective. Dirk was covering three other captives, including one of the biggest men Ana had ever seen. He must have been at least seven feet tall. Dena was dragging something up from the ground.

"Navy, get Hercules and his friends up here where we can talk to them. We need some answers before the local rapid response squad arrives."

"You heard the man," Dirk yelled at his prisoners. "Hands high, walk up forward. Dena, leave it, it's too big."

"Like that's ever been true before." Dena stooped to examine a gun. "That one doesn't work on me. I've used it too many times myself. Oh, Dirk, Dirk, Dirk, this is the biggest gun I've ever seen."

"Navy, get up here. Nature Girl, what in the Emperor's name are you doing?"

Dena stood the gun vertically. It was as tall as her, with a foot-wide drum ammunition magazine attached. "The big guy there had this. He must have taken it off the back of the truck. I want to see it fire."

"What is it—no, not that way."

Dena yanked the gun into her arms and staggered back under the weight. Staggering caused her to shift her balance, which made her move her hands. Which made her pull the trigger.

At full automatic, the recoil slammed her around in a circle, and the gun barrel lifted skyward. It fired next to the heads of her prisoners, through the closer truck windshield, and over the heads of Scruggs's captives. Shots punctured the far truck's fuel tank and blasted two overhead electrical transformers to bits in a shower of sparks. The burning transformer swung down and blew out a neon beer sign and smashed a store window containing children's shoes. The sparking wires dropped and danced. The leaking fuel tank exploded with a whump, knocking crew, captives, and onlookers down with a wet smoky shockwave. A smaller bang blew shoes over the crowd.

Dust blew around the intersection. A police car edged in from the far side, lights flashing but no siren. It stopped in the light of the burning truck, Gavin climbed out and surveyed the ruins.

Dirk helped Dena up. Three of the prisoners had already vanished into the gloom, two more climbed up and ran into the darkness. Ana walked to the one remaining. He was unconscious but still breathing.

"So much for finding out who they were. Sound off."

"Here, Centurion," Scruggs said. "Unwounded. One rifle."

"I'm fine, Centurion," Dirk said. "I'll help Dena as long as I can waddle along. She's a little stunned."

"Engineer?" Ana said.

Gavin gestured at the police car. "I grabbed us a car. I talked to Lee. We kicked up an ant's nest. Now there are cars responding from all over town in all directions. One more won't make a difference. Let's get out of here."

"Outstanding. Everyone pile in and let's go. Nature Girl, you need help?"

"A little."

"Problems walking?"

"Surprised more than anything. First time that's ever been true."

"What's true?"

"What I said."

"And what, Nature Girl, did you say that's so surprisingly true?"

Dena pointed at the machine gun. "Over there. It's true." She nodded. "That's the biggest one I've ever seen."

CHAPTER TEN

"Form input error thirty-seven," Devin, the Lord Lyon, brother to the Empress, fabulously wealthy noble and Imperial Tribune, read. "Unanticipated over-storage of collected totals. Ensure that quantities on hand, in storage, in transit, and expended are included in current totals. Ensure that losses are correlated to approved actions, subject to conditions on ammunition expenditures required by Imperial form hxa-235-3/c."

He rubbed his eyes and stared at the screen on his desk. His desk and credenza were polished dark wood that said 'expensive.' The paintings on the wall said 'taste,' but the comm equipment on the desk said 'Navy.'

"Conditions on ammunition expenditures," he said. "What conditions?" He brought up a search screen and typed "What are conditions on ammunition expenditures?"

The computer returned 43,216 hits. Devin cursed. He tapped his fingers, then searched for form hxa-235-3/c. It popped up on his screen. "Thirty-six pages." He tapped the screen again. "And one hundred twenty pages of addendum." He opened his liquor cabinet and selected a glass carved from a single quartz crystal—a gift from his sister—and poured a stiff drink. "I serve the Empire."

Then he typed.

Four hours and two more drinks later, his intercom bonged. "Yes?"

"Imin sir. Have some people at the main hatch to speak with you sir. You might want to ask them some questions."

"Some people?"

"Friends of mine, sir. Friends of a friend, actually."

"Fine. Come in here for the interrogation, Imin. And send for the Subprefect."

"We're on our way, sir."

Devin poked at his computer for a few more minutes, sighed, and sat back in his chair. The door bonged and Devin buzzed Imin in.

"The Empire runs on forms, Imin."

"It does sir."

"We have just achieved a great victory over the Confederation forces, Imin."

"We have sir."

"At minimal losses, we have recaptured an Imperial system, destroyed thousands of tons of enemy warships, spoiled their transport capacity, and regained the glory of the Empire."

"Indeed sir."

"Do you know what form input error thirty-seven is, Imin?"

"You used the wrong units somewhere, sir. Double-check your numbers."

"I have double-checked, triple-checked."

"Still an error somewhere sir."

"Did I mention our great victory?"

"You did sir. Great victory."

"Why am I compelled to fill out these stupid forms?"

"Regulations, sir."

"To a tabbo's tusk with regulations. There's a death warrant out on me. I think I'll just ignore these forms. I'll have you send them in."

"Oh no sir." Imin shook his head. "Can't ignore regulations. Or forms. And you don't want to mess with the supply bureau sir. Very dangerous."

"Imin, you just followed me into battle. Into a battle we nearly didn't win. We took on a ship five times our size."

"And won, sir."

"Yes, but the issue was in doubt."

"Not with you in charge, sir, it wasn't. You'd figure it out."

"You could have died."

"I'll take my chances with you, sir. I trust you."

"Does that mean you'll file these forms for me?"

"No sir."

"You'll follow me into battle, risk death at the enemies' hands, but you won't file a form?"

"No sir."

"Why?"

"Scared of the supply people, sir. Rather be in a bar fight with the whole crew of an ore freighter than face them."

"Scared of the—"

The door bonged, and Subprefect Lionel's face appeared on the intercom. Devin waved him in and pointed at a chair in front of his desk. "Steward Imin here says he'll risk death for me but won't fill out my ammunition replenishment forms for me."

Lionel slouched down into the chair. "Smart man, your steward. Always knew he had a good head on his shoulders."

"Would you be—"

"No. Don't even ask. Ordering ordnance is always the captain's responsibility, says so in the regs."

"I could order you to do it."

"Still won't do it."

"That's mutiny."

"I have a better chance of coming out of a court martial with a commendation and three weeks' extra leave granted than winning a fight with the supply bureau. You have to fix it yourself."

"It's this stupid error, thirty-seven."

"You used the wrong units somewhere. You have to triple-check your numbers."

"I already did that, I—"

The door bonged again. The Marines escorted a young man in an ill-fitting Imperial uniform with no insignia in front of his desk, and a woman dressed the same. Devin waved the Marines out and steepled his hands and settled in to listen.

"They were all dead? You're sure they were dead? All of them?" Devin regarded the two spacemen in front of his desk.

"We didn't check every compartment, sir." The man in

front of him was taller than anybody on Pollux, and so thin, his uniform flapped on his arms. But he gave off an impression of aggressive sharpness, reminding Devin of an old-style letter opener he'd once seen. He also stood at attention, proper attention, like he'd been in the Navy. "Everybody we saw was dead. Engineering had been blown open to space, so we could only get into the hab modules. We hovered nearby, hopped on, and did a quick walk-through. It was all corpses, mostly not suited up. Somebody came up close and popped them good. Whoever was on duty in the control room had managed to get a helmet on, but they'd been shredded."

"Shredded?" Devin turned to the woman to his left. "What does he mean, shredded?"

The woman was just as thin, but not as tall. Her coveralls fit but were worn at the knees and elbows. She exuded the same feral sharpness as the man did. She also stood at military attention. She looked at Imin, standing at her side. He nodded.

"Automatic gun sir," the woman said. "Ship-mounted frightener. Half inch. Somebody got in close and sprayed everywhere."

"Frightener?"

"Short-range ship weapon, sir. Nonexplosive kinetic projectiles, sir. Chemical propulsion, belt fed. Usually a thousand-round belt. Whole thing goes on a powered turret on the outside of a ship hull, in a single package. Or mounted axial on a small craft."

"And you know this how?"

"Characteristic damage, sir. Those half-inch bullets are

powerful enough to damage a ship. Powerful enough to break sensors, cut control lines, and de-air the ship with pinholes. That's what we saw on that freighter. But they're not explosive, so they won't ignite the oxygen and blow the ship to pieces."

"I misspoke," Devin said. "Not, how did you know the attack was made by this type of weapon, but how do you know the characteristics of this type of weapon? I've never heard of a 'frightener' as a weapon."

The woman's eyes flicked down. "It's common in some circles."

"And low velocity, short-range, unguided bullets, against a warship?" Devin popped his feet up on his desk and tapped his ship slippers. "You might as well take off your slippers and throw them. You'll have more chance of damage then. Isn't that so, Imin?"

Imin bustled to the sideboard. "Tea, sir?"

"Thank you. Imin, have you ever heard of such a weapon?"

"Yes sir. Common in some circles, as the lady said."

"Which circles?"

"Circles that don't attack warships, sir. Not much use against a reinforced hull. But merchant ships aren't reinforced."

Devin held up his hands. "But no range, no guidance? How do you hit anything?"

"Have to get up close sir. Like if a ship is refueling, or stuck in cargo transfer, or doesn't keep a good watch. These guns are small, they look like a sensor if you do it right. Or put a fabric bulge over them to hide them, so they look like part of the hull."

"Why in the Emperor's name would you attack a merchant ship's hull with weapons that kill the crew, but can't go through any sort of serious metal? All ships are metal. Even cargo containers are metal. Can you shoot through the side of a container, then?"

"Not easily sir," the woman said.

"Then what's the point—Emperor's toenails, you're pirates." Devin glared at Imin. "You brought pirates onboard to see me?"

The steward clicked a counter on a microwave. "Hot water shortly, sir."

"Imin, are these people pirates?"

"More along the lines of smugglers, sir. I heard some rumors about things, about the Confeds and why they attacked Sand Harbor. I contacted some people to check things, see what the word on the street was. Some things didn't add up, some folks had seen some strange things, they had been in the Confederation and heard rumors, so I asked some questions, and that led me to ask these folks to come and share their stories with you."

"Share their stories?" Devin looked at the man in front of him. "You're here to share your story, are you?"

"Sir." The man braced.

"Were you ever in the Navy?"

"No sir."

"Never?"

"No sir."

"What's your name again?"

"John Smith, sir."

"What ship?"

"Presently between ships, sir."

Devin turned to the woman. "Let me guess. Jane Smith? Also between ships?"

The woman nodded. "Yes sir."

"Imin, is that their names?"

Imin pulled a cup from the microwave. "That's the name they were using when I was introduced, sir."

"I see. You two—you know I could just have you scanned to get IDs, do you?"

John Smith gulped. "Mr. Imin said you wouldn't do that, sir."

"He did, did he?"

Imin put a steaming cup on Devin's desk. "I did sir. It was in the way of a promise, like. I'd rather you didn't do that, sir."

"You wouldn't, would you?"

Imin drew himself to attention. "Rather not, sir."

"Right." Devin stirred his tea. "You, John Smith."

"Sir?"

"Give it to me. The whole thing. What you got there, why, the whole bit. Tell the truth, and you can go. No ID checks. But no holding anything back. If you do, I'll know."

John raised his eyebrows.

"Okay, I won't. Imin will, though. You can discuss it with him if you like."

John shook his head. When he'd first slouched in, he

had dropped into Devin's red-fabric visitors' seats. At Imin's frown, he'd hopped up and braced to attention. Imin then glared at the chairs—like he was contemplating burning the chairs and spacing the charred remains out the air lock. Or perhaps that was his plan for the visitors. "Rather not, sir. We were in the... a system. I don't want to say where—"

Imin interrupted. "I have a good idea of the system name, sir. No need to discuss it with these folks. That way, they'll be able to say they didn't tell you."

Devin waved. "In a system. Doing what?"

"Meeting people to exchange some goods."

"Stolen goods? Smuggled goods?"

"Wasn't my job to track the origin, sir. But nothing we should clear at a customs port, that's for sure. We jumped in, just outside the jump limit. No settlements. No rocky planets at all. But an ice giant to refuel if you were short. It was a meeting place, like. Our ship had been there before. We jumped and the ship we were supposed to meet was there already. But drifting. Not answering hails, not moving, no responding to anything. We were in a hurry, so the captain, she hustled us over—"

Devin pointed at Jane. "You the captain?"

She shook her head. "Weapons tech, sir."

"What's your job, then?" Devin said to John.

"Spacehand, sir. Outside. Docking, cargo transfer, general maintenance, and uh... portable weapons."

"Fine." Devin folded his hands. "Continue."

"Well, we closed up to this ship... Mr. Imin has the name, maybe..."

"I do, sir."

"We closed up to her, didn't take more than twenty minutes. We always met up very close... I mean, if we had been..."

"Stop prevaricating," Devin said.

The man tilted his head. "Sir?"

"Don't lie. Just get on with it. Stop being evasive."

Imin grunted. "Don't waste the Tribune's time. Tell it like it was, straight out."

John spoke in a rush. "We go to this system every few months. Meet two different ships. We know them, and we always meet in the same place. Quick jump in, trade containers of stolen items, and hop out. It was all arranged beforehand, somebody else shipped us the goods. We went out to the dark and swapped them. The other freighters were usually Confed. We swapped stolen Imperial goods for stolen Confed goods. That way, nobody would get caught. They gave us proper import paperwork showing they were duty paid into the Empire. Once we got the new stuff, we'd head for an Imperial port and sell it. Go back trading, then we'd do it again. Good money. This time, somebody got there before us. They'd chewed up that other ship."

"Tell the rest," Imin said. "Tell the Tribune how it happened. And what you told me."

"We weren't there, but the way this works is, we come up close and swap, and then go our way. Somebody must have come up close and blew their engine room. Then riddled the ship and killed everybody. Why do that?"

"Because they're pirate scum," Devin said.

"Maybe, Tribune, maybe. But where's the profit in it?

They could have shot up the whole hab module, then boarded it, made repairs and sailed away. Or at least rifle through the containers attached for something good to sell. But they didn't do anything like that. They blew the engine room, and shot up the rest. Carol—I mean Jane…"

Carol/Jane glared at the man's slip, then compressed her lips. "It was a proper starship weapon. A laser probably, big one, big as on this ship, Tribune."

"And you know this because you were in the Navy, correct?"

Carol nodded. "You know I was, Tribune. Gunner's mate. John… Derek… there was a Marine. His specialty is boarding. We're not pirates, Tribune. No way. But people talk. The way it works, if you're out hunting, you want the ship, the cargo, and the crew in that order. Take the ship somewhere and sell it, or at least strip it for parts, and you want the cargo to mix around and sell. Then the crew, well, the thing is, somebody has to fly the ship back. You can put our own people on board, but why bother? Some of these captains aren't too bright. They treat the crew like slaves, and if you shoot the captain and the officers, oftentimes, the crew will cheer you on. Specially the Confed crews, they do not like their commissars. You'd be surprised how many sign on with us later, or take a cut and go live somewhere else. Some other planet."

"Where are these swap places? And where do you break your cargoes up?"

Carol/Jane shook her head. "I can't navigate a starship. Don't know where we go. But there's lots of borders near here. We go to systems, meet a depot ship, which can fix things or strip them down and do what needs to be done. They go back to Imperial Space, stooge around, and do it all over again."

"And this whole shooting up a merchant ship was unusual?"

Both Carol and Derek nodded. "No profit in it, sir. What's the point of shooting people up if you're not making any cash out of it?"

"Some of us do it for honor," Devin said.

"We'll leave that to you rich people, Tribune," Carol said. "Some of us can't afford honor."

"How do you make a profit out of this?" Devin wondered. "There can't be enough gold or jewels, or currency in cargoes to make this worthwhile. How do you make a living?"

"Food," John/Derek said. "Food is the best."

"You pirate a ship for food?"

"Best haul we ever had was maple syrup, sir. You can sell a liter of maple syrup for a hundred credits. That's a hundred thousand credits a ton. Molasses is good too. You get a full container of molasses, that's a million credits, maybe. Everybody wants some, for cooking, or pancakes. They'll pay big for the natural stuff."

"Or shampoo," Jane/Carol said. "Container load of shampoo bottles. Easy to sell on frontier planets, or anywhere. Nobody asks if you stole your shampoo."

Devin looked at Imin. Imin nodded. Devin tapped his fingers on his desk. "You'll kill a man for a box of shampoo? Kill a man that never did anything to you?"

"You'll kill a man for having a different-colored uniform. A man that never did anything to you."

"But you do it for money."

"So do you." John/Derek grunted. "Everybody needs to earn a living."

Devin stared silently for twenty seconds. "Why are you telling me this?"

"Mr. Imin asked us to, sir."

Devin snorted. "Mr. Imin asked you to? So you just did it?"

"Yes sir."

"Why?"

Carol looked at Imin, then back at Devin. "We're afraid of him, sir."

Devin laughed. "That's the most truthful thing you've said yet. You're afraid of him?"

"We don't do what he says, we're dead."

"My steward will kill you if you don't speak to me?"

"Not personally, maybe, sir. But we work for some scary people. People I don't plan to cross, ever. Mr. Imin, he went to see them. Spoke to them. They treated him real respectful. Called him 'Mr.' And 'sir.' He talked to them, and next thing we know we're told go with him and speak to you. Tell everything. Even the stuff we're not supposed to talk about amongst ourselves. They said we should leave out names and places, though. Names of ships, systems. Mr. Imin would deal with that."

"No worries there, Tribune," Imin said. "I've got all that."

"Good to know." Devin regarded the two pirates. "What else do I need to know?"

Carol scowled. "Somebody shot up that ship for no reason, sir. Somebody rich. Otherwise, they would have taken the cargo at least. And they didn't negotiate or anything, just got in close and fired. And they've got at least one big weapon, warship like you, they didn't blow that drive room with half-inch bullets."

"Who was it?"

"Not a pirate, sir. Unless they were insane."

Devin nodded. "An insane pirate? Isn't that normal?"

"No sir. Crew wouldn't stand for that type of destruction, not regular. They want to get paid too. That shooting can happen once, by accident. Twice, and the captain would go out the air lock. We're not murderers. This is a job."

Devin cracked his fingers one at a time. "Imin, anything I missed here?"

"No sir."

"We're done with these folks. Walk them out. And give them something for their time. Something to make it worthwhile."

"Yes sir."

"You two. Keep silent about this. But if you find out more, and you let us know, there'll be more money for you."

"Don't need more money," John/Derek said. "Just want to go."

"Nevertheless, there will be some. Imin will see to that. And if you talk about this, well, Imin will see to that as well. Imin?"

Imin braced to attention. The others did likewise and filed out.

Devin flexed his fingers one at a time, thinking. It was almost fifteen minutes until Imin returned. As Devin's personal steward, he didn't have to knock.

"All taken care of, Imin?"

"They'll keep quiet, sir, and let us know if anything else comes up."

"You know a lot of pirates, Imin?"

"These folk are more smugglers, sir. That part is the truth. I know a lot of people, sir. Some of them owe me favors. Ask a friend of a friend of a friend of a friend, and you can learn a lot."

"Can we trust pirate scum, Imin?"

"No sir. Unless they're frightened. Very frightened."

"Indeed. Do you know where this system is, where they met up?"

"I know of three it could be. Could be any of them, but they're all within easy jump. I... uh, took the liberty of contacting the navigation watch and suggesting you might be looking at those three systems. They should have the calculations up shortly."

"Of course you did." Devin tapped his comm. "Helm?"

"Here sir," a voice said.

"Ready to depart?"

"Sir, we've recalled the working parties on the station. We have a course to the jump limit laid in, and we'll have the jump calculations your steward suggested done by the time we get there. "

"Wait 'til they get back, then head out. I'll review the jump courses before we go."

"Review the jump courses? You, sir, you'll—I mean. Yes sir. Of course. Standing by for your review. Of the jump courses. Sir."

Devin clicked off the channel and held his head for a moment, then turned to a stone-faced Imin. "Do. Not. Laugh. Not now."

"Wasn't thinking of it sir. Not for a moment."

Devin tapped the channel again. "Strike my last. As soon as the Subprefect authorizes it, leave the station. To the jump limit, and then navigator's discretion for courses."

"Yes sir. Um, you'll need, I mean…"

Devin clicked the channel off and rubbed his head again. Imin made a strangled noise and bent over some dirty teacups.

"Something to say, Imin?"

"Never, sir."

Devin clicked the channel again. "Helm?"

"Sir?"

"Execute. Execute-execute-execute."

CHAPTER ELEVEN

"Lifting." Lee maxed the thruster slider. "Once we're in orbit, I have a course to Pilot's friend."

Gavin clambered into the seat behind her, rubbing blood from his nose. "Good deal."

"Where is everybody? What happened? And you stink."

"Those alleys behind those houses were disgusting. Not sure that town ran to sewers yet. They must poop in the streets, like you do, Rocky." Rocky the whippet had jumped into the adjacent seat. His tail thumped as Gavin strapped him into his harness. Harness meant strange motions, but then no gravity, and no gravity was fun. The crew would throw his ball for hours and he could chase it by bouncing off the walls and ceilings.

"Ick. Did we get the software?"

"We got software, all right. I don't know what type."

"Anyone hurt?"

"Nothing bad. Dena got banged around, the old man is

putting her in the med unit. Scruggs is helping the skipper take off his clothes."

"What?" Lee jerked. "Scruggs is…"

"Taking Dirk's clothes off. It will be difficult. He's all swelled up."

"Oh." Lee blinked. "I see."

Ana and Dena crowded into the control room. Dena rubbed her hips. "That's the biggest one I've ever seen, Old Man. I think it broke me."

"Nonsense," Ana said. "I've seen bigger. Why, I've got bigger myself. Mine is huge."

"I'd like to see that sometime," Dena said. "For comparison, you know."

"If we're in atmosphere, I'll even let you play with it. Fire it off a few times."

"That would be fun."

"Always is. Hello, Rocky! How's my favorite whippet!"

Rocky's tail thumped. Ana had saved him from suffocating a while back, even putting a temporary breathing bubble around him. And he helped him find the best toys to play with on the planets, like squirrels and lizards. Rocky liked chasing lizards.

"Slide over, furred one, and I'll strap myself in." Ana lifted Rocky up, slid underneath and did up his own harness. "Thanks. Nature Girl, run a scan like I showed you before. I'll do my own and we'll compare. Engineer, anything we should know?"

Gavin shook his head. "Systems nominal. Still nominal for us. The Tribune's people did a good job on their installations." Tribune Devin had his engineering people do a quick and dirty overhaul before letting them go chasing into the core. It had also been his suggestion that they find some sort of weapon for the Heart's Desire, as he had nothing that could be mounted on a merchant ship.

"Dena," Lee said. "You said you wanted to—"

"Play with the centurion's gun. I want to see how it rates to the others. Has Scruggs called up yet?"

"No," Lee said.

Dena tapped her comm. "Scruggs? Have you got his pants off yet?"

Scruggs's voice came over the comm. "No. He's all crowded and stuck together. I'm having to use both hands. But I'm making progress."

"How much longer?"

"A few more yanks and I've got it all. It will make a huge mess on the floor, though."

"Scruggs," Lee said. "Maybe the two of you should go to your room."

"My room? Why?"

"Well, you know. Privacy, and... well, hygiene."

"Hygiene?"

"You know. I don't want a mess on the table." Everyone in the control room looked at her.

Gavin raised his eyebrows. "You don't want a mess on the table."

"No," Lee said. "I mean. Well. We eat there, right?"

Three jumps and a month later, they were at the edge of Imperial Space. Lee had seen pictures of Dena's former big gun. Ana brought out his own big gun—or as he called it, rifle, automatic, bi-pod-mounted, belt fed, squad support, for the use of. Lee found herself on the defensive when the incident was mentioned.

"I just... you all sounded weird is all," Lee said. "I misunderstood."

"Keep your mind out of the gutter, Navigator," Dirk said. "I'm surprised at you, thinking that I would have sexual relations with a member of my crew."

"I'm right here, Navy. I can hear you." Dena sat next to their computer console. She inserted a puce-colored cartridge into the computer. "867-11-11 is another cargo program. Description says, 'Container optimization for cross-loading in deep space with no air locks present.'" The crew was working through the piles of software they had stolen. They'd found four different single-function laser-targeting programs. If they could get a laser that matched the program, they would be in business. The rest was control software for equipment they didn't have.

"Put it in the database with the rest." Ana grunted. "Keep trying. We want a general navigation or piloting program with a description like 'evasion' or 'random walk' or something like that. Some sort of laser-control program would be great as well."

"Next one." Dena put a blue cartridge into the slot and waited for the contents to display. "Says—Food and beverage ordering program for voyages of more than sixteen months or ten thousand people, with vitamin supplement module. Who uses that?"

"Battleships. Long-range exploration ships. Keep trying." Ana tapped his scan board. "Nothing weird going on in the system. No pursuit, nothing. We got clean away, for once. Once we're at the limit, we can jump."

"Should we accelerate?" Lee asked.

"Nope. Slow and steady. We're just a simple trading freighter moving along. Not a bunch of software-stealing arsonists. Nothing to see here."

"Which means I'll have lots of time to ask the pilot-navy guy here what constitutes sexual relations, since what we did in the past was something else."

"You were, well, you were more a volunteer than a crew member. More like a passenger. Not really crew."

"Sounds like I still have a chance, then. Whatcha think, Centurion?"

"Hmm." Ana looked up from his screen. "Sorry. About what?"

"Whether I have a chance with the pilot here."

"You're female and you're breathing. You have a chance. Perhaps only as a target of opportunity, but a chance." Ana tapped his screen. "And I added the breathing for politeness's sake, I'm not sure that it's an actual requirement."

"See? So even Scruggs has a shot. Centurion, this one says 'ordnance storage.' That's ammunition, right? You can use that one?"

Ana tapped his screen. "Hmm?"

Dena snapped her fingers. "What is it?"

"What? You have software?"

"What are you looking at, Old Man. You only get that

look when you see something you might want to kill. Stop acting strange."

"This isn't strange. I see things I want to kill all the time."

"Which is why we're all familiar with that look. What's on your screens?"

"A big freighter... making a gentle turn. It was headed to the outer system—not in our direction—but it shimmied to the side a bit."

"Shimmied? How?"

"Like they were clearing some sensors to scan us. But they swept back, still going the other direction."

"Don't our sensor detector things bong from that?"

"If they did an active scan, yes. But not if they only used optics. Or passive IR. With passive, they could get a pretty good look at us."

"At this distance? A freighter?"

"Not a freighter. But a ship with military equipment."

"Does it look military to you?"

"No. No. Just that maneuver, it was like they wanted to do an all-round scan, then back on course. Unusual."

"Should we do something about it?"

"Nothing we can do. We ready to go on jump soon?"

Lee tapped her board. "In twenty-two minutes. We should set travel watches now. I could use a nap."

Ana stood. "Good idea. All this talking about showing my big gun around has made me tired. I'm going to bed as well. Wake me up when it's my shift."

"I'm on first, Lee," Dena said. "You'll have to do the jump, but then I can watch the board. While I'm checking all these software cartridges."

Dirk stood. "Now that we're in the navigator's good hands, I think a period of rest for myself might be warranted."

"Love how they talk in the Navy." Ana stretched.

"So, I'll be by myself, and bored," Dena said. "Need something to talk about. So, Pilot, just so we're clear, you wouldn't sleep with Scruggs."

"I would not," Dirk said. "She is far too young, and she's still coming into her looks. She'll be a beautiful woman someday, but now is not the time."

"Got it." Dena punched the comm. "Scruggs, you there?"

"Yes?"

"Pilot says nobody wants to sleep with you because you're such a kid!"

"I'm not a kid!"

"And he says you're still too ugly for anybody to want."

"What? I'm coming up."

Dena slammed the comm shut before Dirk could complain.

"What's that in aid of?" Ana wondered.

"Any second, Scruggs will come up here and start yelling at the pilot."

"Much as I enjoy that, why?"

"Because he's an attractive man, she's young and frustrated after all this fighting. If we get her riled up enough, she might come up here and prove all his statements wrong."

"You want Scruggs to sleep with the pilot?"

"No, no. I mean, she can if she wants." Dena shrugged.

"But she's still learning. So far, all her romantic adventures have ended in physical fights."

"And...?"

"She thinks it's foreplay." Dena grinned. "We get her horny and angry enough, she'll come up here and smack him around!"

Several systems back, Dirk had met a former Navy buddy who mentioned that his good buddy Cass had left the Navy and gone into business for herself as an equipment broker. Dirk remembered Cass fondly and arranged a meeting with one of her suppliers. He asked about getting some offensive and defensive systems installed on the Heart's Desire. The equipment was available, but the software wasn't. That led to a discussion about how to buy it, which led to firefights and explosions and shootings in Archan. But now that they had software, they could get a laser.

"Scheduled to come out of jump in a half-hour, everyone." Lee gagged as she drank down the bitter-tasting basic that Scruggs made for them every week. It contained vitamins, minerals, sugars, anti-radiation meds, and a variety of other health promoting powders that Scruggs mixed in. "This is particularly worse this week."

"I agree, Navigator." Ana gulped his cup down without a change in expression. "This is the worst of any of your mixes I've ever tasted. What's in it this time?"

"I added selenium and shark cartilage," Scruggs said.

"Why selenium?" Dirk pinched his nose, drank his down, and then closed his eyes and grimaced.

"What's a shark?" Gavin asked.

"For that matter, what's cartilage?" Dena pulled her cup into her lap and glared down at it. "Yuck."

"It's the connective tissue that holds bones together. I looked it up." Scruggs slurped hers down and licked her lips. "And sharks are like big fish. They're strong and fast and smart and mean, and very flexible. Shark cartilage keeps them supple and flexible, and it does the same for people."

"That's what it's called? I've eaten something that tastes like this before. When I was lost in the woods, starving and nearly dead." Dena stretched, dipping her hand below the table.

"I see what you're doing," Scruggs said. "And I know you're going to try to spill that on the floor so that Rocky will lick it up. Don't bother."

"If it's good for people, it should be even better for dogs. More... joints for the cartilage thing."

"It is good for dogs." Scruggs got up and pulled a pan out of the cupboard next to the microwave. "Which is why he gets his own, every week."

Scruggs poured a generous measure into the pan and set it on the deck. Rocky the whippet wagged his tail happily as he slurped it all down.

"I can't believe he's drinking that," Ana said. "Then again, I can't believe that Scruggs likes it so much either."

Scruggs was running her finger around her glass and licking the rest of the basic off. "I like the taste."

"The Emperor help us all," Ana said. "Pilot, what happens when we come out of jump, according to your friend Cass?"

Dirk rubbed his hand across his mouth and wiped it on a

cleaning rag nearby. "We'll be met. Some people have to check us out, make sure we're who we say we are."

"So, false IDs, that sort of thing? Hide our weapons?"

"Nope. Regular IDs. Normal ship's papers. And any weapons you want visible, that's fine too. In fact, it might be best if we were all armed when they come aboard."

"Come aboard, whooo, nobody said anything about that."

"As you keep reminding me, Centurion, when we're on the ground, you're in charge, but when we're in space, I am."

"Lee, did you know about this?" Ana demanded.

"Now you're on my side, Centurion?" Lee asked. "Before, you were all suspicious and dismissive."

"I've reformed. Also, I didn't know you worked for the Empress. I like her. She has good judgment. Met her once."

"You met the Empress?" Dena asked.

"Unofficially, yes. One time. Long time ago."

Dirk swished his glass. "Was this relating to you killing some people?"

"It was, actually. She was very pleased that I'd killed those particular people, and the method. She gave me a medal."

"I'd like to see that sometime," Dirk said.

"Don't show my medals," Ana said.

"Or talk much about them," Gavin said. "Or about which side you were on at the time."

"You're no chatty Cathy either, Engineer."

"Was she prettier than me?" Dena asked.

"What?"

"The Empress. Is she prettier than me? Come on,

Centurion. Dirk knows her, Lee works for her, Scruggs probably sold her some real-estate.”

Scruggs jerked. “How did you know that?”

“You sold her real estate?”

“My family—you didn’t know, you’re just messing with me.”

“Yes. Everyone’s seen her except me. One of you has to introduce me.”

“Next time we’re in her Imperial Majesty’s presence, I’ll do it,” Ana said. “I’ll talk you up. Tell about how you can start fires in the snow, and kill wolves with rocks, and steal cars by seducing the men in them.”

“Thanks, you Imperial turd,” Dena said. “Thanks for nothing.”

“She’d probably be impressed with those skills,” Dirk said. “She’s pretty practical.”

“Why won’t you tell me what she looks like?” Dena asked.

Scruggs stuck her tongue out at Dena. “Maybe he thinks you’re too ugly and too young for any man to want, like he does me, and he doesn’t want to insult you, like he did me.”

Ana laughed. “Outstanding. But back to our boarding...”

“We’ll meet them at the air lock. Answer a few questions, show some money, and get directions.

“Outstanding. You never did tell us about your friend, Cass, the mastermind behind this whole shipyard setup.”

“She was a few years older than me, but the same rank. She didn’t get promoted as fast as she could have, there were some... questions about some things she was accused of. In the end, they decided not to promote her, and she left the service voluntarily after being passed over. It's a shame. She was a good officer, aggressive, brave, diligent, and resourceful."

"What was she accused of?"

"Stealing."

"Stealing? What? Naval stores? Money?"

"Nothing as minor as that."

"What did she steal, then?"

"Nothing. Accused but never proved."

"Fine." Ana shook his head. "What was so important that she was passed over for promotion for potentially but not proved stealing?"

"A task force."

"What?"

"Warships." Dirk shrugged. "She stole an Imperial task force."

CHAPTER TWELVE

"Commence in two minutes. Make sure you start on time." Kapitan Kruder hung up the hard phone in the corridor. "Hans, let us proceed." Kapitan Kruder and his first officer had left the bridge on an inspection tour.

"Are you sure this is necessary, Kapitan?"

"Constant drill keeps the men sharp, you know that."

"The weapons crews have performed well during our test firings. More practicing will make the crew tired, without additional benefits in efficiency."

"If not the weapons crew, then perhaps more sensor practice would be useful. For some of the crew."

"I am still upset, but the young idiot was correct. I didn't prohibit it." Kruder was referring to Third Officer Blomberg's maneuvers in the last system they had visited. While conducting a routine passive sensor scanning exercise, Blomberg had been unable to get a full picture of some departing freighters. Rather than waiting for the plodding merchant ships to inevitably move into his sensor cones, he'd pivoted the ship to scan the target. Only warships did that. Any Imperial naval ships watching would have been very suspicious.

"You did not prohibit it, but he does need to understand we are pretending to be a merchant ship."

"I'm sure you'll take care of it, Hans. But for now, we need to keep everyone else sharp."

Hans Fusterheim braced to attention, then led the way down the corridor, settling his helmet and gloves on his belt. At the next air lock, he stepped past the open hatch and called out, "Kapitan arriving."

Eight members of the gun crew jumped up from where they were playing cards at the central table. The petty officer in charge stepped up and saluted. "Petty Officer Gerlach, reporting for compartment 1-3-12-W, Kapitan."

Kruder returned the salute. "How are things here, Gerlach?"

"All is in order, Kapitan. We stand ready."

"Explain your duties here to myself and the executive officer."

"Sir. We control projective weapon L-6, and we—"

BONG. BONG. BONG. BONG. Red strobe light flooded the compartment.

"ALARM!" Gerlach ran to his locker. "To stations."

Kruder and Fusterheim stepped smartly back. During an alarm, even officers had to stand clear of crew movements. The crew grabbed helmets and gloves. Two rushed sternward into the next compartment, locking the hatch behind them. Two more collected portable firefighting equipment and hull patches and rushed forward. The petty officer ran downstairs to the spinward compartment and strapped himself into a dual console. One sailor seated himself beside him, and the other two grabbed handholds at either end of the compartment and waited.

"Decamouflaging." Petty Officer Gerlach slapped his screen. Lights flashed red. The petty officer tried again, then tried a third time. "Karlheinz, I cannot decamouflage, my screen is not responding. Try yours."

The other sailor slapped his hand on his screen. "Same here, chief."

Gerlach punched his intercom. "Central, this is station C-16-R-13. We have—"

PRESSURE. PRESSURE. The random bonging changed to words, and the red strobe switched to twice per second. Kruder and Fusterheim checked each other's seals and confirmed green lights on the back of the helmet assembly.

The petty officer switched to the radio and tried again. "Central, this is C-16-R-13. Central? Please respond, this is C-16-"

The radio signal died in Kruder's ear as the drill master cut radio communications in this part of the ship. The petty officer turned to his console companion and tapped his ears, the universal 'radio out' symbol. His partner responded with the same, then pointed at the ratings in the back. His blinking red light showed a bad seal.

The bridge had cut acceleration, and thus gravity, when the drill started. The PO unstrapped, rolled over his chair, grabbed the wayward sailor, and gave a quick twist until the helmet locked green. Then he returned to his seat and commenced a test on his console. He shook his head, then looked across at his partner and opened his two hands in an interrogative. The PO and backup touched helmets for twenty seconds. The PO released, gave a thumbs-up, then locked helmets with each of the seamen. The PO's partner pulled over to the far wall and unlocked a hatch, disappearing into it.

The two sailors approached the captain and waved. Kruder waved back. What was going on? They were under strict orders not to speak to monitoring officers during a drill.

The two men waved again. Kruder, annoyed, leaned in to touch helmets. "We are not here, ignore us."

"Kapitan, you are blocking the equipment locker. You must move."

Kruder looked over his shoulder, cursed to himself, and pulled out of the way.

The two sailors opened the locker Kruder had been blocking, and pulled two large winch handles free, then proceeded to the open hatch on the far side and slipped in.

Kruder gave them thirty seconds, then drifted up to glance through the hatch. The two ratings were mechanically cranking the camouflage cover off the external hull. The petty officer was peering through a telescope, his hand on a trigger. His partner manually elevated and traversed the weapon, until it matched the numbers displayed on the telescope.

Kruder gestured Fusterheim back. Once in the compartment, he plugged his suit into a special radio link to speak to the drill master and discuss details. The drill went on for another twenty minutes before the ringing bells canceled, and red lights turned to green.

Kruder and Fusterheim removed their helmets. "Not bad at all, Hans. Not bad."

"It should have been faster."

"The mechanical backups are heavy and take some time to maneuver."

"Are they really necessary, Kapitan?"

"You never know when a backup system will be necessary."

BONG. "Secure from drill. Kapitan to the bridge."

Kruder keyed his radio. "Kruder here."

"Sir, please come to the bridge. We have spotted a ship approaching the jump limit," the drill master said.

"Understood." Kruder clapped Fusterheim on the arm. "It begins."

Kruder sat at the command console. The forward screen displayed the system primary, and the Pinguin's location, in an elliptical orbit beyond the first gas giant past the jump limit.

Third officer Blomberg turned from his console and smiled at Kruder. "Our first catch of the day, sir!"

Fusterheim zoomed the display in and put a red ring around the planet. "Don't jinx it."

"She'll be passing the jump limit soon, sir. I have a course laid in to intercept her before she does." Blomberg was short, neat, and particular. His uniform was always immaculate—he paid several of the spaceman ratings to clean and press his clothes and shine his shoes. He was cheerful, outspoken, enthusiastic, and completely unburdened by anything resembling competence. He'd been appointed to the ship at the last minute by the Konteradmiral, and Kruder assumed he was the committee spy onboard.

"Do not engage," Kruder said. "Continue our current vector."

"Sir? Are we not going to capture her?"

"Leutnant," Fusterheim, the first officer said. "I don't know how things were done in your previous posting, but here, we do not question the Kapitan's orders."

"Sir, but she's getting away."

"She's not getting anywhere, Leutnant," Fusterheim said. "Now be quiet while the Kapitan thinks."

Blomberg closed his mouth, but he glared sideways at the first officer.

Kruder put several vectors up on his screen, as well as a display of the orbit necessary to fuel at the gas giant. Kruder had chosen this orbit on the assumption that ships departing would take the opportunity to fuel for free outside the jump limit. They would suspect him of doing the same if they even paid him any attention.

"Sensors, what do you have on passive?"

"We've got their beacon, sir." Wilhelm Alvarez, the sensor operator, had served with Kruder before. "Tsar Edward, a Confederation ship. One hundred twelve containers, life support for twenty-four persons, standard power settings. Nothing on passive sensors to refute that. Dimensions, albedo, heat, all within what our records say."

"Are they scanning anything active?"

"Nothing we can see, sir. No radar or radio at all. And their passive would be unlikely to see much. The planetary atmosphere generates substantial infra-red interference. We can barely see them ourselves."

"If they even bother to look around. Are they equipped for atmospheric refueling?"

"I can't make out scoops, but our visuals are poor. According to records, she wasn't built with any, but she is very, very old. Almost a hundred years. She could have been modified since constructed. Also, Kapitan, the planet will block our sensors in seventeen minutes."

"Very well." Kruder tapped his intercom. "This is Kruder. Away Kapitan's boat. Contact me when ready to launch."

The bridge officers exchanged significant looks and eyebrow lifts. The captain was planning something clever. He was a wily one, Kapitan Kruder. He'd see them through.

Six minutes later, one of the ship's boats launched and generated a vector at ninety degrees relative to the Pinguin.

Kruder resumed putting numbers into his screen. Alvarez reported his sensors blinded by the planet. Kruder discussed the recent drill results with his first officer. They planned a series of other practice operations. Blomberg seethed at his console.

"Hans, I am still not happy with our firefighter's response. They must be quicker."

"With respect, Kapitan, I think the men are doing well. We have no integral internal suppression systems like with a warship, and the portable equipment is bulky. Maneuvering it through companionways and up ladders is difficult. We will have to assign more men to fire suppression tasks if we want to decrease response times."

"But then we will have fewer repair parties."

"We cannot have both, Kapitan."

Kapitan and the first officer discussed the matter for a few more moments. The rest of the bridge crew went sedately about their tasks, but Blomberg was near twisting in panic.

Kruder noticed a particular strong twitch. "Leutnant Blomberg, are you well?"

"Very well sir. Just…"

"You appear agitated."

"Sir. I. Permission to speak freely?"

"Of course. What is it, Leutnant?"

"The target ship. The freighter. You are letting it get away."

Kruder raised his eyebrows. "I am? Has it escaped while I was not looking?"

"Sir, we do not know. Our sensors are blinded."

"They are. That is the plan."

Blomberg shook his head. "I do not understand, sir."

"Well, no need to keep you in suspense." Kruder examined his screen, then pulled up a radio channel and got the pilot of the captain's boat online.

"Do you have a view of the target?"

Being smaller than the freighter, the boat could pull higher acceleration. It had pushed itself clear of planetary interference. Now it drifted, with a clear view of the area behind the planet hidden from the Pinguin.

"Sir, we see her. She has continued on her course with no change."

"She's passed the jump limit?"

"Confirmed, sir. She could have jumped minutes ago but has not."

"No deceleration yet?"

"Not yet, sir, we don't—wait—she's pivoting, and there it goes. Her drives are firing. Exactly where you indicated, sir. She's moving into a fueling orbit around the planet."

"Very well. We will be maneuvering shortly. I will send you a course. Follow this and we will pick you up in two hours. No active sensor sweeps during that time."

"Understood."

"Kruder clear. Helm, I am transmitting a course. Conduct it with no further reference to me but warn the ship for acceleration as necessary. Hans, I am going to my cabin for a quick nap. Wake me in thirty minutes." Kruder stood, yawned, and left the control room.

The other officers grinned and exchanged winks. Kapitan Kruder was going to get them their first capture.

Blomberg muttered in confusion. He echoed the helm station on his screen and stared at it. The ship executed a desultory course change and dropped into a lower orbit—deep in the atmosphere. He shook his head.

"Questions, Leutnant?" Fusterheim asked.

"Sir, I don't understand. Why are we not trying to catch the other ship?"

"There is no need to catch it. The Kapitan has made it come to us. Did you ever serve in freighters?"

"I have been on regular duty since I left training."

"Well, youngster, if you had spent any time on a freighter, you would know that freighters need fuel, and fuel costs money. This freighter captain executed a least fuel course to bring himself into atmosphere. He'll cruise around the planet sucking up fuel as economically as possible. Once he's got a full load, push gently out of the gravity well, and he can jump right away. Our Kapitan, our brilliant Kapitan, I might add, deduced this, and predicted the other ship's course. We are now on our own meandering course that will put us alongside that other ship as she comes around to this side. In practice, she'll sail up to us, and park directly under our guns, with no effort on our part. We just lie here and wait."

"Had a girlfriend like that once," Alvarez said.

"Hid behind a planet and tried to run away?" Tannen, the female comm officer, said. "Smart woman."

The bridge crew laughed, then continued with their duties. Information flowed to Fusterheim's screen, repeated from their ship's boat. Nothing deviated from the Kapitan's plan.

Blomberg continued to run vectors on his screen. Fusterheim grinned. "Questions, Leutnant?"

"Sir." Blomberg tapped his screen. "We just orbit until they come up next to us?"

"That is the plan."

"Seems, well, it seems…"

"Boring?"

"Yes sir. A bit."

"If the plan works, it will be boring."

"And if it doesn't?"

"Well then, youngster, you'll get all the excitement you want."

CHAPTER THIRTEEN

"I still don't understand, Pilot." Lee pushed a software cassette into the main computer and read the summary. "How did your friend steal a task force? That's a big deal. There are ships, and people, and weapons, and supplies, and, well, you can't hide that sort of thing."

The Heart's Desire had made two more short jumps to the system where Cassandra was supposed to be. The crew amused themselves by testing the stolen software. They spent their bridge shifts popping software in, reading and copying the summary in a log file, repeatedly. Ana and Lee had taken over the task of examining anything with an interesting title in more detail, but the work was slow. So far, the only one they had installed was a fuel-optimization program that Gavin was testing in engineering, and a ground vehicle simulator that Ana had put Scruggs and Dena to practicing with.

Dirk belted himself into the pilot's chair and brought up Lee's suggested course. "She didn't try to hide it. She did it in plain sight. Lots of different burns here, Lee."

"The system is crowded, Pilot. Lots of asteroids, and minor planets to avoid. But back to the task force. How did she do that?"

"She used her secret superpower."

"What's that?"

"The power of paperwork. She used paperwork to have them given to her."

Lee cocked an eye. "She ordered them up, like a food delivery in an orbital hab?"

"Almost, but not exactly." Dirk keyed his screen to bring the control functions up. In truth, except for tricky dockings and landings, he didn't change Lee's intra-system burns anymore, just let them play out. And her jump calculations are better than mine. She could be navigator on an Imperial Flagship if she wanted.

"How exactly?"

"She was in charge of ship taskings for a sector. An old corvette, ISS Agassiz, came in for overhaul. She posted the regular crew to another ship and left a different skeleton crew onboard to watch it 'til it was turned over to the dockyard. She reserved a dockyard slot for it, a few weeks ahead of time, but the slot wasn't ready. The Agassiz got shifted to a holding orbit by a towing company. Since it was being towed preparatory to refit, the dockyard took administrative possession of it. Another task force came in. She took the Agassiz off the dockyard's strength and put it on the new task force's. The shipyard didn't care—the Navy paid a penalty for re-activating the ship, so they took their money and shut up. The task force disbanded and the ships in it went their own way. But according to the computers, the task force still existed, which meant the Agassiz belonged to it."

"But didn't the original task force commander—"

"Her ship was the first to be released, then the next senior, then the next. They were to turn over command of their ships to the next-most senior officer, and in a day, the last manned ship left the system, turning over command of the task force to the 'senior officer on remaining ships' on Agassiz, which was nobody."

"Didn't anybody notice?"

"Commander of the last ship should have, because in theory, she was in command. Her orders would have been generic 'turn over command of any remaining ships.' She figured she was the last one, so didn't inquire. She didn't know he was assigned a new ship that morning."

"Cassandra got a ship."

"Three ships. She did it again, twice more, ships coming in for refit or whatever. Had them parked at the dock, sent the crew away, had them towed to a parking orbit, then assigned them to the non-crewed task force. The shipyard didn't care —ships come and go, and once it was removed from their responsibility, they didn't even check. The crews did as they were ordered and left the ships."

"How did she get them moved?"

"They sat there for almost a year. She had them labeled as impaired-functional then put up a proposal to have them stricken and sold."

"You can't sell an Imperial warship like a tray of tabbo meat."

"Well, if the sector administration and the senior officer onboard certify that a ship is missing key components, there is a process to have the ship stricken and sold. Hard to do, but possible."

"How did she do it?"

"She didn't. Ships considered for disposal can be transferred instead. She arranged to have them sold to an allied government, a planet nearby—that was some big bribe, I'm sure. She had herself assigned to the existing task force. When the planetary government came by with crews, she signed the ships over to them. Two corvettes and a military supply freighter are happily chasing pirates in the Siarcuse system right now, courtesy of my good friend Cassandra. The Siarcuse government got a small navy, with all the paperwork done correctly. All the crews got sent to better ships or got promoted. The shipyard was paid a substantial cancellation fee, and everybody was happy."

"What happened to her?"

"She was court-martialed. Didn't stick."

"Why not?"

"She followed all the regs, filled out all the paperwork, and she didn't get anything for herself. Not a single credit. Well, not that they can prove."

"She got away with it?"

"Yep, she got away with it."

"Got away with what?" Dena slid into her seat behind the two.

"Friend Dena, you don't have to be here," Lee said. "It's not your shift."

"Yeah, but I don't need as much time on the driving sims as Scruggs does. I've had my fill of so-called low-tech vehicles. Half the 'primitive transportation' in that program are things I had to use back on Rockhaul. And don't get me started on the 'basic maintenance' that has to be done."

"You can maintain vehicles?" Lee asked.

"Primitive vehicles, as you high-and-mighty Imperials would say. But yes, I'm used to working with what we've got back home. Simple stuff by Empire standards, but a diesel truck can still carry cargo and people to a starport, and knowing how to refill a radiator or fix a flat tire in the field can be useful. At least that's what Centurion says."

Dirk laughed. "He's Centurion now, is he? Not the old man?"

"Sometimes he's the old man, and an insufferable one at that. Gotta admit, though, he knows things. He knows more about how to change the oil on a diesel engine than Old Man Murphy did back home. And you always call him Centurion. And you call Gavin Engineer a lot too. You're Mr. Polite these days."

Dirk stretched. "Centurion is competent in his realm. As is the engineer. Remember, the engineer says he can get this laser mounted on the hull, if we get all the major parts and the software."

"If that ever happens."

"What makes you think it won't?"

"I may not know much about spaceships." Dena activated her screen and started the limited scanning programs. "But I do know that connecting a bigawatt or however much powered thing that will take more than a quick weld and hitting it with a hammer. Power means electricity, and how is he going to get that much electricity out through the hull? Need a power cable as big as a giant spruce trunk, and where are you going to put it? Drape it through the air locks and leave the hatches open? Needs to cut a hole, and I don't see that type of equipment stuffed under the lounge table. And the control cables have to come in too, right? That software that you all keep whining about needs something that can let you aim at things, and I don't know where that would go either. Scruggs and I sitting here and pointing a telescope won't let us hit something in space."

"How did you figure all this out?" Dirk asked.

"What?" Dena shrugged. "We were poor and backward on Rockhaul, but nobody ever said we were stupid. I know a scam when I see one."

"I'm sure that the engineer has a solution for all of this," Lee said.

"Have you asked him?"

Lee bit her lip. "I just assumed he'd, well, he's fixed things before."

Dirk nodded. "He's fixed things, things that are already installed. And he can repair broken parts and replace fixtures and modules. But this is a complete re-build of part of the hull."

"Need a shipyard for that," Lee said.

"Yes, you do. I didn't think about that."

"Well, great Duke-Pilot-in-Command, maybe he knows

where there's a shipyard that will install illegal weapons." Dena activated the intercom. "Hey, Old Man!"

"What is it, Nature Girl?" Ana's voice answered.

"I did that scan like you told me to."

"And?"

"And nothing. There's nothing broadcasting radar, and nothing on the radio bands either."

"What about infra-red?"

"Where, in this giant system, do I point our discounted infra-red reader? And even if I see a heat source, how do I know it's not natural or supposed to be there? Like you told me, we check for differences, and we've never been here before."

"I'm coming up." Ana pulled himself up against the gravity a minute later and strapped himself into his seat. "You don't see anything? No beacons? No radio? Nothing?"

"Your hearing is finally going, Old Man. Or your brains. I already said that. I knew you'd go senile eventually, it was just a matter of time—"

"Thank you for your input, Nature Girl. It's noted. Shouldn't there be a shipyard here, Navy? Something to do with lasers?"

"I did expect more," Dirk admitted. "But Cass always ran a loose show."

"And it doesn't bother you that a lady who stole three Imperial warships has lured you and your ship out to the middle of nowhere, where nobody knows where we are, and there are no witnesses to anything going on? Anything like boarding a ship and killing everybody on it so they can steal it?"

"Cass wouldn't do that." Dirk frowned. "Would she? We were friends."

"Were you lovers?" Dena asked. "Because, if you were, she might have a few issues with you afterwards."

"Can we stop talking about that?"

"For sure. It's not a big subject with me." Dena laughed. "Not a big subject. That's a good one."

"Navy, check the systems," Ana said. "I'll do another sweep."

Dirk already had a test sequence running on his screen. "These are only internal self-tests, Centurion. We'd need something external to check against."

"We close enough to put the telescope on the planets, and the primaries?"

"Sure."

Ana tapped his screen. "Nature Girl, check the albedo of the planets against the sailing directions, and check the luminosity of the stars in the system as well against the star charts."

"Check the what against the what and the who?" Dena shrugged. "Speak Standard, Old Man."

Ana hit the intercom. "Scruggs, cancel that training. Get up here and show Nature Girl those new features of telescope that the Tribune's people put in."

"What's going on?" Dena asked.

Ana ignored her. "Navigator, are—"

"I'm checking right now, Centurion," Lee said. "But I'm pretty sure we're in the right place."

"Is our beacon up?"

"Yes, we're broadcasting."

Scruggs pulled up into the control room. "What's going on?"

Dena waved her hands at the rest of the crew. "All the spacy people started using big words and getting all excited. You're supposed to show me what an albedo is."

Ana looked up from his screen. "Scruggs, you and Nature Girl check the albedo of the planets and the luminosity of the primary, and then compare it to our records. Tell me if there's a difference."

Scruggs and Dena exchanged looks and shrugs, then Scruggs showed Dena how to get the numbers. They loaded them up and compared.

"Telescope reports match the sailing directions and the star chart, Centurion," Scruggs said. "Why are we checking this?"

"Tells us if the telescope is working properly. Pilot? Navigator?"

"All the tests run good," Dirk said. "Everything should be working."

Lee mirrored her position screen for everyone. "We're in the right system, in the right place, inbound to the fourth planet. Nothing special showing from the planet."

"Nothing here?" Ana asked.

"Right."

Dena laughed. "You're all getting pretty excited about nothing." She dug an elbow into Scruggs. "Excited about nothing. Get it? Get it?"

"There should be a settlement, or a port, or ships," Dirk said. "We're supposed to meet Cassandra here to buy some weapons."

"And telling people you want to buy weapons usually means you don't have any. People who want to take your ship away from you, one of the things they can do is tell you to be at a certain place at a certain time, wait for you, and then take your ship away when you get there."

"You think Dirk's friend would do that?" Lee asked.

Ana grunted. "I'm not sure the words 'Dirk' and 'friend' should ever be in the same sentence, unless the word 'former' is also there. If this lady was smart enough to steal a taskforce, she's smart enough to hide an armed ship right where we're supposed to be, hide it somehow, and have it sneak up behind us and blast us without warning."

"How will we find them if they're hiding?" Scruggs asked.

BONG BONG BONG. The radar warning scanner screamed at top volume. A powerful radar, or a weak one that was very, very close had just scanned them.

"We'll know, "Ana said. "We'll know."

CHAPTER FOURTEEN

"Korvettenkapitan closest approach in thirty minutes," Blomberg reported. "Target is still decelerating for almost zero-zero meeting."

Pinguin's sensor operator, Alvarez, had detected the Confederation freighter Tsar Edward as it appeared around the planet in a chasing orbit behind them. He had also previously reported it to the entire bridge in a loud voice, making Blomberg's repetition superfluous.

"Thank you, Leutnant," Fusterheim said. "But it is not necessary to repeat the sensor operator's statement. I am not yet so ancient that my hearing is gone, so that I cannot understand Wilhelm when he talks."

"Sir, regulations require the junior watch officer to repeat reports to the senior watch officer."

"Kapitan Kruder discourages such things, and for that matter, so do I."

"Sir, the regulations are clear."

"Indeed they are, Leutnant. But. We are not on a home fleet

battleship inspected by a Council representative each day. We are a converted freighter operating in the Verge, and our mission requires us to act as such. Freighters apply more relaxed rules to communications, and we will operate that way."

"Sir, but—"

"That is not a suggestion, Leutnant. Relax. That is an order." Fusterheim tapped his intercom, ignoring the giggling from a corner of the bridge. "Kapitan."

Kruder's voice answered. "Yes, Hans?"

"All is as you specified. Closest approach at nearly zero-zero in thirty minutes."

"Very well. General quarters with camouflage at this time."

"Yes sir."

"Don't let them know we're coming."

"Of course sir."

"Right, sorry, Hans."

"I will assemble a boarding party as well."

"Yes, please. But you know what, Hans, let young Blomberg take the boarding party over."

"As the Kapitan wishes."

The longer-serving bridge crew stifled sniggers. Many had served with Fusterheim and Kruder before. Fusterheim's responses followed a pattern. 'Yes sir' meant—I'll take care of it, don't worry. 'Of course sir' meant that it was already taken care of, and why are you asking again?' 'As the Kapitan wishes' meant that Fusterheim thought the Kapitan was out of his freaking mind but was too well-disciplined to say so.

"Everyone has a first boarding party, Hans."

"As the Kapitan wishes."

The first part went off without a hitch. The Tsar Edward approached, slowly, until she was in a least-cost orbit to take on fuel. Pinguin meandered along ahead, also sucking in fuel to maintain the illusion in case the other ship bothered to check. Kruder appeared on the bridge, in full dress uniform, and ordered a course adjustment to match orbits. Once that was complete, he pressed a buzzer.

The buzzer signaled the crew to execute the operations they had been practicing these past weeks. Fake hull plating rolled out of the way. Weapons powered up, extended, traversed, elevated, aimed, and settled on targets. Lasers and microwaves lashed the adjacent ship, measuring distances, angles, and vectors, and reporting to computers. Fire control made minute adjustments and locked their tracking. Manual backups at each station flashed warnings. Sailors stood ready to intervene if necessary.

Tannen killed their false beacon, then brought up the new beacon. She confirmed with the captain's boat that they were broadcasting their warship status. Kruder had insisted on that—no shooting until he had confirmation that they were broadcasting the appropriate beacon.

"Go for shooting, Kapitan," she reported.

Kruder touched his all-ship intercom. "Continue phase two. Gun four. Fire."

The rearmost slug gun, which happened to have the best view of the target, fired a five-second burst of slugs across the bow of the Tsar Edward. Tannen flooded the other ship with notices of cargo inspections and warnings about holding course and not using the radio.

Blomberg leaned over and scowled at Tannen. "That was not a proper report. You should provide the details according to regulations." He was nominally the same rank as the older Tannen, so he felt he could get away with some discourtesy.

Tannen grinned at him and leaned in so the Kapitan couldn't hear her. "Leutnant, I do as the Kapitan says. And that's how he likes his reports. Short, direct, and clear."

"I think—"

"Leutnant, in a crisis, we need to know exactly what to do next. For example, the Kapitan could say 'Please, Leutnant Tannen, could you ensure that Leutnant Blomberg is informed that he should not be second-guessing bridge orders during a crisis? But then I don't know how or what, exactly, I should do. On the other hand," Tannen tapped Blomberg's forearm, "if the Kapitan said, 'Tannen, if Blomberg speaks again, break his wrist.' Then I know exactly what the Kapitan wants done, and when. Much easier to understand, don't you think?"

Blomberg blinked. "You'd break my arm?"

"If the Kapitan ordered it? Without a second's thought." Tannen flexed her bicep—it was bigger than Blomberg's. "I work out."

Kruder lounged in his seat, relaxed. He'd sent Blomberg off when the boarding party was ready, and now they waited. The relaxation was feigned, but the crew needed to see his confidence expressed. "Happy to be a pirate now, Hans?"

Fusterheim looked up from his board. "We are a Union of Nations warship broadcasting our identity. We are conducting an inspection for escaped prisoners, searching for contraband and prohibited cargo. We are operating in space claimed by the Union of Nations."

"A claim which the other Empires do not recognize."

"That is their issue, not mine, Kapitan."

"How many did you allow in the boarding party?"

"Eight."

"How many did Blomberg want?"

"Thirty-two."

Kruder laughed. "How would we even get them over there?"

"Multiple runs, suited up on the hull? I don't know."

Tannen held up a hand. "Boarding party reports ship secured. Light resistance."

"Light resistance, what does that mean?"

"No information, sir. Our repeaters cannot punch through the hull. A rating returned to the shuttle to give a verbal report."

"Tell them to get Blomberg on the radio."

"Sir, the report says... ah... the petty officer in charge is returning with the Tsar Edward's captain and crew, and he asks if he can bring her—the Tsar Edward's captain—to the bridge to report."

"Where is Blomberg?"

"Sir, Petty Officer Wann has requested four additional ratings report to the dock to escort Blomberg to the medical bay."

"Ratings? Not a medical team?"

"He has not asked for a medical team."

"Escort? He said escort, not evacuate?"

"Begging the Kapitan's pardon." Tannen shrugged her shoulders. "I apologize. I mis-repeated the PO's report. He didn't say escort, he actually said 'carry'."

Kruder looked at Fusterheim. Fusterheim shook his head and shrugged. Kruder laughed. "Bring that captain to the bridge to report—right away."

The comm officer returned to her duties and reported the shuttle inbound. Twenty minutes later, a stone-faced petty officer reported to the bridge with a disgruntled-looking Confederation captain in tow. She scowled at everyone, and her left cheek was bright red with a trickle of blood on it where she had hit something. Or been hit by somebody.

Kruder clicked his heels and extended his hand. "Korvettenkapitan Felix Kruder, at your service. You are?"

The Confed crossed her arms behind her back, ignoring the proffered hand. "Samovitch. Captain. Tsar Edward. I protest this act of piracy."

"This is not piracy. We are a Union of Nations Warship conducting anti-smuggling patrols. You were captured in space claimed by the Union, operating a foreign beacon. And in violation of a multi-national treaty regarding foreign commerce. We are currently inspecting your ship for contraband, and you are liable for incarceration. The contraband and the ship are liable for seizure or destruction."

"We do not recognize your claim to this area, and we are not signature to any treaty restricting our access. We carry no contraband. Common usage and innocent passage—"

"Does not apply in this case."

"Says your government."

"It does. The contraband list is also very long."

"I protest—" Samovitch waved her hands. "I protest everything. All things for the record. But we are unarmed, we could not fight you on our ship, and we certainly cannot fight you here. What happens now?"

"You will be interred onboard the Pinguin. We have suitable quarters for you and your crew. You will be housed, fed, and clothed at our expense. You may have private quarters as befits an officer, or you may house with your crew. It is your choice. If you house with your crew, you may impose such discipline as you see fit. Otherwise, they will be under National naval regulations."

"I will stay with my crew. They will listen to me. We have been together forever, we are like family."

Kruder consulted his comm. The relevant information had been sent to him by the boarding party. "Very well, you and your crew of six others will be assigned quarters."

"Kapitan," the petty officer broke in, "we only located five others. The political commissar was missing."

"You did a sweep?" Kruder asked.

"Twice, Kapitan. The habitat section was empty, and we found no other sections aired up. We checked engineering and the bridge most closely. The remaining boarding party has secured themselves while they perform their checks."

"I see. Captain, where is your missing crew member?"

"Missing crew member." Samovitch smiled. "I don't know what you are talking about. You said that you have five others. That is the sum of my crew."

"Six, with the political officer."

"We carry no political officer. That is an error on the manifest. We had one, but he left us... two jumps ago, while we were deep within our own borders. Some party event he had to attend."

"All Confederation ships carry political officers."

"We did not."

"You deny his presence?"

"Yes."

The petty officer cleared his throat.

"Yes?" Kruder asked.

"We did find an open air lock, Kapitan. Inner door locked, but outer swinging freely. Like somebody left in a hurry...or triggered it remotely."

"I see." Kruder glared at Samovitch. "Did you murder your political officer?"

"I murdered no one," she said. "Our records are wrong. You have our complete crew."

"Minus one political officer."

"Who left on his own accord. Previously."

"Under suspicious circumstances. What of this air lock?"

"In the confusion of your attack, who knows what my crew did? We are a merchant crew. Not used to such things. And in any event, Korvettenkapitan, I am declaring for the record that my crew is complete with no casualties. Such things as happened before your attack are none of your concern, nor of your responsibility."

Kruder shook his head. "I have much to do, so I will leave this for now. Wann, escort the captain and her crew to their assigned quarters and return here when done. Captain, if you have any questions, you may speak to me at any time. Simply ask one of the crew and they will bring you to me, any time, day or night."

Kruder stepped back, saluted, then extended his hand. After a moment, Samovitch returned the salute, shook the offered hand, then left with her escort.

Kruder turned to Fusterheim. "Tell me of this ship."

"Food, some supplies. Some general cargo, a large amount of processed metal pellets. Nickel and titanium. Definitely prohibited as contraband."

"Take pictures and keep good documentation."

"Already done, Kapitan."

"Anything of use in the general cargo?"

"Two containers of fabric. I can have that moved by the tug in about two hours if you give the word."

"We won't wait two hours for fabric. Electronic parts, perhaps, but not that. Have the boarding party set to scuttle the ship in the planet's gravity well and return as quickly as possible."

Ten minutes later, Wann, the petty officer, returned and saluted. "Reporting as ordered sir. The Confed is in the prisoner section with her crew."

"Call her Captain Samovitch, please. We will address our new guests correctly by their proper ranks at all times and grant them the respect you would accord a member of our own navy."

"Yes, Kapitan."

"What happened on the boarding?"

"Everything went according to plan, Kapitan. We arrived.

The crew was gathered at the air lock, they did not resist, and we secured the ship with no issues."

"Except for Leutnant Blomberg. What happened there?"

"Sir, I don't know. I saw what happened, but I do not understand."

"Start at the beginning."

"We boarded as ordered. Myself, the leutnant, four ratings. The ratings were armed, visibly armed. The engineering specialists were behind us. We met the Confeds—we met Captain Samovitch—and her crew at the lock. She demanded an explanation. I identified myself and read the boarding request as written. I had it on my comm."

"You read it? What of the leutnant?"

"The leutnant sounded stressed, Kapitan. He had some problems speaking, so after ten seconds, I stepped in."

"Why did you do that, PO?"

"Sir, things were tense. There were many weapons present on our side, and on their side, who knew. Best to get things moving along before anything bad happened."

"But something bad did happen?"

"Sir, while I was conducting the operation. I had informed Captain Samovitch of our intent to board, inspect the ship, and remove her and her crew to Pinguin, and stressed that she was under superior weapons. She was not happy, but she seemed reasonable. Her crew was also unhappy, but they were careful. They kept their hands where we could see them and made no protest. Mostly older folks, Kapitan. My age. Experienced sailors. I could tell."

"What happened next?"

"The leutnant recovered himself. He interrupted and told me he would deal with this—he used a Russe word. I do not speak Russe, but I have heard this word before. It is not polite. I have only used it myself once."

"What for?"

"To start a fight. In a bar. I was bored." The petty officer looked worried. "When I was off duty, of course, Kapitan."

"Of course. And then?"

"The leutnant continued speaking to Captain Samovitch in Russe. The conversation escalated to near shouting. I didn't know he spoke Russe."

"Neither did I. Did you understand anything?"

"A few words. Similar to the ones he used before."

"He was calling her names?"

"At first. She called him some as well. And then—"

"Yes?"

"He slapped her."

"What?" Kruder's voice rose. "He slapped her?"

"Hard. Her face snapped sideways."

"Had she offered any resistance? Physical resistance."

"No sir. She and her crew stood easy, without weapons. No threat at all."

Kruder ground his teeth for a moment. "What did you do?"

"Well, nothing sir. It was a bit of a surprise, but not much."

"Not much? Slapping is not much?"

The petty officer straightened his shoulders. "We are used to the leutnant's ways."

"What do you mean, his ways?"

"The leutnant is sometimes very... enthusiastic in enforcing discipline."

Kruder turned to Fusterheim. Fusterheim returned a grim nod. He'd get to the bottom of this.

"I see. Then?"

"She hit him back."

"Struck him?"

"Not at first, sir. First, she kneed him in the balls. Then she hit him in the face, twice. Knocked him out."

"She knocked him out?"

"Yes sir. I was so surprised, I didn't do anything. I just stared. Then she turned to me and ordered me to take her to you."

"Ordered?"

"I don't remember her exact words, sir, something like, enough of this puppy, take me to your Kapitan right away. That sort of thing. She ordered the ratings to collect the leutnant and take him back. And boarded the shuttle with her crew."

"She ordered our sailors?"

"Sir, I—" The petty officer shrugged. "She talks like you, sir. Like a captain. She told us what to do, and we did it. I'd no more argue with her than I would argue with you, sir."

Kruder nodded. "I see. I see." He returned to a console and sat, drumming his fingers. "Very well. That will be all, PO. You behaved appropriately. Well done."

The petty officer saluted, turned, then stopped. "One more thing, Kapitan."

"Yes?"

"Next bar fight I'm in, I'd like that captain to be on our side." He whistled. "For such a small woman, she throws a mean punch."

CHAPTER FIFTEEN

"Jump emergence in three minutes, Tribune," the helmsman said.

"Thank you, Trevor," Devin said. He smiled at Lionel, at the console by his side. "Well done, Trevor."

Lionel rolled his eyes. His continued lectures were having an effect. Devin now called his officers by their names rather than their stations.

Mostly.

Devin tapped his screen. "Subprefect, I am unhappy."

"Unhappy, Tribune?"

"Yes."

"What are you unhappy about, Tribune? That you defeated a larger Confed armada, recaptured Sand Harbor, and have now secured it against re-capture by the judicious use of Marines and semi-repaired ships?"

"No, that was well done. I enjoyed that."

"Or are you unhappy that you have sent, in your words, 'a crack team of spies and special agents' into the core to determine the cause of a secret warrant being issued against you? Said team, including the heir to one of the richest families in the Empire, one of your sisters' fanatically loyal Jovians, and is headed by a Duke of the realm, one with a claim to the Imperial throne himself, come to think of it."

"Dirk is, what, three hundred thirtieth in line to the throne? Something like that. It would take a catastrophe of galactic proportions to put him on the throne."

"It would be a catastrophe of galactic proportions if he was on the throne, but that's another story."

"Escorting merchant ships out here is boring."

"The safe and timely arrival of the convoy at its destination is the primary object of the escort."

"What idiot said that?"

"You did. It's your standing orders for ships under your command."

"It's in my orders? I don't remember saying that. Or reading that."

"You signed them. I'm not sure you read them."

"You gave them to me, didn't you, and told me to sign them?"

"Yup."

"Why didn't you tell me to read them?"

"We need you here to sign things, Tribune. Not to read things."

"Thanks for your vote of confidence. What are we doing here again?"

"Look, Tribune. We keep escorting convoys, or even single ships for that matter, we give the others time to figure things out, coreward. And, moving through the trade routes, we have a better chance of tracking down whoever is shooting up merchant ships."

"Confeds," Devin said.

"Or Nats."

"Could be Nats, yes."

"Or plain old pirates. That's the most likely."

"Yes."

"Or somebody else. Somebody in the Navy."

"Not likely."

"You know anybody else with positron guns?"

Devin shook his head and looked around the bridge. "Not here."

Lionel nodded.

"And then what, Subprefect?"

"If we can figure out the who, we'll figure out the why. I'm much more interested in why somebody is shooting up freighters out here."

"Theories?"

"Could be pirates, in which case it's only money. We hunt them down, blow up a few ships, you get all stabby on some of the pirates, and then we have a nice lunch with more of those canoes."

"Canoes? You mean canapes?"

"The cracker things? Is that what they're called? Not canoes?"

"You know very well what they're called. Stop changing the subject. What if it's not pirates?"

"Then it's either the Confeds or the Nats, and they're

trying to put the blame on us, so that we attack the other. Classic disinformation."

"Where do you place your bet?"

Lionel brought a list of ships up on his screen and tapped each description. "We can't tell, exactly. We know some of our ships went missing, and we know when and where. But they're all over the place—some near Confed space, some near Nat space, some in unaligned planets. It's all random. There's no pattern that I can see. We need more info."

"What type of info?"

"We know what they're doing. We need some idea of how. Warships? Armed freighters? Which?"

"How do we find that?"

"Move around. Collect intelligence. Wait for your crack team of 'spies and agents' to report back."

"They said they would check in once they got their weapons sorted out."

"And how will they find us?"

"The Jovians. Lee's people will keep her informed of where we've been and where we're going."

"As long as we remember to tell them, yes."

The jump timer counted down. Devin tapped his fingers on his chair. "I'm worried about her, Lionel."

"She's fine. You were right. You've only got a frigate. She has a fleet."

"What if, what if..."

"What if what? All we know is that regular communication to the core has been cut off. There are a dozen reasons that could have happened, not all bad."

"You don't believe that, do you?"

"Not for a second. Somebody is starting something. The Confeds. The Nats. Our people. The Chancellor. Pirates. Sunspots. Who knows? There's too many Empires, too many ships out here. We're too far away to make a difference to things, but we can provide somebody with an excuse to start something bigger."

"I want to go help her. Never mind what I said."

"We need more information. Who the players are, what they want. Why do they want you out of the picture? Dirk will figure it out. He's not incompetent, just lazy. And your sister trusts Lee—she'll tell her the truth. One way or another, we'll find out what's happening there."

"And if they don't come back, don't come back here at all?"

"That's a message in itself, isn't it?"

Trevor interrupted. "Emergence."

The Pollux, the Valhalla, and the Hydrogen Queen were uniquely qualified to run convoys out in the Verge. But they were only three ships, and given the immensity of space, they couldn't convey everything everywhere. Lionel had come up with a unique solution. Rather than forcing the merchants into convoys they didn't want to wait for, for the last few weeks, he'd given them the chance to participate on routes of his choosing. Routes that made substantial commercial sense but were usually bypassed by mainline shipping companies because of the existence of lower risk routes. Routes that frequently let them investigate systems that may have contained pirates.

"I understand your constraints, Captain Temas," Tribune

Devin said, confirming the name from a list on his comm. "But we will be leaving the system in four hours, with the good ship K D Pearson, or without. We already have three other freighters with us, and we will be making two long jumps, and refueling in the dark. If you don't think your fuel capacity is up to it, or your navigation for that matter, then don't come. We're cutting the corner to Weave's world, and the intermediate stop has no fueling capacity. No population either. We'll protect you if you want to jump there, but you need fuel for a second immediate jump."

Captain Temas grunted on the video screen. His beard was neatly trimmed, he wore starched coveralls and a starched hat, with a bald skull peeking out from below. He looked like the sort of person who borrowed money casually, and never paid it back unless reminded at least three times. "We can't afford to spend that much money—a double fuel load will kill our profit. We normally refuel at a gas giant or a comet when we're passing through systems."

"You can try. I don't recommend it. Either way, we're leaving in three hours and fifty-seven minutes from now. See you at the jump limit, or not at all."

"You're crazy. Nobody can afford that."

"All evidence to the contrary, in the form of three freighters accompanying us already."

"You nobles are all alike. Don't understand that commerce drives the empire." The captain's eyes glinted. "We'll meet you there and follow along."

"With sufficient fuel?"

"Yes, of course." Captain Temas smirked. "Always happy to follow naval instructions."

Devin regarded the screen in front of him. That had been too easy. "Captain Temas. You said I was crazy earlier, did you not?"

"It's just an expression, Tribune."

"It is. I understand that. But you know, most people don't call me crazy. They call me mad."

"Tribune?"

"You've heard of me, of course. The Mad Dog of the Verge? The Empress's crazed brother? Wealthy, arrogant, completely nuts? Executes random pirates?"

"I don't listen to gossip, Tribune. I'm sure you're a fine officer doing your duty."

"I am, I am. But ask yourself this, Captain Temas. Let's say that you were the Mad Dog of the Verge, and you had jumped into the dark, and you discovered that one of your ships had misrepresented how much fuel it carried. Rather than jumping right away, the whole convoy had to wait while fuel was transferred. Do you think the Mad Dog of the Verge would wait for that? Or would he simply jump away and leave the other ship out there alone, in the dark?"

Captain Temas swallowed. "Take the crew off and leave the ship there? Abandon it?"

Devin shook his head. "Nobody said anything about taking the crew off, Captain."

Captain Temas nodded rapidly. "Understood, Tribune. We'll see you at the jump point in four hours."

"Three hours, fifty-two minutes, Captain."

"Three hours, fifty-two minutes, understood."

"Pollux out." Devin killed the connection. "Well?"

Lionel looked up from his console. "Well what?"

"Did I scare him?"

"Don't see why not. You frighten me all the time, and you're not even trying."

"You're scared of me?"

"No."

"You just said you were."

"I didn't say I was scared of you. I said you frightened me. Different thing. What will happen to me when I'm following you around? Now, that, that gives me nightmares. Trevor, where's that freighter going, the one the Tribune was just talking to?"

Trevor played with the comm console. "The K D Pearson has left orbit. Course is... directly for a cluster of fueling barges."

"The course it's taking, is it least time or least fuel?"

"Least time, Subprefect. He's burning money to get fueled up faster."

"Yup." Lionel nodded. "You scared him."

Three warships and four freighters cleared the jump limit, en route for the seldom visited 736-3636 system. Four days later, they emerged at their destination. Twin cold white dwarfs. Outer planets were worthless balls of rock. The nearest gas giant was uncomfortably far inside the jump limit. Refueling ships would have to coast inward for at least a day before refueling and burn a portion of their collected fuel getting back outside the jump limit.

No pirates or other ships.

"We'll never catch anybody this way," Devin said, scanning the empty threat board.

"Tribune, we can't be everywhere at once, and besides, we're not counting on catching any pirates here."

"Poor fueling capabilities," Devin said.

"Not here. But we've picked up a few hints, and Imin wants to chat—"

"Anomaly around the third gas giant," Lieutenant Lukas, the sensor operator, said.

Devin perked up. "What type of anomaly?"

"Visual flares. Items reentering atmosphere and burning up."

"Thats an anomaly? That happens all the time, officer..." Devin shut his mouth. She was the one who couldn't drink wine, but he'd forgotten her name. Was it Lukas?

"Metal objects according to the spectroscope, sir."

"Asteroids are... no, they're not usually, are they?"

Lionel was tapping his screen. "Nope. We need a better view, Tribune. Suggest thrust ninety degrees to the ecliptic, get a clearer view."

"Very well."

"And... maybe...."

"Yes, general quarters." Devin checked his restraints and made sure his gloves and helmet were close by.

"Sir." Lukas was throwing courses up on the main screen. "Valhalla has good sensors as well. If she drops down, and we exchange data, we'll be able to triangulate and get better results."

"Send her a course, and tell her she's ordered to follow it," Devin ordered. "And include your sensor requirements as well."

"Sir."

Warning bongs echoed on the bridge. Red lights flashed the maneuvering pattern. Devin first floated against his restraints as the ship pivoted, then pushed back into his seat as the main drives fired. Lionel had that 'I'm busy' look on his face and was throwing orbits up onto his screen. Lukas was sending instructions to the Valhalla and answering queries from their sensor people. Lieutenant Carroll, the comm officer, had taken over the sensor sweeps. The weapons officer had taken advantage of the Leeway that general quarters offered to power up backup radars and aim them.

"Sir, Captain Temas is on the line," the comm officer said. "He wants to know why his radar warning sensor is going off."

Devin mirrored the bridge screens of his officers. "Lieutenant... Huusko... what are you doing?"

Huusko tapped his screen to share it on the main display. At general quarters, he didn't have to salute, or face the captain, and he certainly didn't have to get out of his chair. "Sir, we are running test firing solutions on nearby ships, to ensure the weapons are ready."

"Nearby Imperial ships, Huusko?"

"Those are the only ships that are nearby, Tribune."

"Is there a reason you picked that particular freighter to run tests on?"

"Seemed like the one we would miss the least if we had to

destroy it, sir. Or at least miss its captain the least. And I note, from my scan, he's been fired on before. Note the repairs to his starboard truss." Huusko put a wireframe diagram up on the screen. It clearly showed where a reinforcing beam had been welded onto the forward truss. The K D Pearson had obviously survived combat at some point.

Devin laughed. "Well, you won't be destroying it today. But if we ever need any Imperial ships destroyed, I'll remember to ask you."

"Thank you sir."

"Sir," the navigator interrupted.

Devin couldn't remember her name. Something with a V. Villars? Verbier? Villa, that was it. "Yes, Villa?"

"We have lost our jump solution, and I am unable to calculate a new one without a steady course. And any moment, the other ships will be complaining about the same thing if we make them shift."

"Tell them to hold their vectors and continue jump calculations and countdowns. I have a feeling we'll be done here shortly. Isn't that so, Subprefect?"

"We're done now, Tribune. We have our information."

"Secure from general quarters," Devin said. "Helm, give the navigator what they need in the way of a course to jump out with the others. Release the Valhalla likewise."

Officers' fingers flashed as they shut down systems and brought items to standby. Alarms bonged as the ship changed aspect and vector.

Devin brought up a private screen with Lionel. "Well?"

"Take a look at this, Tribune." A grainy picture appeared

on Devin's screen, pieces of twisted metal, tumbling and already flaring as the gas giant's friction burned it up.

"I see burning metal things."

Lionel froze the picture mid-tumble and superimposed a wire-frame diagram on it. The wireframe showed a regular module, and the tumbling metal fitted nicely into one quarter of it. "Better now?"

"That's part of a ship."

"Yes."

"An important part?"

"Very. It's a standard hab module. Fitted to dozens of different kinds of freighters."

Devin scratched his chin. "Don't they need that? The freighters, I mean?"

"Yup."

"They wouldn't leave it behind by accident, would they? Jettison it, maybe?"

"Nope."

"Why did they leave it here?"

"Because somebody scuttled a freighter by blowing it to pieces and let the pieces crash and burn up in the atmosphere here, and this is all that's left."

Devin shook his head. "Doesn't compute. Why blow it up if they were going to scuttle it. Why not just aim it into the gravity well and let nature take its course?"

"Perhaps the people onboard the ship were anti-nature and didn't want to burn up in a fiery flame. Perhaps they fought back."

"So they had to be persuaded. They didn't survive the persuasion, do you think?"

Lionel zoomed in on something next to the debris. "Bodies."

"Jove bless them. They're too far in the gravity for us even to recover." Devin peered at the picture. "Are those Nat skinsuits?"

"Hard to tell. Could be. Notice anything else?" Lionel flipped between two displays, one a hab module with six internal bulkheads, one with eight. The debris more closely matched the eight-bulkhead model.

"The bulkheads are different. That's significant?"

"It's much more common in the Union, but not totally unknown in the Empire."

"Where's the rest of the ship?"

"Gone, probably. This will be as well in a shift or less. We're lucky we caught it. If we were here two shifts later, we wouldn't see anything at all."

Devin tapped his chair. "Some pirates attacked a ship, boarded it, and..."

"Dragged it way out here? In the middle of nowhere? Pirates? Why bother?"

"Somebody who's destroying ships and doesn't want anybody to know that they're doing it, somebody who doesn't want to tip their hand."

"Who?"

"I want to find out. I need to find out."

"Yes Tribune."

"In fact, I will find out," Devin grunted.

"Yes Tribune. Better do it soon." Lionel threw a list of ships up on the screen. "Lots of freighters in this sector. Lots of targets."

CHAPTER SIXTEEN

"Everyone gun up." Ana unlocked the arms locker across from the main air lock. "All of you have something lethal in your hands when Navy's friends get here. And full suits as well. And put on shoes. Private, get my shotgun out of my room for me, and one for yourself."

"You don't want your rifle, Centurion?" Scruggs asked.

"Too long for inside a ship. Get one for yourself as well."

"I've got my favorite in my room. I'll get that." Scruggs pulled herself down the mid-ship ladder. Heart's Desire was floating in space. A mean-looking freighter had lifted off a nearby asteroid and zapped them with a powerful radar, then ordered them to heave-to for inspection by 'Cassandra's friends.' Requests for more information were met with silence.

Dirk and Lee had complied and set them coasting. Ana checked the signature of the radar scanning them and discovered it matched Imperial weapons, then ordered them all back to the air lock.

"Scruggs has a favorite shotgun now?" Dena asked. "Does that mean she has more than one?"

"Why not?"

"What do you need more than one shotgun for?"

"You need three. One lightweight with a short barrel for confined spaces," Ana said. "Something heavier to absorb the recoil if you're firing slugs, and something more rugged if you use it planet side."

"Empress's shoes," Dena said. "What have you turned that girl into?"

"Don't you have a favorite slingshot?"

"It's a piece of wood with a rubber band."

"How many different leather outfits do you have?" Ana asked.

"I don't kill people with a leather bustier."

Ana shrugged. "But you use them to convince people to give you what you want. I don't look good in a bustier, so I use guns. Engineer, get up here and gun up."

Gavin climbed through the floor hatch, then patted a wrench on his belt. "I'm better with this, at least on ship. And I don't look good in a bustier either."

Ana picked out the largest revolver from the locker and handed it to Gavin, along with a thigh holster. "Strap this on where people can see it. You can use your space-hammer all you want in a fight, but guns are more intimidating, and it's good to have a ranged weapon, just in case."

Scruggs climbed through the hatch behind Gavin, two shotguns strapped over her back. She handed Ana a shotgun.

He checked the action, then loaded it with solid slugs, and slung it over his shoulder.

"Solid slugs on yours, Private."

Scruggs did as she was told.

"Scruggs," Dena said. "Centurion says you need three shotguns."

"Well, respectfully, I disagree," Scruggs said.

"Aha." Dena smiled. "See, Centurion? Not everybody buys into your weird gun fetish."

"Five is the correct number." Scruggs clicked a shell in. "Long barrel for accuracy, short barrel for ease of utilization. One each in light weight for mobility, and heavy weight to deal with recoil, and I have one specially greased for wet and moldy environments. I could take it underwater if I had to."

Ana laughed then pulled a small revolver and tiny belt holster from the locker. "Outstanding. Lee, take this and strap it on your belt, please. No, better idea, strap the holster, but have the weapon in your hand when that lock opens. Not pointing at anybody, but ready."

Lee clipped the holster to her belt, then removed the revolver and examined it. "Not too big. Fits in the palm of my hand."

Ana pulled four loads of frangibles from the locker and handed them to her. "You're tall, but not a lot of mass. If you try firing something with heavy recoil, you'll bounce all the way to engineering and out the thrusters. This is the smallest recoil item we have. If things go sideways, just aim in the general direction of the bad guys and keep pulling the trigger. These frangibles won't kill them, but dust, noise and smoke will distract them while Scruggs and I get a bead on them. Scruggs, make sure you load it with slugs. You too, Nature Girl."

"Me too what?" Dena asked.

Ana offered a shotgun from the locker to Dena. "Load that up for yourself."

"Forgive me for doubting you, O psychopathic-murdering old guy, but I thought you restricted these solid slugs on the ship because you didn't want us to blow holes in things."

"Right tool for the right job." Ana pointed at Gavin. "He's a big guy, and he can swing that wrench. Somebody gets too close, he beans them, but no general shooting, so we can still have a discussion with our new friends. Something surprising happens, these Jovians may be freaks, but they're quick freaks, and ours doesn't panic. She can watch from behind me, and if she gets bothered by something, she can have dust and noise happening right away. That gives time for Scruggs and me to observe the threat, orient ourselves, decide to engage, and then destroy our opponents. That's why we've got the most powerful weapons. Neither of us is likely to destroy the ship by accident, because our shots will go where we point them."

"What does that have to do with me?"

"Navy will be up front, to talk to his friend. Then Scruggs and I, with Engineer between us. We can step up and deal with any immediate threats. Lee's tall, so if something bad starts behind the first few people, she can decide to fire, then we'll know and engage."

Dena crossed her arms but still didn't take the proffered

shotgun. "And I'm supposed to hang out in the back, because I'm a scaredy cat who doesn't like to fight?"

"You hunt a lot with that slingshot, back on Mudhole or whatever it was?"

"Rockhaul, as you know—never mind, that's a fair characterization. Yeah, I hunted."

"And you killed the animals, of course."

"We'd eat them after, but sure. If we didn't kill them, they'd come for us."

"If you wounded something, but didn't kill it, and it crawled off into the brush, how did you feel when you had to go in after it?"

"That's scary," Dena said. "Wounded animals are dangerous. You have to put them out of their misery, but you need to be careful, and make sure it doesn't get behind you."

"Exactly." Ana racked the shotgun. "This is a strange situation. We're meeting some pretty dangerous people out in nowhere. If things go bad, in the end, there will be only one crew left alive here. I intend for that to be us. If they start shooting, we shoot back, and then we charge in and eliminate any other threats. I need somebody I can count on to make sure there are no wounded animals sneaking up behind. I figure, next to me, you're the most experienced in that area." Ana shoved the shotgun into her hands. "You'll take care of the strays."

Dena nodded, took the shotgun, and racked the action. "I'll need more slugs."

Everybody gathered at the air lock, brandishing weapons —except Dirk. He waved his hands at the others. "I'm not saying I need a laser rifle, for Empress's sake. But I think I should be armed."

"No," Ana said.

"I remind you that—"

The others all chorused the reply "I'm the pilot of the ship."

Dirk jerked back at the answer. "Yes, and the captain should be armed."

"The captain is only armed if he expects a mutiny, Navy. Are you expecting one?"

"I think I've already got one."

"Look, you overeducated noble cretin, take a look at what you see here, at what your friends will see when they come through the air lock."

"A group of desperadoes—"

"Stop being a jackass. Describe this group as you would the side party of a ship you were inspecting, when you first arrived. Uniforms, weapons, the whole bit."

"Well." Dirk stepped back and examined the group. "I see three, well, three armed... spacers. All in the same uniform, or close. You and Scruggs have identical skinsuits, and the same coveralls. Even Gavin's look similar. Your weapons match, sidearm and shotgun. Gavin has a sidearm. You two are dressed like a standard ship security detachment. Gavin's a bit greasy, but sometimes the Marine detachment helps in engineering, so that's not a surprise if he were in too much of a hurry to change. You've got full suits and boots, look dressed for boarding."

"Shined boots too," Scruggs said.

"Yes. And ship patches. That's a nice touch."

"Lee has ship patches too, Pilot," Scruggs said. "So does Dena."

Dirk twisted. Both Lee and Dena wore skinsuits and hard boots. Lee covered hers with loose pilot-type coveralls. Her thigh pockets were stuffed with a comms unit and two med-kits. Dena's skinsuit was tight and as revealing as possible, but she had a web belt with pouches and equipment, and a bandoleer of slingshot slugs across her chest. She rested a shot-gun on a cocked hip. Both women had ship patches on their shoulders. All five had helmets racked behind their shoulders or on their belts.

Ana jerked his head. "Do we pass inspection, Navy?"

Dirk nodded. "You do, in fact. You look like, well, you could be a naval crew, almost."

"Kind of scary, isn't it?"

"Yes." Dirk looked down at himself. He had got back into the habit of wearing emergency air-loss gear, so he carried his own helmet and gloves, and wore vacuum-safe boots. His thigh pockets had a comm stuffed in them. Except for rank markings, he had dressed like this during his time in the Navy.

"Well, look at us. We look competent."

"Looks can be deceiving, at least for some naval members of our group. But yes, this isn't a group that you'd get into a random fight with, without good reason."

Dirk surveyed the group in front of him. "You do know, Centurion, that they could just stay back and blast away."

"Not if they want the ship intact."

"What if they don't?"

"We can't do anything about that at all, can we?"

"Nothing."

"I like to focus on what I can control, not what I can't." The ship rocked gently as something mated to the air lock. "And they're here."

Dirk stepped up to the air lock and drew himself to attention, like he was meeting an admiral. "Crew, prepare for boarding."

The air lock lit red as the outer door opened, then blinked green as it closed and the fans filled it. There was atmosphere behind the outer door, because the flashing red turned green in less than a second. The air lock door swung open.

A tiny blond-haired, black-eyed woman hopped out. She was shorter than anybody on the crew, even Scruggs. Her skinsuit was fitted even closer than Dena's, and over it, she wore a short, pleated skirt that would do nothing to stave off vacuum but emphasized her legs. A laced blouse did the same for her breasts. She wore gold sandals, the same color as the leather thong holding her two pigtails.

"Durriken Friedel, you hound you, you look good enough to eat." She grinned, then hopped up and straddled his waist, threw her arms around him, and planted a full mouth kiss on his lips.

When she showed no sign of stopping nuzzling Dirk, Ana lowered his gun. "Well, looks like they do know each other."

Cassandra pulled her mouth back, unbent her legs and hopped down, pigtails swinging. She put her hands on her hips and licked her lips. "I promised myself that's the first thing I'd do to you when I saw you again. And I promised myself this was the second thing I'd do." She stepped forward and slapped Dirk hard across the mouth.

Dena rolled her eyes. "Not only friends, but old friends. She knows him for sure."

"Adventure awaits," Ana said.

CHAPTER SEVENTEEN

"Dirk and I go way back. Way, way back. Back to the Navy. Early Navy days. We were in some classes together, and then we went to that officers' school. The one with all the presentations. Dirk kept falling asleep and I would try to balance things on his nose. First, I got one of my rule books up there, then I managed to balance it across his nose and onto his forehead. Then I put a sandwich up there. I think it was cheese. Was it cheese, Dirk? I remember you liked cheese." Cassandra flounced along beside them. After she'd confirmed it was the real Durriken Friedel calling, she'd given Lee directions to the next rendezvous—a rough spaceport on one of the volcanic islands. After a patented Dirk re-entry, they had thumped into a rough but ready settlement.

"Yes, Cass, I do like cheese." Dirk was holding her hand while they walked, and he looked guilty about it.

"That's right. You liked all those cheeses. The squeaky ones. And you made us drink all those icky wines, the ones that you said brought out the flavor. The white ones. And we had to swirl the wines in the glass. I can't swirl them. I always mess up and splash them around. Do you still splash the wines? I'll bet you do."

The ground rumbled under their feet, and the whole landscape shook. The crew stumbled a bit, but the shaking lasted only seconds.

"Don't worry about that, everybody," Cassandra said. "Just the volcanoes and the earthquakes. We get that all the time. Follow me, and I'll take you to the market."

"Was it absolutely necessary to board us like that?" Dirk asked. "With the guns and all?"

"Can't be too careful. Some ships have gone missing recently. Merchant ships, on regular runs. Some tramp freighters too. Best to be careful."

The rest of the crew, except Lee, trailed along behind them. Cassandra kept babbling on as they walked down the loading ramp of Heart's Desire onto the surface. Rocky darted down the ramp, stopped to pee on the strut, and raced around, sniffing happily. They'd landed in a clearing at the bottom of a volcano, and there were all sorts of new smells and critters to chase.

Innocent-looking snow covered the top of the volcano—but the crater emitted a steady stream of white smoke. Below it, a trickle of reddish-white volcanic rock flowed out to form a red patch.

"And what a great doggie he is," Cassandra said. "Hello, doggie. Nice doggie. Who's the best doggie ever? Such a cutie. He's so cute."

"Cass, what's with the volcano up there? That lava can't be good."

"Don't worry about the lava, Dirk. That's normal. It trickles out every day." Cass picked up a stick. "You want a stick? Will you chase a stick? Good doggie."

Rocky happily chased a stick back and forth. Dirk and Cassandra continued leading, the others fell behind.

"Does she ever shut up?" Scruggs hefted her shotgun. They'd all kept their weapons, and Cassandra didn't seem to mind. Or notice.

"Not so far," Ana said. "She does go on."

"She can't possibly be any sort of arms dealer."

"Know a lot of arms dealers, do you, Baby Marine?" Dena asked.

"And who dresses like that?" Scruggs said. "It looks ridiculous."

Dena tilted her head to get a better view. "It looks good on her. Makes her legs stand out. And she's got that breathy little girl thing going on. Some men like it."

"Men like that?" Scruggs asked. "Really?"

"Some do. Like Dirk. See how he's holding her hand?"

"He never does that."

"He does with her."

Dirk stopped, faced the crew, and cleared his throat. "Um, Cass and I have to have a private discussion first. Arrange a few things, iron out the details. You all understand?"

"Take your time, Navy," Ana said. "Take your time."

"Thank you. Thank you all."

Gavin nodded. Ana and Dena smirked.

Scruggs looked confused, then her mouth formed an 'O.' She shook her head. "I don't understand men."

"That's pretty obvious."

"To be fair," Ana said, walking behind them. "Men probably don't understand you."

"What's to understand?" Scruggs asked. "I'm quiet. Polite. Friendly. I like to fit in. Follow instructions. Not make waves."

"And shoot people." Dena kicked the ground.

"I don't, I haven't. Not many. Not very many."

"Blow up tanks. With rockets."

"It wasn't a tank. It was a wheeled self-propelled tank destroyer. Tell her, Centurion." Scruggs had helped the centurion destroy a planetary tank that was trying to blow up the Heart's Desire. She'd been very badly injured during it—she still limped when she was tired.

Ana laughed. "Yes, it was a wheeled self-propelled tank destroyer. But you can't expect Nature Girl here to call it that. Her vehicle identification skills are poor."

"Bite me and my vehicle identification, Old Man. You shoot people, and you blow up tanks, you once clubbed a lover over the head with a handmade sculpture."

"I didn't hurt him." Scruggs smirked. "Well, not badly."

"Then you came back and fought off four armed hijackers with cans of beans and a camping stove."

"They were the best weapons I could find at the time. And I couldn't let those two be captured. Or hijacked."

"And you cheat at poker."

Scruggs smiled. "Yeah, I do. I kind of like that."

"What I'm saying, Baby Marine, is don't judge a book by

its cover and all that. Looking at you, people wouldn't think you did all those things. Looking at her, she looks like a complete bimbo. I'm sure it's misdirection, and that there's much more there than we see. This is just a way of making people underestimate her."

"I guess so." Scruggs smiled. "I wonder if I could borrow her skirt."

Other than the regular earthquakes, Carousel seemed like a semi-nice place to live—once they got off the blackened landing pads and into the jungle. The crew sweated in their skinsuits. They were kept hidden from orbital thermal scans by volcanic activity. Sulfuric clouds blocked visual scans. If all the ships kept radio discipline, they'd even be invisible to radio detection. The air was moist, and the perfumed scent of bright red and yellow plants warred with the occasional whiff of sulfur from the distant volcano. A great place to relax for a few days, if not for the feeling of impermanence surrounding them—everything seemed temporary.

"This feels like a high-end Army field post," Ana said. "Look at that bar over there."

A collection of rough wooden tables and benches surrounded a single prefab container building under the forest canopy. The container was open at both ends, displaying a kitchen and storage coolers inside, with electric stoves and microwaves. Metal cables supporting yellow-orange panels draped between the trees.

Dena mopped her brow. "Smart, shading from the sun."

"That's not shade. Those are solar panels," Ana said. "That's a military field kitchen module. The panels pack up inside, the whole thing locks up for shipping. You can move it into place in an hour, and all you need is supplies. Over there. Engineer, is that what I think it is?"

Gavin shaded his eyes as they walked between the trees. Earth oaks, part of some long-forgotten terra-forming package, extended up dozens of feet, with branches drifting out in all directions. The sunbeams danced across the clearing as the green tops swayed in the wind. A cluster of containers lay ahead, the nearest with dozens of finger sized power cables running out the front and connecting to the others. "If you think that's a portable switching station, then you're right. If that's the switching station, then there should be a feeder cable around here somewhere."

"Would this be it?" Dena hopped up onto five tree trunks that had been cut down and laid out as a footbridge across a small creek. A fist-thick cable snaked along the creek, disappearing under the trunks.

"That's it. Follow that back to the pads and you'll find it hooks up to one of those ships."

"Quite the setup our skirted friend has here," Ana said. "Freighters modified to provide shore power, a full portable electrical distribution plant, and all the trimmings."

"This doesn't make sense," Dena said. "Why bother with all this? You can just bring portable generators, or something like that. Or solar, like you said."

"You can buy temporary construction containers on any world, anywhere." Gavin pointed to the containers visible through the trees. "They're designed for contractors building in cities or on civilized planets. You can get office containers, meeting room containers, entertainment centers, gyms, everything. They all have heating and air conditioning built in, and lights and hard comm links. Which helps to stay undetected from ships scanning from orbit. They all have standard power couplings with standard comm links. Any planetary environment that humans can move around in, they work. They pack up easy for transport, they're durable, and rugged. Some can even be luxurious. I've seen hot tub ones, lounge and bar ones, even a yoga studio once."

"Yoga in a container?"

"Better than doing it outside in the snow, or the rain," Gavin said. "Or the dust or what have you."

"And best of all, nobody is going to ask questions if you buy some, or transport them," Ana said. "Perfect for the aspiring illegal weapons seller."

"Easy to set up," Gavin said. "Easy to tear down. No questions asked."

Ana watched Dirk and his friend retire into one of the containers in a group under a tree in the distance. "I think the pilot is beginning his negotiation for our new laser."

"What should we do?" Scruggs asked.

"Let's go to the bar and order a drink or two while we wait," Ana said.

"Just order one," Dena said.

"Why?" Scruggs asked.

"Trust me. This shouldn't take long." Dena laughed. "Not long at all."

CHAPTER EIGHTEEN

"I only have one drink when we're doing something sketchy," Dena said to Scruggs. "I want to keep my wits about me."

Dirk and his new paramour took so long, they needed to order a second set of drinks. The bar-container was well equipped, if pricey. Gavin drank bottled beer, while Ana took a huge mug of brandy. Dena sampled a bottle of white wine and declared it good. Then she flirted the bartender into giving her two more glasses for free, but she only drank the first one.

"But why talk him into two, then?" Scruggs asked.

"Keep in practice."

"Private," Ana said, "What is that vile orange thing in front of you?"

"It's called a Rocket Launcher, Centurion. It's not very good. I don't think I like gin."

"If you don't like gin drinks, why in the name of the Emperor's back hair did you order one?"

"I didn't really, I just—"

Dena laughed. "The bartender asked what her favorite weapons of destruction were, and she said she liked rocket launchers, because she'd destroyed a tank—"

"A wheeled self-propelled tank-destroyer!" Scruggs interjected.

"A whatever. The bartender laughed and said she was a funny kid and mixed this up for her."

"I'm not a kid."

"He doesn't think so either. He gave her the drink for free."

"He's just being nice."

"He wants something from you. Care to guess what?"

Ana pointed across the clearing. "Speaking of people wanting things from other people, I see the pilot has managed to finish his discussion."

"Perhaps he acquired a discount."

Dirk sauntered over to them, Cassandra grasping his hand. His face was flushed, and he was breathing heavily. "Cass and I have been talking. I thought that you all should see the item in question."

"Always good to know what you're buying," Ana said. "Isn't that so, Engineer?"

Gavin nodded. "It is."

"You're the starship's engineer?" Cassandra asked.

"Yes."

"Oh. My. God. That is so cool. Did Dirk tell you that I wanted to be an engineer! I studied for it in college, but there wasn't a spot in the academy. And my adviser, she was former Navy, and she suggested I go regular officer path, you know, but then I'd have to take a whole bunch of other courses. More history and that, because all the math I'd taken for engineering, and I loved math so much. I still love math, why—"

Cassandra continued speaking non-stop for the next ten minutes as she led them through the trees, around the landing pads, and to a group of containers stacked together in the trees. The crew followed along behind. She had graduated from holding Dirk's hands to grasping his side, and continued to babble on about math, and school, and the Navy.

"She can't possibly be that dumb," Gavin whispered to Ana. "She's supposed to be a super thief who stole a task force."

"She did date Pilot Dirk there for a while," Ana said.

"But this would be a new level of dumbness. The height of dumbness. Who would possibly be that dumb?"

"The man dating her?" Ana said.

Cassandra brought them to a group of four containers stacked side by side at the edge of the clearing. A rugged-looking freighter, fifty years old, sat a few dozen meters away in the middle of a burned patch. Clearing vegetation required daily fires on Carousel.

"We'll be inside the blast radius here if she takes off, "Gavin said.

"Why not put them somewhere safe, then?" Ana asked.

"Easiest place to put them is close by if they're offloaded from the ship. And easiest place to get them back on if you're leaving in a hurry."

"I think she probably leaves a lot of places in a hurry."

"Everybody," Cass called. "Come close, please. You come closer, Dirk."

A weary-looking Dirk walked up to her, and she stood on tiptoe to kiss him. "Thanks, Dirk, sweetheart. Now, let's take a look here." She dragged the container's door across the muddy grass until it was open. A view screen covered the inside. Cassandra flicked a switch. Blinding white lights illuminated the inside of the container, and the screen powered up, displaying a schematic of the item inside.

"Right, this is the BL-4, Mk IX laser. 4.572 meters max length, including focusing mechanism, 101.6mm diameter of the laser focusing tube, max weight 1814.37 kilograms, excluding targeting radar, power and data cables." Cassandra brought up a different picture. "Let's focus on the base. Here, you can see that it's attached to the hull by 32 hexagonal bolts. The base itself is good for up to 7G, but all the stress of acceleration is taken up by the attachment, so you need to ensure that the attaching bolts can handle the stress."

Cassandra kept prattling on, as before, except this time, she was spewing out engineering specifications. Memorized, because she didn't need reference materials. Gavin grinned at the beginning, then frowned, and finally pulled out his comm and made frantic notes.

Ana wrote his own notes. "Engineer, what's a Young's Modulus?"

"Measures a material's resistance to being deformed elastically. This woman knows her bolts."

"Don't want it falling off when we punch the engines, do we?"

"Or try to pivot." Gavin made another note.

Cassandra switched the screen display. "Now the laser and focusing elements themselves are the external parts of the system. You need high-capacity capacitors..." She giggled. "That's funny. Capacity-capacitors. You need at least one, and there are connections here, and here, for four. Unlike regular electrical systems, these aren't plug and play. You need permanent, hardwired connections here. They take up to four—"

"How big are the connecting cables?" Gavin asked. "What's the size?"

Cassandra giggled again. "Silly man, I know you're just teasing me. You know as well as I do that the size depends on the output of your plant and the distance they have to run. But that being said, with the capacitors we offer, a four-centimeter-diameter copper wire—"

The capacitors she offered were apparently the best on the market with high storage values, and easy to recharge. They spat out their power in approved chunks that maximized the output of the laser, without reducing it to a melted pool of crystal and metal.

Ana raised his hand.

"Yes, big fella," Cassandra said.

"Assume we just weld it on top of engineering and plug it directly into the ship's power systems, how do we aim it? And how accurate is it?"

"Ideally, you'd have four different radars working in concert," Cassandra said. "We'd put four of them in different spots on your ship and tie them into your computer. You'll need an interface module, of course, and you'll need to have the appropriate software to make it work—"

"The appropriate software, multiple radars, interface modules. That's a lot of electronics," Ana said.

"Can the engineer install all of that, Centurion?" Scruggs whispered.

"I don't know. And that's a lot of things to go wrong."

"Do we have the correct software?"

"Maybe." Several weeks' diligent checking had located five weapons control programs, but since they were only identified by serial numbers, their capabilities were still a mystery.

Gavin was making more frantic notes as Cassandra kept talking.

Scruggs gestured. "She seems a lot less goofy now."

"Indeed. "

"Which one is the real Cassandra? Goofy Cassandra or Competent Cassandra?"

"Shhh." Ana waved her down.

Cassandra talked data-link integration, and how different ships could transmit 'encrypted target profiles and vectors with future time-adjusted aiming point predictions' and Gavin kept writing. Ana was nodding his head. Even Dirk paid attention.

Scruggs wandered behind Lee and Dena. She petted Rocky as he sniffed the shrubs. "Lee, is this the truth? Do you need all these radars?"

"Yes, Sister Scruggs. Space combat is challenging. We're moving, the target is moving, there are planets and stars and gravity, and they affect everything. And if the laser moves as well, even a small difference in turret speed or elevation angle, and we will be off by hundreds of meters at any sort of distance."

"How does anybody ever destroy another ship, then?"

"Naval ships have powerful customized computers, specialized software and specialized crew. They all work together. The targeting software knows the ship's intended moves and compensates for it."

"But if everything is moving…"

"All the time. And we're not aiming at where the targets are, but where it will be."

"Sounds like you know about fighting in space?"

"I took a basic class at school to learn the different terms. As a navigator, I had to be able to talk to the gunners, tell them what the ship is doing."

"This sounds impossible. We don't have the people to do all of this."

"Do we need to?" Dena asked.

"Why get a laser if we can't hit things with it?"

"Well, but we're not some super-duper warship, right? We're like a bus with a shotgun. If we're going to use it, we'll drive up close and then fight. Shoot from touching distance, right?"

"Sure."

Cassandra was talking about 'time-dilation effects in large gravity fields and high-speed orbital passes.'

Dena pointed at Ana, who was taking notes as fast as Gavin. "Remember what the old man said about revolvers and range?"

"He said you should only deploy a revolver if the range was such that you could do equal damage by throwing it at your target."

"My hunting buddy said the best way to make sure you hit with a revolver was to stick the barrel into their belly then pull the trigger."

"I don't think we'll be able to get that close," Scruggs said.

"Why not? We gotta get the boys off this 'spaceships dueling from thousands of miles thing.' What if we got the ship closer, and counted on that?"

"That could work."

"We need to eliminate variables," Dena said. "When you're trying to punch out a flock of ama-grouse, the best way is to fix your shotgun on a stand and have the birds fly into it."

"Like that wheeled self-propelled tank-destroyer we blew up," Scruggs said.

"You mean that tank thing?"

"It's not a tank, it's—never mind. Call it a tank. But it didn't have a turret. It could only fire forward in a straight line. And because the gun didn't have to move, it could be more powerful and longer ranged."

"So get rid of the turret?"

Scruggs waved her hand. "Hey, uh, Cassie?"

Cassandra stopped her spiel. "I prefer Cass."

"Uh, Cass, we think we have a simpler way to do this. The three of us."

"You girls?" Cassandra asked.

"Yes."

"Ladies," Dirk said, "as much as I think that you have

something to contribute to this discussion, I remind you that I'm a former naval officer. Centurion is very familiar with field artillery, and Engineer here has been around the ship-weapons block a few times. I'm sure we've got it covered."

"Of course, Pilot." Scruggs bobbed her head. "You have much more experience in this than we do. But we would like to ask Ms. Cassandra a quick question."

"It can't hurt, Dirk," Cassandra said. "Let's find out what the ladies want."

"Well, sure. We do need to let everybody have their say."

"Thanks. Ms. Cassandra?"

"Yes."

Scruggs pointed. "All those computers and software, and special targeting software, and all of that. We don't have most of it."

"Right."

"And those radars will suck up power, right?"

"A lot of power."

"Power that we could use for the laser?"

"Has to come from somewhere, for sure."

"Okay. And the turret, and the motors, how accurate will they be?"

"They have to be re-aligned every time the ship shakes excessively. There's self-test software, or you can do a firing test on a known grid."

"I don't think we have a known grid. And what's excessive shaking?"

"Well, high-G landings for one."

"How high is high?"

"Anything over three-G for sure."

Dena, Scruggs, and Lee looked at Dirk then back at Cassandra.

Cassandra grinned. "Ohhhhhh. I forgot about that. Yeah, the way Dirk drives, you'll need to re-calibrate the turret mountings after every landing. And takeoff too."

"Every single time?"

"You have landed with him, right?" Cassandra shivered. "Scares the beJoves out of me, let me tell you."

Dirk interrupted. "I'll have you know that everyone here has walked away from every landing we've had so far."

"We've had to walk away," Ana said. "Because you only get us next to the target about half the time—we end up walking to where we need to be. But that is a problem, if this equipment is that sensitive, we'll never be able to maintain it."

"It's very sensitive," Cassandra said. "It's a military package after all."

Scruggs raised her hand. "What if we don't use it, the military targeting package, the turret, all the fancy long-distance radars. What if we simplify it?"

"Simplify how?"

"Just weld the laser into a fixed mounting—facing directly forward. Wherever the ship points the laser points."

"That's ridiculous," Dirk said. "How'd we know if there was anything in front of us to fire at?"

Lee gestured at Cassandra's notes "Just point that radar forward and measure the dispersion cone. When a target hits the sensor cone, the radar triggers. Then delay the laser firing a tenth of a second to let the target move in front of the laser, rather than track the laser onto the target.”

“How would you handle the software?” Cassandra wondered.

“We don’t need any. Hard wire the laser to the radar. Put in a switch in the cockpit. Turn the switch on, and the laser fires right away when the radar triggers. Turn it off and it won’t. We won’t have to worry about recalibration if we use two radars pointing forward, because the radars’ interference will tell us how far apart they are. Simple, easy to set up, easy to fix. Then we’ve got a gun.”

“That might work,” Ana said. “Straightforward.”

“Easier to weld fixed mounts than moving ones,” Gavin said. “No chance of something seizing or shaking lose. We don’t even need to be accurate during installation. Once they’re in, we adjust.”

“Very irregular,” Dirk said. “Not like we did in the Navy.”

“Dirk, none of us are in the Navy now. I think it’s brilliant,” Cassandra said.

“Thanks,” Scruggs said.

“You said you had two questions?” Cassandra asked.

“Yes,” Dena said. “We do.”

“Well?”

“That skirt.” Dena pointed. “Could I borrow that, later at the bar? Try it out?”

CHAPTER NINETEEN

"We need to see it working." Ana drank his brandy. "A test firing."

"Don't tell me, Old Man, tell it to Pilot. He's doing the negotiations."

The group was sitting on the rough wooden benches surrounding the bar container. Ana had his draft, Gavin his bottle, the others had glasses. The primary was setting, and the high canopy produced a gloomy twilight. Dirk and Cassandra had wandered off alone, holding hands.

"Negotiations? With Ms. Cassandra the bimbo? Is that what the cool kids call it now?"

"Call it what you like. She had every engineering specification for that laser memorized. Any question I asked, she had an answer. An answer right away."

"Maybe she makes them up."

"Maybe you're a paranoid freak, Old Man. I wrote some of them down and cross-checked some of them with the documentation I found. She had them right, to three decimal places."

"Even paranoids have enemies. Three decimal places? Not two?"

"Three. She knows her guns. I figure you would too."

"I fire 'em, I don't fix em."

"Pffffst." Scruggs, at the end of the table, spat out a mouthful of drink. "That tastes horrible. It's like grain alcohol mixed with turpentine."

"Lee," Ana said. "What are you doing to the girl?"

Lee downed a swig of her drink. "Teaching her how to drink a vodka martini. It's not going well."

"Who drinks these vile things?" Scruggs shuddered and shoved it away. "You finish it, Lee. I knew I didn't like gin, and now I know I don't like vodka."

Lee drank Scruggs's drink off. "Picky girl. What did you drink at home?"

"Nothing."

"Nothing?"

"Nothing at all. No alcohol. No caffeine. No drugs."

Dena swished into view and sat at the table. "Sounds horrible. What did you drink at dinner?"

"Juice. Or water. Official functions, they had wine, but they didn't much like underage kids drinking, so they doused it with water."

"What did you drink when you went out with your friends?"

"Nothing. I didn't spend much time with my friends."

"You never went anywhere? Didn't leave the house?"

"We left the house. We went places."

"Like where?"

"Well, school, and study hall, and dance class, and clarinet practice, and family events at church, and well..."

"No wonder you don't drink. Wait, are you saying that you never..."

"I never had alcohol 'til I was on the Heart's Desire."

"Never?"

"Nope. That's why I ran away. Part of the reason."

"So you could get stinking fall-down drunk?"

"Because I wanted to decide for myself what I should do. And how I should do it."

"That's weird. Hey, Old Man, when did you have your first drink?"

Ana took a slug of brandy and leaned back. "Long time ago. Think it was when I fought Banda Singh. He said something to me that I didn't like, so I slugged him."

"You celebrated winning your first fight with a beer?"

"Winning? No. I slugged him, then he got up and beat the crap out of me. He was a foot taller than me, and maybe a hundred pounds heavier."

"Why did you pick a fight with a guy that big? He sounds humongous."

"Not really. About the punk's size here."

"But if he was a foot taller..."

"I was ten. He was seventeen."

"Ten? You started fights when you were ten?"

"I won fights when I was ten. Just not that one. It taught me a valuable lesson."

"Don't start fights with guys bigger than you."

"No. Don't stop hitting. And once they go down, use your feet. If I'd kicked him more when he was down, I would have won. I didn't make that mistake again, let me tell you. You know what you need to win a fight?"

"A clear conscience and a pure heart?"

"Friends with steel-toed boots."

Dena raised her eyebrows. "Inspiring story, Old Man. Really gets the heart going. Gavin, when was your first drink?"

"Guys at the shop had a beer after work on a Friday. When I was working there the summer I was sixteen, they'd give me one. Just one. But I developed a taste for beer."

"Lee?"

"My family had wine with dinner starting when I was six. Mixed with water, but not as much as Sister Scruggs's. We all did it."

"That's pretty trusting for a young kid."

"It was practical. Our family traveled a lot. When you're on a frontier world, the water or the juice might have some local bacteria that would make you sick. Alcohol kills most everything, so if you mix alcohol with the water, you won't get sick."

"Practical."

Lee sipped. "What about you, friend Dena?"

"When I was younger on Rockhaul, we had lots of distilled liquor. Plenty of grains, fruits, and stuff. Most places mixed some up. The boys would try to get me drunk and sleep with me."

"Did you?"

"Get drunk? No."

"They must have been unhappy that their plans didn't work."

"Didn't work? What do you mean?"

"Well, they wouldn't get to sleep with you..."

"Oh, I slept with them. I just didn't get drunk. I have a high alcohol tolerance. It was great fun. I got all the sex I wanted and free booze too." Dena downed her glass of wine. "Speaking of plans, time to see how this skirt of Cassandra's works."

Dena sauntered up to the bar and engaged the group there in conversation. Cassandra had loaned both her and Scruggs a pleated red skirt and matching top, and she had attracted covert glances from the men at the bar.

The ground rumbled and shook, and the drinks sloshed in their glasses. Lee grabbed her drink. "Earthquake. Should we be worried?"

Gavin held his drink. "Crowd doesn't look too concerned."

"Is this a problem?" Ana asked. "Will it affect the ship?"

"Not sure," Gavin said. "We're leveled out with the landing legs. Even a big earthquake wouldn't tip us over, but shaking is not good for electrical and mechanical connections."

"I wonder if that's why everything is so temporary here," Ana mused. "All these temp bars and suchlike."

"If I was running a secret pirate base, I'd want to be able to pick up and go."

"Even so. What the hell?"

Rocky, who had been roaming the bar meeting people, wagging his tail and getting petted, ran back to their table. His eyes were white around the edges. He hopped up on Scruggs's lap and licked her face.

"Stop it, Rocky. You're all spit."

Rocky scampered to Ana and plopped on his lap. He licked Ana's face as well. "Stop it, furball. What are you doing?"

Rocky whined then peered into the dark and growled.

"What do you see there, Rocky? Bad people?"

Rocky growled again, and Dirk appeared from the darkness.

"Right in one, Rocky." Ana said. "Well, Navy, did you get us a good deal?"

"Sort of. We agreed on a price. A good price."

"And we get to see it fired before we take it?"

"We're still talking about that."

"Nothing to talk about. We need to see it."

"She says it's too difficult to set up for firing."

"That's what I'd say if I had a non-functional gun I wanted to sell."

"To be fair, Old Man," Gavin said. "We'd need to connect it to a ship's main drive to test it out properly."

"First, when have I ever been fair, and second, I see a half dozen ships here, all with main drives, as far as I can tell."

"She says she'll try to arrange a test tomorrow, once she's moved the containers closer to power sources. She's doing that now. If the test goes well, then I've agreed to pay for it. But she wants to sell it now."

"We want to buy it now, but why is she in such a hurry?"

The ground shook again. Rocky whined and hid under the

table. Ana grabbed his cup before it could slop over. "Maybe she doesn't like earthquakes."

Several relaxed beers, or mango juices, later, the crew retired to the ship to sleep. Except Dirk, who they assumed was 'negotiating' the price with Cassandra. After several unfortunate events, as Dirk called them, or near-death experiences, as everyone else named them, they now always maintained a twenty-four-hour sentry. The person on watch monitored the ship's status boards, comms, and exterior cameras. Occasionally, they also had a sniper on the top of the ship next to the dorsal hatch.

Ana woke and reached for his gun. Something unexpected had intruded on his consciousness, and he didn't like the unexpected. The ship shook and the ground rumbled. Another earthquake.

"That's not it," Ana said out loud. "Something else."

Scritch. Rocky was outside his door. He added a whine. Ana got up and opened the door. A white-eyed Rocky ran inside and pushed up against his legs. "What's bothering you, boy?"

Rocky panted and pushed harder against his legs.

The ground rumbled again. "It's just the earthquakes, boy. Nothing to worry about." Ana frowned. "Except, that wasn't an earthquake. That was a ship drive."

Rocky following close behind, Ana stepped out and walk-crawled along the main tunnel. With the Heart's Desire planet side in a gravity field, up and down had shifted. The ship's central tunnel was now more of a crawlspace than a ladder.

Ana reached the hab module. All the interior lights came on and the fire alarm bonged.

"Outstanding," Ana said, increasing his crawl speed to a sprint. He raced into the control room. "Where's the fire?"

Dena had the shift. As soon as Ana arrived, she killed the alarm. "Isn't one. But this is the only emergency alarm I know. Look outside. Forward cameras."

The main screen showed a bright light over the forest. "You woke us up for dawn?"

Scruggs, Lee, and Gavin surged in behind him, all yelling variations of "where's the fire?"

Ana pointed at the screen. "Out there. About fifty million miles away. Burning hydrogen and helium. Some lithium, depending on where we are in the star's life cycle. Nature Girl got all excited and woke us up to showcase her artistic sensibilities."

"You woke us up for that?" Gavin asked. "To see the dawn? First, we didn't need a fire alarm for that, and second, who cares?"

"You ship-born twits, the fire alarm is the only emergency alarm you ever showed me, and you're behind on fixing the intercoms so I can't use them. What time is it?"

Lee pulled up her comm. "It's the middle of third shift. We should be sleeping."

"Yes," Dena said. "It's the middle of third shift."

"Right."

"Figuring out sunrise isn't your thing, then. What's that big light in the sky, then, 'cause dawn ain't for another four hours."

"Uh oh." Lee dropped into her seat and busied herself with the screen.

Ana leaned over Dena's shoulder. "What do the other cameras show? The upper hull ones?"

"Nothing, just black." Dena cycled through the cameras. "Some sort of malfunction."

Ana squinted at the displays. "Not a malfunction. You can still see a glow. That's dust. Uh oh. Make a hole!" Ana pushed back through the others to the air lock and yanked the wheel. "Emperor's sweaty armpits. Dena, call the pilot on his comm. Get him back here now. Engineer, get ready to lift."

The air lock had three exterior hatches. Up, down, and to port. Ana swung the inner air lock hatch open, climbed up the ladder on the wall, and spun the upper hatch open.

Air lock hatches always opened against pressure, so that a major air leak would slam it shut. In this case, as soon as he dropped the hatch, a cloud of fine dust billowed in. Everyone coughed. Ana climbed up and out onto the top of the hull. The darkness reeked of sulfur and fire. Red light flared from the horizon, obscured by the clouds of dust. Heart's Desire's hull didn't clear the forest canopy, but gaps in the trees gave a clear view of the horizon.

Bright red magma poured out of the volcano, drifting down the mountainside like burning blood. Steam and smoke billowed above it, blotting out the stars and showering the surroundings with black dust.

"That's so cool!" Scruggs climbed up next to Ana. "I've never seen a volcano this close before. It's really neat! Look at those red magma things."

"Those red magma things are thousands of degrees hot," Ana said. "They'll burn you up like a piece of paper, knock forests over and incinerate them, even melt metal and rock 'til it's just a pool of liquid."

"Like I said, cool." Scruggs took out her comm and took pictures.

Lee stared. "Jove is angry at somebody."

Gavin stepped up and looked over. "Hope it's not us. Centurion's right. We need to be away from here if that magma is coming by. We can't take those temperatures on our landing legs."

"What about the dust?" Ana asked. "That's going to be a problem."

"I've already shut off the air-exchange," Gavin said. "We close this hatch and we're sealed up, we'll be fine for a while. Mostly. But we do need to vent noxious gas, remember. Our air purification system is cryogenic—we freeze CO and such out of the air and vent it outside. But if our vents get gummed up with dust, we'll have to go out and clear it."

"Let's get out of here before we have a problem."

Dena poked her head out. "That's not something you see every day."

"Not this close. Where's the pilot?"

"He just commed. He'll be here any second. He said he snuck out on Cass while she was sleeping."

"And that is something you'll see every day."

Dena looked down, and then climbed up onto the hull. "Look who's here. Come on up, Dirk. We're all gaping at nature in her might and majesty."

"Might and majesty?" Scruggs asked.

"Read it in a book. Dirk, much as we like your girlfriend, which we don't, we don't like being burned to death in volcanic fires even more, so let's get out of here. She can pick up her guns and sell them to us somewhere else."

Dirk climbed onto the deck of the ship and looked at the display. "She wants her skirt back, she said."

"Sue me. We need to go."

"Well, there's a tiny problem," Dirk said.

"What did you do, Navy?" Ana asked.

"I got us a better deal on the lasers," Dirk said.

"Great. We'll lift and we can talk about it."

"No, you see. It was a great deal. Cheap. Very cheap."

"We talked about this, we needed to see a demonstration."

"Well, Cass was in a hurry to get things moving, so..."

"I asked before. I'll ask again." Ana gritted his teeth. "What. Did. You. Do?"

"I bought the laser. As is. Great price."

"You bought the laser?"

"Yep. It's ours now."

"Cancel the deal."

"Can't. Already paid."

The crew groaned. Tribune Devin had given them a lot of money. Plenty to run a starship. Enough to eat extravagantly well at every port. Sufficient to buy a ship-mounted laser.

Not sufficient to buy it twice.

"We'll cancel the deal. You and I go over there and talk to her. I can be very persuasive."

Noise blew in from astern. Two pads behind them, a starship revved its main drive and lifted, a crash orbital insertion.

"Unless I miss my guess, Old Man," Dena pointed at the ship lifting over them, "the person you need to persuade just left on her ship."

"Nothing to worry about," Dirk said. "Cass said she'd leave the containers where they were right now. We just need to pick them up when we're ready."

Fire lit the night. The volcano had switched from steam and dust, now burning magma blew skywards. Shards of white-hot burning rock rained from the sky. Pieces landed on the trees, glowing red with inner fire.

"We just need to pick them up." Dirk kicked a small burning rock from the hull. "I think now would be a good time."

CHAPTER TWENTY

"Imperial Freighter Dieppe, this is the Union of Nations Auxiliary naval cruiser Pinguin. Cut your acceleration and hold your course. Do not attempt to use your radio or we will fire on you." Tannen disconnected the call and monitored her board. Her radio receivers were scanning for local traffic originating from the nearby freighter. "Acknowledgment, Kapitan. No other comms at this time."

"Very well. Boarders away."

Blomberg, the third officer, spoke into his comm. Fusterheim led the boarding party this time, while Blomberg sat in the control room. "Shuttle away, Kapitan."

"Very well. Good to see you back on duty, Leutnant. How is your head?"

"Healing, sir." Blomberg's head jerked around as one of the bridge crew stifled a giggle. "Healing very well."

"Very good. And your, umm... personal areas? Are they well?"

Blomberg spoke through clenched teeth. "Everything is

fine, Kapitan. I have no problems." Blomberg had gone to Fusterheim to demand the Confed captain be punished for hitting him. Fusterheim told him to make a formal report. He also told him that if Blomberg did that Kruder would brig the Confed captain in solitary, and then court-martial Blomberg for not following his orders. Slapping prisoners was not permitted.

Blomberg backed off.

Kruder ignored the tittering going around the bridge. Blomberg would either survive this mistake and rebuild his reputation, or he would not. It was up to him. But he was on notice now—the other officers were watching. "Good, good. Glad to hear it. Tell me about this ship. What does the registry say?"

Blomberg consulted a list on his screen. "Hundred-container ship. Longer-ranged design—fifty percent more distance in jumps before refueling. Fuel-processing capability."

"Self-unloading?" Kruder asked.

"No Kapitan." Kruder was asking if the ship had its own tugs or shuttle that could move the containers around on frontier worlds. "She needs a port with tugs and orbital storage. It's strange to see her this far out. The planet in this system barely warrants the name. No orbital infrastructure at all, just isolated farms across the main continent."

"What do you think she was doing here?"

"I don't know, sir."

"Something for you to investigate. Yes, Edda?"

The comm officer had raised her hand. "If you've got a

longer jump capacity, you can cut the corner of a major shipping route here and save several weeks of travel time."

"What is the point of that?" Blomberg said. "These freighters operate on fixed rates regardless of how long it takes. And the longer jumps take extra fuel. Which costs money."

"Yes," Edda spoke slowly. "But if you can get there faster, Leutnant. Even if you spend more on fuel, you can do more deliveries in the same period of time, which makes more money."

"It's all about money with these bandits," Blomberg grumbled.

Edda snorted. "You dislike money, Leutnant?"

"It's not an honorable way to earn a living. These freighter captains are little better than thieves. Scum, the lot of them." Then he gulped and shut his mouth, remembering too late that Kapitan Kruder had been a freighter captain for many years.

Kruder laughed. "Worse than thieves in many ways, Leutnant. Much worse, some of them. Do you agree, Edda?"

Edda grinned from ear to ear. "Merchant spacers are the very scum of the earth, sir. I should know."

"I recall you serving in several merchant ships."

"As the Kapitan knows, that is where I met my husband."

"And your oldest girl is at the trade school now, isn't she? She should graduate soon."

"Already done, Kapitan. She's fourth officer on an insystem bulk carrier. Nothing glamorous or lucrative, but she's getting her hours in. She'll be merchant scum, just like her parents."

"Wonderful. Well, I'm truly blessed to have such talented scum on my staff, don't you think, Leutnant Blomberg?"

"As the Kapitan says." Blomberg's face was red.

"And I haven't heard from the boarding party. Edda, get them on the radio, please."

Two minutes later, Fusterheim came on the line. "Kapitan?"

"How are things over there, Hans?"

"All is in order sir. We're waiting for the crew to finish packing their personal effects, and the master to secure his personal liquor storage."

"Where are you now?"

"In the master's cabin. Helping him with the securing."

"How much longer?"

"We're the last ones. The engineers have already laid a course in. Once I deliver the master to the shuttle, I go to the bridge and slap a button or two, and in two hours, this ship will be clouds of gas down below."

"Any problems?"

"None." Fusterheim lowered his voice. "The master and crew own shares in the ship, and I think they over-insured it. They don't seem unhappy at all that it will be destroyed. Their insurance covers war risk, and they're looking forward to a big payout."

"They'll be sad when they find out they're being interned."

"That doesn't seem to bother them. They claim that the Tribune out here, the one they call the Mad Dog of the Verge, will come and get them."

"How's he going to do that if he doesn't know where we are?"

"They're confident he'll figure it out. Do you want me to bring back any fire hydrants when I return?"

"That's the cargo? Fire hydrants?"

"And manhole covers, and different lengths of iron pipes, and valves, and bolts and all manner of pipe things. Imperial colony water systems, they all use iron pipes."

"Why not plastic or some such?"

"Cheap, very strong, and the new ones last up to three hundred years before they need to be replaced. They're nearly indestructible."

"I didn't know you knew about pipes, Hans."

"The master here has a brochure. It's quite interesting. I think I might go into water management when I retire."

"Let me know how it works out. Do you need anything?"

"No sir. We'll be out of here in ten minutes."

"Very well. Kruder out." Kruder leaned back in his chair. "Sensors?"

"Board is clear, sir. Nothing to report."

"Comm?"

"No communications except yours, sir. Board is green."

"Anyone does not have a green board, sing out." Kruder waited. His officers were attentive but relaxed. "Navigation, resume our orbit once our boarding party is back. I'll be in my cabin. Did you find that exciting, Leutnant?"

"Sir?" Blomberg asked.

"The boarding. Anything exciting about that?"

"No sir. It all seemed very routine."

"And that's the way it should be. Routine." Kruder left the bridge.

Pinguin lay over in the system for the next nine days, loafing around the jump limit. Four other freighters arrived in that time. Skillful maneuvering allowed Kruder to capture and scuttle them. Kruder was surprised at the amount of traffic, given the size of the system, until one of the freighter captains admitted they sent hunting parties to the main continent for fresh meat and exotic animal parts, like horns, or gall bladders, or bones.

"Animal part trade is prohibited in the Union, and in the Accursed Empire as well, Kapitan."

"Why?" The freighter captain shrugged. "There's millions of them on that giant continent, and all the others. There're hardly any people here. They'll never be hunted out. This planet is too far from the trade routes, and there isn't much demand for them. It's a niche market."

The only settlement in the system, a tiny, Imperial-affiliated colony, had no idea what was going on over their heads. Since they were farmers, they wouldn't have cared either. There was no new traffic for eight days. The Pinguin's crew were getting bored when another freighter arrived at the jump limit.

Kruder arrived on the bridge and proceeded to his seat. "Anything to report, Hans?"

"One target, Kapitan. Imperial registered. Hundred containers or so. We'll know more when she's closer. Arrived a few minutes ago. Still outside of the jump limit."

"Anything to report, comm?"

"Imperial beacon. No other communications, sir."

"Sensors?"

"She's sitting there, sir."

"Getting her bearings, no doubt. Let me know when she heads insystem."

Fusterheim amused himself by playing with his screens. "Kapitan, she's not shaping a course for the system. She's just running on the ballistic course she carried on arrival. Still outside of the jump limit."

"Outside? Still?"

"Yes." Fusterheim tapped his screens. "Far outside, in fact, according to my readings."

Kruder cocked his head. "Far outside and not moving?"

"Yes." Fusterheim tapped his screen again. "Sensors. Double-check me. Confirm that the Imperial freighter is drifting."

Alvarez sat up straighter. "I see it that way too, sir, but I will confirm my instruments." He flipped through several screens and consulted with a colleague next to him. "Confirmed sir. No drive plume, not even attitude adjustment. She's just drifting."

"An accident?" Kruder wondered.

"She's warm," Alvarez reported. "And the navigation lights are functioning, and her beacon is reporting—Zingari, one hundred ten containers—there's another one. New ship arrived sir."

"A freighter? Another one?"

"Looks like it sir. Approximately the same size. Also Imperial beacon."

"Two ships." Kruder looked at Fusterheim. "Two Imperial ships. Odd to see two here at the same time."

Blomberg grinned around the bridge. "What excellent luck, Kapitan. We should be able to take both of them before we leave."

"Why are they floating?" Fusterheim tapped his fingers on his chair arm.

"Why indeed." Kruder slapped a button on his console. Alarms rang. "This is Kruder. Stations for ship-to-ship combat. This is not a drill. Do not decamouflage. All stations double-check camouflage in place before reporting ready." Kruder disconnected and sealed his skinsuit, slapping his gloves and helmet onto his harness. "Helm, bring us onto a least fuel course for the inhabited planet, do it right now, but do not exceed one G during any maneuvers. Sensors, go dark. Nothing active at all without my permission. Blomberg?"

"Sir?"

"Contact engineering. Get them to shut down as many of our power systems as they can. Reactors too if possible. Cut any possible emission sources as much as they can."

Blomberg's brow creased, and he turned to his comm.

"They probably didn't see us," Fusterheim said, sealing his own skinsuit. "They won't have good sensors. And they'll be too busy with their own affairs to take a close look."

"Let's hope so," Kruder said.

"Status change, Kapitan," Alvarez, the sensor operator, said. His earlier relaxation had disappeared. "Another freighter. No, two. Two more arrivals. Imperial beacons. Total four."

Kruder grunted. "Four freighters? Navigator. The new arrivals. Where are they in relation to the other ships?"

The navigator put dots up on the main screen. "Close, Kapitan. Closer than I would be comfortable with if I was their navigator."

"Engineering reports all non-essential systems shutting down," Blomberg said. "They say reactor shutdown is complex and will take twenty-one minutes, but they are starting now."

"Very well." Kruder busied himself with his screens.

"Kapitan." Blomberg spoke quietly. "Is it permitted to ask a question?"

"Ask away, youngster." Kruder didn't look up.

"Are those freighters armed?"

"Imperial freighters? Of course not. Well, perhaps one of them might have some weapons, it's possible. Not likely. And certainly not all of them."

"Why are we running? Even four of them, even if they were armed, we could capture them all."

"We might be able to. We might not. We certainly couldn't do it without at least one of them getting a message through to the planet. And one of them might be able to jump, and then we're in trouble."

"Kapitan, we are a naval vessel. We should not be scared of freighters."

Fusterheim looked up from his screen. "Leutnant, are you saying the Kapitan is scared of going into battle?"

"Sir. With respect, I am just asking why we are... retreating from an inferior force."

"Leutnant, we are a commerce raider. We raid commerce. We need to stay alive to do this. Our job is to take calculated risks, not die gloriously for no good reason."

"How will four un-armed freighters cause us to die gloriously? They have no weapons. We should be closing with those freighters, putting ourselves in a position to seize them, for the glory of the Union of Nations."

Kruder threw a picture of the ships up on the board. "It is a worthwhile question. Why am I scared of this convoy, because four ships are definitely a convoy. Do you think I'm scared of four merchant ships, Leutnant?"

Blomberg spoke carefully. "The Kapitan's actions confuse me. If you are not afraid of freighters, then why are we running?"

"We are not running, Leutnant. More... sneaking. We're sneaking away and hoping they don't notice us."

"Because you're scared of four freighters."

"I am not scared of freighters." Kruder rotated the screen display slightly. "See these positions? Four freighters in line? They all went into jump together. Why did they jump together? That is the question. And I'm not worried about them. I'm worried about what will be... here." Kruder highlighted an area in front of the four ships.

"There is nothing there, Kapitan."

"Correct."

Blomberg shook his head. "But... there is nothing there, Kapitan."

"Not yet. Watch."

The bridge was silent. Kruder took various reports, confirmed their slow, freighter-like inward-to-the-planet course, and had a long conversation with engineering about emissions and heat profiles.

After five minutes, Blomberg cleared his throat. "Kapitan—"

"Status change!" the sensor operator announced. "Activity at the jump limit. One, two—multiple ships arriving. Imperial beacons."

"What type of beacons?" Kruder asked.

"Stand by." The sensor operator tapped his screen. "Warships. Imperial warship beacons. An Imperial task force has entered the system."

CHAPTER TWENTY-ONE

"I'm not interested in your complaints, Captain. My priority is the safe and timely arrival of this convoy. That's my sworn duty. You cannot stay behind by yourself, even if it is a good commercial opportunity, and you cannot suck free fuel from the gas giant. You must use your internal stores. If you do not fuel on time, I will take measures." Devin fiddled with his screens, ignoring the testy merchant skipper's response. He was just as irritated as the merchant captains at having to traipse through this marginal system, but for different reasons.

A light speed delay later, the merchant captain's response sputtered back.

Devin's face reddened. "I don't, there is no reason—Weapons Officer Huusko?"

"Sir?" Huusko said.

"Are you still practicing targeting all the ships in the vicinity?"

"Yes, Tribune. You didn't say—"

"Remember I told you that you'd be the first I'd call if I wanted an Imperial ship destroyed?"

"Sir."

"Well, now's your chance, sort of. Fire something close to that idiot. Something bright and scary. Shoot across his bow, let him know that we're serious. Do it now."

"I'd love to sir, but I can't."

"Why not? You have the firing solution?"

"I do sir. But Positron weapons only make a... display if they hit. No visible lights like lasers. No intimidation value."

"Joves's greasy nostrils."

"Tribune." Huusko tapped his screen. "Marines are pretty intimidating. And they have lasers."

"Comm," Devin said. "Secure channel—no. Regular unencrypted channel. Make sure everybody can hear it. Message reads: This is Tribune Devin on the Pollux. Close that freighter—" Devin looked around. "Anybody?"

"Coquimbo," Lukas, the sensor operator, said.

"Close the Coquimbo and ensure she jumps with the others. If she doesn't, put Marines onboard and seize her in the name of the Empire. Devin out."

Lionel rubbed his forehead. "Tribune, you cannot go seizing private property..."

"There's a war on."

"Says who? War needs to be declared by the Senate. I haven't heard that they did."

"I'm a senator."

"And I'm a Virgo. Gives me as much authority in this matter as a single senator has. And speaking of senators, what are they going to say about other senators firing on friendly ships?"

"It's not Tribune Devin speaking, it's the Mad Dog of the Verge speaking. Known crazy person."

"Yet, not sufficiently crazy that they don't quote their executive officer regarding the safe and timely arrival of the convoy."

"Good turn of phrase, that. Thought it sounded good."

The comm officer interrupted. "Sir, Valhalla is pivoting to intercept the freighter."

"What's the freighter doing?"

"Suddenly on a straight course sir. No pivots or rolls."

"Outstanding," Devin said. Calculating jumps was hard. Ships, especially merchant ships with inferior computers, had to keep a steady course while they ran their jump calculations. "Comm, tell me about this system."

The comm officer put details up on the main screen. "Daube's world. Habitable, barely. Marginal living conditions. Warm and wet. Main flora is... ferns."

"Ferns?"

"Ferns. Big ones. Up to a hundred feet tall."

"I've never seen a hundred-foot fern."

"Less than ten thousand people."

"How many less?"

"No idea sir. That's the lowest number on my scale. Subsistence farming on the offshore islands. Animal husbandry. No minerals of note. No mining or manufacturing. Lots of grazing animals, and predators, big ones on the main continent. It's uninhabited."

"Why?"

"Hippopotamus, the sailing directions say. Big grazers, adapted to swamps. Extremely dangerous. Violent, unpredictable. And a rhinoceros-type animal, complete with horn. That's why everyone lives on these tiny islands off the main continent. They exterminated the big animals, and they never go to the main island except to hunt."

"Outstanding. What do they do for excitement? Or money?"

"Some tourism. Big game hunting. Big demand for the horns of the rhinoceros in some places."

"Glad I don't live there. Anything else?"

"One ship inbound sir. Freighter. Big one. A couple of hundred containers or more. Earl of Clydebank, according to the beacon."

"Pretty big ship to be out here by itself. Anything unusual about them?"

"Nothing on the sensors sir. But we have some interference. Our scans aren't conclusive at this distance."

"Ask 'what ship' and 'query intentions.' What's our status for jump?"

"Three of the four freighters report ready for jump. Course laid in. Hydrogen Queen is ready. We're ready. Valhalla says seven minutes for calculations once you release her from operations."

"Very well. Release Valhalla. Hold the convoy here 'til Valhalla and that other freighter report ready. How long will it take for the freighter to figure things out?"

"Twenty minutes if they're on the ball and have a decent computer and a competent astrogator."

"They have that?"

"Not a chance in Jove's whiskers sir."

"Your recommendation?"

"Set the jump clock for forty minutes."

"Very well. Navigation, you may jump in forty minutes. Inform the other ships."

"Tribune," Carrol, the comm officer, said.

"Yes?"

"Automatic response from that freighter. Replays beacon data and adds they are conducting 'miscellaneous trade' in the system. No firm next port of call."

"Automated message?"

"Yes. The crew is probably asleep, Tribune. I just sent a standard query—their computer won't wake them for a routine message. I could send a high-priority query that would trip alarms. Of course, it's a freighter, so they could have disconnected the alarms."

"Don't bother. Subprefect, what do you think they're doing here?"

Lionel squinted at the main screen. "Could be smuggling, I suppose. But nothing here worth smuggling, and it's inconvenient for transfer, and any pirate-type transfer would be out here, beyond the jump limit, not all the way in there."

"Watch them for now. Unless something interesting happens, get us out of this boring system. Take me somewhere we can find some pirates."

CHAPTER TWENTY-TWO

"Everyone's accounted for," Dirk said. "Centurion and the others are clear into the woods. Flare now."

"Firing." Gavin pulsed the main engines, and Heart's Desire rocked as the drive ignited.

BOOM. The whole ship shook. Lights flared on the external cameras, and two went dark. The air vent blew the smell of burning metal.

"Engineer," Dirk said. "What are you doing back there?"

"Wasn't me, Skipper," Gavin said. "I gave the engines a nudge. Is somebody firing on us?"

"No."

"Methane," Lee said.

"What?"

"Methane. That volcano, or the earthquake is squeezing out explosive gas. The heat of the main engines ignited them."

Lee, Dirk, and Gavin got the Heart's Desire ready to lift. Dena, Scruggs, and Ana suited up and ran across the clearing to check out the containers holding the laser.

"Navy," Ana radioed. "What in the name of the seven devils are you doing? Stop lighting planetary farts, you idiot."

"Methane, Lee says. We've got another problem. Gavin says the dust buildup could be an issue. If it gets too thick, when we fire the drives, we might melt it in place rather than blast it out. We need to pulse the engines and the thrusters to keep it away."

"Well, we have a problem here too. Your girlfriend's ship is gone, and all her people."

"We knew that. Is the laser there?"

"One container lasers, one container capacitors, and one container miscellaneous stuff, that we saw yesterday. All here. What we don't have here is a forklift, or a drag lift, or a tractor, or anything to move them to the ship."

"Then we'll bring the ship to you. I'll fire up, pivot and land over there. We'll be there in five."

"Forgive this uneducated, simple-minded ground pounder, but my understanding is that starships, even ones commanded by idiot Imperial duke pilot peoples, leaving aside for the moment the competency of said duke-pilot-peoples, can't land IN THE MIDDLE OF A FREAKING FOREST OF GIANT TREES."

Dirk slammed the radio off.

Lee muttered next to him.

"Yes, Navigator, you have a suggestion?"

"Yes." Lee turned to him. "Find different girlfriends."

Ana swung his axe. "Join the Army!"

WHANG! The chain rang as he slammed the ax into it.

"See the Galaxy."

WHANG!

"Meet new and interesting people."

WHANG!

"Then kill them."

WHANG! SNAP!

"Nature Girl. Another length of chain for you." Ana inserted the axe blade in the cut of the chain, braced it with his foot, then pried it open. "Come and get it."

Dena and Scruggs raced out from the trees, grabbed the chain and towed it into the woods. Gavin had unclipped all the docking and cargo chains they could find and strung them end to end. They still didn't reach the ship's winches. Now Ana was cutting the drag chains off the existing containers and splicing them into a longer set, hopefully long enough to reach the ship.

Ana's heart hammered in his chest, and his vision darkened. "Not today." He yanked a pill bottle out of his pocket, twisted the top off and shook out a pill. He swayed for a second, cursed, shook a second out, dry swallowed them, then leaned against a tree. "Getting old sucks."

Heart's Desire was on one of the burned landing pads, a hundred yards away. Normal, civilized landing pads were two-hundred-yard circles of rock, cement, or some sort of dense nonflammable material, surrounded by a ten-yard-tall berm. Ships could safely crash and burn in the middle, and not bother the neighbors. Here on Carousel, a hundred yards worth of trees had been cut or burned down and compressed by ships landing on top of them. At least it was dirt underneath, not swamp.

Scruggs appeared out of the gloom. "Centurion, what's wrong?"

"I'm fine. Just resting. Do you have enough chain?"

"Twenty more feet, Gavin says. Did you... I mean, will you..."

"Twenty feet. I can get that." Ana climbed up. "Let me cut it for you. And yes, I already took two pills."

Scruggs snatched the axe and ran into the dark. "I'll get it. Go check in with Gavin."

"Check in about what?"

"You're a centurion, Centurion. Co-ordinate. Give some orders. Yell a lot." Her body was lost in the dark with her voice.

"Young puppy," Ana said, standing. He stumbled toward the ship, following the chain. He had to stop walking twice to catch his breath. This was the worst attack yet.

The ground rumbled. "Incoming, take cover," Dirk radioed.

Ana threw himself to the ground and covered his head. Burning pockets of lava whooshed through the sky, hitting trees and starting fires. His tree shook, and limbs cracked above. Leaves and branches rained down, some burning.

Ana rolled over, dusted himself off, and looked up. A dollop of white-hot rock had slammed into a limb above, and the tree around it was already burning. He shook his head and stumbled off along the chain.

Fifty yards later, he found Dena sitting in a tree, four feet off the ground, saw in hand. "Gavin says he can get the container around the bend here, but he can't make it duck." She sawed at a tree limb. "I need to cut these three branches off."

"Have another saw?"

"Nope."

"Outstanding. I'll go ask him what else needs to be done." Ana broke into the clearing and clomped to the ship. Gavin waited by the landing struts, next to an open toolbox.

"Shouldn't you be doing something?" Ana asked.

"I am. I'm waiting to attach the last length, then take it up and wrap it around the winch."

"And tow the container in?"

"Maybe." Gavin held up a chain link, with attached snap shackle. "The breaking strain of these quick links is lower than the chain itself. I need to double or triple them up."

"So?"

"So they'll jam the winch. I have to feed them through one at a time, or unclip them when they're at the drum, and replace them with a longer one. Which means time."

"We're on a bit of a schedule here."

The ground shook. Dirk's voice came over the radio again. "Dust cloud."

Both men pulled breathers and face masks over their foreheads. Hot dust rained down from above, obscuring their faces.

"More than you know."

Scruggs ran out of the dust, sweating. "Last piece. Should be long enough."

Gavin snapped the quick links into place. Ana helped him

wheel the chain back to the ship. Scruggs ran to find the axe and help Dena cut the rest of the trees.

Gavin fed the chain around the docking winch three times, then handed the slack end to Ana. "Keep tension on this, don't pull, just keep it feeding away as it takes up the strain."

Gavin checked on the radio, got affirmatives from everyone, and tensioned up the strain. "Everyone be ready. I'm putting the power on now." He threw the control lever forward.

The chain moved up, strained, pulled forward an inch, then stopped. It strained, then with a noise like a rifle shot, it jerked forward and started reeling in at speed. Gavin throttled back.

Dena radioed in. "The chain just shredded a small tree, knocked it over."

Gavin slid the lever forward an inch. The chain rolled in easily, then tightened, then stretched, then held.

"Be ready." Gavin pushed the winch throttle another inch. An electric motor screamed below him winding the chain in.

Scruggs cheered. "First container is moving. Dragging over the ground."

"Upright?"

"Straight up and down. It's coming up to the first tree, the corner chains are bending around... pivot! It pivoted. It's working."

"Outstanding!" Ana said.

Gavin watched the links spool up, slowed his pull, then stopped.

"What? What now?" Ana asked.

Gavin pointed. "Quick links won't go through the feeder.

We need to disconnect them here, drag this long piece out there, and re-attach it to make one single chain with as few breaks as possible."

"We have to do that for every one of these quick links?"

"Every single one."

"How much longer do we have 'til that big fire pit over there breaks something?"

Dirk yelled, "Incoming. Looks big on the radar. Everyone under cover."

Gavin and Ana dove under the ship. Fire-tinged rocks rained down all over them.

A red-hot rock bounced down the landing struts and smacked into the ground, burning the grass.

"Not long," Gavin said. "Not long."

Gavin connected and disconnected links. Dena and Scruggs chopped trees. The first container was successfully yanked to the ship, attached to the cargo chains, and winched up. Ana, Scruggs, and Dena raced to re-assemble the disconnected chain and attach it to the next container. Gavin fed it through the winch, the other three connected everything. Ana raced back from the container along the chain path, checking for kinks.

"Listen, everyone, we might have a problem." Lee was watching the sensors. "I see something."

"More bad on the radar?" Scruggs asked.

"Don't know, but it looks different. Hotter. Dirk?"

Dirk had been checking the winds for launch. "Nothing new. Smoke, dust, explosions. All sorts of explosions."

"You think you could tell us about the explosions, Navy?" Ana said. "Before they drop things on us?"

"There's one every minute," Dirk said. "I only warn you if it blows high or far enough that it's going to hit us here. Don't want you to worry."

"Don't worry about the explosions," Lee said. "Worry about this. Infrared shows that whole mountain heating up. There's some super-hot magma coming out of the vents. Lots of it, burning down the hill, and it's spreading."

"Exactly how long 'til it gets here?"

"I don't know, Centurion. Why don't I consult our special magma speed indicator sensor? I think it's right next to the calendar with the next unscheduled maintenance issue."

Ana cursed. "Right. Best guess."

"It's moving at a couple of miles an hour, plus or minus."

"How far away are we?"

"A couple of miles."

"Plus or minus?"

"We hope plus. Either way, we need to get these containers out of here before they melt into a puddle of metal and laser pieces."

"Right, Engineer, you heard the lady. Crack on."

Gavin took up the strain on the winch. The chain tensioned and reeled in. "Cracking on, whatever that means."

"Centurion," Scruggs said over the radio. "This one is sliding over rock, not dirt. It's scraping the topsoil free and we can see a black rock underneath."

"We care why?"

"There are ridges and bumps and things."

"Nothing to do but wait." The winch slowed, then slowed some more, then ground to a halt, quivering.

"Scruggs, Dena, what do you see?"

"It's caught up on a ridge of rock, sort of, half caught. The front edge is caught on the left, but on the right, it's free."

"Should we keep pulling?"

"I think so. It should pivot over, like it did before."

"Engineer?"

Gavin pushed the throttle lever in, giving it as much juice as it could. "I heard you."

"Scruggs?"

"It's straining, Centurion. Hard, I think—"

CRACK.

The chain parted inside the tree line. It whiplashed sideways and backward directly at Ana's face.

CHAPTER TWENTY-THREE

"Incoming!" Ana dove. Mud splashed in his face and the wind from the recoiling chain brushed his back. He lay still, counted to five, then rolled over on his back, and keyed his microphone, keeping his head low.

"Ladies, talk to me."

"Container's stuck, Centurion," Scruggs said. "Chain jerked back and now it's coiled in there."

"Everybody okay? Dena? Where are you?"

Dena's voice cracked. "I'm in a tree. That was scary."

"Yes, yes, it was. Engineer?"

No answer. Ana stood. "Gavin? You okay?" The Heart's Desire loomed above him. The returning chain had recoiled and wrapped across the landing leg, and then across to the far landing leg, and piled up there. Gavin leaned against the near landing leg, pinned by the chain.

"Lee, we need a medic. The engineer got hit by that recoiling chain. Get out here."

Ana ran toward Gavin, slipped in the dust and fell to one

knee, cursed, stood, and continued at a slower stride. A hatch opened over his head. Lee dropped out.

Lee reached Gavin first. She checked his pupils with a small penlight.

"Well?" Ana asked, behind her. Gavin slumped against the landing leg. The recoiling chain had wrapped itself around the struts, but he was free.

"Pupils, fixed, dilated, and different sizes. Concussion."

"Chain caught him. Glancing blow." Ana tapped the strut. "This shielded him. Good thing. If it had caught him at chest level, he'd have been cut in half. If it had hit his head, it would be mush."

Lee ran her hands lightly up and down his extremities. Gavin jerked and gasped when she checked his left forearm. She probed again, and he jerked again. "Bad sprain or broken arm. Either way, he's out of things for a while. Help me get him up to med pod."

Ana and Lee each grabbed a shoulder. Gavin mewled again when they jostled his arm. Lee gave him a pain shot. They counted to thirty and lifted him again. This time, Gavin flopped about until they hauled him into the med bay. By the time they got him undressed and strapped in, the others had returned from the field, and Dirk had come down from the control room.

"Is he okay, Old Man?" Dena beat the dust from her outfit. "Dammit. I got a decent skirt for once and now it's ruined."

"Good to see you have your priorities straight," Ana said.

"We're here, and we're asking about him. I can be worried

about him and my outfit at the same time. Unlike some people, I can think about more than one thing at once."

"Lee, will he be okay?"

Lee didn't look up from the med pod. "He banged his head pretty good. I have to run some programs to stabilize him."

Dirk stuck his head around the corner and peered into the med pod. "Lee, your thermal thing is heating up. Um, you can see his arm is broken, right?"

Ana grunted. "Really, Navy? Because of the angle it's bent at. Lee—"

"I'm busy." Lee flicked through screens on the med pod. "I don't think this is bad, but I have to get this right. Leave me alone for a while."

"Let us know when you have more info." Ana tapped Dena on the shoulder, and pointed down the hall, and they left the med pod. Scruggs and Dirk followed.

Ana brought up an external camera in the lounge. All it showed was dust. "Pilot, what's that thermal thing doing?"

"Heating up and getting ready to explode."

"When?"

"No idea. I'm not a vulcanologist. And that lava, magma, whatever is out there, and it's sliding down the mountain. We need to get out of here."

"We need to pick up your stupid laser, that's what we need to do. Private, unravel that chain out there. Nature Girl, come help me with the engineer's winch. We can set it up—"

Scruggs shook her head. "Centurion, we shouldn't do that."

Ana crossed his arms. "And why not?"

"Because that chain broke once in the middle somewhere, not at a specific weak point, so we're exceeding the breaking strength of the whole thing. It'll just break again."

Ana cursed. "Ideas?"

"Fuel hoses," Dirk said.

"We have plenty of fuel, Navy. And we're in the middle of a burning firestorm, with red-hot rocks falling from the sky. Mixing volatile hydrogen and oxygen with that might not be a good idea."

"Water, Centurion, water."

"Going to spray the volcano with water, cool it down? Great idea, except we'd need an ocean—"

"Mud, you ground-hopper clod," Dirk barked. "Mud. Something you should be familiar with, since you normally live in it."

"Yes, we ground pounders live in mud. So what?"

"What's mud like?"

"Wet. Sticky. Dirty. Unpleasant. Hard to maneuver in."

"And slippery."

"Yes, great naval pilot. Mud is slippery."

Dirk crossed his arms and waited. "It's slippery."

Ana nodded. "Correct, Pilot. It is slippery. Private, Nature Girl, unwrap those chains, lay them out, and I'll get to fixing them. Soon as they're unraveled, report to the pilot."

"Report for what, Centurion?" Scruggs asked.

"Lawn care."

It worked like a charm. Gavin had been snapping pre-made quick links onto shorter pieces of chain, something that Ana copied easily. Scruggs, with Dena, maneuvered the fueling hoses out of their storage area, then walked them out to the container. Dirk figured out how to spew water out, making a slippery mud path between the next container and the ship. It slid so easily that when Ana stopped hauling, he had enough slack that he could unwind and re-wind the chains to make the pulling easier. It rolled right up underneath the ship and slid to a stop.

"Right, help me get the lifting chains attached again and we'll haul it up. Put it in the top rack. The lasers will be heavy, we'll drop them in on the bottom." Ana uncoiled the chains from the winch and loaded up for the final pull, and the women headed off into the woods, dragging the tow chains.

Red-hot rocks dropped from the sky, hissing when they hit the mud trail, or smoking and starting small fires. Curses ran over the radio. Ana ducked back under the ship and listened to the bangs as red-hot gravel rained down onto the ship.

Lee came down the ramp. "What's that noise?"

"Local weather. Sunny, with burning red-hot rock hail. The engineer?" Ana asked.

"Stable. He's strapped in, we can lift. But he's not going to be much use for a while."

"Who's taking engineering?"

"Pilot and I can handle it while we lift." Lee looked at the container strapped in. "I'm surprised that Dirk's idea worked."

"I'm surprised that he knew where the water valve was."

"He's not incompetent, Centurion, just lazy. He needs to be given a challenge from time to time so he can feel like a real pilot again."

"What do you mean?"

Lee pointed around. "The rest of us all have something. Running around in the mud, shooting people, blowing up tanks, that's your thing. You're good at it, you're used to it, and you like it. I've had more varied injuries working with this crew here than anybody I worked with outside of a trauma center. And we're always doing some weird navigation thing to get away from chasing warships or hiding in rings or whatever. The girls are still young. They just have a lot of energy to burn, and as long as there's excitement, they'll be happy."

"Thank the gods for that." Ana pulled a bottle from his pocket, popped a pill out and swallowed it. He took three deep breaths. "No way I could drag those chains off into the woods after climbing all over the hull. Getting old sucks. What's this have to do with the pilot?"

"He's bored. He used to be a military shuttle pilot, or pilot on a warship. He was a Duke. An important man. Now he takes a beat-up old freighter and dumps it onto a planet and pulls it off. He said it's like driving a waterbed."

"He would know."

"Not much of a challenge for him."

Ana shoved the pill bottle into his pocket. "Why didn't he go with the Tribune? Save the Galaxy?"

"Tribune didn't ask him."

"Really? I didn't know that."

"Tribune Devin doesn't look it, but he is a very, very smart man. He knows people, and he knows nobles especially. He doesn't suffer fools gladly."

"Your point?"

"The Tribune didn't ask him because he didn't think Dirk was ready, after his accident and trial and all that. And Dirk knows he knows. The Tribune's waiting for Dirk to get his confidence back."

"He may be waiting a while."

"Centurion!" Scruggs's voice came over the radio.

"Yes, Private."

"Problem. The chains won't reach. The last container is too far away."

"How far?"

"We need another hundred feet, at least."

Lee and Ana looked up onto the ship, assessing the containers. Gavin had already removed all the towing and lifting chains. There wasn't a hundred feet left.

"We should have kept that old towing chain we got from that station guy."

"We didn't," Lee said.

"No, we did not." Ana keyed his comm. "Private, describe where that container is. Can we run it downhill, or drag it physically? I need ideas."

"It's not looking good, Centurion. It's at the bottom of a depression, and some of the water has already collected there. We'd have to stand in the mud and drag it up."

"Wonderful. What's the forest there like? Could we land the ship there?"

"Forest, the same as before, Centurion. Not as dense, lots of open space, we can see the sky easily. But the ship won't fit."

"Outstanding. Can we cut the trees down?"

"With one axe? There are like fifty trees."

"Never mind that."

"Centurion, we can see the sky, and we can see the volcano. Have you looked at where the magma is?"

"No, because you're going to tell me."

"It's down off the sides of the mountain and coming across the plain. Burning up the trees as it comes."

Ana stepped out from under the ship and shaded his eyes to peer at the mountain. Red lava glowed through the smoke. "Outstanding."

"It's speeding up. Probably will be here in fifteen minutes." Scruggs coughed. "Too bad we couldn't light up the trees ourselves. We could burn them down and then land."

"Big trees take a long time to burn."

"These aren't big trees, not here. The biggest ones are only three to four inches in diameter. Others are only an inch or two. We could almost knock them down."

"Yes, we could." Ana keyed his comms off, smiled, then keyed it on again. "Yes, we could. Get back here. I need your help carrying something."

Dirk came down the ramp. "We need to get out of here. That lava is heading this way."

"Just one thing we need, Navy."

"What?"

"Got a challenge for you." Ana grinned. "You always like a challenge, don't you?"

"But how wide, exactly?" Ana wiped sweat from his forehead. The lava was only a few hundred yards from the laser container, and he sweltered in the heat. The smoke and red-hot dust didn't help either.

"As wide as possible," Dirk replied. "We need to lift soon. That lava is nearly here, and the smoke is affecting visibility."

"Nature Girl—not that far out!" Ana yelled. He, Scruggs, and Dena had filled a box with his supply of ready-use grenades. They were lashing them to the bigger trees with rope, taking care to make sure the pins were accessible.

"It's a big tree, Old Man." Dena rapped it with her knuckles. "Won't fall down."

"It's far enough away that we don't need it gone. Navy can land next to it. Move on to the next one."

Scruggs wrapped her hands around a trunk. They didn't touch, so she tied a grenade at knee height. Ana's rule was, if they couldn't get their hands around it, attach a grenade. Shrapnel from blowing the big trees down should drop enough of the smaller trees. If necessary, the ship could stomp down the rest.

In theory.

"Centurion, this is my last grenade."

Ana pointed at one larger tree. "Put it right there. Nature Girl, how many have you got?"

"Three, including this one."

"Give 'em here. Then you two get out of here, back onboard the ship. I don't want anybody near me while I splice the pull cord in, in case something happens."

"We can help, Centurion."

"Private, do you honestly think in the middle of a volcanic eruption, ducking showers of red-hot dust and burning rocks, is a good time to learn how to wire grenades to explode with a pull cord?"

Scruggs started to protest. Dena grabbed her. "Baby Marine, he needs us to lower the locking chains so that he can clip it in when Dirk drives over. Come on, I need you to help me with that."

They had dispersed fifty grenades through the trees. Ana had guessed the diameter that Dirk needed to land the ship in and tagged the biggest trees for destruction. He started from the inside closest to the laser container and tied a length of fishing line to each pin in succession. He used six different lengths of lines for forty-one trees, each time looping and knotting the line to the pins. He left a big chunk loose on the end. He couldn't have the lines taut. The trees flexed in the wind, and an early detonation while he was setting his pins would be lethal.

He stopped at the edge of the clearing, pulled each line gently until he felt tension, then tied the different lines together. When finished, he had a bundle with a loop. If he grabbed the loop and ran like a bandit, the fishing line would pull all the pins out, and the grenades would fire soon after.

In theory.

Dirk keyed the intercom. "Get ready to lift."

"Not yet, we're still getting to the chains," Dena said.

"Hurry it up. Things are getting worse."

"Really? I didn't notice, except it's hot as Hades out here, there's dust everywhere, and those firebomb things keep falling."

Dirk clicked through the cameras. Dust and smoke only gave an indistinct glare, no idea how near the lava was. "Lee, get to the air lock, lean out, and tell me how far away that lava is."

Lee unbuckled and scampered down the corridor to the air lock. She pulled the side hatch open. Dust, smoke, and heat billowed in. She coughed as she breathed the sulfurous air and leaned out.

The boiling dust swirled. In the distance, the volcano glowed red as streams of blood-red lava poured down the sides of the mountain. Streams of it stretched out across the plain. One stream ran in front of the Heart's Desire. It flowed about two hundred yards away, a fifty-foot-wide red-black path, with a coal dust surface. Burning trees bordered it. A scorched oak tipped over and splashed into the molten rock, flaring up in flame.

The lava flow ahead was wide enough to consume the entire ship, but it was passing well forward. But one part, not so much a trickle, more like a tiny stream, had split off and flowed at them. This one was only two feet wide, small enough to jump over if you were suicidal. It had curled to within two feet of the port landing leg and was still burbling forward.

Lee hammered the intercom. "It's nearly at the landing legs. Feet away. Lift us now."

"Do we have time—"

"NOW. LIFT NOW!" Lee yelled.

"Everybody hang on," Dirk said over the main channel. He pulsed the engines. The thrusters fired, burping explosions as pockets of methane flared. The Heart's Desire lifted, moved forward, pivoted, and spun.

"Lee, can you see the centurion? The cameras are all dark here."

Lee grasped the edge of the air lock and leaned out. Dust and steam swirled, blocking her view of the centurion, but she gave Dirk a heading.

"I see him! Five hundred meters, three degrees port. The girls are just ahead, running to us. We can pick them up on the way."

"Understood. Tell him to pull those cords, we'll drop and lift that laser. And tell him to get away from there before we start maneuvering.

"Um. Dirk."

"What?"

"Lava flows moved around him. He's covered on three sides, and the other two will meet up downhill shortly. If he doesn't move right now, he's going to be trapped."

CHAPTER TWENTY-FOUR

"Head south to get away from the lava, Centurion." Scruggs's voice rang out over the radio. "You need to get out of there before you're trapped."

Ana carefully set his fishing lines on the ground. This side, they terminated in loops for easy pulling. On the far side, they were tied to fifty grenades clamped onto the larger trees. Wouldn't do to yank that accidentally before he got farther away.

The nearest tree was an oak, with numerous thick branches. Ana grasped the lowest one and hauled himself up, climbing steadily. "How long 'til Navy gets the ship over here?"

"He says he's not coming. It's too dangerous, the lava's too close."

"Really? Tell him I say he's a cowardly weasel who is a disgrace to the uniform."

Scruggs paused, then responded, "He says he doesn't wear a uniform anymore and reminds you that there are four other people on this ship."

Ouch.

Ana coughed as he cleared the lower branches and paused to wipe the sweat from his face. The lava shimmered with a hot rage, even a hundred meters away. A little higher and he got a view across the forest. The rings of lava were advancing. Two narrow streams, faster than the others, had surged around this part of the forest, making a nearly closed ring. He might be able to beat it if he ran that way, but that would mean abandoning the laser container. Single trees were tipping over and bursting in flame. The area in the middle of the ring was still empty of boiling rock, but full of pointed trees.

"Tell him I'm going down and pulling the cord. Explosions in two minutes."

"Centurion, I don't think you have two minutes."

Ana reassessed the rolling lava. "I think you're right. Ten seconds to detonation."

"Ten seconds? How are you going to get—"

Ana jumped.

He was thirty feet up the tree, but the ground was soft mud, and he aimed for a lattice of mixed branches and crashed through them. The springy, snapping branches slowed him, rolled him over, and dropped him on his back into the mud.

"Ooooough." Ana gasped a breath, then another, then started laughing. "The old guy still has it."

He'd lost his earbuds, so he couldn't hear, but his microphone was intact, so they could hear him. He grabbed the loops of fishing line from where he'd draped them, and raced forward, feeling the little tugs as the grenade pins pulled out. He jumped over a rock, slipped in the mud, rolled but kept his hands on the loops, and slid in behind a big tree. "Fire in the hole."

"I can see hardly anything in the cameras," Dirk said over the intercom. "I don't know where he is, exactly. We've got four pointing down, and—whoa!"

Bright flashes marched across all four of Dirk's screens, sprawling out in a spiral pattern. Ana had arranged the central trees to blow first, then circle out, so they would have room to fall. The explosions cleared the smoke and dust. Dirk got a quick view of a flattened clearing, with splinters of large trees lying in all directions, smaller ones tipped sideways, and a large blue painted container dead center.

"Got it. Scruggs, Dena, hang on. I'm maneuvering."

Ana called over the radio, "My earbuds are out. I can't hear you. I'm going back in and climbing up top of that container where the chain hoists are. Drop the lines to me, and when I signal, haul away."

"Scruggs, Dena, get those chains ready. I'm going in. Direct me."

Dena and Scruggs scrambled up the ramp while Dirk hovered. Now they climbed onto the hull and back to the container truss. Dirk edged the Heart's Desire gently to the side. Random winds buffeted him from side to side.

Dirk pushed the controls sideways, trying to follow the shouted directions. "Lee, find me three reference points—the top of that mountain, a hill way off to one side, and a tall tree far away. Point one of the laser rangefinders at each and get a distance. Put the three distances on my screen. Shut up, ladies. Never mind." Dirk slapped a button on his screen, and his headphones died. "Lee, put the screen up now."

Lee gave him a sideways glance while fiddling with his radio. "No, I don't know what he's doing. Stand by." She paged through her screens, found two rocky peaks miles away, and pointed a rangefinder at them. The excellent laser scanner Devin's people had installed read off the distance to the tenth of an inch. She hunted and found a prominent tree in the distance and focused another radar on that. "Like this?"

"Yes." Dirk ignored the cameras, ignored Lee's queries, and stared at the numbers. They jerked and changed as he focused on them, flicking the thrusters, until he had a feel for how they changed as he maneuvered.

"Right, Lee. Get the girls to give me a direction to that container. Distance in meters, then direction, north, south."

Lee chatted for a moment. "Centurion is fifty meters north, thirty meters west."

Dirk examined the screens, glanced at the—gyroscopic repeater, and memorized the necessary numbers. He edged the ship slowly left and forward, until he was where they said he should be.

"Now?"

"He's ten meters south, six west."

Dirk puffed the thrusters.

"Two meters north. One west."

Dirk puffed again.

"Scruggs says stand by."

Scruggs and Dena had yelled curses at Dirk—first he ignored them, then he dropped off the channel. But by dint of

Lee repeating their directions, he had moved up so they were almost over the laser. Ana climbed up on top of the battered blue container and waved his hands, the forward lifting strap at his feet. Scruggs and Dena had retired to the truss connections. They were spooling the lifting chains down, watching Ana on the cargo connection cameras.

"Go, Baby Marine. Bow first," Dena said.

A shockwave of air surged over them, rocking the Heart's Desire. In the camera, Ana bent down and shielded his head. Burning rock chips pattered down around him. One struck his arm, and he shook it off. Scruggs dumped more chain. Ana stood, grasped the swaying chain, hauled it down, and clipped the cargo hook onto the front connection of the container. Seconds later, the Heart's Desire slipped sideways, and the container slewed under Ana. He dropped to one knee, grabbing the chain, and held on as the container shook under the chain.

"Scruggs! Lava on my screen!" Dena yelled. The burning lava over-topped the bank, and was now flowing down the sides, searing everything in its path.

"Pilot wants to know if he can lift?" Lee asked.

"Not yet. We're only connected with one chain. We can't go yet."

The wind shook the Heart's Desire again, and the ship slewed sideways. The landing legs snapped a still-standing tree. The ship pivoted again, and Ana grasped the dangling chain to his chest, cursing.

"No, we need him to. I want—"

"I need a direction."

"We need." Scruggs stopped. The forward chain was attached. They could winch it up any time. But the stern chain wasn't attached. A pilot would tell her she needed to have Dirk to keep the ship steady, but yaw it on its Z-axis fifteen degrees, aligning the rear chain over the connector. The problem was, she wasn't a pilot, and she didn't have the vocabulary for that.

"Tell him to pivot, Lee," Scruggs said.

"What direction?"

"Direction?"

"Clockwise or counter-clockwise?"

"I—incoming." A rain of burning rock obscured her view.

Ana was holding the chain with one hand but saw the falling rocks. He ducked his head and grabbed the chain with both hands as another patter of burning rocks fell from the sky. One smacked his shoulder and he yelled.

"Scruggs, give us directions," Lee said.

"Baby Marine," Dena said. "Lava's passing my camera. It will be at that container any second. Once it's there, everything will burn. Container, laser, Ana."

"Lee, tell Pilot to lift three feet and hold there."

After a two-second delay, the Heart's Desire lifted three feet. The container in Scruggs's vision jerked up, dangling at the end of the chain. Ana clasped the taut chain with both hands. Scruggs waited for a beat. "Now lift twenty meters and take us one kilometer south. Now. Go. Go."

The Heart's Desire surged into the air. Suspended from only one chain, the container dangled below. A cursing Ana hung on the single chain, scrambling to stay on top.

CHAPTER TWENTY-FIVE

"It's the ISS Pollux, according to their beacon," Alvarez said from the sensor station. "A frigate. The Lord Lyon commanding. They are exchanging communications with their consorts."

"The Mad Dog of the Verge," Kruder said. "We meet at last."

The whole bridge laughed.

Fusterheim put the sensor outputs up on the common screens. "Big for a frigate. Out-guns us, Kapitan. More weapons. Better weapons. Longer-range weapons. And fast—no way to escape."

Blomberg faced Kruder and saluted. "We will fight to the death, Kapitan."

"Fight to the death? Why?"

"For the glory of the Union, of course sir."

Kruder looked sideways at Fusterheim. Fusterheim shook his head and addressed Blomberg. "Sit down, Leutnant."

"But sir—"

"Be still. There will be no fighting to the death. The Kapitan will deal with this. Be seated. Now."

Blomberg dropped to his seat. Fusterheim glared at him, shook his head, and focused on Kruder. "This is a new class to me, Kapitan."

"And me," Kruder said. "Sensors, how many lasers?"

"None, Kapitan," Alvarez said. "A new technology. Positron beams, the summary says."

"How effective? How long-ranged?"

Alvarez paged through his screens. "I'll have to look her up in the warbook sir. This is new construction, and I didn't expect to see any out here."

"Carry on," Kruder said.

Blomberg frowned at Alvarez. "It's your job to have this information available for the Kapitan."

"Blomberg!" Fusterheim had heard. "Thank you for your comments, but Alvarez needs to work."

Alvarez rolled his eyes as he posted the Pollux's specifications on the main display. "Here is what the warbook says about the Positron beams. Shorter range than lasers, and less damage. But a faster recharge rate, and smaller physical footprint."

Fusterheim shook his head. "Exchange longer-ranged, more powerful weapons for shorter-ranged, less powerful weapons. What idiot designed that?"

"What about speed and sensors?" Kruder asked. "Any notation on that?"

Alvarez paged through his screens. "Less acceleration than older models, same sensor package."

"But physically bigger," Kruder said. "Something doesn't add up here. Why make a bigger ship with inferior weapons, but the same power plant and sensors? Makes no sense."

"It could be an export model, sir, designed for co-belligerents, or colonial use. Using older technologies so it could be constructed in peripheral shipyards." Alvarez highlighted an area of the display. "These could be extra fuel tanks. Same power plant and jump drive but longer duration on station."

Kruder looked over his shoulder—the comm officers sat behind him. "Comm, anything from the Pollux?"

"Just the standard 'what ship,' sir, and we gave the automated response. We're pretending to be asleep."

"Keep doing that. I'm going to my cabin." Kruder unbuckled himself and slid back to the central corridor. Pinguin's 0.25G gave enough gravity for him to hop down the corridor and pull along the rails.

Fusterheim asked for an analysis of the other ships in the group. A fleet tanker and a modern assault carrier accompanied the Pollux, along with four large freighters. The bridge crew assembled the passive scans and displayed them on the screens, then argued about their meaning. Fusterheim countered each point, and the bridge crew struck back, citing displays and readings. Twice they called up petty officers or regular spacers who had experience with ship designs or who had spent time in the Empire to clarify matters.

Kruder returned to the bridge. "Well, Hans? What do you think?"

"A naval task force composed of three modern ships. The

assault carrier is larger than normal for the Verge, but not unprecedented. They could simply be swapping Marine units from one station to another. The fast tankers double as fleet supply ships and delivery ships. One of the engine room crew has been on one at a party. She says they are longer ranged than they look, the jump drives are powerful. They're big enough that the Accursed Empire uses them to supply entire sectors, so it's not clear who is escorting who. They might be with the frigate as part of a task force, or the frigate might simply be their escort. We can't tell."

"The freighters?"

"Nothing unusual except all are newer than average for the Verge, and longer ranged. Solid ships, our people say, they recognize at least two of them. Big shipping lines, competent officers. Not your regular tramp ships. And Edda pointed out, if you have a long-ranged jump drive, extra fuel, and aren't scared of pirates, this system is an excellent short cut between the main shipping routes."

"And with a tanker and a military escort, most of those problems are solved. Interesting." Kruder leaned back and flexed his fingers. "Sensors, put the warbook specs for that frigate up again."

Alvarez obligingly displayed information about the Pollux's class, including size, speed, weapons, range and so on.

Blomberg grinned at the screen. "Kapitan, with those weapons being that short ranged, we could almost take her in a straight fight."

"There might be some issues regarding construction methods, as we do not have the normal military redundancies built in. Our biggest problem would be the rate of fire. Pollux will recharge much faster than us. But if we could get in close, it would be an interesting fight, if those specifications are correct."

"That's assuming, Kapitan," Fusterheim said, "that the warbook is correct."

"Of course. Hans, come over and give me your opinion of this report, please."

Fusterheim obediently unclipped. Kruder's screen displayed a report of ration consumption by the engine room overnight watch. Kruder tapped a blank space on his console and traced '90%' with his index finger.

Fusterheim knew that Kruder had retired to his quarters to look up the frigate in the top-secret database provided to ship captains. The captain's database not only had more details than the warbook, but also how reliable the intelligence department considered them. Ninety percent confidence was extremely unusual.

Fusterheim shook his head. "Not possible," he whispered. "How?"

"Human intelligence and plans."

"They have copies of the plans?"

"They say they do."

"Still not possible. Do you believe it?"

"Not really. But I don't know what to believe. This bothers me."

Fusterheim shook his head again. "Best avoid that one, Kapitan."

"Agreed," Kruder said. "We need to do something about young Blomberg..."

"Leave it to me." Fusterheim winked and returned to his seat. "Sensors?"

"Sir?"

"I find myself agreeing with Leutnant Blomberg. It is necessary for you to have the specifications for all possible from the Accursed Empire instantly available."

Alvarez saluted. "Sir. I am quite comfortable that I can respond to any question about the units regularly stationed here. City-class corvettes, the older destroyers, and such. But the more esoteric ships are harder. We did not expect the Accursed Empire's most modern frigate to be in the area."

"Nevertheless, you must acquaint yourself with all the possible Imperial designs that are available."

"All of them sir?"

"All of them. How many are there?"

"Hundreds sir." Alvarez grimaced. "I shall begin my studies at once. I will do my best."

"Excellent. But I will provide you with some help. Leutnant Blomberg?"

"Sir?" Blomberg said.

"Does this sound like a good idea to you? This memorizing of all the different Imperial ships?"

"It does sir. In the fleet, we strive for excellence."

"Indeed we do. Well, you'll help sensors, then. Prepare a presentation on the Imperial ships. You will give it during morning briefing from now on."

"Which ships sir?"

"All of them."

"What?" Blomberg frowned. "I mean, yes sir. Of course sir. Where should I start?"

"Wherever you wish. I will simply pick one at the start of each meeting."

"Sir? You mean, I..."

"Will memorize the specifications of all Imperial ships, and be prepared to present on any of them, starting at tomorrow's meeting. I'll choose a different one each day, you will present a briefing on that ship during officers' call. That way, our sensor officer, and all the other officers, will learn a new ship a day."

"But, with no knowledge of what ships you will ask..."

"Yes, yes, it will be difficult." Fusterheim grinned. "But in the fleet, we strive for excellence, do we not?"

Blomberg looked sick, but he nodded. "Yes sir."

"Excellent." Fusterheim beamed around the bridge. "Excellence is its own reward."

Alvarez interrupted. "Activity at the jump limit. Freighters are jumping. One gone. Two. Now a third. Last one. All the freighters have jumped."

Kruder's head jerked up. "Just the freighters? And all at once?"

"Yes. That's a very close jump spacing sir."

Kruder reran the display showing the ships disappearing into jump space. "Closer together than I would have done."

"The warships are on the same vector... there they go. All three together. Excellent jump spacing for the warships."

"Somebody over there knows how to drive a ship," Kruder said. "Navigation, get me a course."

The navigation officer sat straight up and hovered his hands over his screen. "Destination sir?"

"The jump limit, and then take us out of here."

"Direction, Kapitan?"

"Opposite direction from that task force. We'll search out some better hunting for a while."

The next few weeks settled into a routine. Kruder jumped in a straight line away from the task force. At each system, Pinguin would head for the nearest gas giant, whether she needed fuel or not. He'd either top up his tanks or orbit, but no longer than three days. Half of the time, they managed to surprise a freighter in orbit on arrival and capture it. Sometimes they caught one per day. The crews always surrendered without firing a shot. Once, he captured a freighter with a cargo of ship components and electronics. He took what he could use and sent it and its cargo back to the Union under a prize crew. He sent the captured Confed crew members back with them as well.

Twice, he loaded up captured Imperial freighters and jammed all the Imperial captive crew members on board. He sent them to the rendezvous he'd been given by the admiral. He provided contact locations, frequencies, and codes, and instructed his prize crews to accept reasonable suggestions from the Imperials contact for routing and delivery. In no cases were they to give up the ship—they needed it to get back to Union space themselves. In three months, he would be returning to a neutral shipyard for maintenance. They were to meet him there.

Blomberg had a miserable time. Every morning at officers'

call, the first officer quizzed him on Imperial ship types and their specifications. It was, of course, impossible to memorize them all. Fusterheim added insult to injury at the first meeting by asking him about the three warships they had encountered yesterday, a test he failed.

But at the end of the third week, Blomberg surprised him.

"Blomberg, our topic for today is the Colony-class cruisers of the Accursed Empire.

"Colony-class sir? Eight-inch lasers in eight twin turrets. A dozen one-inch lasers in single mounting for small craft and missile interdiction. Capable of jumping three parsecs at once. Fuel for twelve parsecs worth of jumps before refueling is needed."

"Weapons range?"

"Range of the main armament is 150,000 miles, but sensors limit effective range to 100,000 miles. Smaller weapons ineffective beyond twenty thousand miles."

Fusterheim raised his eyes. "You are sure of this, Leutnant?"

"I am sir."

"Interesting. Enough on this for now. Captain-class frigate?"

"Four-inch lasers in four single turrets. Two one-inch lasers in single mountings. Range 100,000 miles, with proper sensors. Capable of jumping three parsecs at once, but fuel for only one jump."

Fusterheim checked his notes. That was correct.

"Very well, Town-class corvettes, a common opponent here in the Verge."

"One four-inch laser in a single turret. One-inch laser in a single mounting. Up to 150 mini-missiles for engaging missile boats. Two parsecs of jump, and fuel only for a single jump, barely."

Fusterheim brought up his displays and checked. "It seems you are correct again, Leutnant. Well done."

"Thank you sir."

This continued for the rest of the week, until Fusterheim put a halt to it. "Leutnant, you appear to have memorized the specifications of the entire Accursed Empire's fleet. I must ask, how did you do it? Will you share your methods?"

"Could I not just have an excellent memory sir?"

"Is that the case?"

Blomberg smiled. "I do have an excellent memory, but what I have done, sir, is memorize the class types, and the standard weapons. Imperial warships follow a pattern, mostly. For the frigates, destroyers, cruisers, and so on, they have similar weapons packages and turret configurations. Corvettes have one turret, frigates have four, cruisers have eight or sixteen depending on class, and so on. Corvettes have four-inch lasers, frigates as well, cruisers six- or eight-inch, depending on class. Maximum range varies by size of laser, modified by the sensor package. I really just have to remember the deltas—for Imperial Light cruisers, for example, they all have eight six-inch turrets, except the Daring-class, which have four eight-inch turrets. They are all effective to 150,000 miles, again except the Daring, which can shoot up to 200,000 miles, but the sensors are only good to 150,000. All have endurance of twelve parsecs, three parsecs at a time. Except the Vigor-class.

They have endurance of only eight parsecs, but at four parsecs a time."

Kruder grinned "That is very well done, Leutnant. There are always trade-offs. Larger guns, and you must have fewer of them in the same size hull. Bigger weapons are longer ranged but need targeting software and sensor support. What about crew size?"

"Crew size is largely irrelevant, sir. They average about the same for each class. Add more engineers to handle bigger drives, you need fewer gunners."

"Very well done, indeed. What about the exceptions?"

"Some of the larger classes can be a bit confusing, and the auxiliary ships are all over the map. The first officer could confuse me very easily with questions about fast combat support repair ships—each is almost unique, but I gambled that he wouldn't ask me that."

"His focus is on war-capable ships, yes. This is the War Navy, after all. Well, in a fight between us and the Accursed Empire, who would win?"

"We would sir. Nobody can defeat the Union of Nations."

Kruder shook his head. "A stout answer, and of course the Council guarantees us success, but it would be unrealistic to assume we would win every battle. What of a battle between equals? Say, one of our destroyers versus one of theirs?"

"Sir, ours would win, of course."

"On what do you base that? Size? Weapons? Crew morale? Or is it just an inevitable function of our superior political system?"

"Sir." Blomberg squirmed slightly. Criticizing the

inevitable victory of the Union of Nations over any adversary was always politically risky, but the officers on Pinguin seemed to value truth above all things. "Sir, we would win. Because of size."

"Go on."

"Class for class, all of our ships are somewhat bigger than most Imperial classes and carry heavier weapons. For example, our cruisers always carry eight-inch lasers, rather than the six-inch. A duel between equals, we should surely win."

"Our victory is assured, then, Leutnant?"

"Sir." Blomberg closed his mouth, then shook his head. "There are a great many of them sir. By tonnage, their navy is three times as large as ours. Individually, we are better ships, but we are gravely outnumbered."

"Indeed we are, Leutnant, which is why, on this cruise, we do not challenge them, but instead take Confederation vessels. I do not want to start a fight with the Accursed Empire on my own—"

BONG. BONG. "Kapitan to the bridge. Enemy in sight."

"Unless I am forced to. Well done, Blomberg. Continue your studies. Everyone to your stations." Kruder stood and hit the intercom. "Kruder here. Report."

"Enemy warships in sight Kapitan. An Imperial frigate. Coming directly at us."

CHAPTER TWENTY-SIX

Two weeks later, the Verge Defense flotilla, as Lionel called it, or the Mad Dog's fleet, as Devin referred to it, arrived in Papillon. They discharged their freighters and planned their next move. They'd been cutting back and forth across the verge for weeks now, escorting merchant ships, collecting data, scanning ships, boarding suspected pirates, and generally making a nuisance of themselves. They took a pause to regroup. Lionel asked for a meeting with Devin.

"Subprefect, be seated," Devin said as Lionel walked into his office. "I'm doing paperwork for supplies."

"We have word from the core?" Lionel asked.

"Nope. No couriers. No high-speed freighters, no yachts. Nothing."

"Regular traffic still working?"

"No indication that it isn't, but it would take any news months to get out here if it came via freighter. How much does a box of gauss rifle ammunition weigh?"

"I have no idea. Are you still filing ammunition requests

to the core? We've got the Hydrogen Queen out here. Surely they have all that?"

"They use the same software as the core requests. And the supply officer was trained at the same school."

"Ask the Marines. They might know. Tribune, I've been cross-checking with the shipping companies for the last two hours. They're finally getting their act together. They are reporting ships overdue."

"How many?"

"Nine are reported overdue. Five that we care about or can make sense of them."

"And of the five?"

"Three of them should be here now. And part of their route came from the direction of Daube's world."

"The direction? Or from?"

"Freighter routes are usually flexible. It's possible that they may have called on Daube's world. Not guaranteed, but they could have. One for sure didn't, but it's farther out. I've plotted the losses, last identified locations, and planned itineraries." Lionel put a display up on the screen.

"How accurate are these?"

"Those two here—" Lionel highlighted two ships. "—are definitely overdue. We've got reports from their turn-around ports from other ships that saw them leave. They definitely started back, they're definitely not here, and it's probable that they passed through Daube's world. The other two, not as sure, but possible."

Devin played with the screen. "You think the raider, or pirate, is out there somewhere, in this highlighted area."

"Yes. Us, the Confeds, and the Nats, we all stick out there and meet up. We border both of the other Empires here, and here." Lionel tapped points on the screen. "There're unaligned systems there, and there. Most of these systems—" Another tap. "Nobody cares about them because they have no resources. If I was a pirate, I'd operate out there, make a quick dash into Imperial Space, and capture some freighters. Then I'd dash back and sell what I stole on the other side of the border."

"Right on the border, then?"

"Not right on the border. If I left Papillon with a cargo of feathers, and a week later came back with electronics, food, vehicles and aerospace parts, it would look suspicious, no matter how good my paperwork was. No, I'd steal stuff, hop back into one of the other Empires, go a jump or two inside their borders then trade with another crooked ship. They head away from the Verge, and by the time they're a half dozen systems away, who's to say where this stuff came from?"

"How do they know where to go?"

"Not sure. Inside information from somebody."

Devin tapped the far side of the screen. "You confirm these ones here, near Papillon are overdue. But you also list those two, way over here, as missing as well."

"Same thing. The ships that left after them are here now, and we don't see them."

"They could have changed their routes."

"Lots of overdue ships could have changed their routes. These ones didn't. Specific cargoes with specific delivery dates. They're taken."

"Nowhere near here."

"It could be they got grabbed near the end of their journey, close to us."

"Close but unlikely."

"Or... there could be more than one pirate out there."

Devin shook his head. "More than one? Two pirates working together?"

"Doesn't have to be pirates. Could be the Confeds. Or the Nats."

Devin leaned back and studied the screen. "This is all well and good, but what does it have to do with the secret warrant to arrest me, and the things going on back in the core?"

"Maybe somebody in the core set it up."

"You think the pirates are from the core?"

"Not sure, but I'll tell you something. There are two groups operating."

"How do we catch two groups?" Devin pivoted in his chair. "We can't even catch one."

"What? Something the Mad Dog of the Verge can't do?"

"Indeed. Suggestions?"

"We should become pirates ourselves."

"We should run out and capture ships ourselves?" Devin shook his head. "Not sure how that would work. We'd need eye patches and a selection of parrots, wouldn't we? Is that what you're suggesting?"

"No, I'm suggesting we work backwards." Lionel put a different display on a screen. "We have been trying to stop them being captured. Instead, let's look at how we would plan to capture a merchant ship, and what we'd need to do afterward."

Devin shook his head. "Where do we start?"

"We need help with this. The senior ratings with merchant service would be best."

"How many do we have?"

"Don't know, but I know somebody who does."

Devin spread his hands. "Please, Subprefect, enlighten me."

Lionel tapped a code into Devin's intercom.

"Imin here, Tribune. How can I help?"

Lionel leaned back. "Imin, it's Lionel. I'm here with the Tribune. Can you get a dozen or so ratings who have served in merchant ships together for a special project for the Tribune?"

"Former merchant sailors sir? Any particular types or skills?"

"A variety. Deck, engineering. Cargo, everything. Different skill sets."

"Of course sir. I can have them gathered in thirty minutes."

"Bring them to briefing room two."

"Yes sir. Do you have a request for lunch sir?"

"Lunch?"

"It's lunchtime sir. I assume the Tribune will want to provide a meal if we'll be working for some time."

Devin laughed. "Your discretion, Imin. And, please bring a selection of eye patches as well."

"Of course, Tribune. Left side or right side?"

The meeting of minds produced results. Imin had whipped up an olive-based salad, and rice stuffed in grape leaves, along with a fish from the planet. Imin, Bosun McSanchez, and seven other selected ratings met with the Tribune and the Subprefect. Devin figured out that his presence inhibited discussion, so finished his lunch and left. Lionel stayed only a few minutes longer, and left Imin and McSanchez to figure things out. Devin spent a frustrating two hours searching for a table of weights of small arms ammunition. He had reached a point where he was trying to figure out how much a packing case weighed when McSanchez asked him to come back.

When Devin and Lionel arrived back at the briefing room, McSanchez had a display up on the screen.

"Bosun?"

"Sir. We've discussed it. The first issue is how to figure out which freighters to hit. No profit in hitting freighters carrying scrap nickel, or grain, or potash. Gotta be something you can sell, use, or eat if you want to stay out there."

Subprefect Lionel leaned back. "Insurance companies could tell you that, if you had an inside man, or somebody at the port office with the bill of lading. Or in customs."

"Or all three, sir. If that was the case, all the cargoes lifted would trace back to a single point—they'd have something in common. They don't."

"Perhaps we don't see it."

"No sir. We think it's not there to see. You gave us a list of the ships you think are missing, captured. We decided to follow the money. Here's a list of their cargoes, broken down by value."

Devin and Lionel watched as the list scrolled down the screen. By the end, both were shaking their heads.

"Bosun," Devin said. "I'm not in trade, but even I can tell there's not much money in reselling stolen cargoes of water pipes."

Lionel nodded. "I see why you said potash. There're three shiploads of potash missing. Where would you sell it?"

"Out here sir?" McSanchez shrugged. "Only to the planet that ordered it, and they'd be suspicious if their ships went missing and I showed up with the exact same amount as they had recently ordered. Wouldn't fly."

"You could run the cargoes into Confed space, or Nat space," Lionel said.

"And who is it that's doing the pirating while you're bringing the cargos back and forth?" McSanchez asked. "And as the Tribune is aware, the logistics of transferring cargo containers in the dark is challenging. At the very least, you'll need small tugs, and crews trained in them, and self-loading and unloading capability."

"Okay, Bosun," Lionel said. "Why not have the captured ships themselves carry their cargos back? They could sail back deep into the Union of Nations and discharge them there."

"Ships would show up sir. Word would get out."

"Fine, then send them into the Confederation. Jove alone knows what type of madness goes on in there."

"We thought of that sir. There's the question of crews." McSanchez put a second list up on the screen. It was the crew lists of the missing ships.

"What of them?"

"If they keep the ships, somebody has to drive them sir. Navigate, patch things in engineering, feed the people doing the patching, the whole thing. And you need multiple watches."

"Why not just murder the crews and replace them with your own?" Devin wondered.

"That would work, Tribune. Put your own crews on. Or threaten the ones onboard to make them do the work. But if you threaten them, then..."

Lionel saw it. "You need guards enough to keep an eye on the captured crews. Or your own crews. Or a combination of both. And they have to be specialists. Engineers. Navigators. What cargo ship carries a dozen spare engineering staff?"

"None, Subprefect." McSanchez put up another screen. "Given the size of the ships on the missing list, assuming you replaced even half of the crews on the list, either by murdering them all or guarding them, then by our estimation, you'd need another hundred crew on your pirate ship. And while you're out pirating, your people have to be fed, and they need life support, and quarters, and supplies. I've never seen a merchant ship with space for an extra hundred crew."

"Passenger liner," Devin said. "No, wait, that's stupid. Passenger liners are always on well-known routes. Everybody would notice a stray passenger liner."

"Yes sir. We need a ship that could be over-crewed from the start. And then there's the question of physically boarding the ships."

"Pull up alongside, point your guns, and demand surrender," Devin said.

"Yes sir." McSanchez nodded. "Works great on a frigate, like Pollux, 'cause we're faster than anything out there. You can drop us into a system, pick any ship on the screens, we can run it down in a few hours at worst. Merchant ships can't. They're all the same speed, specially the smaller ones. And even if you wanted to speed them up, they don't have the space to install better equipment."

"I'm hearing nothing small, then." Lionel nodded. "Your pirate ship has to be big, with lots of room for crew, and fast, with powerful drives to produce the energy for all this. Plus weapons. That says warship."

"My understanding is that nobody has reported any warships recently, Tribune." McSanchez said. "The way things are right now, anybody spots a warship in any system, they're going to head for the nearest planet, or jump away, or broadcast a mayday, or all three."

"What are you saying, Chief?"

"Needs to be a big merchant ship sir. Largest size you can find out here, to handle the crew requirements. And it has to look like a merchant ship—lots of regular container racks, the whole bit. Might have a tug visible. It can be faster than a regular merchant ship, but not warship fast."

"If it's not warship fast, how does it catch anybody, then? How do they find the freighters to capture?"

"Goes where they are sir. We think—" Imin indicated the nodding ratings sitting behind him. "We think they catch 'em while they're fueling. Space is big, freighters don't usually run into each other, except at starport or orbital transshipment points. And any sort of fighting there would be noticed. If you're on a freighter in a sparsely served system, anybody changes course to come toward you, that's suspicious, you get out of there quick, especially with the news going around now. Or you run for the planet—they might have some defenses— maybe a custom boat with a slug thrower. But fueling…"

McSanchez took a drink of water. "Fueling. You're out-bound from a planet, and you see somebody loafing around the local gas giant sucking fuel in, you don't even comment on it. Even if they're taking a long time, they might not have good processing capability. Nothing unusual. And the orbits will be the same. Everybody always wants the most fuel-efficient orbit—deep enough in the planet's gravity that you can suck up a lot of atmo, but not so deep you have to burn a bunch to get out. They teach standard orbits in merchant academies, and they publish them in the sailing directions. You jump into a new system, the captain will say 'take us into a fueling orbit around XYZ,' and the navigator knows exactly what he means. Even if he doesn't, he looks it up in the book. If there's another ship there, so what? Everybody needs fuel."

Devin nodded. "Right, Bosun. We need to search for a large container-carrying merchant ship, big enough to hide modifications for a large crew, with tugs for self-unloading, trading in the Verge."

"Yes sir. We made a list. It's pretty long. But one other thing."

"Yes?"

"We're thinking it's got to be hanging around the jump limits of lightly visited stars with a gas giant around the jump limit—inside or out. Nothing too high-tech of a world, or they'd see what was happening."

"How many have you found?" Devin asked.

"Seven systems, sir."

Devin hit the intercom. "Recall our on-station people. Discontinue any loading operations. Prepare to leave orbit. Inform the Valhalla and the Hydrogen Queen."

Devin dropped the intercom and looked at the room. "Subprefect, any comments?"

Lionel shook his head. "Let's go hunting."

CHAPTER TWENTY-SEVEN

"It will look great, Centurion," Scruggs said. "And it will be much more hygienic. Let Dena do it."

"The only way that Nature Girl is going to get near me with those scissors is if I've stabbed her so deeply with them that they're lodged in her hipbone and can't be removed."

"They're not scissors, it's a shaver," Dena said. She buzzed the shaver in front of Ana's face. "See? Shaver. And as a side note, if you did stab somebody so deeply with scissors, why would you want them to get close?"

"To get the scissors back, of course. Good scissors are hard to find," Ana said. "Especially sewing ones. My sewing scissors are specially made. If you find a good pair, you want to keep them handy."

Dena, Scruggs, Ana, and Rocky were sitting in the lounge. Dirk had successfully lifted them away from the burning lava, and landed on a cliff top where the smoke and dust were less. Dena attached all the chains on the containers, and Scruggs winched everything back into place and made it safe for orbital flight. Ana would have helped, but Dirk hadn't picked up enough altitude when he crossed over one of the bigger lava flows—the burning hot lava flows. Ana's skin suit, glove and boots had protected most of him, but his head above his hard collar was one giant sunburn, and the skin had started to peel.

"What do you know about sewing?" Dena asked. "Not a very manly pursuit."

"Much more manly than walking around an assault carrier with your uniform pants falling down because you don't know how to tailor them. I'm good with needles and thread. And you're not shaving my head."

"Yes, yes, she is." Lee entered the lounge, bent down and rubbed Rocky's neck. Rocky's tail thumped.

"Her and what army?" Ana asked.

"Medical, meaning me, says so. I've got tubes of antiseptic that we have to smear over your whole head, and there can't be any hair. Otherwise, you'll get infected, and if that happens, your whole head will end up being a giant ball of noxious pus."

"His entire head a ball of noxious pus." Dena laughed. "How will that be different from now?"

"Shut up, both of you," Ana grunted. "Fine. I'll shave it down. Gimmie."

"Better if I do it, Old Man." Dena held up the shaver. "This is going to hurt, with all those burns, and I'll do it quickly. I used to do this for my brothers. I can do it for you."

"What do you think, Rocky?" Ana asked. Rocky's tail thumped in reply. Ana grunted and closed his eyes.

Dena and her shaver made short work of the hair on Ana's head and face. True to her word, it took less than thirty seconds until he was bald. With his bald pate, sunburned skin, and his normal snarl, he looked like a bad-tempered tomato.

"Outstanding." Ana rubbed his head. "I feel cooler already."

Lee slathered on the ointment, taking time to work it in behind his ears and down to his shoulders. Ana gritted his teeth. He was badly burned, and the touch hurt.

"That burns."

"Yes. It's antiseptic."

"Isn't it supposed to deaden the pain?"

"That's the other ointment," Lee said. "I figured since you were so tough and all, you didn't need it. Want me to get it?"

"No." Ana's eyes were tearing. "I'm fine."

"You look great, Old Man," Dena said. "I just—no, don't smile. You know how that makes everybody feel. And it's even worse now."

"That was a grimace, not a smile, and I need a mirror," Ana said.

"Don't worry, Centurion," Dena said. "You look just as..."

"Handsome," Scruggs said.

"Military," Lee said.

"Hideous." Dirk arrived from the control room.

"Well, it can't be too bad if Navy here hates it, so that makes me feel better," Ana said. "Navy, I've got a bone to stab you with."

"What? A bone? Stab me?"

"It's an expression."

"I think the expression is a bone to pick with you."

"Really? You sure?"

"Pretty sure."

"Well, I've already picked the bone. I don't need your help with that. I need to stab you with it."

"Well, that can wait," Dirk said. "I've come back to apologize to you."

"Of course, you would say—wait. What?"

"Apologize. I took us out too low, and I didn't account for the heat. It's my fault you're wounded. Well, wounded more. I couldn't help the falling rocks. But I want to apologize and let you know that it won't happen again."

Lee, Ana, Scruggs, and Dena exchanged glances.

"Pilot," Lee said. "Are you well?"

"Very well, thank you. What's the prognosis on Gavin?"

"Medical pod says he's out of danger, but the protocol is to keep him knocked out for the next twenty-four hours while the drugs fix his brain."

"Gonna need a lot longer than twenty-four hours to do that," Ana said.

Lee held up the tube of ointment. "Want some more rubbed in?"

"Never mind. I'm good."

Dirk shrugged. "Excellent, thank you, Navigator. Or in this case, Medic. Right, we've got our laser. Now we have to figure out if we have software for it and find somewhere to have it installed."

"Didn't Miss Cass say…"

"I'm not too happy with her right now, given the way she sold things and how she left it."

"She did recommend a shipyard, didn't she?"

"Yes. And I'm not keen on going to a shipyard that she has her hooks into."

"What do we do?"

"The engineer said he might know somebody. Let's head to the jump limit, and reconsider once we're out there."

Dirk didn't stress the ship, so it took two days to climb out of the gravity well and meander to the jump limit. Of the four other ships that had been present, three, including Cass's ship, jumped in different directions. One circled the planet and dropped back onto a different island. Now that they were watching, it was clear that every single island was volcanic. Every day, a different island blew up. Any settlements down there would have been washed into a fiery ocean every few years at the most.

Gavin woke up demanding food. Ana demanded anti-itch cream as his entire scalp peeled off in a giant sunburn. Scruggs and Dena demanded a better simulator program than the one that Ana had installed. Rocky demanded treats.

Lee came back to the lounge after her shift. Dirk and Dena were watching Gavin eat his third tray since coming out of the med pod a half hour ago.

"I've never seen anyone eat so fast," Dena said as Gavin shoveled the food into his mouth.

"He's not even stopping to taste it. We should have given him those vile Red-Red-Red trays." Food trays were all color-coded. Red-Red-Red was stewed tomatoes, stewed apples, and stewed red sweet potatoes, all mixed together.

"That's what I gave him," Dena said. "We've got so many extra, and he didn't specify, so I figured, what the heck."

Gavin stopped shoveling the food into his mouth, sniffed his tray, and wrinkled his nose. "It does smell horrible." Then he shrugged and shoved another spoonful into his mouth.

Lee came back from the control room. "I have news."

"Give us the bad news first," Dirk said.

"There isn't any. It's all good news. Guess what this is?" She held up a software cassette. They had continued plodding through their collection of stolen software while on shift.

"A complete listing of all Imperial Navy shoes issued for the last hundred years?" Dirk asked.

"Surprisingly, we did find something like that. An entire program devoted to ordering uniforms. Did you know the Imperial Navy has over three hundred different uniform types?"

"I would have guessed higher," Dirk said. "But what's on that one?"

"A random-walk program, combined with an auto-helm."

"A genuine random-walk program?" Dirk asked. "For real?"

"What's a random walk?" Dena asked.

"The pilot plots a course, engages the random walk, and it moves us up, down, left right, slow, fast, the whole bit. We can program the dimensions and how often we want the changes made, and it even suggests how much of a change it should make. We can have it always return to a base course so we're always going to get to the same point in space, or just let it move us without regard to destination. It even has a fuel-economizing mode."

"That's outstanding," Dirk said. "That will make things a lot easier when we meet people who we're not sure are hostile."

"Which is everybody, these days," Dena said. "But how does that benefit us?"

"If you do it manually, it's hard to not fall into a pattern," Dirk said. "Even if you don't think you are, you probably do. They had us do random course changes at the academy, and plotted them on a graph anonymously. After the third time we did it, we could tell whose graph we were looking at without the name. Everybody had a style. Real random-walk programs use external stimuli to make changes unique."

"Cosmic rays," Lee said. "Strength and direction give it the seed, and continue to feed in. Lots of cosmic rays in space."

"Do you need to set a course?" Dena asked.

"Only a destination," Lee said. "Get on screen, pick a planet, choose an orbit, and it will take us there, changing vectors."

"Sounds great." Dena frowned. "What do we need Dirk for, then?"

"Thanks for your support, Dena," Dirk said. "Lee, what's the other one you have there?"

"I want you and the centurion, and I suppose the engineer, to double-check me, but I think this is the monitoring and firing program for an Imperial Navy four-inch laser. One of which we have in a container attached to our ship at this point."

"Much more outstanding," Dirk said.

Dena clapped her hands. "Yay. We've got guns. And Dirk's been replaced by a plastic package."

"We have guns, but we don't have them mounted," Dirk said. "We need some sort of sneaky shipyard that doesn't mind dealing with stolen Imperial technology and taking illicit payment for illegal work. Somewhere close."

Everyone looked at Gavin. He swallowed the last of his red slop. "What?"

"Oh come on," Dena said. "You're so sketchy, you're bound to know somebody."

"Just 'cause I made some mistakes in the past doesn't mean I'm a criminal mastermind," Gavin said.

Rocky sat up and barked. Gavin looked at him, and Rocky's tail thumped against the seat. Thump Thump Thump.

"Even Rocky doesn't believe that," Dena said.

"Fine." Gavin put his spoon down. "I know a guy. Happy?"

"How far away?" Dirk asked.

"It's not how far exactly, that's the problem," Gavin said. "It's who else is there."

CHAPTER TWENTY-EIGHT

"It's a complete shipyard." Gavin displayed a map on the screen in the lounge. "Full facilities for repair and replacement, berths for ships up to two hundred containers. Only four, admittedly, but there you are. Construction facilities for small craft. There's substantial belt metal deposits insystem, so metal fabrication is inexpensive. The planet below is habitable, barely, but it's mostly grassland and river. The axial tilt is seventy degrees, so the seasons are insane, but you can get water and oxygen cheap. There are even some greenhouse-type places that grow food, so you won't starve. Small fishing fleet that follows the coast for more protein. Everything a small station could want."

Gavin tapped the display screen as he briefed Dirk, Dena, Scruggs, and Lee. Ana had taken some sleeping pills and was trying to sleep through his enforced itching period.

"No gas giant," Lee said. "Just rocky planets."

Gavin shrugged. "You can't have everything. You can land and process fuel, but have to do it quick. Thirty-five-day orbital period, so summer is a week. Winter's a week too, so you can wait it out and hope you don't freeze."

"Sixty feet of snow?" Dirk studied the specs. "In a week?"

"More like ten days. It piles up quickly."

"So you're either in a frozen arctic night being buried in snow for a week, or a blazing hot twenty-four-hour day, surrounded by giant floods pouring down from the melting snow."

"Got it in one," Gavin said. "Spring's nice, though. Comes on a Tuesday, usually. Standard terraforming package applied hundreds of years ago."

"Any crops?" Scruggs rubbed black grease into a belt on her lap. "Anything we can eat?"

Lee flicked through the display. "Cabbage and cauliflower. Lots of asparagus, kale, things like that. Things that can survive water. And most of the bugs are edible."

"I've never eaten a bug," Scruggs said.

Dena swallowed the glass of basic in front of her. "Yuck. And really? You haven't. You've eaten every other strange thing going."

"After you fed me that moldy cheese, I decided to try different things."

"Didn't you get decent cheese and food when you were growing up?"

"My mom was always on these health kicks. We got a lot of vegetables and grain stuff. It tasted okay."

"Well, knowing you and your weird palate, they'll probably become your favorite breakfast meal."

"I'll ask Centurion, he'll know how to eat bugs." Scruggs

rubbed more of the black grease into her belt. "Does that look dark enough to you?"

"Dark enough for what?"

"To hide. Before, you said that you could see me in the dark."

"Not see you, exactly." Dena traced her finger across the table. "More like a straight line where there shouldn't be a straight line. And a gleam where there shouldn't be. You need to blur the lines. I used to do that when I hunted in the woods."

"Centurion gave me this grease to work into the clothes. He says it darkens them and cuts down on the outline."

"Fine if you're in a dark forest. What if you're in a desert, or a red-tinged swamp?"

"Dunno." Scruggs shrugged. "But it gets dark everywhere, so this has to be good for nights. That makes it worth it."

"Speaking of worth it," Dirk said. "This shipyard sounds great. Good repair facilities, certainly enough to mount a laser on the ship. What about price?"

"They'll deal," Gavin said. "They'll take precious metals or trade, even Imperial credits."

"They'll take credits? Outstanding," Dirk said. "We can use the money Tribune Devin gave us rather than scrounging around. Or trade them some of that software."

"About that." Lee held up a cassette from the coding software they had found. "This needs to go back to the Tribune. Or at least one of his people. After we get the laser installed, we should track him down and drop it off."

"We don't know where he is."

"We can ask the other ships while we're here. This is the sort of place that asking where Imperial forces have been seen is reasonable, so people know where to avoid them."

"That's true enough," Gavin said. "They interact with Imperial ships a lot, so they could sell them software or trade them it. And the captains who call here will have some idea of where 'The Mad Dog of the Verge' has been operating."

"Is this a pirate base?" Scruggs rubbed black grease on a belt buckle. "I've never been to a pirate base. Even if I'm kind of on a pirate ship."

"Not a pirate base, no," Gavin said. "More of a free port than a pirate base. They've got a half dozen small cutters—custom-type cutters, but they're armed, so they don't put up with any nonsense. Fire on somebody and they'll swarm you."

"We could take a cutter in a fight," Dirk said.

"Yes, Pilot, if we had a laser," Lee said. "Which we don't, yet. But could we take six?"

"Good point." Dirk nodded. "So. They can do repairs. They can install a laser. We can pay. How long?"

"Don't know, but it's not the type of place that you book into a year in advance. Mostly you show up, say what you want, and find out then."

"And we can get supplies, fuel, water, and all this. What's this place called?"

"Casarubrum."

"Never heard of it," Dirk said. "Is it in the Verge?"

"Sort of," Gavin said. "Close enough for our purposes. It can do what we need, it's going to be fast, affordable, and it's within a couple of jumps."

"If it's so good, why haven't I heard of it?"

"It's a sketchy type of place, Skipper," Gavin said. "You don't see a lot of Imperial aristocrats there."

"Dirk is pretty sketchy these days," Dena said. "He'll fit right in."

"I'll need to keep a low profile," Gavin said. "There might be some people who know me, and if they remembered, there would be complications. I don't exactly want to be seen there."

"Why suggest it, then?"

"There's not guaranteed to be complications. The people I don't want to talk to aren't there all the time. If they are, I'll hide on the ship."

Dirk crossed his arms. "I should have heard of it, though."

"It's not in your regular orbit, Skipper."

"It's a full shipyard. You vouch for the quality?"

"I've had repairs done there before, Skipper. They do good work."

"And reasonable price?"

"I'll negotiate a good deal."

"Well, let's go, then. Anything else we need to know before we set a course?"

"Yes, Pilot," Lee said. "I looked up the co-ordinates that the engineer gave me. One other thing."

"That is?"

"It's a Nat naval base."

The discussion got heated enough that it woke Ana, so he climbed up to the lounge. Dirk, Lee, and Gavin huddled at a navigation display. Dirk was shaking his finger in Gavin's face.

Gavin was arguing back. Lee waved her hands from time to time to try to calm them down. Dena relaxed across the compartment on the bench next to Scruggs, sipping from another cup of basic, grimacing every time. Scruggs continued to rub grease onto her clothes.

"What's all the noise, Private?"

"The engineer wants us to go into Nat space and have our laser installed at a Nat naval base. Pilot is against it."

"Nat naval base? Which one?"

"Place called Casarubrum."

"Casarubrum." Ana snapped his fingers. "Of course. I should have thought of that myself. They have a tidy little shipyard there. But it's not a naval base. It's an independent world."

"You've been there?" Scruggs asked.

"I can neither confirm nor deny. Good progress on your grease, Private. Keep that up and you'll be invisible in the dark."

"Thank you, Centurion."

"And good deflection on not answering the question." Dena screwed up her mouth. "Emperor's thigh bones, Baby Marine, what did you put in the basic this week? It tastes like acid."

"That's because I put acid in it."

"That explains it." Dena sipped again and nearly gagged. "Why are you feeding us acid?"

"Vinegar," Scruggs said. "Acetic acid."

"Don't care what it's called. Why that?"

"You complained about some of the chemical tastes last time. I like vinegar, so I used it to mask the chemicals."

"Why vinegar? Why not sugar or something sweet?"

"Oh." Scruggs frowned. "Never thought of that. I like the tangy tastes."

Dena sipped again. "I don't. So, Old Man, truth, you ever been to this Casarubrum place?"

"I have."

"And is it a Nat naval base?"

"Not exactly. The Nat Navy uses it sometimes, but it's not Nat territory. It's a free port. The system is disputed between the Nats and the Confeds. Not worth fighting over, but neither wants the other to have it, so it's kind of a gray area in the middle."

"Like Papillon?" Papillon was the Verge world they and Devin's forces had been frequenting. It was at the end of several Imperial trade routes, the farthest out courier route into the Verge.

"Papillon is a free world, but since the Empire runs the starport, a lot of Imperial trade comes through there. Here, they are an entire free port. The locals handle everything themselves. A rough place."

"Rough?" Dena sipped again. "If you say it's rough… what does that mean?"

"Best to go in groups. Four would be good. And be armed. Obviously armed."

"Anything fun to do there?"

"Dancing, food, casinos, brothels, you name it, you got it."

"Maybe I'll finally be able to get Baby Marine laid."

Scruggs sputtered her drink out, then wiped her face. "I don't need your help with that."

"All evidence to the contrary." Ana turned as voices rose. "Has Navy taken to carrying a concealed revolver?"

Dena looked up. "He does have his hand near what could be a holster. I wonder who will draw the fastest? Dirk or Gavin?"

"Neither," Scruggs said. "Lee will beat them both."

Ana looked at the two women. "Twenty credits on the punk."

"I am not going to a Nat naval base, and that's final." Dirk reached for his revolver. Gavin made a grabbing motion, then his eyes widened, and he froze. Dirk unbuckled his holster, hidden under his shirt, but a slight breeze and a light tickle made him pause.

Dirk coughed. "Engineer?"

"Yes?"

"The navigator has her revolver out, doesn't she?"

"Yep."

"Pointed at my head?"

"Yep."

"Big gun?"

"Nope. Small. Fits in her hand."

"Big enough?"

"Absolutely."

"And if I draw, she'll probably shoot me before I can make it."

"You can ask her, but I'd guess yes."

"And why aren't you moving?"

"She's got two guns. One's pointed at your head, the other at mine."

"I'm going to snap my holster shut." Dirk clicked it closed. "And cross my arms on my chest. Engineer?"

Gavin raised his hands, palms out, ever so slowly. "Just going to keep my hands up here. Lee, we get your point."

Lee rolled the two small revolvers in her hands until they pointed at the roof. "I wasn't going to shoot you."

Ana stomped over and held out his hands. "Lee, can I have those back, please?"

Lee handed the two tiny revolvers to Ana. "You said I could borrow them."

"One of them. To practice with. Not to shoot..." Ana paused. "Well, I never said you couldn't shoot these two. But it might be inconvenient."

Dirk dropped his hands. "Killing us would be inconvenient. Well, we wouldn't want to inconvenience you, Centurion."

"Maybe. Nature Girl, I don't remember, who's on cleanup duty for the lounge this week?"

Dena jerked her thumb sideways. "Your girl here."

"In that case." Ana pocketed one gun, flipped the other up, and handed it, grip first, to Lee. "Feel free to shoot a crew member of your choice."

"I won't be shooting anybody. I only wanted to get their attention."

"Shooting somebody normally gets their attention."

"She could have yelled—" Dirk said.

"Shut up, Navy, you cost me twenty credits. I'll say,

Praetorian, that was a slick maneuver, the speed draw. Where did you learn that?"

"One of my uncles taught me," Lee said.

"Outstanding. Navy, why won't you go to a Nat Navy base? Casarubrum seems like a great place to get this laser thing fixed up."

"Remember the death warrant on me?"

"Death warrant is on Scruggs here," Ana pointed. "Not you. You're worth cash. And that's in the Empire anyways." Ana cocked his head. "Was that alive, or dead or alive?"

"The Confeds want me for crimes against humanity, remember?" Dirk had originally been sent to prison because of an incident at New Madrid, where he'd gotten hundreds of Imperial and Confed troops killed.

"This isn't the Confederation, it's the Union of Nations. And the Nats don't want you for anything, do they?"

"They have treaties with the Confeds. They might hand me over."

"We can keep you safe, Pilot," Scruggs said. "I'm not scared of the Nats."

"See?" Ana laughed. "Don't worry, Navy, Scruggs will keep the bad men from hurting you."

"And how would Scruggs fare against Confed regulars?" Dirk asked.

Scruggs glared. "As well as I did at New Oregon, against regular troops there. Or as well as I did against a wheeled self-propelled anti-tank gun, or kidnappers, or regular Imperial Navy troops, or Imperial Security operatives, or crazed insurance guards."

Dena laughed and tilted her head. "Normally, I don't see how a shoe would ever fit in Dirk's mouth, but then he goes and jams it in, proving me wrong."

"I'm sorry, Scruggs," Dirk said. "Of course you can take care of yourself. And me, if need be."

"I can more than take care of you." Scruggs glowered. "Thanks for the twenty credits, Dena, Centurion. Come on, Rocky, it's time for your treat."

Rocky the whippet's ears perked up at the word 'treat,' and he hustled to follow Scruggs to her room. Catching her glare, he turned to Dirk and bared his teeth, and growled as he left.

"I love that dog," Ana said. "Navy, we need a laser mounted. Casarubrum is relatively close, as I recall. Lee?"

Lee nodded. "Three jumps."

"Well, let's go get some weapons installed. Engineer can deal with his friends, Lee can be the pilot of record. Anything that needs to be done on station, Scruggs and I, or for that matter, Dena here, can provide security. You hide for a while if necessary. We didn't go to all this trouble to get this laser just to leave it in a box. A few weeks of relaxing, new weapons, and then we can finally head coreward to do some research for your Tribune friend."

"All right, but we need a different captain of record. Somebody has to be in charge. Somebody rough, tough, looks hard as nails."

"The navigator can—" Ana stopped.

Lee shook her head. "I couldn't pull it off, Centurion. I'm a medic, and, well, I'm not mean enough."

"Can't be me," Gavin said. "I'm known there as an engineer."

"I could do it. No, it has to be somebody who isn't Army, right?"

"You're too ground pounder," Gavin said. "Nobody would buy it. Army people don't command ships."

"Scruggs is too young," Dirk said.

Ana turned to Dena, and grinned.

Dena shuddered. "Stop that! Urgh. I told you, Old Man, that grin gives me nightmares."

"That's part of the attraction. Do you have any extra ammunition for that slingshot of yours?"

"Slugs? Of course, buckets of it, for practice."

"I wonder," Ana smiled, "what you'd look like in your leather outfit with crossed bandoleers."

CHAPTER TWENTY-NINE

"How did they catch us?" Kruder asked, sliding into his chair. "We've been jumping in the opposite direction for weeks."

"Clever, these Imperials," Fusterheim said.

The Pinguin had been doing its usual loafing along at the gas giant. This system and the last one they visited were well traveled, and merchant freighters turned over cargo quickly. He'd only stayed two days in the last system. Even if somebody saw him on both their inbound leg and outbound leg, he'd look like a refueling ship taking an extra day to conduct routine maintenance. He didn't dare stay longer in case any of the passing freighters reported his presence to the starport. In case they sent a ship to investigate, or worse, 'help.'

"What beacon are we showing?"

"Confederation beacon. St. Nicholas. Freighter," Comm Officer Tannen said.

"How close are we to the real specifications?"

Tannen shook her head. "Close enough to pass a cursory scan, Kapitan. But if they get close, we're in trouble."

"General quarters, stations for ship-to-ship combat. Do not decamouflage," Kruder ordered.

"We're being hailed," Tannen said. "'What ship' and 'state intentions'."

"Vonavitch to the control room—there you are. Your moment to shine, Vonavitch. You know what to do."

A short, swarthy rating climbed up from the hab module. He opened a locker and pulled out Confederation-style outfits. Thirty seconds later, all the bridge officers wore a Confederation merchant ship shirt, tunic, and hat, with red star prominently displayed. The Nat dark blue undershirts were sufficiently neutral-colored to not give away their origin. If the calling officers got a close look at their skinsuits, though, the game would be over. Confed skinsuits used totally different glove and boot fittings than Nat ones.

Vonavitch sat at a console in the middle of the control area and nodded to Kruder. "Ready, Kapitan."

"No talking except for Vonavitch from now on. All radios silent." Kruder gestured to Vonavitch.

Vonavitch slapped a control on his board. The main screen lit, the face of a black-haired man in an Imperial captain's uniform appeared.

"St. Nicholas, state your business in this sector," the man said.

Vonavitch answered, clearly, coldly, loudly, and in fluent Russe.

The man on the screen blinked. "Another one of those stupid peasants who don't speak Standard."

"I speak Standard good enough," Vonavitch said. He thickened his accent so he could barely be understood. "Understand better."

"Who are you, and what is your ship doing here?"

"I am Vonavitch, Captain, Confederation freighter St. Nicholas. Who is asking?"

"I am Captain Saxon. I command this warship. You are in Imperial Space."

"Not Imperial Space. This space protected by Confederation. And we are trading."

"Trading what?"

"Whatever we wish. You have no authority here. Free planets insystem decide what the trade is."

"Now it's free trade, is it?"

"We are Confederation-flagged merchant ship, we are trading here."

"Have you seen any other Imperial ships recently?"

"Many freighters. Peace-loving Confederation people encourage trading."

"Any warships? Imperial warships."

Vonavitch blinked. "I have seen many Imperial warships over the years. At your planets when I trade in."

"Any out here? Nearby?"

"Nearby?"

"Have you seen any warships that look like us?"

Vonavitch snarled. "Like you? Please to send specifications, we will check database."

"Never mind. Ross, speak to this man."

The main display on the bridge changed. A second man appeared, younger than the captain. He started speaking to Vonavitch in halting Russe. Vonavitch replied, increasing his speed until the other man was struggling to keep up. After several exchanges, Ross turned sideways on the screen and nodded. "Fluent, Captain. Better Russe than mine sir. Much better."

"Very well. Dismissed." Ross's face disappeared, but Saxon continued to glare at them. "We are seeking a rogue Imperial warship. You should be careful if you encounter any other Imperial warships. There are rumors of them attacking neutral ships."

"I have found best to always mistrust Imperial ships when I see them," Vonavitch said.

"Is that a fact?"

"Yes. I am mistrusting you right now, as fact."

"Careful what you say, Captain."

"We need no approval from you. No further questions, we wish you good day and good trading." Vonavitch turned to the comm operator, and made a cutting motion across his neck, but in such a way that the motion was visible to the camera. The comm operator waited a two count, then cut the channel.

Vonavitch's breath whooshed out.

"Well done, Vonavitch," Kruder said. "Arrogant, dismissive, everything a Confederation captain would be. Well done."

"We are being hailed again, Kapitan," the comm officer said. He pressed his earphones. "He sounds angry."

"Good, we want him angry, and not thinking. Helm, standard merchant course for the jump limit after our next orbit."

"Understood, Kapitan." The navigator and the helm officer conversed quietly.

"Sensors, tell me about that ship."

"Similar size as the frigate we saw before, Kapitan, but probably not the same ship. Slight differences in power signature."

Fusterheim exchanged glances with the Kapitan. "Two brand new Imperial frigates out here? That's a surprise."

Kruder leaned back in his chair. "That makes no sense. Are they scanning us?"

"Since they came out of jump, Kapitan, but nothing intrusive. They got a good look at us, externally at least, but no targeting radar yet."

"Can they see through the screens?" He meant the metal and fabric screens hiding the weapons.

"Unknown, but unlikely sir. Tests with our own systems indicated they would have to get closer to be sure."

"Keep us on course for the jump limit."

"Kapitan, that will bring us closer to them…"

"Can't be helped. Sensors, what are they doing?"

"Scanning heavily, Kapitan. Everything is firing off over there. But not targeted at us. They're bouncing radar all around the outer system. Looking for that other frigate, perhaps?"

"What's their course?"

"Station keeping outside the jump limit, Kapitan."

"Best guess when their scans can penetrate our disguise?"

The sensor operator played with his screens. "Half hour, Kapitan, perhaps. Forty-five minutes, at best."

"Helm, drop our speed... ten, no eight percent. Take it off a percent at a time, make it look like engineering is having efficiency problems, like with poor fuel, understand?"

"Got it, Kapitan."

"Kapitan," Fusterheim said. "Are you thinking of engaging her?"

"We can't run, and we can't hide for much longer if they stay there. Our other option is fight. What do you think, Hans?"

"I am forced to agree sir. We will give a good account of ourselves."

"We will."

Fusterheim whispered to Kruder, "Is it possible that they are our Imperial contact?"

"An Imperial warship? Why would a warship be involved in piracy? And they didn't use any of the code words, and why would they meet us here?"

"Not sure, but we're not that far from the co-ordinates we were given. Three jumps perhaps?"

"If things get desperate, I'll try our codes with them."

"They came out of nowhere."

"That is the benefit and the problem with wallowing along by the jump limit. Ships can appear at any time." Kruder drummed his fingers. "Still, it is curious the questions they asked. Vonavitch?"

Vonavitch waited at a spare console in case he was needed. "Kapitan?"

"How was that officer's Russe language skills?"

"Horrible, Kapitan. My four-year-old speaks better Russe."

"I thought there were good linguists in the Accursed Empire. Their Germanish speakers are excellent."

"I have spoken with many port captains and not a few customs officers in Russe in my time, Kapitan. Change the uniform and they could work in the Confederation with no problem."

"That good?"

"That good, Kapitan. And common. But not this one. If he was the best speaker they had onboard..."

"They didn't expect to be out here close to the other Empires...or to have to speak to Confed ships."

"Status change," the sensor operator interrupted. "Jump signature. Enemy vessel has left the system."

"Can you track them?" Kruder asked.

"Not even a general idea of direction, Kapitan. They're too far away, and we didn't have any active sensors on them."

"Very well. Navigation, take us to the jump limit and get us out of here."

"Sir." The navigator typed on their screen. "Destination, Kapitan?"

"We need to disappear for a while."

"We are running low on supplies, Kapitan," Fusterheim said. "We will soon need provisions."

"Good point. Hans, where can we go to hide while we load up some supplies?"

Fusterheim smiled. "I know a place. Helm, stand by for co-ordinates."

CHAPTER THIRTY

"I look amazing," Dena said. "Ask anybody. Ask me."

"Don't you think it's kind of... revealing?" Scruggs marched beside her.

"Yes. That's the point." Dena sashayed along the corridor. After docking, they called the construction manager's office and requested a meeting. Dena had dressed for the meeting. Over her skinsuit, she wore leather pants and crossed bandoleers of shotgun slugs. She even included a pouch of heavy ball-bearings for her slingshot, and a short leather jacket. Her skinsuit was tight and unzipped down her chest to show off her cleavage.

Ana dubbed this outfit 'Pirate Princess.'

"Aren't you cold?"

"Yes, that's the point too." Dena pulled her slingshot from its holster and spun it in her hands. Ana had adapted a thigh holster specially for her, and on her left hip, she had the biggest revolver in the ship. He'd told her if she shot it, to use both hands rested on a flat surface. Otherwise, she risked a broken wrist. "It keeps the boys focused somewhere else other than my gun hands."

"You do give off this 'don't mess with me' attitude," Ana said, trailing behind, his shotgun at the ready. "Very useful in this sort of work."

"I wish I looked like that," Scruggs said, sighing.

"Baby Marine." Dena pointed. "You're carrying that giant shotgun—"

"I need the heavy one for the recoil, and the barrel for accuracy."

"With that knife thing on your belt. Revolvers in a thigh holster, grenades clipped on, all that other belt pouch stuff—"

"I don't want to run out of ammunition," Scruggs said.

"And Jove knows what else is in your backpack. Which, with that new sludge or whatever you rubbed into it, now it looks like you just came in from a month in the jungle eating snakes and shooting prisoners."

"I've never tasted snake," Scruggs said.

"Ask Rocky, he'll get one for you."

"I'm not sure I give off the same... dangerous vibe you do."

Dena stopped again, folded her arms and considered. "What do you boys think?"

Gavin had been trooping along behind. "Well, the weapons fit the whole mercenary thing, but the freckles and the hair don't look the same way."

"What's wrong with my hair?"

"It's very... nice..." Gavin said.

"That means it looks horrible, and I agree with him," Dena said. "We need to put you in pigtails."

"Pigtails? Then I'll look like I'm even younger than I am now!"

"Exactly," Dena said. "Young, fresh-faced, and heavily armed. Cute but crazy." Dena grinned at the two men. "Cute but crazy. I like it."

Gavin laughed. "We have a new nickname. CBC."

Scruggs shook her head. "I don't like it. Don't call me that."

"Doesn't matter," Dena said. "You don't get to choose your own nickname. Right, Old Man?"

"That's the truth," Ana said. "Why, I was on an operation once, and they decided to call me... never mind. It wasn't flattering. Cute but Crazy it is."

"Don't call me that."

"The more you say that, Cute but Crazy, the more I'll call you that." Dena walked down the hall. "You know how it works. Let's get to these shipyard people."

"Lee, they're making fun of me," Scruggs said. Lee was behind the group, med kit evident, fiddling with something on her hip.

"You're big enough to handle it now, Sister Scruggs. Stab them with your metal stick thing."

"Bayonet. And I'm not sure how, exactly. I'm still practicing."

Ana shook his head. "I told you, Private, shotguns don't get bayonets."

"You said you'd never seen a shotgun with a bayonet, not that it wasn't possible, Centurion. I made a note."

"I'm sure you did." Ana drifted back until he walked next to Lee. "Well, Navigator? Status?"

After two short jumps, the Heart's Desire had coasted into the Casarubrum system. It was as Gavin had described. A small but functional shipyard orbiting the primary. When they approached the jump limit, they were met and scanned. Two cutters escorted them in. Four others orbited, leading and trailing the station. Two tugs shuffled containers between the station and a trailing container farm. Weapons tracked them as they sidled up.

The station design was a standard three-ring type. Spinning rings provided gravity, with one unusual addition. The central axis extended far beyond normal. At each end, a web of non-spinning struts with rails stretched out, forming two open hangars—dry docks—where a parked ship could be secured. Once locked in, mobile cranes and welders on rails could attach or detach pieces or open up hull plates to work inside a parked ship. An initial request for docking and a meeting had been answered with a slip and directions, but no more information.

Lee tapped the comm she had been fiddling with since they left the ship and shook her head. "Jamming. Can't talk to the ship. Or to each other. No comms to the station's system either. We're on our own."

"Best not get lost, then," Ana said.

"We won't. I'm making notes of what we pass."

"What's your assessment so far?"

"My assessment? You want a freak's assessment?"

"I haven't called you that in a long time, not since I found out you worked for the Empress. She's a sharp lady, and she only employs the best. Which means that I underestimated you. That embarrasses me, so I don't mention it. So yes, what do you think of this station?"

Lee looked left and right as they walked the ring. They had to move spinward from their lock to find the main spokes and a set of stairs wide enough for them to climb together. "Normal station. Regular offices. I saw a dentist a while back, and an electric motor repair shop. There's a snack bar." She pointed ahead. "They have a lunch special."

"Coffee and a cheese sandwich, three credits," Ana said. "What a deal."

Ahead of them, on the corner of the spoke stairs and the outer ring was a set of stools facing a window, with a small kitchen inside. Four crewmen in matching uniforms sat drinking tea. The uniforms were old but tidy. All four had the red star of the Confederation.

"Confederation crews in town," Ana said. "And we passed two Nat officers earlier. Nobody gave me a second glance. We could be in Imperial Core space."

"One thing is different," Lee said.

"What?"

Lee gestured at the Confeds as they passed. "Weapons. Everybody's armed."

The main construction office was on the last ring before the core transfer tubes. Spin gravity there was about one-third of normal. Low, but not uncomfortable.

Dena led the crew into the main office, and announced that they wanted to talk about maintenance, repairs, and installation, and that they had money. The clerk at the front desk, an over muscled, bearded gym rat who looked like he never missed an upper-body day, pointed to a line of chairs. He stepped into an inner office behind him, closing the door. When he stood, it was plain that he didn't miss leg days either.

"Yum," Dena said as he closed the door. "Think he wants to come see my starship?"

"I don't think that line will work on him," Scruggs said.

"Why not? It worked on me. Several times."

The silent clerk re-appeared, swung the interior door wide open, and gestured them in. He held it as all five filed by, then swung it shut behind them.

Inside was an executive office—wooden desk with fabric chairs, a conference table to one side, and a seating area. The random art on the wall impressed Dena with its style and variety, but would probably have been sneered at by Devin, or Dirk. The color combination was odd-green and yellow. Striking, but relaxing.

The woman who stood to meet them was old—gray hair, lined face, age spots. But she stood straight and extended her hand. "Keflavic. Station Construction Manager. You would be the crew of the Heart's Desire."

Dena checked for a second, then shook her head. "No, our ship is Heavyweight Items."

"Also known as Heart's Desire, in its original incarnation. But that's none of our business. Who are you?"

Dena introduced everyone, but only by position. Lee was the navigator and pilot, Gavin was the engineer, Ana and Scruggs were just their guards.

"I'm the captain."

"Kind of young, aren't you?"

"Do you care?"

"Do you have money?"

"Yes." Dena shoved a chip across the table.

"Then I don't care, no." Keflavic inserted the chip into a slot on her desk, read the result, and nodded. "You're responsible for your own security 'til the yard takes control, then it's on us. We'll give it back to you in the condition we got it from you, subject to your repairs. Which we'll discuss. Let's sit over here." She led the way to the conference table and sat. "Coffee? Tea? Something harder? I'm drinking wine."

"Wine, please," Dena said. Lee took wine as well, and the others ordered beers. Except Ana, who had his usual brandy.

Scruggs shook her head. "Do you have basic?"

"Sure. Citrus-based or vinegar-based?"

"There're different types!" Scruggs almost bounced in her seat. "Vinegar, please."

Keflavic's eyes tracked down Scruggs, inventoried the visible weapons, contrasted the youthful face, blanked her expression, and touched a button. Five seconds later, a different young man entered. He was the exact opposite of the muscled bruiser outside, slim, elegant, fine featured, extremely tall—taller even than Lee. He wore a cravat. Keflavic gave their order, and he disappeared. Dena's and Scruggs's eyes tracked him as he left. Even Lee watched.

"You're in luck," Keflavic said. "We've got a slot that opened up. We were supposed to do maintenance on a freighter, but he hasn't arrived, so the space is available. We're extremely busy, normally."

Gavin stirred. "Doesn't look that way. We saw two open slots when we arrived. That's half empty."

"One is the guy who didn't show up, the other is a replenishment job that didn't know exactly when they would be here, so they booked a big window. Paid in advance."

Lee stirred. "Have you had a lot of ships that were supposed to be here not show up? Go missing?"

Keflavic tilted her head. "Why do you ask? Do you know something?"

"Just rumors," Lee said. "Ships going missing."

"Ships go missing. Drive failures." Keflavic sat up. "But this is the second one in six months. More than usual. We haven't heard from them since. We kept their deposit."

"And the other freighter makes three."

"No." Keflavic shook her head. "We've dealt with that organization before. They're still coming, but they don't know their exact schedule, that's all."

"What type of freighter doesn't know its maintenance schedule?" Lee asked.

"The type that we don't ask questions to," Keflavic said. "As we won't ask to you."

The waiter-assistant re-appeared with a tray. He was accompanied by another man the same age, but a moderate build, handsome, with broad shoulders. The two men distributed the drinks and a bowl of snacks, then left the room without a word.

Dena watched them disappear, her eyes lingering on behinds. "None of your staff can talk?"

"I tell them to keep quiet," Keflavic said. "Young men's talk bores me."

"What if they have something important to say?"

Keflavic smiled at Dena. "Young lady, I don't hire them for their vocabulary."

"You don't—oh. Oh." Dena grinned. "Really?"

"I'm old, not dead. And everyone needs a hobby, and I don't like knitting very much."

"How old are you?"

"Not that's it's any of your business, but eighty-two this year."

"When I grow up." Dena leaned forward, very serious. "When I grow up, I want to be you."

Everyone laughed.

"Thanks. Now that the hospitality part is over, what do you want?"

Dena took a sip of wine. "This is marvelous. We want certain... items installed on our ship."

"Items?"

"Items that we may have acquired, somewhere, that..."

"Who did you acquire them from?"

"What?"

"You're Imperials. You're outside of your borders. There're plenty of good shipyards in the Empire, but they won't do certain things. This thing—you got it from one of three people. If I know who, I know what you got. And there's no need to be shy here."

"We can't tell you who—"

"Man with a big scar on his left cheek, petite woman with

a nice selection in skirts and leggings, or a middle-aged fat guy? The fat guy looks like somebody who issues permits for new fish farms."

Dena blinked again, then said. "I borrowed one of her skirts. It fits great."

"Cassandra. That will be ship weapons, then. A four-inch laser, for certainty."

"How do you know that?"

"Most common laser in Imperial Service. Easiest to steal."

Dena downed her wine. "You win. Yes."

"Nope."

"What?"

"Nope, can't do it."

"I thought you could do anything."

"Oh, we can do anything, install anything, and we're happy to take your money. But your ship is the problem. Not enough power."

Gavin interrupted. "We've got plenty of power."

"For a merchant ship, sure. Insystem drive, life support, anything electric like entertainment or computers, heat, all that. Even for jump. Not enough for lasers."

"We've never had a problem with power before."

"Do I need to explain?"

"Yes," Ana said. "You do. We've come a long way to talk to you. We were told you can do this, but now you're saying no without a reason. That sort of exposure could hurt your reputation. This place lives on its reputation."

Keflavic sipped her tea, then placed it carefully on the

table. "I'll play. Ever notice you can't jump whenever you want? That there's a delay?"

"The jump calculations take time," Lee said, sipping her drink. "You have to wait for them to be complete."

"And recharge. Jump drives have built-in capacitors. They charge up while you're driving along. It's automatic—you don't even notice it. The jump drive draws power 'til the capacitors are full, then fires it out to build the jump field, and start your jump space bubble moving."

Ana put his brandy down. "I know if we want to jump twice, we need to wait between jumps, but I thought that was the calculations, not the capacitors."

Keflavic tapped the table, which doubled as a display screen. A navigation diagram of the system appeared. "Calculations take time, yes. The better your computer, the faster it is, the faster those calculations are done. The easier the calculations, the faster they're done. That's why you keep a constant vector, or at least merchant ships do, to simplify the calculations."

Ana looked at Lee. Lee nodded. "It's true, Centurion, it often takes up to two hours for some merchant ships."

"Your jump calculations don't take that long," Ana said.

"I take some shortcuts. I pre-calculate potential massive objects between us and potential destinations."

Ana shook his head. "I don't get it."

Lee pointed at the display on the table. "From this system, there are... four places we could jump to."

"Okay."

"To jump to any of them, we'd have to get to the jump

limit. I guess which planets we'll be visiting, program in a theoretical jump point, and have the navigation system do a search for anything between us and our ultimate destination —outer planets, comets, rogue moons, brown dwarfs in deep space, rogue planets, anything. And I set the time frame to be anytime over the next month. That will take the navigation computer hours to produce a result."

"What's the use of that?"

"If it finds that there will be something in the way, then nothing, I need more data to plot a course when we finally leave. But if the navigation computer finds nothing in the way over the next month, when we do leave the system, I head for one of my pre-plotted points, and I can zero out that section of the calculations, which saves time." Lee shrugged. "In effect, I pre-calculate a couple hundred potential jumps, let the programs run for a couple days, and I have those numbers available when we do decide to go."

Keflavic slow-clapped. "Only the best military navigators do that, and only the best civilian ones. It's a lot of extra work. You must have been in the military or trained by some."

Lee sat silently and sipped her wine.

"Well, you're Jovian, so I think we all know where you got your training. But my point, before we found out what an excellent navigator you have, is that there are two limiting factors—how long it takes to do the calculations, and how long it takes to charge the capacitors for the jump drives. Normally, the calculations take so long, that the capacitors are fully charged and ready when we're done."

"What does this have to do with our laser?" Ana asked.

"Given the standard engines you have on this model, they'll take a long time to charge up a laser. By my calculation, you'll be able to fire your laser..." Keflavic played with some numbers on the screen. "Once every seven minutes. Do you want to spend a fortune installing a weapon you can only fire eight times an hour?"

CHAPTER THIRTY-ONE

"It's not worth it," Dirk said. "A laser that only works every ten minutes is no laser."

"Eight minutes," Scruggs said. "She said eight minutes."

"Once every ten minutes, once every eight minutes. Might as well be once an hour."

"It's not once an hour. It's once every eight minutes," Scruggs said. "If she'd meant every ten minutes, I'm sure she would have said it. She seemed like a precise lady."

The crew had returned to the Heart's Desire and briefed a scowling Dirk. After explaining Keflavic's math, Gavin had suggested they look at the devices in question.

"What's the point of that?" Ana asked.

"Get the exact model numbers of those capacitors and see how long it would take to charge them. We can look up the specs, or they might even be printed on the units themselves."

"And how's knowing that going to help us?"

"Just confirms what she said. She might be lying to us to drive up the price."

"Fine. You crawl around in an unheated container, and I'll watch and make helpful suggestions."

"Your suggestions aren't usually much help for me."

"Who said helpful for you? I have myself to look out for here. Never mind, let's go. Nature Girl, what the heck are you doing?"

Dena made finger pistols and pointed them at the crew. "Pew. Pew. I'm Pirate Captain Dena, the Scourge of the Spaceways. Do as I say, spacescum, or me and my trusty crew will blast you to smithereens."

"Laser cannons don't blast things to smithereens," Lee said. "They tend to burn through control lines, destroy thrusters, that sort of thing. Smaller pieces fall off, unless you hit the engines, then the whole ship blows up."

"I'll hit the engines, then."

"What's the point?" Dirk asked. "You blow up the engines, you blow up the whole ship. Nothing left to pirate."

"Spacescum?" Scruggs asked. "Is that us?"

"No, you five would be my trustworthy..." Dena looked at the group. "Well, untrustworthy... you know, maybe I'll just hire new crew."

"High standards, Miss Scourge of the Spaceways has, indeed." Ana said. "For your new crew. I'm sure that we wouldn't meet them, regardless. Let's get this over with. Engineer, lead the way to this container of wonders."

"Standards. Hmmm." Dena tapped her chin as they walked. "For the crew. Need to have high standards."

"Education," Scruggs said. "That would be important."

"And experience too," Lee said. "If you're going to be a pirate queen, you'll need experience."

"Tight butts," Dena said. "They'll have to look good in the uniform. Like Ms. Keflavic had for her boys. Tight pants. Tooled leather belt. Some sort of open shirt."

Ana called back, "Open shirts don't work with skinsuits, Nature Girl."

"Shut up, Old Man. All I want is a crew with tight butts. No need to ruin it for me."

"How about me?" Ana stopped and cocked a hip. "Would I meet your criteria?"

"And now it's ruined." Dena sighed. "All I want is a bunch of hot young things, athletic, who like to work out a lot, very fit, look good in tight clothes."

Lee laughed. "Only person who meets those criteria is Sister Scruggs."

Scruggs blushed. "Don't say that."

They arrived at the first container truss alcove. Gavin brought up the displays on the environment connections. "Scruggs, can you open the access panel, please? Check the connections inside before I open up, make sure we don't lose our atmo while we're in there."

Scruggs unlocked a wall panel and bent inside to trace the wires.

Dena watched as Scruggs bent into the wall. "I'm more looking for a male version of her. But I will say she looks fine in that skinsuit. What do you all think?"

All the men looked. Dirk and Gavin smiled. Ana shook his

head but nodded once. Even Lee gave her a once over, in an academic sort of way.

Scruggs pulled herself out. Her face was bright scarlet. "Stop looking at my butt."

"Why?" Dena asked. "It's a great butt. You should be proud of it. Much better family trait to have than, say, double-jointed thumbs."

"Don't make fun of me. Centurion!"

"Private," Ana said. "As I've mentioned before, were I fifty years younger, single, and not your boss, we'd be having a different conversation. But as I am none of those things, my suggestion is enjoy it while you can. But you don't have to take any guff from these three."

Dirk and Gavin were grinning now. "It really is extraordinary. Cute."

Scruggs put her hands on her hips. "Cute? Like in cute but crazy?"

"Well, yes."

"Fine." Scruggs slapped her own butt. "Here's the cute. Everyone thinks that's cute."

The men nodded.

"It is," Dena said. "And now that I think about it, body style is usually a family trait. Scruggs, do you have any brothers?"

"Brothers?"

"Yeah. Brothers. If you do, maybe you could introduce me." Dena waved her hand. "Think they'd like to be the scourge of the spaceways, work with the pirate queen Dena? I'd provide cool uniforms."

"I have sisters."

"Too bad. Are they crazy like you?"

Scruggs ignored Dena and turned and bent to give them a better view. "Enjoy the cute, because now you hear the crazy. You make one more comment, and I'm going to go get my shotgun with bayonet and pull your guts out, like Centurion taught me."

"Absolutely not, Private." Ana shook his head. "You will not do that, understand me?"

Scruggs nodded. "Yes, Centurion. Sorry, Centurion. I won't hurt them."

"Don't hurt them?" Ana shook his head. "I didn't say that. I said don't stab them with a bayonet on a shotgun."

"Because you don't want her to hurt us?" Dirk asked.

"No." Ana shook his head again. "Because that's an inappropriate weapon to use in close quarters like this. Difficult enough to maneuver a shotgun in a hallway, even a short one. Add a bayonet and you'll keep bumping into things. No, Private. Take the bayonet off the shotgun and use it to stab like I taught you."

"With the swords?"

"Yes. Thrust, step back. Thrust, step back. Repeat." Ana demonstrated, stamping his right leg forward and pushing with his right arm, then stepping back. "You set your left foot, then you can pivot forward and back, but it's better if you can step, but there's not always enough room. This way, you don't have to worry about banging into water pipes or anything like that."

"That's good advice, Centurion."

"Mine always is."

"Say, Scruggs," Dena broke in. "No brothers, but do you have any cousins? Male cousins?"

Ana ignored her. "When was the last time you practiced with swords?"

"Not for weeks, Centurion."

"Exactly. Where is your bayonet? Is it already disconnected?"

"I put it on the rack in my room. I haven't found anybody to use it on."

"Well, we can fix that right now. Turn around." Ana twiddled his hands, and Scruggs spun so she had her back to all of them.

"Like this, Centurion?" Scruggs glared at the men. "They're looking at my butt."

"Outstanding. But that's the point. Time for some practice. You need some motivation to stab somebody. So, who wants to go first? Say something about her appearance. First one to jump in, Private Scruggs will take you on."

Dirk and Gavin shut up.

"What, no comments? Are you going to deny this young lady her sword practice?"

"That's crazy talk, Centurion," Dirk said.

"Of course it is. And I believe, since we're calling her crazy, we've all decided she's just the lady to do it. Private, go get your bayonet. And bring your shotgun, just in case."

"Yes, Centurion." Scruggs ran off.

Ana crossed his arms and waited. Everybody stared at him.

Finally, Dena said, "You are one freaky psycho killer guy, you know that? Always talking about killing people."

"Everybody needs a hobby. You always talk about sleeping with the men you meet."

"I enjoy that."

"I enjoy my thing too."

"Killing people? Why did you pick that to enjoy?"

Ana shrugged. "I didn't. I just discovered it. Can you control what you like? Or did you just find out that you liked it? Did you get up one day and say, I think I'll start to like tormenting men? Or did it just happen?"

Dena laughed. "It happened."

"I found out I like fighting, and shooting, and nearly getting killed. The killing is part of it, it can't be separated. I like excitement. You like excitement too. So does the navigator. She might not like violence, but she could have stayed back in Jovian school modifying trade route reports if she wanted. The engineer could have stayed home, wherever that is, and fixed backup diesel generators his whole life. He didn't. We're out here because we find it exciting, and we like the excitement. Oh, we like other things, like sleeping with men, or math, or machines, or violence. But mostly, we don't want to be bored."

"I'll agree with that," Dena said. "On a general level. For most of us. But what about Scruggs? She's still a kid."

Ana nodded. "She might be crazy. It's possible. She might be psychotic, and like killing people, that's possible too. Boredom is part of it. But I think it has more to do with ruthlessness. She's related to some super rich guy. He probably didn't get to be that rich by being nice to everyone he met. She's got some of that, and she's been suppressing it for a long time."

"She's shy," Dena said.

"She's embarrassed, different thing," Ana said. "She knows what she wants, but she's been taught that she should be embarrassed for wanting it. Once she figures that out, she'll sort her priorities out pretty quickly, and move on to what she really wants."

"You're a psychologist now, are you?" Dena asked.

"Just old. I've seen a lot, and I have a lot of older friends. Nothings sadder than people who never did what they want, not even once before they die."

"Very interesting."

"Not as interesting as trying to get this laser thing working. Engineer, if I were you, I'd get those measurements or part numbers or what have you now, before you have to explain things to a lady with a bayonet."

"You won't let her stab us."

"No, no, I won't." Ana smiled. "Not 'til after this laser is up and working, at least."

There were no stabbings. But Scruggs did bring her bayonet back, and after having her practice with it, Ana also showed her how to use the sheath and the knife as a wire cutter.

"Fit it over the notch like this." Ana demonstrated. "Put the wire in this slot at the end of the sheath, and you use the reverse side of the bayonet to clip it. Watch your hands."

Scruggs snapped the wires holding the crate together, then used the bayonet to pry another box open, which was the real reason Ana had sent her for it. After checking the life support connections, Gavin threw the container door wide open and brought in a portable heat and light unit. He and Dirk ransacked one crate and were muttering over the contents. Lee stood next to them, looking part numbers up on her comm.

"Very versatile knife," Dena said, hanging with Scruggs and Ana. "I should get one."

"You'll need a belt fitting, and a sheath too," Scruggs said. "But I've got another one. You can try mine."

Ana laughed. "Look at you two girls. Sharing stuff. Next thing you know, you'll be sharing fuzzy sweaters and complaining about stretching them."

"I have some great fuzzy sweaters, Old Man," Dena said. "I look great in them. And I'll bet Cute but Crazy here will look good in them too."

"I'm a girl, Centurion," Scruggs said. "I can wear fuzzy sweaters if I want to."

Ana looked at Scruggs, then at Dena. "So you can. Of course, you can. Carry on."

Scruggs and Dena exchanged grins. Ana went in and poked around inside an open crate.

"Ha!" Everyone jumped when Dirk yelled. "I knew Cassandra wouldn't let me down."

"I think, Navy." Ana stood and rubbed his back. Bending over that long hurt. "That the discussions were more focused on you letting her down, rather than the other way."

"Tell 'em what we found, Lee."

Lee held up her comm. "Targeting radar."

"We knew it came with a targeting radar, otherwise, we couldn't hit things."

"A very good targeting radar. Total military-grade, with its own phased array. We don't have to worry about pointing them, or anything like that. Install them on the ship and we'll get almost three-sixty squared views."

"Almost?"

"We're not built like a warship, so the panels won't overlap properly, so there will be some gaps, but it's an excellent system. I trained on it with my navigation—I can show you how to use it."

"Outstanding," Ana said. "Having a decent radar is worthwhile. What about the laser itself?"

"There's a laser here, in the other container. This one has capacitors." Gavin pointed at one crate. "They're big capacitors. And Lee and I looked up the recharge rate. Ms. Keflavic was right—it will take a long time to charge up a capacitor."

"We get a shot every ten minutes, not much use," Ana said.

"Yes, but these capacitors are bigger than the ones she mentioned. And more efficient."

"They charge faster?"

"Nope. Slower. Well, slower for us, at our power output. But they hold more power."

"More power means bigger shots?"

"In theory, if the laser can handle it. Or more smaller ones. And if I'm reading this manifest right, there's eight of them. Not the main and backup that a laser usually has."

"Spell it out," Ana said.

"We need to charge up for two hours. But once we do, we'll get ten full power shots before we have to recharge."

"Ten full power shots?"

"You bet."

"Outstanding." Ana slapped the ship's hull. "I'll finally be back on a warship."

CHAPTER THIRTY-TWO

"Hard dock, Kapitan. The magnets are all green." Spieler, the Pinguin's helmsman, threw up pictures of the four docking spars the ship had mated to. "Deck crew is asking permission to attach the chains."

"Yes. Proceed. Once we are chained, the watch is released, except those assigned to anchor watch." Kruder stood and brushed dust off his outfit and pulled his cap on. "Hans, are we ready?"

"We are, Kapitan," First Officer Fusterheim said. "We will commence with the maintenance and loading and locate our detached crew." The prize crews from captured ships had been instructed to return to Casarubrum and await the Pinguin. This was the only port that Kruder could guarantee he would return to on any sort of schedule.

"Locate? How many are there here?"

"None appears to be in transient housing. At least none have responded yet."

"None? That is a surprise. When did you send your messages?"

"Right after you commed the station, Kapitan."

"Hours ago."

"Yes. Probably they are roistering in the local bars, Kapitan. I will locate them and punish them appropriately."

Kruder locked eyes with Fusterheim. None responding? Even the drunkest sailors would keep one of their group sober enough to respond to a recall.

Fusterheim's eyes drifted to Blomberg, seated at his console, then back to Kruder. He shook his head minutely.

Kruder nodded. Hans thinks something bad is going on, and he doesn't trust Blomberg to hear it. "Very well. Carry on. Anything else?"

"One new problem."

"What now?"

Fusterheim waved four other bridge officers to stand beside him. All wore gray merchant coveralls and standard skinsuits. The suits sported departmental shoulder patches and merchant rank badges. The three men and two women all shared looks then grinned at the captain.

Kruder narrowed his eyes. "Are you all ready to proceed?"

"Indeed sir. We stand ready."

"Then what is the holdup?" Kruder asked.

Fusterheim stared at Kruder's feet, ran his eyes up to Kruder's face and made a 'what about that' gesture.

Kruder looked down, realized he wore shined boots, bloused pants, and the full uniform of a Union Korvettenkapitan. "Faugh. This will not do. I must change. The management here is prickly about their prerogative. They will be unhappy if we are all late for our meeting. Do not wait for me, Hans."

"As the Kapitan wishes, of course."

"I will catch up with you."

"We leave now, Kapitan. Who will be your escort?"

"My what?"

"Standing orders, an officer of your rank cannot leave the ship alone. Not at this station. You must have an escort, or at least a companion. An armed companion."

"I do not need a guard."

"Regulations, Kapitan. I and Katerine are both armed." Fusterheim pointed to his belt holster. Katerine, the logistics officer, tapped her holster. "You must have an armed escort."

"The crew are busy preparing for the maintenance. We'd need to get a weapon issued, and find somebody who is currently qualified, and wearing proper clothes. I should not bother them."

Blomberg stood and braced to attention. "If it pleases the Kapitan, I am rated expert with a pistol. I can easily sign out a weapon while the Kapitan changes his uniform."

"The quartermaster is otherwise employed. You cannot acquire a weapon."

Kruder glared at him. "You have other duties to perform, Leutnant."

"I am unaware of them sir. And as the Kapitan has released the watch, I have no further duties on the bridge, and the first officer had not assigned me other tasks."

Kruder turned to Fusterheim and raised his eyebrows. "He did not, did he?"

Fusterheim shook his head.

"And sir?"

"Yes, Leutnant?"

"I am already correctly dressed for a station visit at this station." Blomberg wore a standard coverall, with a single rank stripe, and a generic deck division logo on his breast.

"Already dressed. Yes, you are. Were you planning on visiting the station, Leutnant?"

"Hoping, Kapitan."

"Hoping? This is an isolated repair station, Leutnant. Nothing to see here. You'll be lucky to get a hot meal. Why do you want to visit here?"

"Kapitan. This is my first tour outside the borders of the Union. You were a young officer once on your first foreign cruise. Surely you remember your first visit to a strange place? New sights, new people. Does it not bring back memories?"

Fusterheim smothered a chortle. Three of the officers with him wore broad smiles. Katerine, the logician, chuckled. "Indeed, Kapitan, your first off-Union trip was quite memorable, is that not so?"

Fusterheim laughed. Kruder glared at him, then at Blomberg, and then back at Fusterheim. "Hans, this is unseemly."

"Now or then, Kapitan. Unseemly? It surely was, at the time."

Now all the officers except Blomberg broke out laughing, and Kruder grinned and hid his face for a moment. Blomberg stood at attention, his eyes darting around.

Fusterheim collected himself and wiped tears from his eyes. "Time presses, Kapitan."

Kruder grinned. "It does. It does. Leutnant, acquire your weapon and wait for me here. Hans, you will have to hurry. I will change and catch up."

CHAPTER THIRTY-THREE

"Pew Pew Pew, I'm Dena, Scourge of the Spaceways!" Dena made a finger gun and banged away at every light fixture in the corridor.

"Please stop that," Ana said. "It makes you look like an idiot." He and Dena waited outside Keflavic's outer office while Dirk and Scruggs delivered the final payment for the work. They watched the corridors for potential ambushes or trouble following them. Scruggs said that Dirk and the money needed an escort. A guard would make him look more important, and she'd keep a close eye on both.

Dena suggested that Scruggs keep a close eye on Keflavic's young male assistants. "Never know what they could be hiding under those pants. Make 'em take them off to check."

Scruggs blushed.

After initial fights and a lot of 'we don't promise this' and 'not sure about that,' along with a liberal application of the Tribune's money, they now had a brand-new ventral laser installed directly below engineering. Keflavic's small but efficient repair crew had mounted it parallel to the ship's long axis, disguised as an extra-large fuel scoop. The eight capacitors were hidden in two different containers and fitted with control lines and sensors.

Dena pointed at another fixture. "Maybe I like being an idiot."

"Even you couldn't possibly want to be that much of an idiot."

"Do you know what an otter is?"

Ana rolled his eyes. "Is it some sort of stupid house pet you kept on Blackrock, and it was cute and cuddly and fun, and you miss it so much it makes you cry?"

"It's like a cat that swims in rivers. You can train them, yes. And they are cute. But you don't get it." Dena pointed at Ana. "Look at you. Military outfit, weapons ready, harness with Jove knows what in those pouches. Looks scary."

"Because I am scary."

"And old clothes, makes you look poor and miserable."

"That's because I am poor and miserable. But I like it that way, at least the miserable part. Keeps me sharp. Lets me focus my rage."

"When somebody sees you, they see this miserable career soldier who would sooner shoot you than talk to you."

"Talking is overrated. Shooting is underrated."

"Now look at me." Dena did a twirl, her jacket tails flaring out. "What do you see?"

Ana looked her up and down. "A shallow idiot who cares more for clothes than personal defense. An overdressed party girl."

"Not very threatening, am I?"

"Nope. Do you have a point?"

Dena held up her slingshot. "How about you stand still, and I'll slam one of these into your forehead? You're all about weapons. Think that will hurt?"

Ana grunted. "Try to shoot me with that and you'll regret it."

"Is it a decent weapon? Yes or no?"

Ana nodded. "It's effective at short range. Almost as effective as a firearm, and easier to conceal, and not as noticeable. Easy to repair. Ammunition is cheap. Good rate of fire in skilled hands. The only issue is short range, and the need to have some distance between you and the attacker."

"Neither of which is a problem on a spaceship, or a station. And I'm smaller and quicker than most men, I can get a shot off before they close. I'm not letting somebody bigger get too close without a good reason. If they can get hands on me, it's over for me."

Ana looked at her with new respect. She knows how to use what she has. "That's actually an intelligent assessment of your strengths and weaknesses."

"A river otter," Dena flicked her sling, "is small, furry, cute, and kind of goofy. Doesn't look threatening at all. Flops around in rivers, makes people laugh. Easy to underestimate. But you get too close, it's got big teeth, and claws, and it'll chew your hand off and run away with it before you can react. You learn quick not to mess with happy, smiling otters."

"You saying that you're a fur-covered aquatic mammal?"

"I'm saying, that in a fight, the first shots will be fired at you, and while you're busily fending off four big guys with sticks who are beating your head, I'm standing back picking them off with rocks."

"Huh," Ana said.

"See?" Dena smiled "I'm smarter than I look."

"You'd almost have to be, really," Ana said.

Dena stuck her tongue out. "Well, I don't care what you think. I'm single, rich—well not rich, but we have some money—we've got a spaceship, a laser, and this new jacket!" She spun in place and her new thigh-length leather jacket spun out. "The world is our oyster!"

"Do you even know what an oyster is?" Ana grunted.

"Some sort of fish, right?" Dena said.

"Mollusk," Dirk said, exiting the office with Scruggs behind. Dirk had been keeping a low profile but had to come because his thumbprint was needed on the chips. Ana's suggestion of bringing only Dirk's thumb, rather than the whole Dirk, had been voted down.

Barely.

"And up your Imperial mollusk as well. Mollusk yourself." Dena twirled her hands. "Pew. Pew. Watch out, Pirate Queen Dena is coming for you."

"A mollusk," Dirk said, "is a type of shellfish."

"Fish with shells? How do they swim?"

"They don't swim."

"They why are they called fish?"

"That's a good question, Nature Girl. But it will have to remain one of life's mysteries." Ana pointed at a box under Dirk's arm. "Is that for me?"

"For all of us. Amiens Brandy. A parting gift from Keflavic. She's doing a final debrief with her crew now. She needs all her staff for some big job on an arriving ship. Mollusks. Didn't you have them on Rockhaul, where you grew up?"

"Don't remember any. They weren't part of the terraforming package that we got. We had oceans, and lots of fish, but I don't remember that. Something about the salinity in the ocean, type of salts or something that made things difficult."

"That's too bad. They're supposed to be aphrodisiacs. Turn here for that chandler."

"What type of ship is coming in?" Ana asked.

"Big freighter. Taking the slot next to us. Keflavic says all her logistics people will be busy, so if we need anything else, we have to load ourselves. We're paid up 'til the next shift, after that, she charges. We should get out of here."

The group assembled and headed down the corridor. Dirk was the only one not visibly armed, but close inspection would have noted a bulge near his belt in the small of his back. Dena had her slingshot on her belt, and the giant, low-slung revolver on her hip. Ana carried his shotgun at port arms.

The group turned left and spotted Lee and Gavin coming in from a side corridor. Keflavic's dockyard security was always strict—armed guards at air locks, and only the six of them plus necessary repair techs were permitted access. Even Ana had admitted the ship was more secure than a warship at an Imperial base, so they'd taken an opportunity to visit the station and do some shopping.

"Hey, Cute-but-Crazy—what do you think?" Dena spun and let her jacket flare out. "Pretty nifty!"

Scruggs had given up complaining about her new nickname after Dena promised to help her dress the part. Dena had done Scruggs's hair in a coiled, braided ponytail. Scruggs fed her braid through a ballcap and down her back and bought a shorter jacket. "Outstanding. I like it."

"Need to get you one," Dena said. "Lee? Want to go shopping with me?"

Lee laughed. She had a box labeled with a green cross under her arm. "We're not exactly the same size, friend Dena." Lee's tall, lithe body was a complete contrast to Dena's shorter, curvier frame.

"The fun is in the seeking, not the finding."

"Wish that applied to parts and supplies." Gavin pushed a borrowed handcart of boxes and bags. Even a small ship needed a steady stream of filters, chemicals, cleaning agents and personal items, not including food and water in quantity. "Got a deal on toothpaste—so I bought thirty-two tubes of it."

"Not that wretched mint stuff you had before?" Dirk plopped his box onto the cart.

"The same. Great price and cleans the best."

"Tastes like mint-flavored ass," Dena said.

"Better than regular ass," Gavin said.

Everybody laughed and slid into a formation. Two weeks at the same station, with their ship securely guarded, and plenty of decent station food and booze had dropped the crew's stress level. They were more relaxed than they had been for weeks. But relaxed didn't mean clueless. The clandestine repair station wasn't dangerous, exactly, but there were a lot of weapons, alcohol, and visiting crew roaming around who could be boisterous. The staff were clear—disputes between ship's crews were to be settled between them, and they wouldn't intervene.

Ana placed himself first, shotgun at port arms. Dena and Dirk came next, Dirk fussing with his comm, Dena keeping her hands free. Gavin pushed the cart in the middle, and Lee lugged her box of medical supplies behind him. Scruggs brought up the rear, shotgun at low port.

"Navigator," Dirk said, "we can still hold back some payment. I want to make sure you're happy with the software integration."

The Heart's Desire now had two radars. Scanning, for navigation and courses, and targeting for the laser. They installed the navigation radar at different points on the ship, and even managed to link it to the navigation computer. They now had a full 360 x 360 view of the space around them, but would light up every radar detector in the system.

"Like I mentioned before, Pilot," Lee groaned. She'd made this point several times. "It's not integrated. The scanning radar will give us an updated course to the target, but we have to manually spin the ship onto that heading to point the laser. It can calculate drift and so on, but we can't feed course directions back in."

"Blah blah blah blah," Dena said. "Speak standard."

"When we want to shoot something," Lee said, "we turn the navigation radar on. It tells us where to point the ship. We pivot the ship and point in that direction. Then turn on the targeting radar, then wait."

"Sounds pretty ineffective," Dena said.

"Best we could do. We're a freighter, not a warship. We can hit things that are close, that are slow, or that are chasing us. Provided we turn to fire at them."

"Outstanding." Ana grinned. "Just having something that will shoot back makes my heart warm."

"That grin makes me shiver," Dena said. "Heads up. Company."

The corridor was wide enough for two to walk abreast, but with the cart, the group would need anyone approaching to press against the wall. Ahead of them was a group of merchant ship's crew, in spiffy uniforms. They angled to the side as the Heart's Desire's crew approached.

"Nice clothes," Dirk said. "Confed trading uniforms."

"Dirk," Dena said. "Those uniforms are brand new. And clean. And starched. And ironed. Nobody has uniforms like that."

"Noted." Dirk's hand drifted to his belt. "Ana, they... walk differently. Like I did when I was on duty."

Ana's hands twitched. He still held his shotgun at port arms, but his finger was now on the trigger. "They're Nats. Pretending to be Confeds. I recognize the skinsuit fittings. Scruggs. Contact front."

Scruggs wasn't as subtle as Ana. Her shotgun came up and she stepped sideways to clear the group to her front and moved up. Ana stepped right. Dirk and Dena reached for weapons. Gavin handed the cart off to Lee and pulled a wrench from his tool belt. Lee dropped the med kit on the cart and took over pushing.

The approaching Nats detected the movement. Three with holstered weapons moved to the front, the others trailed behind. None of them slowed down.

The two groups moved down the hall. Three meters before a collision, Ana stopped and held up his left hand, palm forward. The Heart's Desire crew paused. The leading Nat officer copied Ana's gesture, and his group halted as well.

"Stand aside," the Nat officer said.

"No," Ana said. "You go back the other way."

"That is not convenient for us."

"Don't care," Ana said. "I'm not turning my back on you, and I'm not letting your people get in close. I don't like the look of them."

"I could say the same about you. You don't look particularly trustworthy." The leading Nat looked down at Scruggs's shotgun. "Are you going to try to shoot someone with your shotgun, little girl?"

Scruggs grinned. "Maybe. Do you know anybody needs to be shot?"

"Many people, but I will restrain myself." He looked over at Dena. "Nice jacket."

"Thanks, I got it today." Dena's right hand stayed at her side, concealing her loaded slingshot. "Shows off my shoulders, don't you think."

"Yes." The Nat nodded. "Very good quality. Double-stitched seams. Inset pockets."

"Yep." Dena nodded. "You some sort of tailor?"

"My father was. He knew clothes. He made some jackets like that for me. But yours is different than mine."

"That a fact? How is mine different?"

"You've got a slit so you can load your slingshot and hold it ready, then pull it up without catching in the lining. Great weapons for a station, slingshots. Disabling if you can put a shot on target, but with no danger of blowing out view ports or anything important. I'm more wary of that than the shotgun."

Dena rotated her hands. Now she gripped the slingshot in front of her, a metal ball-bearing in the pouch, the rubber band extended. She only had to lift, aim, and release, and somebody would have a very bad day.

Both sides milled for advantage. Hands hovered near weapons. Hands on weapons tightened or drifted to triggers. Gavin gripped his wrench—one of the Nats had one as well. Everybody tensed, waiting.

"What happens now, then?" Ana asked. "We need to get to our ship. We don't want a fight, but we're not backing up."

"The same with us," the Nat officer said. "We have business to take care of, and no time for recreation. You should back up."

"Not in the cards. Say!" Ana snapped his fingers. "That's it. We could cut cards. What do you say to that?"

"What is going on!" A new voice entered the fray. A man in a similar uniform, with a captain's stripes, arrived behind the Nats. "Let me by."

The Nats shifted as Kapitan Felix Kruder shoved through. "Imperials," Kruder said. "I should have known."

"They want to cut cards for passage, Kapitan."

"You want to cut cards. Well, that is not a problem. We

will do so, high card goes forward, in victory, low card must retreat in disgrace. What do you say?"

Ana looked at the newcomer. "There's no way we are cutting any of your cards. Three stripes. A Korvettenkapitan, no less."

"Indeed." Kruder put his hands on his hips. "And what rank are you now?"

"Senior Centurion, before my... retirement."

"Retirement? Did you kill somebody?"

"Several somebodies." Ana removed his hand from the trigger of his shotgun. "But I only shoot people who deserve it."

"You haven't shot me."

"You didn't deserve it. Yet." Ana grinned. "Hello, Felix."

"Hello, Anastasios. It's good to see you again."

The two men embraced while the crews goggled.

CHAPTER THIRTY-FOUR

"First Centurion," Dirk asked. "You know this man?"

"Felix and I go way back," Ana said.

"That is Kapitan Kruder to you," a young Nat officer in the back said, glaring at Ana.

"It's alright, Leutnant Blomberg." Kruder waved his hand. "Anastasios and I were on the same ship for a while."

"Felix was the captain, and I commanded the Marine contingent," Ana said. "A long time ago. Good times."

"Imperial Marines?" Dirk asked.

"No."

Dirk surveyed the bemused Nat crew members in front of him. "Union of Nations naval landing forces?"

"No."

"If not the Union, or the Empire…" Dirk said.

"It was a… private endeavor," Kruder said. "Nothing official, but my superiors knew where I was, as did the Senior Centurion's, I suspect. And you are who?"

"I'm the pilot." Dirk said. "This is our crew. Heavyweight Items is our ship."

"That highly modified freighter they are finishing buttoning up in the slip next to us," Kruder said. "An unusual configuration. And Imperial registration. Strange to see one such as you out here, nearly in Union of Nations space."

"You're that giant container freighter next to us," Lee said. "I saw you coming from the outer system. Your beacon says the Earl of Clydebank. Your Imperial beacon."

"The Earl of Clydebank, yes."

"Strange to see such a big ship out here," Lee said. "In a tiny starport, a tiny repair port. I'd expect you to be at one of the major shipyards. One of the major shipyards well within Union of Nations space. Not an unaligned station on the border of the Confederation. With an obviously fake beacon."

Kruder smiled. "We get a good price here. They give us a discount for quality."

"We pay almost twice as much for supplies here," Lee said.

"So will we, but we'll make it up on volume," Kruder said.

"That makes no sense," Lee said. "You're all Nats. Why is your ship showing an Imperial beacon?"

"It's rude to ask too many questions."

Blomberg had been fiddling with his comm. "Kapitan."

"Not now, Blomberg."

"But, Kapitan, we don't have—"

"Comms, I know. This station blocks unauthorized internal traffic. Which ours surely is. Anastasios, I didn't recognize you. Have you lost weight?"

Ana spread his hands. "Just all my clean living. You look the same."

"I don't feel the same." Kruder grimaced. "I feel very old, some days. Ana, it is wonderful to see you. It reminds me of good times. But I have business."

"Of course you do." Ana nodded. "As do I."

Kruder clapped Ana on the shoulder. "What did you say? Free Trades, wasn't it?"

Ana laughed. "I don't do that anymore. Now it's 'The Empire,' but thanks. Keep your chin up."

"You too." Kruder spoke to his crew. "We will be about our business. Stand aside and leave these Imperials be. We have no quarrel with them."

"Kapitan," Blomberg said. He switched from Standard to Germanish. "We cannot let them go. We must seize them. Our mission, and the possibility—"

"First, do not question my orders. Second, we have business with the station authorities here, and they do not look kindly to us interfering with their other visitors. And third, and most important..." Kruder grimaced at Ana.

"Third," Ana said, switching from Standard to Germanish, "I understand Germanish, you worthless puppy. If you think you can stop me from moving, you're welcome to try, but it won't end well for you. Oh, and stop embarrassing your Kapitan in front of strangers."

Blomberg's mouth gaped. Kruder repeated his order to stand aside, and his crew lined up along the wall, Blomberg at the end. Ana marched until he was past them, turned, and waved the Heart's Desire's crew forward. Gavin took back the cart. Dena, Dirk, and Lee filed past the Nats, exchanging pleasantries. Gavin kept his head down and pushed the cart. Scruggs followed behind, her hands on her shotgun, but no longer ready to fire.

Gavin's cart reached the end of the line of Pinguin crew members, but in his haste, he slammed it sideways and into the wall. A pile of boxes tipped over, and two dozen air filters fell off. Gavin scrambled to pick them up. Scruggs waited for him to finish. Blomberg bent down and picked up a box and popped it back on the cart, then stood. He came face to face with Gavin. His mouth gaped, then he drew his pistol and pointed it at Gavin. "Halt."

Gavin froze, seeing the gun inches from his face.

"Gun!" Ana and Scruggs yelled together. Ana drew his shotgun up and pointed it at the side of Blomberg's head. Scruggs brought up her shotgun, and pivoted, ramming the barrel into the stomach of the woman next to her. The two armed Pinguin crew pulled their pistols and pointed one at Scruggs, the other at Ana. Dena drew her slingshot, and Dirk and Lee both produced revolvers.

"Wait," Kruder yelled. He held his hands high. "No shooting. No shooting."

"In the Empire's name, Felix," Ana yelled. "Control your boy."

Kruder kept his hands up. "Blomberg, you're under arrest. Give your weapon to the first officer. Hans, get that pistol off him."

Blomberg shook his head. "I cannot do that, Kapitan."

"That is an order."

"I cannot follow that order, Kapitan."

"I will speak harshly to the officer candidate selectors when I get back, that is for sure." Kruder said. "Hans, Katerine. Lower your weapons. Step clear."

Hans, the first officer, lowered his pistol instantly at the Kapitan's command. He extended his hand. "Blomberg, give me your weapon."

Katerine kept hers pointed at Scruggs. "Kapitan, she has a shotgun in my belly."

"Ana..." Kruder said.

"Scruggs," Ana said. "Step back and clear of that lady. Keep your gun up. Step back far enough that you can point it at Felix."

"Who's Felix?"

"The Nat Captain."

Scruggs stepped sideways, then slid along the wall, keeping her shotgun up. Once backed far enough, she pivoted and pointed it at Kruder's head.

Kruder didn't even look at her. "Blomberg, if you shoot that Imperial, his friend will blow your head down the corridor and ruin my new uniform, and I will let him. Thank him, in fact, for removing an insane crew member from our ranks. Drop your weapon."

"But he's not, Kapitan."

"He's not what?"

"An Imperial, Kapitan. I know this man, I have seen his picture, it is in the special intelligence database. He is Gerhart Sorge. A citizen of the Union of Nations, and a spy and a murderer. He has been sentenced to death by special session of the committee, for spying and treason. All officers of the War Navy are instructed to shoot him on sight."

CHAPTER THIRTY-FIVE

"We've cracked the code," Lionel announced to Devin, striding into the gym.

"What code?" Devin banged a punching bag "We had a code to crack?"

"What are you doing, Tribune?"

"Boxing." Devin threw another punch. He was in the corner of the Pollux's gym wearing huge red boxing gloves, banging away the hanging bag. Other crew members were at different stations, exercising.

"That's not like any boxing I've ever seen. It's more like slapping."

"It's harder than it looks," Devin said.

"You've never boxed before in your life. Why are you doing it now?"

Devin slammed the hanging bag as hard as he could. It swayed, moving an inch. "I need to work out my frustrations."

"That's what you do sword work for. Why aren't you practicing with that?"

"I feel guilty."

"About practicing?"

"About breaking another sword dummy. I've been shredding them faster than Imin can build them. And now he's out of wood. We need to load up on a shipment of wood, so I can hack it apart." Devin swung again.

"Trees for the Tribune, then." Lionel shook his head. "You're supposed to hit it, not just slap it."

"I can't get into boxing. It seems so... common?"

"Common?"

"Sword work is an upper-class pursuit. Boxing makes me feel like a commoner, the stinking masses, you know, grubbing along in the dirt."

Lionel crossed his arms. "Really? Commoner?"

"Yes."

"Grubbing in the dirt?"

"Yes—oh." Devin remembered that the Subprefect wasn't a noble. "Not that there's anything wrong with dirt."

"Or grubbing, apparently," Lionel said. "I begin to understand those long ago Francais guys and that blade thing—the one that cuts off heads. What's it called?"

"Guillotine."

"Odd word for you to know."

"They taught it to us in Tribune school. Wanted us to understand what we were getting into. The code?"

"What?"

"The code you were talking about. That you cracked."

"Right." Lionel activated the wall screen and displayed

the sector map. Then he overlaid a series of starship courses. "Courses of the ships that went missing."

"Yes."

The course display changed, each one now being a string of different-colored segments, chained together.

"Looks like what would happen if you mixed broken pieces of colored spaghetti together," Devin said.

"Spaghetti comes in colors?"

"I'll have Imin make you some. Green, blue, whatever you want. You can glue them to paper to make pretty pictures. So what?"

Lionel brought up a legend on the side. "Darkest red is eighteen weeks ago, light red, seventeen, orangish, sixteen, and so on."

Devin saw it immediately. He reached up and tried to touch the screen, cursed, and held out his hands. Lionel unlaced the gloves, then Devin pointed. "On this side, there's a course starting here, and going to here, and here." He started with the oldest color and traced across the colored lines. "A ship—the pirate ship, or raider ship, it started here, and it moved across the space lanes like this." He traced from the oldest colors to the newest. "Taking each ship where it crossed. Outstanding. Finished off here, no activity for a few weeks. Where did it go?"

Lionel put up a nationality symbol for the missing ships. "Where do you think?"

"This guy here—you called him Raider-A, I see—is taking only Imperial and Confed ships. No Nats. But would we know if he took Nats?"

"We'd have heard something. Like we did with the other ship. Raider-B."

"The other ship? Oh…over here?" Devin pointed to the other side of the screen. "This cluster."

"Separate ship. Taking Confed, Nat, and Imperial. We know at least two Nat ships were taken because they had additional Imperial routing that they didn't make. There might be others."

"Right," Devin considered. "Two ships?"

"Yes."

"And that… special damage we saw?"

"That would be Raider-B, the one that doesn't care about nationality. And our pirate advisory board says that Raider-A matches the profile of a well-stocked freighter moving through the spaceways, collecting captures as it moves along, and ending up here." Lionel pointed.

"Confed space?"

"A free port. He could have gone in there to re-supply."

"And the other?"

"He's operating out of a central base, hopping out from it, grabbing what he can, then hopping back."

"This makes sense. What's your conclusion?"

"What we see here, Tribune." Lionel adopted his 'briefing' pose. "What we see is one large converted freighter, taking a meandering course through Imperial and Confederation edge territories, pirating only Confed and Imperial freighters, then taking their crews and cargos away, never to be seen again. And the fact that it's only Confed and Imperial crews means…"

"It's the Nats. It's a false flag operation. They're trying to increase tension between us and the Confeds."

"Remember what that friend of Imin said? That they were capturing freighters and killing the crews?"

"Even the Nats wouldn't do that. They have freighters of their own to worry about. But what do they do with the crews?"

"The Union of Nations is a pretty big place. They can stash a lot of people in out of the way places there and keep them 'til they need them."

"In a war. That's Raider-A. What about Raider-B?"

"All its captures are in the same area. We think a central base it jumps in and out of."

"A base? An actual base?"

"Probably not. More likely some sort of depot ship or crooked system administrator, one who buys the cargo and so on."

"Very well. But which one?"

"Imin is looking into that. He's talking with some of his friends, and they'll give him some ideas. He thinks he can narrow it down a bit. He's off ship right now."

"Where is he?"

"Like I said, Tribune, he's off the ship..."

"Meaning I don't need to know where. Right. How soon can we leave the system and get out there?"

"There's a convoy we should escort, at least partway. It's assembling now, it will take a couple days. We can load up, fuel up, and bring the Valhalla and the Hydrogen Queen with us, help protect the convoy."

"I want to go after that warship, whoever's it is."

"If we go tearing out of here in a hurry, they'll know something is up."

"Who are they?"

"There must be some sort of spy ring feeding these ships info on targets."

"I don't have time to figure that out, and we don't have the skill set either."

"Imin might."

"Huh." Devin flexed his wrists. "My hands hurt."

"All that fake boxing. We need to wait for Imin to come back."

Imin arrived an excruciating six hours later. Devin had been pacing, demanding reports, snarling at his crew. The crew hid. Lionel rolled his eyes but kept working.

Imin arrived in Devin's office minutes after reporting onboard. Lionel followed him in, a big grin plastered on his face.

"Imin!" Devin said.

"Tribune." Imin saluted. A sloppy salute. Very sloppy. With the wrong hand. And he swayed. His other hand was buried in the pocket of the dirty jacket he was wearing.

"I want you to tell me... wait. Have you been drinking?"

"Absolutely sir!" Imin grinned. "Lots!"

"Are you drunk?"

"Absolutely, sir!"

Devin opened his mouth but stopped at Lionel's wave.

"What is it, Subprefect?"

"I'd like to point out that Steward Imin was on special detached duty. So his condition is... authorized."

"Authorized? You told him he could get drunk?"

Lionel shrugged. "I didn't say he couldn't."

"Just because you didn't say he couldn't, doesn't mean he should do it. You have to explicitly tell him he could."

"Understood, Tribune. Does that also mean he's not supposed to push people down stairs? Because I didn't tell him he could do that either."

Devin closed his eyes for a moment, then returned his view to Imin. "Imin, did you push anybody down stairs?"

"I did sir."

"Who was this person?"

"People sir. More than one."

"Which people?"

"Bad people sir. Very bad people."

"Tribune," Lionel interrupted. "Why are you asking questions that you don't want to know the answers to?"

Devin raised his eyebrows, shook his head and pointed. "Everybody sit down. Imin, take that chair."

"Best not, sir." Imin pulled his hand out. "Bleeding, sir."

"Is it serious?"

Imin waved his hand. Blood dripped from a bandage and stained the floor. "Flesh wound, sir."

"How did you get—" Devin stopped. Lionel was shaking his head again.

Devin nodded and reached for the intercom. "Medical to my cabin."

A voice came from the open door. "Already here sir." The ship's medic entered. "Subprefect already called. Have a seat, Imin, we'll set you up. Um, Tribune, all this blood…"

"Put him in that chair." Devin pointed at a stained chair in the corner. "He won't be the first one to bleed into it."

It took the medic ten minutes to fix Imin's hand to his satisfaction. Subprefect Lionel grinned the whole time. Devin fumed.

Imin fell asleep.

"He's all yours sir." The medic left.

Lionel shook Imin awake. "Imin?"

"Wassup? Oh, I'm on the ship. Subprefect, Tribune? Is it dinner time already? Sorry, I'll whip something up."

"Not dinner, Imin. You've been drinking."

"Yes sir."

"Tell the Tribune why you were drinking."

"I was nervous, sir."

Devin leaned forward. "Why were you nervous?"

"Wasn't sure I'd get the job, sir."

Devin looked at Lionel. "The job? What job?"

"Cargo boss on the Hector Dixey. They needed a new deckhand, with cargo experience. I said I could do it if they gave me a shot. Offered them a good deal on wages, in return for a share of any profits."

"I'm excited about your economic acumen, Imin," Devin said. "But how does it relate here?"

Imin explained. He'd gone to the station and tracked down a few of his shadier contacts. He said he needed to make some money in a hurry, as he had to jump ship from the Navy—a little matter of some missing money in the steward's account. He had a day, maybe two to get away, and he needed a berth on a ship heading away from the station, and some serious money. The discussion consumed a great deal of alcohol. His contact said he'd speak to his captain, who valued skilled spacers who could keep their mouths shut. There'd be a job in it if he was willing to leave right away. And pay a finder's fee.

"So you paid the finder's fee," Devin said.

"I did sir. He said he'd get back to me. Then I went back to his ship, to the Hector Dixey, to apply for the opening."

"What opening?"

"Cargo boss sir. They had an opening."

"You said that. He told you?"

"No sir. Wasn't an opening when he started talking."

"Then how did you know there was an opening?"

"The two of them fell down the stairs on the station on the way back to the ship."

"They fell down the stairs?"

"Truthfully, sir. They were pushed."

"Pushed? By who?"

"Oh, me sir. I did it. Pushed him and his buddy down the stairs on the station."

"Wait, you threw him down the stairs?"

"Yes sir. Needed there to be room on his ship. Needed a way that wouldn't be suspicious."

"How is he?"

"Dead sir. Both of them. Broke their necks."

"Wow." Devin sat still. "Wow. That's...."

"Resourceful," Lionel said. "Very resourceful, Imin. Well done. Carry on."

Imin nodded, his eyes growing heavy. "Thank you sir."

"And lucky," Devin said. "Lucky that they both died, I mean. They could just have been badly hurt."

"Oh, they didn't die at first sir. Just got beat up badly." Imin held up his hand. "That's where I got this. He stabbed me while I was carrying him."

"Carrying him?"

"Oh, yes sir." Imin smiled. "He didn't die the first time. Had to carry him back up and throw him down a second time, make it look good. Heavy, that bastard. And he puked all over me."

CHAPTER THIRTY-SIX

"Surrender yourself or die, traitor!" Blomberg kept his pistol pointed at Gavin's head. "In the name of the Council, you are under arrest."

Gavin stood still, Blomberg's pistol pointed at his head from two feet away. "I think you have the wrong guy, pal."

"I was looking at your picture yesterday. I know who you are. And a genetic scan will prove it."

The two crews stood frozen in the corridor. Blomberg covered Gavin. Ana covered Blomberg. Scruggs had stepped back and covered Kruder. The two armed Pinguin crewmen had lowered their weapons, but they could raise them quickly. Lee stood behind Gavin.

"I'm not doing any genetic scan," Gavin said. "You've got the wrong guy, Leutnant."

"How do know my rank? How do you know Union ranks?"

Ana kept his shotgun pointed at Blomberg's head. "You

stupid young puppy. Everybody who has been in space more than a day can read ranks. It's on your sleeve."

"Blomberg, put up your weapon," Kruder repeated.

"I will not, Kapitan. He will get away."

"That is an order."

"I'm sorry, Kapitan, I have orders that supersede yours."

"Really?" Kruder lowered his hands. "From who?"

"I operate under direct orders of the Council. My authority is in my quarters."

Fusterheim hissed. "I knew they would have a spy."

"Leutnant, did you ever think of coming to me in confidence and telling me this?"

"We can discuss this later, Kapitan. You, traitor, raise your hands."

"You don't get it, puppy," Ana said. "I'm going to blow your head off if you don't move that gun."

Blomberg's eyes flipped to Ana. "I do not take—aaraugh!"

Gavin had grabbed Blomberg's wrist and pushed the pistol away from his head. Blomberg struggled. Everybody yelled.

"No shooting. Weapons hold. Hold." Ana reversed his shotgun to club Blomberg down. The unarmed Nat stepped in front of him and grabbed Blomberg's hands and pointed them at the ceiling. Blomberg cursed and pulled the trigger.

Blomberg's pistol fired the entire magazine with a br-rrrapppp. In defiance of Kapitan Kruder's standing orders, and common sense, he'd loaded with heavy slugs, rather than station-safe frangibles. The station crew would have spaced him if they found them first.

His bullets stitched a pattern on the ceiling. Tiles shattered, lights smashed, and a roof plate started a pinhole leak. Three pipes blew. One was cold water supply, the second hot water. The other pipe was the sewage return pipe.

The wall lights shorted out, only the emergency lights giving any illumination. The hot water exploded to steam, the cold water pipe provided volume, and the sewage pipe combined to blow them all down with a hot, steamy, stinking cloud of liquid feces.

Scruggs took it full in the face. She staggered back, and, as trained, aimed in the general direction of her last target, and fired both barrels. She was already falling back as she did it, and the gun rode high, so she blasted above everyone's heads.

As soon as the lights went out, Kruder, veteran of a thousand bar fights in his youth, dropped low and tackled his nearest crewmember. Both thumped into the wet stinking floor, banging their heads on the metal, but avoiding any ongoing gunplay. Kruder caught a ricochet from Scruggs's frangibles as he dropped.

Gavin slammed Blomberg's hand into the wall, once, and again. Blomberg's gun dropped into the dark. Ana took advantage of this to club Fusterheim, his nearest armed opponent, in the back of the head. Fusterheim dropped, boneless.

The ceiling pipe flapped from the pressure, burping liquid crap. It spun in a circle, hitting both Dirk and Dena and making them stagger back.

Dena had had enough. She stumbled back to clear the group, raised her slingshot and rapid-fired at any Nats she could see in the dim light. She caught Blomberg on the shoulder, and he yelled and dropped as Gavin released him.

The remaining Nat, still able to see and quicker of thought, hopped over Blomberg, ducked past Ana's clubbing attempt, shoved Dirk and charged Dena. She fumbled a new shot load when he barreled into her. He out-massed her by fifty percent, so he bowled her over and slammed her down. He rolled over her, leapt up, and kept running, disappearing into the darkness at the end of the hall.

Ana put his back to the wall. "Everybody, count off. Scruggs?"

"Here, Centurion. Can't see too well. Unwounded. Two Nats on the ground here."

"Keep 'em there. Engineer?"

"I'm fine." Gavin bent and inspected Blomberg. "The Nat kid's shoulder is messed up. He isn't going anywhere."

"Lee?"

"I'm fine." She bent in the dark. "The one you hit is still down. He'll be out for a while."

"Not dead?"

"Not yet."

"Double-check him, and the two Scruggs has. Dirk, Dena?"

"We're here, Centurion." Dirk pulled Dena up. "One got away. Ran Dena over. He's probably on the way back to his ship."

"Let's get out of here."

"Centurion!" Scruggs called. "Your Nat captain wants to talk to you."

"He's not my captain. Everybody, collect your stuff, get ready to head back." Ana stepped down the hall and bent over Kruder. "Felix, how bad is it?"

Kruder gritted his teeth. "Your gun girl caught me with a graze, I think. Or that idiot child did. I'll live." He sniffed. "You smell bad."

"You called me back here to suggest I shower?"

"I'm sorry, Ana. I did not know about this youth. Or his appointment by the Council."

"I figured. Um, my people and I, we could take him along and just—"

"No, no. Much as I would like to see him tossed out of an air lock, mine or yours, my crew, some of them, will not stand for it. But I will be forced to retaliate, you understand? If we see you again, or your ship, I will have to act. The War Navy will not allow otherwise."

"The War Navy, huh? You want to tell me something special about your ship and your promotion, maybe? Big ship out here, naval crew."

"I think you already know. A Korvettenkapitan in uniform, a regular crew..."

"Have you by chance been sailing along through the Empire, hijacking Imperial and Confed ships?"

"Of course not." But Kruder snorted when he said it.

"I figured as much. Good for you, Felix. Good trick. How long will you stay?"

"I need supplies. Blomberg will insist I chase you and chastise you, but I will be able to delay it, perhaps a day."

"We'll be long gone by then."

"Go far and go fast. We have bigger engines than we look. That is a good plan. And, Ana, I mean this in the best possible way. I hope I never see you again."

"Because I'll be at the end of a targeting sight."

"Centurion!" Dirk yelled from the front. "We're ready to go, and that fellow is probably back at his ship, getting reinforcements."

"Move out, back to the ship," Ana ordered. The crew jogged down the hallway. Ana stopped and kicked Blomberg twice, hard, as he ran by. Scruggs stopped and kicked him once, then moved on.

They reached the end of the corridor, Ana paused and turned. "Felix."

"Yes, Anastasios?"

"Congratulations on your promotion!"

CHAPTER THIRTY-SEVEN

"Burn some fuel," Ana said, sitting down in his seat behind Dirk and drying his still nearly-bald head. "Get us out of here."

They had left the Casarubrum shipyard in a hurry. Dirk had given the final payment authorization codes as soon as he got back to the Heart's Desire, and port control had let them drop right away. Lee had them meandering to the jump limit at her usual fuel-conserving course.

Dirk feathered a thruster. "Lee has the course programmed in already. If we modify it, one of us will have to stay here, and I'd like to have a shower. Oh, and by the way, this is a ship thing, we only take your advice when there's some sort of ground combat. Which happens a lot more than I want. From now on, let's not go to the surface of planets."

"Or stations." Lee flicked switches.

"Or stations," Dirk agreed. "Or anywhere. Let's never leave the ship again."

"You can stay locked inside your closet if you want, Navy. I don't care. And I'd like you to have a shower too, but we need to get away from the Earl of Clydebank before they catch up with us."

"They're not moving now," Lee objected. "They're docked."

"They can undock anytime."

"Even if they did, they can't catch us. We can accelerate twice as fast as any merchant ship."

"Any standard merchant ships, yes, you keep telling me. But we're not a standard merchant ship. Which means there are other types of merchant ships. And what kind of non-standard merchant ships do you think are out here in the middle of the Verge? Ones that warrant the equivalent of an Imperial Lieutenant Commander in charge. How many freighters have a crew big enough to have that many officers onboard? We saw six in the fight there, and they weren't the only ones, I'm sure. And they had that stupid kid with his Council orders."

"We found one of the pirates that we heard rumors about, didn't we?" Lee said.

"Probably," Ana said. "That kid talked about their mission. A ship that big, how can it make money trading out here, and what was it doing at that secret shipyard? If they needed supplies or maintenance, they could have gone to a dozen closer Imperial planets."

"They didn't want anybody getting a good look," Dirk said. "Got it. Well, we'll have to put up with the smell."

"No, we don't have to," Ana said. "You got all that fancy software. What about that random-walk program? Point us at the jump point, push us as fast as we can, and it will steer the ship, right?"

"We can do that," Lee said.

"Gets us there faster, safer, and most important, at least regarding you, Navy."

"Yes?"

"You can have that shower. You stink."

Two hours later, a scowling Dena and a grumpy Scruggs wandered into the control room. Ana was watching the board.

"You flying things now, Old Man?" Dena asked.

"Computer does it. One of those new programs." Ana sniffed. "You smell much better. Kind of like... minty."

"Toothpaste," Dena said. "Mint-flavored toothpaste."

"You washed with toothpaste?"

"Turns out Gavin found a sale on mint-flavored everything. Toothpaste, soap, mouthwash. We're all going to be minty fresh for the next few months."

"Better than the alternative."

"Centurion?" Scruggs buckled herself into the chair. "Do you believe what that Nat said about Gavin?"

Ana shrugged. "It could be true. Don't care."

"Well, he's a spy. And a traitor, according to them."

"Last I checked, we've got enough problems following Imperial laws, never mind Union of Nations ones. And who is he a traitor for, anyways?"

"What do you mean?"

"The Nats say he's a traitor and a spy, and that he used to

be in the Nat Navy, and that he spied against them for... who? The Empire? In that case, he's on our side, isn't he?"

Scruggs grimaced. "Never thought of that. Is he?"

"Ask him. None of my business."

"I wonder if there's a reward?" Dena asked.

"Probably," Ana said. "Want to try to collect it?"

"Well, I mean..."

"Would be easier to collect the one on Scruggs here. Aren't you still worth a hundred thousand credits to somebody?"

"Last time I checked, yeah," Scruggs said. "And the engineer is nice. He helps us out. We shouldn't turn him in."

"Plus, what would we spend the money on?" Dena said. "Nat clothes? I don't like Nat fashions. Kind of dowdy."

"It does give us a bit of an issue, though," Ana said. "We can't go into Confed space because they want to hang Navy, we can't stay in Union space because they want to shoot the punk, and the Empire, except for Tribune Devin, wants Scruggs dead—manner unspecified. I think Lee's people are looking for her. And I've got a few problems of my own in the past."

"Wherever we go, we're criminals?" Dena asked.

"Yes."

"Boy, I know how to pick em," Dena said. "Say, Centurion, what did your Nat Navy friend say in your little private chat before you left?"

"He didn't admit to anything, but I'm pretty sure that he's playing pirate, capturing Confed and Imperial ships, to convince us to go to war with each other. Oh, and his ship is much faster and more powerful than it looks, and he'll have to blow us up next time he gets us in his sights."

"Good to know," Dena said. An alarm bonged on the board. "Is that good?"

"Probably not." Ana tapped the intercom. "Navigator, your board is screaming at me."

"What's it say?"

"It doesn't. It says 'custom alarm thirty-seven.'"

"I have to look that one up. Stand by." Lee went offline for a moment, then came back. "I'm coming up. We need to pick up more speed."

"Why?" Ana asked.

"That alarm means another ship undocked from the station. Want to make a guess which one?"

Kruder was not happy with his orders. Or he should say his new orders. A pale and sweating Blomberg, after a spell in the med pod, had arrived with a sheath of directives pulled from a secret cache he had.

"You are in the Security Directive, then, Leutnant?" Kruder asked.

"I cannot confirm or deny—"

"Oh, never mind. You must be. I expected a spy onboard. I do wish they had saddled us with one with a tiny amount of competence."

"Kapitan, that is unjust. We were—"

"Nearly killed, because of your stupidity, and our main mission is compromised due to your actions. We will have to abort and return to base."

"Our orders there—"

"I will review them when I have leisure, Leutnant. In the meantime, I am concerned about our missing crew members. While you were taking your medical cure, the first officer scoured the station. Our people are not here."

"With respect, sir, you should review them now. I have highlighted the relevant portions."

Kruder grimaced, tabbed through the orders, sighed, and hit his intercom. "Helm?"

"Sir?"

"Undock. Full speed for the jump limit."

"Kapitan, if we show our full capabilities for speed this close to the station—"

"I know. But full speed it is."

Blomberg smiled as Kruder closed the channel. "Thank you, Kapitan."

"Don't thank me. I admit those orders are properly formatted. But the only reason I am moving with such dispatch is that they will take us in the direction of one of our rendezvous points where I expect our crew members to be waiting. "

"Don't worry, Kapitan, we will catch this traitor yet."

"You better hope so."

"Why is that, Kapitan?"

"Because you have blown up our primary mission with this meaningless chase of a single man. If for some reason we do not catch him, you will have to explain to the Council the failure of both missions."

CHAPTER THIRTY-EIGHT

"Just jump us somewhere, anywhere," Ana said. He watched his screen. Pinguin had left the station and was chasing them outsystem.

"Somewhere is not a position I can put in the computer," Lee said. "We need to put an actual destination."

Ana cursed as he bumped into the laser controls. The control room of Heart's Desire had originally resembled an old garage where electronics went to grow old and peacefully die, but since the laser, the Tribunes upgraded gear, and the new radars had been installed, it felt more like a closet with too many boxes stuffed into it. Boxes piled randomly, with sharp edges, ready to explode outwards if you touched the wrong button.

And it smelled of burned electronics, hot plastic, and dirty toilets.

"This place is worse than the heads," Ana said, stretching to strap himself in. "Smelly and crowded."

"Nobody said you needed to be here," Dirk said. "We can

handle this part, thank you very much. If you leave, it will be less crowded."

Lee coughed. "And much less smelly."

"Just jump us somewhere," Ana repeated. "Because if we don't get out of here soon, then Felix's freighter—"

"The Earl of Clydebank," Lee said, entering data into her navigation computer.

"I'm sure it's not called that," Ana said. "But whatever. We need to get away."

"What's he going to do, ram us?"

"You think that big a ship, with a Nat Commander in charge and all those Nat Navy officers, doesn't have some sort of anti-ship capability built in? He as much as admitted to me that he's been pirating ships in the Empire."

"We'll be at the jump limit shortly. We can head back into the Empire," Dirk said. "We'll ditch this Nat, and Lee can have her chat with the Tribune, if we can find him."

"We'll need to do the calculations, which will take time," Lee said.

"Why?" Ana glared at Lee. "You gave us that song and dance about calculating jumps and not having to wait for computers."

"I told you that if nothing was in our way—rogue planets, comets, other stars, between us and our destinations, then we can zero out a whole bunch of the calculations, and it speeds things up."

"So zero away."

"We can't, Centurion." Lee shook her head. "All our paths back to the Empire, there are obstructions—other systems, cold dwarfs, dwarf planets. The zeroing out won't work in that direction right now. We need to do the full calculations. We can't calculate a jump back the way we came in less than two hours. "

"Navy, do we have two hours?" Ana asked.

"Nope." Dirk played with his board. "Lee, can you put up whatever courses you have that you can calculate?" Dirk plotted a point on the board. "Use this point at the jump limit, which we will be at in less than thirty minutes. Show me where we can safely calculate a jump from at that time. Just give me directions, not destinations."

Lee nodded and put data on the screen.

Dirk overlaid the pursuing ship's vector onto his screen. "Your friend's freighter is surprisingly fast. Good acceleration curve."

Ana cursed loudly, repeatedly, and continuously. "Damn that stupid engineer."

"You going to shoot him?" Dirk asked.

"Why do you ask that?"

"It's your usual reaction to problems."

"Only when the shooting would solve the problems. Which this won't."

"Not going to do it for fun?"

Ana shook his head. "Surprisingly, I'm not that mad at the engineer. This isn't his fault. He's been hiding from an entire Empire, he's done a pretty good job, and to be fair, didn't he say there could be serious complications if we went to this yard? And besides, shooting him would be too much work."

"There's the Ana we know and love." Dirk keyed the intercom. "Engineer?"

"Yes, Skipper?" Gavin's voice answered.

"I have some questions."

"Am I that super spy Gerhart Sorge?"

"That wasn't one of them, but academically speaking, are you?"

"Does it matter?"

"Not to me. You haven't done anything to me. Or the Empire that I can tell. But it does seem to matter to those Nats."

"Do you believe them?"

"Doesn't matter if I do. They believe it, so they'll act accordingly."

"Going to turn me over to them?"

"Nope. One, we need an engineer. Two, they seem to want to shoot you, and they probably won't be too concerned if they have to shoot the people with you as well."

"You think Ana's friend will shoot all of us?"

Ana leaned close to the intercom speaker and pushed the button. "Shoot all of us? He'll do it twice, without hesitation. If Felix Kruder thinks it's his duty to shoot us, or if he's ordered to, he'll do it right away." Ana tapped the button again. "He'll be really sad about it afterward."

Dirk shook his head. "There you go. One, I need an engineer. Two, death. But three, it's not the right thing to do. I'm an aristocrat. I should be supporting the people who work with me, like Devin."

"Odd time to become all honorable. Have you been drinking?"

"Not in a while. But Devin reminded me of a few things. We're not giving you up. But we do have a problem."

"A shipload of crazed Nats who want to shoot me, and anybody with me?"

"Yes. And a slow jump computer. What sort of shape is the jump drive in?"

"Tip-top, Skipper. The yard people did a full tune when they installed the power conduits—they had to move some of the jump drive connections, and it was part of the service."

"We normally have enough fuel to make at least two jumps. Two long jumps."

"Sure, Skipper. We're stuffed full of fuel as well. Fuel costs were minimal compared to a new laser."

"Could we make three?"

"Well... Let me check." Gavin went offline.

"Pilot?" Lee asked. "What are we doing?"

Dirk highlighted one of Lee's courses on the board. "We normally jump to inhabited systems, or ones with fuel sources. Safer that way. But we can jump out into the dark, here, using one of your precalculated safe zones."

"And then we're in the dark, Pilot. How long do we stay? Ana's friend can just wait us out, 'til we come back."

"Not if we keep going. Jump there, into the dark, plot a new course in this direction, take you three-four hours, whatever, then keep going. Jump to this system here. 429-6666. Unremarkable, seldom visited, and the sailing direction says no fuel."

"So we're stuck in an empty system with no fuel...oh." Lee nodded. "If we can do one more jump, we're able to jump back into the Empire."

"Right. Safe at home, far away from the Confeds and the Nats, ready to do the job the Tribune gave us. Armed and dangerous."

"If the engineer says we can make three jumps, we can do it. Cross this rift, get back into Imperial Space."

"Let's ask." Dirk keyed the intercom. "Engineer? We have to decide soon. There are people with guns behind us."

Gavin's voice came up. "We can do it. The numbers check out. Might not be able to do it again, ever, but this once, right out of the yard, we can do it."

"Outstanding." Dirk plotted the three courses up on the screen and double-checked with Lee. After they both agreed, he opened the ship wide channel. "Attention, attention, this is your captain speaking. As is usual for us, after a hasty departure from somewhere, there's a group of angry people pursuing us. Unfortunately, in this case, they have guns, a well-armed and long-ranged ship with a trained crew, who is upset we shot and/or beat them up. They're catching up, so we're modifying our course to jump away from the Empire into deep space, where we will conduct two additional jumps, total seventeen days in jump space, to escape. The navigator, engineer, and I have conferred, and we think it is a reasonable and safe effort to make." Dirk clicked the microphone off, thought for a moment and clicked it back on. "Also, the people behind us will kill us if we don't do this, so no choice really. Stations for jump."

Scruggs's voice came from the speakers. From the echo, she was in the lounge. "Where are we going?"

"First in the dark, then another hop, then we'll be at a border system, with facilities."

"Does it have a name?"

"Sure." Dirk played with his screen. "Nowhere important. Place called… Fawkes. Looks small and unimportant. I'm sure nothing ever happens there."

CHAPTER THIRTY-NINE

"Jump complete, Tribune," the Pollux's helmsman said. The blue light of jump space faded from the screens, and the cameras showed the current system.

"Very well." Devin stretched in his chair. "Anything to report?"

"Beacons," the sensor operator said. "Seven merchants plus our convoy. Scanning them now. None of particular interest. Two of the merchants are heading for the far side and will be obscured by Tappacala-1c within the hour."

"Tappacala-1c is the habitable planet?"

"Mostly habitable planet. Goldilocks zone. Temperate climate, half water, not much orbital eccentricity, moderate weather. Low but acceptable atmospheric pressure. Widespread Terran plants. Moderately small population."

"I'm sensing a but in there?"

"Low levels of oxygen. Terraforming is still kicking in. You can survive, sort of, but the sailing directions says carry supplemental oxygen."

"Do you need environmental suits?"

"Not according to the book, sir."

"That's a lot of beacons for an edge system that we'd have trouble breathing on."

"Some orbital and belt operations, Tribune. Gas giants for refueling. And people need more oxygen, but the plants are happy with the carbon dioxide. Big agricultural works here. Grains, exotic woods. Teak plantations are a big thing, according to the sailing directions."

"A planet of teak. Too bad we're not staying. I could use some for my sword dummies."

"Yes sir. Two of the attached merchant ships are requesting—nope, my mistake, they didn't wait. Sir, two of the attached merchant ships have left the convoy without asking permission."

"The ones who were scheduled to detach here?"

"Yes sir."

"Let them go. Wish them bon voyage or some such. What about the Hector Dixey?"

"The Hector Dixey, sir?"

"Yes, they joined at the last minute. Make sure they have the correct routing instructions. And check with the Valhalla and Hydrogen Queen as well, confirm their routing instructions. Take care of that and report back when done."

"If comm will help me out..." The sensor operator huddled with the comm officer. He must have opened a private channel, because then the helm and navigation officers stiffened, and a four-way discussion started.

Devin tuned out and brought up a channel with Lionel. "Subprefect?"

"As we discussed. We hop ahead two jumps and get ahead of the convoy. We'll be drifting when they drop out of jump. The Hydrogen Queen and Valhalla will jump away immediately they arrive. The convoy will disperse, and Imin, on the Hector Dixey, will either comm us via the planet, or we'll just shadow them when they jump next. From the spatial geometry, it will be two, at most three jumps for them to get where they're going."

"Tell me again that they're the right ship."

"Imin thinks they're involved in something shady, and he seems to have a lot of... unusual knowledge in that area. Our pirate advisory committee came up with a list of goods to track for our hidden pirate-warship, and the Hector Dixey has most of them."

"What type of goods? Ammunition? Weapons? Food?"

"Air filters, appliance parts, and cleaning supplies. Things that you'll use up if you have way more people on your ship than normal, and you're stressing your environmental systems. People will ask questions when you buy guns, but if you order ten times as many water purifiers as normal, people just think you're bad at ordering supplies."

"Food?"

"Every ship you pirate has food. Food isn't a problem. Filters and consumables, on the other hand, are brand-specific. Chances of another ship having the right type of spare vacuum cleaner bags is pretty low."

"What did Imin say about that?"

"I didn't let him mention it. Didn't want cross-contamination of the data. I made the group evaluate the cargo loads of a dozen ships and asked which one they thought could be supplying pirates. They all picked the Hector Dixey. "

"Well done. We'll catch ourselves some pirates."

"Maybe. Or one of the pirates. What about Raider-A?"

"They're next. But this Raider-B bothers me. It's a bit more random than the other, and there's that... odd damage issue."

"And it might have come out from the core and know what's going on there."

"Yes. There are a lot of things happening out here that may be related to the core. Any new courier boats arriving?"

"Nothing that I haven't told you about. Um, one thing."

"Yes?"

"There's the small matter of this arrest warrant for you everybody knows exists, but nobody has officially seen."

"Until a courier boat arrives with an official copy, it doesn't exist. Focus on the problems in front of us."

"You're not one to bury your head in the sand, Tribune."

"Sometimes that's the only way to get things done."

"Convoy is dispersing, Tribune," the sensor operator announced. "Two freighters inbound to the container farm. One heading for a refueling orbit. Valhalla and Hydrogen Queen are signaling imminent jumps."

After two weeks of the most boring jumps through deep space that Devin had ever seen, they had beat the convoy into the Fawkes system. Pollux had jumped in a week earlier, plotted to hit the outer system. They turned their beacon off and entered a ballistic orbit inbound to the inhabited area. They weren't emitting any active sensor sweeps, and they didn't have their drive on, so they were invisible to merchant ships. Any warship doing a sweep would have had a better-than-even chance of catching them, but they didn't expect any warships there.

"Maintain course. Who's heading for the refueling orbit?"

"Hector Dixey, sir."

"Very well. You're monitoring her transmissions?"

"I am sir. And there's one going in right now, in code. One of your codes, sir."

"Good lad, Imin." Devin grinned. "He's letting us know he's there." Devin rounded on Lionel. "Subprefect?"

"Tribune?"

"How did Imin convince that master of that ship to let him send messages?"

"Well, Imin said he had to leave your service because he was stealing your money and he wanted to get away before you discovered it."

"Good story, but hard to believe."

"It would be. But we arranged for him to steal money from you and use it to bribe the captain. Imin is taking money out of some of your accounts and splitting it with the captain of the ship as we speak. He's going to do it in every system with a bank where the Hector Dixey passes through."

"Actually steal....oh." Devin tilted his head. "You arranged a scam where he pretended to steal money from me, so that it would look like he was a thief."

"Not exactly."

"What exactly, then?"

"We used your real banking codes, and we used them to actually steal money from you."

"You stole my codes?"

"Well, we didn't technically steal them from you, Tribune. You gave them to us."

"I gave him banking codes?"

"Me. Him. Both. Sure."

"How?"

"He and I were talking about it, so we talked to you and said we needed your banking codes for a project. You gave us some."

"I didn't ask why?"

"Nope. You were doing some important Tribune work and didn't want to be disturbed."

"Tribune work?"

"I think it was dessert. Custard, if I recall."

Devin had a dim memory of something happening before they started a jump, during a meal. "I thought... I thought he needed them to pay bills."

"Bribes are kind of like bills."

"Oh." Devin surveyed the screen. "Did he steal a lot?"

"I hope so. He has to give me ten percent. He's taking the risk, but I wanted a finder's fee."

"You demanded a finder's fee for stealing from me?"

Lionel looked up. "Ten percent is very reasonable, Tribune. You should be happy that it's so low. Most people would want twenty. You should thank me for being so generous."

"Thank you. Wait, am I thanking you for stealing less money from me than you could have?"

"No need to belabor the point, Tribune. It will just embarrass me. I know how lucky you are to have people like Imin and I looking after your welfare. But if you're feeling extra guilty, you could always show your appreciation."

"I should show extra appreciation?"

"Sure. A tip. A bonus for a job well done."

"I should give you more money?"

"Sure." Lionel looked up from his console. "Twenty percent more would be fine."

Fawkes had no habitable planets, just stations and gas giants. Factories extracted minerals from the outer rings of the largest gas giant, Fawkes-1d. The two main-line freighters sped into the floating container farm, intent on transferring their containers loaded with grain and wood for local manufactories, like sheet and bar steel. Then, they'd head deeper into the Empire, to trade the raw materials for manufactured goods. Then back to Tappacala and do it all over again. A steady, prosperous trade, interrupted only by the fact that the shortest path between Tappacala and Fawkes was exposed to pirates. Which explained why the freighter captains had joined the convoy in the first place.

"Hector Dixey in a fueling orbit, sir," the sensor operator said. "Twenty-four hours to refuel, by our estimate."

"Watch them. As soon as they move out of orbit, call me." Devin climbed up. "No matter what shift, day or night. I'm going to have lunch."

The Hector Dixey didn't move until the middle of second

shift two days later, and even then, it meandered. Lionel didn't bother to call, just left the bridge and buzzed Devin in his office.

"Enter."

Lionel walked in and recoiled. "Yuck. What's on fire?"

"Lunch."

"Hector Dixey is moving. Slowly."

"Two and a half days to refuel?"

"Not everybody has a crack crew like you do, Tribune. Or an outstanding first officer. That smells burnt."

Devin pushed the plate in front of him away. "It is disgusting. I'd been eating meals that Imin froze before he left. But now they're all gone, and I'm left with this slop. Let's go chase them."

"We don't need to. They're not even making a quarter G. Are those food trays on fire? What did you do to them?"

"Why only a quarter G?"

"Saves fuel. That's why they took so long to fuel up. I figure they must have some sort of auxiliary tank hidden inside somewhere, and they probably had to fill the main tank, process it, pump the main to the auxiliary, then refill the main again."

"Sounds inefficient."

"Sounds like they're going somewhere they can't count on refueling, somewhere without plants, comets, or gas giants. And they need the fuel to get back."

"Very well. You'll leave word for the Hydrogen Queen and the Valhalla, telling them where we've gone?"

"We're dropping an answer-only beacon before jump.

They know the code to activate it. Your desk is scorched. How long did you microwave those trays for?"

"An hour."

"An hour?" Lionel grabbed his forehead. "Jove preserve us. Why so long?"

"The recipe said fifteen minutes per pound."

"Per pound of what?"

"Potatoes. It's a regular tray. Mostly potatoes. About four pounds."

"Four pounds of potatoes… What recipe?"

"Here." Devin put the message up on the screen. "See?"

"This is for baking," Lionel said. "Baked potatoes. Not microwaved potatoes. Haven't you ever baked before?"

"Baked. Microwaving." Devin shrugged. "Aren't they the same thing?"

Lionel slumped in a chair. "I'm glad you're a better Tribune than a cook."

Devin pushed his food aside. "We're following them?"

"Two can play at a quarter G. They're breaking orbit and heading to the jump limit. We'll be right behind them as they jump. Literally. My course will have us in line with the planet—unless they have a sensor pointing through their drive plume, they won't find us at all."

"What happens then?"

"They jump, we track the jump."

"You are sure we can do that?"

"No."

"No? NO? Imin's on that ship."

"We have an excellent chance of following him, but not a

hundred percent. We talked about it. He was willing to take the risk."

Devin thumped the table. "What if I wasn't?"

"You told us to do something, we did it. We used the best possible information and made a decision."

"He'll be killed."

"He didn't think so. I don't think so."

"I should have been informed."

"Tribune." Lionel sat. "Devin. Your job here is to decide what needs to be done, then step back while we do it. You said find the pirates. We think we've done that. We'll know in a jump."

Devin pushed the food tray away. "What happens after the jump?"

"We get in the next system, we look for a pirate. If we see one, it's time for one of your death-or-glory charges."

"I'd prefer glory, if it's all the same to you."

"I would too." Lionel shrugged. "But, with you, that's not always the way to bet."

CHAPTER FORTY

"Only warships have sensors which can track jumps," Dirk said. "There's no way they could have done that."

"Then they must be a warship," Lee said.

The Pinguin had followed them into the dark.

They'd had a normal trip. Lee fixed everyone's scrapes and bruises collected during their escape from Casarubrum. They worked out every day. Scruggs practiced weapon training with Ana. Lee, Gavin, and Dirk followed up on their professional training. Dena worked on simulators to learn more about the ship. Scruggs and Dena sparred. Ana cleaned and maintained his extensive collection of weapons.

Rocky pestered everyone, except Dirk, until they threw his ball. They were all veteran spacers by now, and they'd learned that avoiding each other during the first part of a jump made it go smoother.

Arriving in the middle of the dark, millions of miles from anything interesting, didn't have much scope for relieving boredom. But even though they often forgot it, Dirk was a career Navy officer, and he'd dealt with jump blues before. He got everybody to go outside and float in the dark, until they had a view of the immensity of the universe. He was hovering just outside the air lock waiting his turn to come back in when he saw a flash and called Lee.

"It was a jump flash," she confirmed.

"I don't believe it," Dirk said. "Run the sensor log again. Are we sure it was a jump flash?"

"Computer says it is," Lee answered. "Better get inside."

"I do not believe this. Why would they bother to follow us out here? Ana's friends are insane."

"Maybe Ana owes them a lot of money?"

"Or they want to shoot a particular engineer really, really badly. We'll need to talk to him."

"You'll need to get in here. Jump clock is started. We jump in fifteen minutes."

Dirk cursed, but locked the ship and came inside. "Crew meeting once we're in jump. Everyone here. Especially you, Engineer." He headed back to his room, climbed into his coveralls and came back to the lounge.

"Where's the engineer?"

"Here, Skipper." Gavin pulled into the lounge.

"That Nat ship followed us. I don't think they're looking for me."

"Probably not looking for you." Gavin grabbed a hand-hold. Lee had brought up point one G on the engines to give an up/down during jump.

"We need to know more about what you did—"

"Do we really?" Ana, followed by a sweating Scruggs and a sweating Dena, pulled into the lounge.

"They're chasing the engineer," Dirk said.

"If they weren't chasing him, they'd be chasing somebody else." Ana pulled a glass of basic for himself. After glancing at Scruggs and Dena, he pulled two more. "Less we know the better. Besides, we're in jump now. Nothing to do about it."

"Knowledge is power," Dirk said.

"Ignorance is bliss," Ana said.

The two women leaned against the wall and drank down the glass of basic.

"Yuck," Scruggs said. "Sugary."

"Yay," Dena said. "Finally something I can drink. Baby Marine, you've gotten better at grappling."

"You're not bad yourself," Scruggs said. "Kind of slippery when you get going. Very slick, and hard to hold."

Dirk closed his eyes and gritted his teeth. "I want everybody to know how hard it is for me not to make a comment about that right now. I assume you two were doing zero-G wrestling just for the heck of it?"

"Centurion had us try to disarm the other," Scruggs said. "It's way harder than it looks."

"Each other? Why not him?" Dirk asked.

"Because I out-mass them by about 50 kilos," Ana said. "I'm a guy, bigger, stronger, and they're not going to take anything away from me that I want to keep. If they want to disarm me, they have to use a knife. Or a bayonet. Or a slingshot."

"What's the point of all this?" Dirk asked.

"Options," Ana said. "If it's a big guy, they need to shoot him. If it's a girl their size, they can shoot her, but perhaps they might be able to disarm her."

"I thought you liked shooting people?"

"I like winning," Ana said. "Sometimes that involves shooting people. But shooting is loud, permanent, and messy. Sometimes you want a conversation after the event, or you're sneaking around so you don't want gunshots, or you might have on your best clothes. I don't want to ruin my clothes. I'm all about options. Which kind of brings up a topic. Engineer?"

Gavin crossed his arms. "What?"

"What's our option for getting to a port? With these guys following us, where can you go without worrying about getting shot?"

"None of your business, Old Man. I don't need your help."

"I'm not offering any," Ana said. "I've got my own problems. But we need to know where we can trade, or travel to, and not potentially have our engineer blown up by angry Nats."

"I'm..." Gavin sighed. "It's best I don't go near Nat naval units. I should be okay with the non-naval people. Same with the Confeds. Regular planets, fine. Or ships. Not naval units."

"You speak Germania?"

"Yes."

"Russe?"

"Yes."

"Good Russe? Bad Russe? Or like a native."

"Like a native."

"Wow." Scruggs clapped. "Three languages. Standard, Germania, and Russe. How do you do that?"

"I'm a good student," Gavin said.

"Or maybe you talked Russe with Dad and Germania with Mom," Ana said.

Gavin was quiet. "Germania with Dad. Russe with Mom. But that was a long time ago. I'm rusty."

"Ever done anything against the Empire?" Lee had arrived from the control room.

"Nothing."

"Nothing, or nothing they know about. Yet," Ana said.

Gavin unfolded his arms and rubbed his head. "Nothing that they know about. And anything they might find out would make them... unhappy, but not outraged."

"Not outraged enough to send a fleet unit after you, you're saying, not like the Nats."

"Didn't know they were a fleet unit," Gavin said. "It looked like a freighter. And it was an accident that they knew me. I didn't know they were there. I told you there might be complications."

"It's a warship," Ana said. "Felix said as much. And the fact that they followed us here means that they have warship-level sensors."

"We've got that laser thingy," Dena said. "And those special radar things. Can't we fight?"

"Yes, we can," Dirk said. "But they out-mass us almost three to one, and some of that mass is probably other weapons. And I'll bet they didn't weld their lasers in place. They'll have turrets to run them. And computers. And crew to man them and control them."

"Yes, we can fight," Ana said. "A short fight. And we'll lose."

"Look, what's the big deal?" Gavin said. "Everybody here has a past. So do I. The Nats are unhappy with me. They're not so happy with Pilot here either. And given how chummy the old man here is with them, I'll bet the Confeds want to talk to him."

"The Confeds might be interested in a chat with me," Ana said. "I'm not going to give them the opportunity, though."

Gavin shrugged. "We just keep running. We weren't going to stop in the next system, this... 425-6666. Just come out of jump, Lee fixes our position, we do the calcs, and we're out of here in two hours. Doesn't matter if the Nats follow us. One more jump and we're in a well-traveled system, and they won't do anything to us there."

"Nope," Lee said. "We can't do another jump."

"We have enough fuel, I already told you," Gavin said. "The drive hasn't been this efficient since it left the factory. We're fine. We have enough fuel to make it."

"Fuel isn't the problem. Calculation is."

"Do your rapid calculation thing, then," Gavin said.

Lee shook her head.

"Why won't you?"

"Not won't. Can't."

"Lee." Gavin raised a finger, then dropped it. "Wait. We can't do the calcs 'til we get there, can we?"

"Nope. Too much uncertainty after this jump. I'll need

our exact position. We're landing clear of the jump limit, but there's too much junk in the outer system. We'll need to either move to get a clear path or run a major calculation update.

"The Emperor's nostrils," Dirk said. "How long will that take?"

"Three, maybe four hours if we stay still. Longer if we're moving."

"I don't understand," Dena said. "How come this jump calculation thing never came up before?"

"It does in warships," Dirk said. "But civilian freighters just do one jump, then go get fuel or orbit a planet. They have days to plot their next jump and get set up. We don't."

"We land, sit still and Lee does these jump calculations, however long they take, and we jump out. What's going to happen?"

"That Nat ship—they're right behind us. They can see where we jumped, and chase us again, if their captain is as mad as he sounded."

"Or as mad as that spy kid makes him," Ana said. "And I think spy kid is pretty mad. Felix told me he doesn't want to see us again. And if Felix Kruder doesn't want to see you again, bad things will happen if he does."

"We finish this jump, we orbit," Dena said. "Lee does our calculations, and this Nat ship jumps in behind us. What happens then?"

The three Spacers—Dirk, Lee, and Gavin—exchanged frowns. Ana shook his head. "You tell her, Navy."

"Well, bad things could happen."

"Bad things?"

"Nature Girl," Ana said. "If we're sitting there in range when Felix comes out of jump, he'll blast us to pieces as soon as we're within the range of whatever guns he has."

CHAPTER FORTY-ONE

"Contact," Lukas, Pollux's sensor operator, announced. "Two ships."

"Took long enough," Devin grumbled from his seat in the Pollux's bridge.

"Indeed, Tribune." Lionel looked up from his screen. "The crew taking seven minutes after we jumped into a strange new system to find two ships without beacons who are attempting to hide themselves. That's unforgivable. Should I schedule the floggings today? Or do you think making the crew wait in anticipation will create the right level of dread-inspired efficiency that you're reaching for?"

Devin bit his lip. "Sensors. Mass and vector?" Pollux had jumped after the Hector Dixey, and then just drifted while the passive sensors went to work.

"Uncertain sir. We saw them transiting that ice giant. We'll need more time."

"Carry on, sensors." Devin slumped in his chair. The system was two not very closely orbiting red dwarfs—429-6666 and 425-6666. It had no habitable planets, no asteroid belt, few moons, and bad solar flares. It was less a star system and more a place where you sent ships that you hated and hoped burned up, along with crews that you felt the same about.

Lionel scanned Devin's sour expression, then tapped a private channel.

"What?" Devin asked. "What's going on?"

"I was going to ask you that myself, Tribune."

"My steward is alone on that ship. Will he be okay? What if they discover he's a spy and try to kill him? What do you think is happening to him?"

"Happening? Most probably, I think he's finished beating all the rest of the crew in poker, has pocketed all of their wages, and he's got the on-board cook fired and is making himself a nice lunch." Lionel glanced at the duty roster on a wall screen on the bridge. "Mid-second shift. I figure he's making soup."

"I miss his soups."

"Very rapid switch from being worried about him being killed, to missing a hot lunch."

"I'd be worried about any of my crew in this situation. But I also worry about lunch. Lunch is the most important meal of the day."

"I thought that was breakfast?"

"It's the most important too. They're all important."

"One must be more important than the others."

"Whichever one you're eating at the time is the most important." Devin rubbed his belly. "When Imin's cooking, at least. I haven't had a decent meal since he left. I'm wasting away."

"This might have more to do with a certain Tribune feeling guilty about doing his duty out on the Verge, rather than rushing back to the core to save his sister."

"That Tribune sounds stupid. If I see him, I'll slap him."

"Let me get a mirror and a camera. I'll be playing this video lots."

"Status change," Lukas said. "We have vectors and sizes. Target-A conforms to the Hector Dixey in mass and drive plume readings. Hector Dixey is closing on a larger target—Target-B—in orbit around the outer ice giant. Target-B is between twice and three times as large as the Hector Dixey."

"Warship," Devin said. "That's our pirate."

"Could be." Lionel said. "But why in this system? Sensors, can you refuel on that ice-giant?"

"Spectroscope says…. says maybe, sir! Not much hydrogen atmosphere there, and most of it would be frozen, but you could scrape some up, perhaps. Take a long time, though. But it's there."

"Why does the sailing directions say no fuel here, then?" Devin asked.

"When was the last time they were updated?" Lionel asked. "If it was two hundred years ago, that ice giant would have been farther out, and no atmosphere to speak of at all."

"Makes sense. Can we sneak up on them?"

"Yes sir." Lukas played with his settings. "They're way outside the jump limit, so they could jump anytime they want.

If we wait until they're both in the planet's gravity well, then they can't get away."

"Outstanding." Devin smiled. "Commence sneaking. I'm going to lunch…" Devin's smile changed to a frown. "No, I'm going to the gym to…I'm just going. Execute. Execute. Execute."

Hector Dixey, presumably with Imin and a cargo of delicious soups onboard, surged into the planet's gravity well, aiming for a zero-zero intercept with the ship there. Pollux crept along behind. Devin sulked in his cabin and ordered engineering to send him a scale, and had the Marines send a selection of different types of ammunition to weigh. He was still fighting his ordering software.

Three shifts later, Lukas confirmed that the two ships were mated. Pollux had crept up behind the two. The second ship was 2.5 times the size of the freighter, which made it either a large freighter or a small warship. Lukas called down to Devin, who collected a pile of ammunition and returned to the bridge.

"Thank you, Marine 1C Jeelin," Devin said to the Marine who came to take the ammunition. "I've finally got a group of weights so I can figure out the units."

"Sir, yes sir. Might I ask, did the Tribune want to weigh them with the sabots?"

"Weigh them with what?"

"Sir. This ammunition can be chambered in a variety of weapons. There are… adaptors… called sabots, special holding cartridges that allow it to be used elsewhere. We don't often use them, but they are available."

"And..."

"They're carried in the same packaging as the actual ammunition itself sir. Available for loading."

"They'd be included in the weight of the packaging?"

"Yes sir."

Devin sighed. "Can you get me some of those sabots, Marine?"

"Right away sir!"

"No. We're about to go into combat. Bring them to me tomorrow afternoon. Dismissed."

The Marine saluted and left. Devin stared at the screen. "Subprefect, give me some good news."

"They haven't seen us, and they can't get away now," Lionel said. "Too deep in the orbit, we're right behind them, a quick vertical maneuver, targeting radar and we can have them for lunch."

"They'll probably taste better than my last tray," Devin said.

"Knowing your cooking, that's more a certainty than a probability," Lionel said.

"Light 'em up, Subprefect," Devin said.

Lionel gave the correct orders. The ship surged down and sideways for a better view. Radars lashed out, examined the two ships, and reported back to the computer. The computer drew a picture on the screens.

"What is that pile of junk?" Devin asked.

"That's not a warship," Lionel said.

"That's not a ship. It looks like...one ship trying to make a baby inside of another ship. And the other ship doesn't want a baby right now."

Devin turned his head sideways. "Over that side, that's the bow of a freighter. But it's in the middle. Sensors. What is that thing?"

Lukas threw some displays up on the screen. "Sir, computer says it's either a tanker or a freighter, but the confidence is very low."

"It's both." Subprefect Lionel walked to the screen and pointed. "This is the bow of a tanker, with the tanks. Engineering is missing. That's the stern of a freighter, but the forward parts, bridge and hab modules are gone."

"Two ships scraped out here, or crashed. Glued together."

"Looks like."

"Well, that monstrosity wasn't shooting up any ships. I don't see any working engines."

"And the Hector Dixey didn't either."

"Right," Devin tapped his chair. "So, no pirates. But where's the warship? Where's the pirates?"

"Status change," Lukas said. "Jump flare."

"Jump flare?" Devin asked.

"Beacon. Imperial Beacon." Lukas looked up. "Imperial warship. They're maneuvering." Lines danced on the displays as Lukas checked his data. "Charging in. Coming right for us."

CHAPTER FORTY-TWO

"They're querying us," Lukas warned.

"Whose warship is it?" Devin asked. "Which warship?"

"Just a general Empire beacon. Scanning now. Stand by." The new warship had replaced the bastardized station on the display. When the station had been displayed, all the bridge crew had leaned back in their seats and laughed. Now, the new warship made them all learn forward and type diligently onto sensor screens.

"Can you block their scans?"

"We can try, but sir, when we radared that station, we turned on our beacon. That was long enough ago they'll know who we are."

"Never mind, then."

"Sir?" Lukas the sensor operator said. "We may have a problem."

"What's the problem?" Devin asked.

"We're much farther inside the jump limit than we thought." Lukas projected a setting up on the screen. "We thought they were just being cautious with their arrival. But after running our scans, it turns out this planet is much more massive than recorded in the sailing directions. The jump limit is almost twenty-five percent farther out than anticipated. We're not just inside it, we're far down the gravity well."

"Outstanding," Devin said. "But only a problem if we have to get out of here in a hurry."

The communication officer spoke. "Incoming message."

"Give it to me."

"Umm. Personal for Subprefect Lionel sir. Private coded to him."

Devin turned to Lionel and raised an eyebrow. "Friends of yours, Subprefect?"

"Not that I know of. But I did order a new set of commemorative spoons recently. Maybe it's my delivery. Give it here."

The comm officer swiped her screen. Lights flashed on Lionel's. He typed a long code into his console, then thumbed a display. He tilted his head and played the message.

"Well?" Devin asked.

"I have the conn," the Subprefect said, and he slapped his screen. "Blast us out, full power. Any direction." The helmsman reacted to the command voice. Lights flashed on the bridge as the Pollux maneuvered. "Get us clear of the planet's gravity well before that unknown arrives. Do it now. Ignore the safeties."

Tribune Devin gaped at the Subprefect. He wouldn't do that unless something very bad has happened.

"Acceleration warning." The helmsman pulled a lever.

Alarms bonged. Devin pressed into his seat, then rose up on his straps as the ship pivoted. His arms floated up. The pivot hadn't finished before he slammed back again. His left arm crashed into the seat. Even with the padding, it hurt. Others on the bridge cursed as hands and elbows slammed into consoles or controls. Devin gasped. He couldn't breathe, and his vision was tunneling. The bonging receded. Did he order it turned off? Stars crossed his eyes, everything darkened.

Devin smelled toast. Was he having a stroke? Why had Lionel taken the conn? Shouldn't he have said something? Shouldn't the helm officer have listened to him? He was the captain. Wasn't he? Was this all a charade, or some sort of dream?

No, if it was a dream, it would be much nicer. He'd have better food. Why did he ever let Imin go? He should have had Imin leave more frozen food. Maybe a lasagna. He liked lasagna.

Why was he thinking of lasagna? Wasn't there a ship? A battle...

The weight on his chest dropped. The bonging of alarms re-appeared. He was stuck in his chair and his wrist hurt.

He could breathe. His eyes cleared. The alarms got louder.

Lionel was yelling at the helm. "I said, goose it, Helm."

Villa, the navigation officer, poked the helmsman. "He's out sir. Dropped the dead man switch."

"Transfer control—"

"I've got it sir." Villa tapped her screen. "I can give another G, that's all."

"Max it!"

"No dead man switch here sir. I might kill us all."

"Change our vector. Course to follow…"

"Sir, with our vectors, and the planet…"

"QUIET!" Devin yelled. "Lionel, Helm, somebody, report. What just happened?"

"I'll answer sir," Villa said. "He's out. Passed out under thrust. When the Subprefect said 'ignore safeties,' he pulled the override lever. Which lets us go into danger mode. That will give us max engines until he lets go. If he passes out, he lets go. I don't have a safety lever, so if I order max thrust, and pass out—"

"We'll all die. Subprefect?"

"We're too deep in the gravity well. I wanted to get out before they trapped us. No time to talk. We can go to standard orbit now."

"Very well. Helm, standard orbit." The bridge exhaled as one person as the Gs dropped to a sustainable limit. "We're safe now?"

"Nope, trapped."

"What?" Devin turned. "What do you mean?"

"Hang on a minute." Lionel sent the Marine to help the helmsman, then called for a medic and arranged for the navigation officer to take over the helm, before responding. "We're in a higher orbit now, but even with my maneuvering jaunt, it wasn't enough. Still inside the jump limit. They can still beat us. On his vector…" Lionel put some courses up on the screen. "We can't get to the jump limit without coming close to him, looks like."

"So we come close to him, why is that bad? it's an Imperial ship, isn't it?"

"They identified themselves in that private message. ISS Castor. A Pollux-class frigate, just like us."

"Two modern frigates in the Verge?"

"Looks like."

"Outstanding. What about your message?"

"And, good news! I've been promoted to Prefect and named in command of a ship."

"Ever better. Congratulations!"

"Thank you sir."

"Which ship?"

"ISS Pollux."

Devin waved his hands around the bridge. "Isn't this the Pollux?"

"The one and only."

"I thought I was the captain of the Pollux?"

"Maybe I should read you the whole message?"

"That would be nice."

Lionel brought up a message on his screen. "Authentications. Then: From fleet HQ to Subprefect Lionel, greetings, the Council..."

"Rather than reading the whole thing, perhaps just the gist of it, Sub—sorry, Prefect Lionel."

"Of course sir. From the Chancellor, in the name of the Emperor... Blah blah... Outstanding officer—I really like that part—loyal service—well-deserved promotion. I like that part too, the well-deserved."

"Prefect?"

"Hmm? Oh, sorry... take command of the Frigate ISS Pollux, and once you have secured command to your satisfaction, arrest the traitor, Devin, the so-called Lord Lyon, and place him under close confinement." Lionel grinned over at Devin. "I relieve you sir."

Devin regarded him. "Well, I stand relieved." He looked at the tactical display, showing the two frigates circling the planet. "Outstanding."

"Thank you sir."

"And the rest?"

"The rest, sir?"

"You're supposed to arrest me."

"Yes."

Devin watched as Lionel tapped on his screen. "And....?"

"And what, sir?"

"Are you going to do this? Arrest me?"

"I'm following orders, sir."

"You're arresting me."

"Not yet sir."

"Not yet?"

"Not yet."

"And why not?"

"I'm hard to satisfy, sir."

"What? Talk sense."

"Orders say I'm to take command, and once I've secured command to my satisfaction, do the rest. I'm not satisfied yet."

"Will you be satisfied soon?"

"Not for a long while. For example, haven't had a decent

meal in weeks. We need to get Imin back here so we can eat something good. Then we need to be fueled up and destroy those pirates."

"Don't we think that the Castor is perhaps the pirates?"

"Most probably sir. Best guess, truthfully. Does make that part a bit challenging."

"I see—"

"Status change," the sensor operator broke in. "Jump flare. Scanning now."

"Very well," Lionel said.

Devin raised an eyebrow.

"What?" Lionel said. "I'm the captain now. You've been relieved and everything."

"But not arrested?"

"Nope."

"Beacon," the comm officer said. "Imperial freighter, Heavyweight Items. Signaling distress."

"Of course he is," Devin said. "Can we comm him?"

"Trying now sir. They asked for a call... but not hand-shaking, sir."

"Keep trying... wait, I'm sorry, Captain. I'm usurping your bridge rights." Devin glared at Lionel.

"No problem, Tribune. Treat my bridge like it was your own."

"Why thank you."

"Except for maneuvering orders, and suchlike."

"Thank you."

"And crew orders, and promotions, and well, I'll make a

list. Perhaps you could confine yourself to positive statements of affirmation?"

"Just that?"

"You can order snacks as well."

"Could I talk to you on a private channel for a moment, Prefect Lionel?"

"Of course, Tribune."

Devin brought up a private channel and put Lionel's face up on his screen. "What in Jove's name is going on, Subprefect?"

"Prefect. That part's real. Do you want to do this in your office? More privacy."

"Aren't you going to claim that it's your office now?"

"Naw it... ya know... is it your private office or is it the captain's office? I should look that up."

"Do we have time for levity right now?"

"Absolutely not, Tribune." Lionel grinned around the bridge. "But we both need to keep smiling because we're in trouble. You were waiting for a ship from the capital, well, here it is. Complete with non-garbled properly formatted arrest warrants. And mail. And proper handshake codes, so they can contact anybody on the ship they want."

"Should we freeze communications?"

"Too late, and, no. You're counting on your people supporting you against the Chancellor and whatever is happening in the core. Best to find out now who we can trust."

"In the middle of a battle?"

"No battle yet. But they can force one whenever they want. They're far enough outside our orbit, that even if we try, we can't make the jump limit without engaging them. We have to climb out of this gravity well first. They can force a fight anytime they want."

"We can take them," Devin said.

Lionel's smile widened, but he shook his head.

"We can't?"

"Smile for the troops, Tribune."

Devin pasted a smile on his face. "We're one of the most powerful warships in the fleet."

"For our size, and there's our mirror image out there."

"Crewed by incompetent officers and the scum of the fleet and time-serving conscripts."

"Captain Albert Saxon, Imperial Space Service, according to my message. You know him?"

Devin cursed.

"Sounds like you do know him, Tribune. Served together?"

"He cheerfully despises me."

"Of course, you're a much better tactician than him?"

Devin shook his head. "No. He's good. Better than me. Almost as good as you, I think."

"Let's not go wild here, but that's what I thought. If we engage, it will be a slugfest. We'll both take damage, heavy damage, unless somebody makes a stupid mistake. Is he the type who makes stupid mistakes?" Lionel cocked his eyebrows.

"No."

"Sounds like we'll batter each other to death."

"Yes.

"Here's what we're going to do—"

Devin interrupted. "You don't give orders to a Tribune, even if you are a Prefect now."

"That, oddly enough, is my point. I'm going to run the ship, and fight the ship, and you're going to figure out a way to save the Empire. You tell me to attack, we attack. You tell me to retreat, we retreat. That's your job. Tell me what you need, and we'll do it."

"Status change!" the sensor operator announced. "Jump flare."

"Dirk jumped out?" Devin asked.

"No sir, Heavyweight Items is still there, but seems to have some sort of communications problem. This is a new ship. A freighter." The sensor operator looked up. "The Earl of Clydebank, according to its beacon, except…"

"Except we talked to that ship some time ago," Lionel said. "And it was going a different direction, and I'll bet you've been scanning everything that shows up and there's some sort of anomaly in the scans."

"It's too big to be the Earl of Clydebank, sir. Too long."

"Tribune, I present you the pirates of the Verge." Lionel swept his hand at the display. "Raider-A, Raider-B, their supply freighter and their support base. Well, support hulk. Delivered to you and awaiting your pleasure. Which one should we attack first?"

"Hmmm—" Devin grimaced. "You swear to follow my orders, Prefect?"

"Follow the Mad Dog of the Verge? Always. Always."

"Very well," Devin said. "Retreat."

CHAPTER FORTY-THREE

"It's an old code, but it checks out, Kapitan," Pinguin's comm officer said. "Should I put him through?"

"Yes, thank you." Kruder tapped his fingers as the call to the Imperial frigate went through. "Wait. Any word from Fusterheim?"

"No sir, he's still in engineering." The jump had been completed normally, but the two jumps so close together had caused... something. Arriving in the system, the ship had shuddered from end to end, and all the power had died. The power came back on in minutes, but engineering was reporting 'ongoing unknown issues.' Kruder sent Fusterheim down to engineering to see what was happening.

"Very well. Let's see this Accursed Imperial."

The static disappeared from the main screen and Captain Albert Saxon, Imperial Space Service, appeared on the screen.

"You're not that Russe guy," he said.

"I'm not," Kruder said.

"And your ship has a different name than before."

"It does."

"And I hadn't seen this code before." Saxon frowned. "You didn't use it last time you saw us."

"No, I didn't." Kruder folded his hands and waited. The silence stretched.

"Do you have anything to say to me, Captain?"

"I'm sorry, are you finished with your questions? You seemed in a hurry, which I assume is why you didn't introduce yourself."

Saxon glared. "Captain Albert Saxon, Imperial Space Service. What are you doing in our space."

"I am Kruder, Kapitan, Union of Nations. That this is your space is subject to some dispute by my government, but regardless, we are here at the… invitation of a member of your government. I was given these codes to request assistance. I did not expect to be asking a mainline Imperial ship."

"I didn't expect to meet a Nat out here either."

"Looks like we've both had a surprising day."

"Is that why your engines are down?"

"I do not go charging blindly in without knowing what I am getting into." And until Fusterheim confirms things are working, I want to stay outside the jump limit in case I need to escape two warships.

"What do you want?"

"There is an Imperial freighter in this system we are tracking. One of our citizens is onboard. We wish to rescue them."

"Rescue away."

"They may attempt to resist this."

"According to my briefing notes, you're some sort of pirate. Can't you deal with their resistance?"

Kruder's' face turned white at the word 'pirate,' and he gripped the arms of his chair. "I am not a pirate. I am operating under orders from my government."

"So you say. But go ahead. We have other fish to fry. In fact, I'd rescue your citizen pretty soon, before that freighter docks at the station in there."

"We have detected another Imperial frigate insystem. It has not responded to our codes. Will you guarantee that it will not interfere with our rescue?"

Saxon leaned back on the screen. "Is this a rescue or an abduction?"

"Can you guarantee they will not interfere?"

Saxon looked off-screen for a moment, then nodded. "Kapitan... Kipper?"

"Kruder."

"Captain Kruder, rescue your crew member. Soon. Stay away from that other frigate and that station. If you attempt to dock with either, I will destroy you. If you pursue that freighter into station orbit, I will destroy you. If the freighter jumps, do not follow it deeper into the Empire or—"

"You will destroy me. Yes, yes, I understand."

"You have four hours to catch your friend and leave. That should be plenty of time."

"It is. Thank you. One more question."

"I'm not inclined to answer any more questions."

Kruder ignored this. "As part of our... arrangement with your... patron... we have sent several ships into a rendezvous here, with crews from captured vessels and some of our own people. What is their status, please?"

"Never saw them," Saxon said. His eyes were flat. "Don't know about any crews."

"Never saw then?"

"None of them."

"There were many, perhaps we can—"

"Don't know anything about that."

"I will send you descriptions and courses—"

"I said I don't know anything." Saxon looked at the corner of his screen. "Three hours and fifty-seven minutes to go. Catch your man, and leave. Saxon out."

The screen blanked. Kruder sat for a long time. Finally, he turned. "Leutnant Blomberg!"

"Kapitan!"

"Do you have anything to add to this conversation?"

"Sir, my explanation of the Council's orders notwith-standing, my involvement in this enterprise is minimal."

"Your minimal involvement is the reason we are in this system."

"I have nothing to add to my orders sir."

"Of course you don't. Helm, plot a course to catch those Accursed Imperials with that spy."

"First officer on the line sir," the comm officer said.

Kruder slapped his intercom. "Hans?"

"Sir." Fusterheim's voice was scratchy. "We've figured out the problem."

"Where are you?"

"Out on the hull at the end of a big tether."

"What for?"

"Needed magnetic readings that weren't going to be messed up by the ship. I jetted out here with some probes and the chief's checking from inside. We jumped inside the jump limit."

"What? Is our astrogation—"

"No sir. No, that's fine. This planet isn't as registered. The notes in the fleet directions are wrong. It's much denser than it looks, much more iron. Lots more iron. The jump limit isn't a standard one, it stretches much farther out. When we came in, the imbalance blew all our circuits. The chief is resetting things right now."

"I see." Kruder blinked. "We're lucky."

"We should be cosmic debris. Or jump space energy. Or something, but not here. The chief wants to double-check all the circuits when he's done. That could take an hour."

"He doesn't get an hour. Tell him we need max acceleration to catch that freighter. There are Accursed Imperials insystem, and they've given us a deadline."

"Can you wait on the max acceleration 'til I'm back inside?"

"Yes, but get moving." Kruder closed the channel. "Helm, call air lock...K13. As soon as the first officer is onboard, bring us after that cursed freighter. It's time to catch a spy."

CHAPTER FORTY-FOUR

"Bring us down closer. I want to nearly dock with that station," Devin stood. "But leisurely. No radical maneuvers. We have plenty of time. "

"Very well, Tribune." Lionel nodded. "Where will you be?"

"In my cabin, watching movies. Once you are satisfied with your course, come and see me. Bring the bosun." Devin left the bridge, but halted as the comm officer called him.

"Tribune, there's a call from the Castor."

"Who for?"

"Private for the captain."

Devin pointed at Lionel. "There's the captain. I'm just excess baggage now. Let the sub—that will be hard to get used to. Let the Prefect deal with him."

Lionel tapped his screen. "What should I tell the Castor, Tribune?"

"You're the captain now, do as you like. I suggest telling him that I'm in my cabin and not available for communications. That should make him think twice."

Devin screened some displays that Lionel had shown him weeks ago. The ones showing damage to ships in battles, and the one system where they had found the remains of a merchant ship. Then he put the Pollux's course around 429-6666 on the screen, then included the station and the Hector Dixey on the screen. Then he added the other ships and played orbits back and forth. After a half hour, his doorbell bonged, and he ushered Bosun McSanchez and Prefect Lionel in.

"Gentlemen, would you like a drink? Or a snack?"

"Not right now. We're on duty, Tribune," McSanchez said.

"That's just as well, because I might be able to find a bottle of something, but food will be beyond my capabilities."

"Thank Jove for that." Lionel flopped into a seat. "Because being forced to eat your cooking might be worse than talking with Captain Saxon for a half hour."

"And how is the good captain?"

"He wants you arrested. And shot. And not in that order."

"And you haven't done that because…"

"I said I needed to read some other messages that he delivered from the core and have a long talk with you."

"What's the news from the core?"

"Nothing about your sister, or her husband. The Chancellor has ordered you detained as an enemy of the state. Imperial seal on the warrant, but not the Emperor's personal seal, so possibly some skullduggery. But the type of skullduggery that we'd need to be in the Imperial presence to sort out."

"Think we should go visit the Imperial presence?"

"I think we should discuss our current situation," Lionel

sat up. "And speaking of our current situation, you're pretty calm about this whole thing."

"What parts of this whole thing?"

"Me being appointed captain. Promoted. Taking over your ship. Being told to arrest you."

"Excuse me sir," McSanchez said. "I've been remiss. Congratulations on your promotion to Prefect sir. Well deserved, and a long time coming."

"Thank you, Bosun."

"And congratulations on being promoted to captain of the Pollux. She'll never have a better captain."

"Thank you again, Bosun."

"Arrramph," Devin said. "Never have a better captain?"

"The Prefect is well-respected amongst the crew, Tribune."

"And me? I was the captain before…"

"You're respected as well, sir. Brave. Honest. Forthright, loyal to the Emperor and the Empire. Courageous."

"I don't hear 'competent' there, Bosun."

"You bring your own set of unique skills to the ship, sir."

Devin scowled, then he laughed. "I'd never have gotten anywhere without you, Prefect Lionel, and everybody knows it. He's right, the Pollux will never have a better captain." Devin stuck his hand out, and Lionel shook it vigorously. "And now I'm going back to being a Tribune, and not getting in the way of the people doing their jobs. Take a look at this."

Devin put the different courses up on the screen. "Our strategic directive. Recover our lost crew member, Imin, here." He highlighted the Hector Dixey. "Destroy the primary pirate presence in the system, here." Devin highlighted the station. "And capture or cripple the other pirate in the system, here." Now Devin highlighted the Castor. "Note I didn't say 'destroy.' I want him intact, or at least minimal casualties. Those are Imperial citizens there, our fellows, and I want as little damage to them as possible."

"Understood, Tribune," Lionel said. "We'll get right on this. After lunch okay?"

"Fine. And there is one other thing," Devin said. "We'll need to chase away that Nat ship, the Earl of Clydebank. We want it out of here."

"Of course you do," Lionel said. "Thank you for your strategic directives, Tribune. Always good to have a concise overview of the strategic situation. Let me summarize our tactical situation. We're on alert, all stations are manned, all weapons ready. We're on a converging course with that pirate station and should be passing almost on top of it in about four orbits. We'll be so close we can throw rocks, so picking up Imin and destroying that base will be no problem." Lionel manipulated the board. "After only a few orbits, we'll have dealt with things down here. Then we will proceed to boost out of the planet's gravity well to meet the Castor in battle. We'll be putting out full thrust, of course, but we'll be hampered by being in the gravity well. Effectively, we'll have about one-quarter of our normal thrust and maneuvering. No dodging any lasers or positrons fired at us. Even if they fire blind box barrages, the target area will be so much smaller that they're bound to hit us before we hit them. Meanwhile, they're weaving and dodging in a high orbit. We'll have to scatter our return fire all over hell and beyond to cover the larger box area they could be maneuvering in. End result, they'll wipe the floor with us as we climb out."

"Thank you for your tactical assessment, Prefect." Lionel smiled. "Bosun, I know that you're not an officer, but I'd like your assessment of the situation as well."

"Well sir, that station isn't going anywhere, so it goes boom as soon as you want. That freighter next to it, same thing. And myself, a shuttle, and a few Marines, we can recover Imin no problem as we pass by. Freighters no threat. Pirates will be wiped out. But the other ship... that's a problem sir."

"Very well, Boson. Well done. One thing, though, regarding the pirates."

"Sir?"

"You'd expect there to be some booty, wouldn't you? Seized cargos? That sort of thing."

"Yes sir unless they sold it somewhere. But they could just jettison it into the sun, if they don't want it."

"Of course, they could. But here's a question where are the crews? All those freighters, we assumed the crews were being held somewhere."

"Yes sir." The bosun turned back to the screen. "Can you expand that base, freighter-tanker thing, please, Tribune?"

Devin pointed at the console. "Help yourself, Bosun. I'm sure you're as good at this as I am. Better probably."

McSanchez manipulated the screen, zooming in and sizing the hab modules with a legend, then bringing up a legend and a chart. Devin made a mental note. He hadn't known how to bring the legend up. Or the chart.

"Only space for about fifty people in those hab modules, Tribune. Even if they're friendly with each other."

"Which captured freighter crews wouldn't be. How many crew members are on those missing ships?"

"Hundreds, sir. Sir." McSanchez stood to attention and saluted. "Permission to attend the boarding party on that freighter, sir."

"Granted. Take Marines. Lots of Marines."

"Yes sir."

"Best you go prepare."

McSanchez saluted again and left. Lionel waited until he left. "What about me?"

"You have your orders. Destroy the station. Rescue Imin. Capture or cripple the Castor."

"While climbing out of a gravity well?"

"You figure it out." Devin shrugged. "I'm strategy, you're tactics."

"That's a little... unfair, Tribune."

"Whatever happens, I'll be sitting right next to you when it does happen," Devin said.

Lionel gave the cross-chest salute. "The Empire."

Devin returned it. "The Empire."

Lionel got up to leave, but Devin stopped him. "Prefect?"

"Sir?"

"Congratulations on your promotion, and on assuming command." He grinned. "I'm sure you'll figure a way out of this?"

"Is dying gloriously a way?"

"It is." Devin bit his lip. "It is."

CHAPTER FORTY-FIVE

"Are you sure it's the Pollux?" Dirk said. "There's two of them."

"It has a beacon, Pilot," Lee said.

"It could be a trick." Dirk glared at the settings. "Gavin, can we get moving yet?"

Dirk and Lee were in the control room reading the scans, Ana seated behind them. Dena and Scruggs had converted two monitors in the lounge to show sensor readings.

"Not yet, Skipper," Gavin said from engineering. "Whether it's a trick or not, we need to find out what happened with our flash." They'd double-flashed upon jump emergence, which was a symptom of either a too-close emergence, or a failing jump drive. "I'm running tests now—It'll take time. You can figure out the trick while we wait."

"You're not important enough to trick, Navy," Ana said. "They don't care what you know."

"Besides," Lee said. "There's only two Imperial ships. If

the Tribune was trying to hide, he wouldn't have a beacon on at all. If he's not trying to hide, then he'd leave it on."

"The ship that's not the Pollux might be trying to confuse us by showing the Pollux's beacon," Dirk said. He shuffled in his seat, his magboots making his seating awkward. For the emergence, he'd insisted they all wear full vacuum-safe mode—skinsuits, hard collars, gloves and boots, with helmets nearby. He'd even gone so far as to trim his beard and put on an officer's cap he found somewhere.

"In which case, there would be two ships claiming to be the Pollux, not one," Lee said. "Why would the Tribune not claim to be himself, if somebody else was there pretending to be him."

"This is why I like you, Navigator." Ana played with his screen. "Smart. Logical."

"You don't like me. You call me a freak. You want nothing to do with the Empire. You're a soulless mercenary who is only out for himself and doesn't care what happens to anyone else. And you're violent and brutal."

Scruggs came up on the intercom. "Lee, you know that he'll take all that as a compliment, right?"

"Yeah, second that," Dena said. "He's probably blushing. Why are you being so nice to the old man anyways?"

Lee shook her head. "Do you want me to open a channel to the Pollux?"

"Before you do," Dena said, "Scruggs fired up that radar thingy, for the stuff close-like, and saw something, so she sent out one of those stripping things."

Dirk tapped his intercom. "You mean Scruggs scanned nearspace, saw a ship, and stripped the beacon?"

"No need to repeat what I said, Dirk. Anyways, there's a ship down there, the Hector Dixey, the beacon says. Freighter."

"Is it for real, or is it a fake beacon?"

"Scruggs says it's real. We looked up the specs in that warbook you got us, and they match. But there's another thing behind it. We don't know what it is. Can I show it to you?"

"Show it to us," Ana said.

"Will do." All the bridge screens went black. They waited. And waited.

"Nature Girl, we've got nothing up here."

"Sorry, that wasn't right. Let me put the picture up here on my screen, okay, here, then I have to zoom in. This is right next to the freighter."

A different picture approached. Dark, twisted lines showed with a white background. There was movement in the corner, and then a pink glare in the middle.

"What is that?" Ana asked. "Doesn't look like a ship?"

"Or a planet. Or a moon," Lee said.

The picture swayed, the pink light moved from right to left and back again.

"Is that some sort of planetary storm? It's pink in the middle."

"Pink?" Dena said. "No, supposed to be white."

"It's not white," Dirk said.

"Could it be another ship?" Ana asked.

Dirk tapped his screen, then zoomed out. "Dena, wrong picture. This isn't a ship?"

"What am I looking at?"

"Don't know what you're looking at, but we're looking at a video of Rocky licking his testicles."

Lee and Ana zoomed their pictures out.

Oooohhhh...gross," Lee said.

"That's a set for a dog to be proud of," Ana said. "Not sure what it has to do with space combat, though."

"Imperial—Scruggs!" Dena said.

The screen flickered, blanked, then a new picture appeared. This was a shot of the planet—the ice giant—with an area in the lower right circled. "Zoom in on the circle," Scruggs said.

"That's a freighter in front," Dirk said as the picture closed in. "Must be your Hector Dixey. And those are ship parts in the back. Not whole ships."

"I don't see a drive," Lee said.

"Because there isn't one," Dirk said. "There's a hab section... fuel tanks. That looks like part of a drive section—the vanes look like from a fusion reactor, but no nozzles. Whatever it is there isn't moving."

"I don't see any weapons," Ana said. "Which is more important than a drive."

"Centurion, there's one of those slug-throwers you told me about, here." Scruggs sent another picture, this time higher resolution, with a machine gun-like protrusion showing on the top.

"Yep, a frightener," Ana said. "But nothing for anybody

more than a klick away to worry about. No other weapons. How did you find that, Private?"

"There's a pattern recognition program in the new software. Run images through it, and it highlights anything that matches the silhouette of shipboard weapons."

"Well done, looks like we've found a secret base."

"More like a secret gas station," Lee said. "And not much of that. Not much fuel in those tanks, and I only see one hab module. Nowhere to keep things, or people, or goods."

"Outstanding," Ana said. "But let's not lose focus. Our current problem—"

"Jump flare," Lee said.

"Our current problem apparently followed us here. But even an over-armed freighter is no match for an Imperial frigate in a fair fight. Certainly not two."

"You are getting all space-like again, Centurion," Dirk said. "Don't you think you should let the space people comment on it, as Dena would say."

"You are correct, Navy." Ana slapped a button and the alarm rang. "General quarters, General quarters. Stations for ship-to-ship combat. This is not a drill."

"What in the Emperor's name?"

Ana brought up his comm. "Attention the ship, attention the ship, Captain the Duke Dirk Friedel will now explain to us how a single armed merchant raider is a match for two fully armed Imperial frigates. Captain?"

Dirk looked at Lee. "When did we get a general quarters alarm button?"

Lee shrugged.

Scruggs spoke up. "I asked the shipyard people to put one in. You complained that we needed one earlier, so I asked the nice boy who was working on the electronics to put one in."

Dirk paged through his screens. "I have a general quarters alarm now?"

"Well, no. You don't. Centurion does."

"We paid for an upgrade to our alarm circuit? For the centurion?"

"We didn't pay anything. I just smiled and gave him my comm code."

Dena jumped in. "Did he call?"

"Don't know. I gave him a fake number."

"Well done!" Dena giggled over the intercom. "Well done."

"If you girls are finished," Ana said.

"Women, Centurion."

"Sounds more girlish to me. But, Navy, you were going to tell us about those frigates?"

"Why." Dirk gritted his teeth. "Why does the ground pounder get the ship alarm button, and I don't?"

"It concerns ship security, right?" Scruggs said. "That's Centurion's job. You just drive."

"I just drive? I'll have you know—"

"You're the captain," Lee said. "Yes, Pilot. Pollux is on the comm."

"Are we sure it's Pollux? The real Pollux?"

"Well, if it's not Tribune Devin on the comm, then don't talk to them," Lee said.

"Good point." Dirk tapped through some screens, and Devin's face appeared. "Tribune. I'm glad to see you."

"I'd like to say the same. Aren't you supposed to be on your way into the core?"

"We got sidetracked getting some weapons. And we met an old friend of Ana's, and we think we've found a pirate base. Or a privateer base."

"You have found a pirate base, and a privateer base as well."

"Oh good, you know about the freighter, the Earl of Clydebank?"

"Know what?"

"Doesn't matter much. You and that other frigate should have no problem taking care of her."

"Yeah, that other frigate." Devin sucked his teeth. "About that."

CHAPTER FORTY-SIX

"Korvettenkapitan Felix Kruder, at your service," Kruder said. "And you would be Lord Devin." Kruder's bridge officers were intent on their duties, but when Kruder spoke Devin's name, another phrase shivered around the bridge. Kruder cocked his head to listen, then grimaced. "Or as we understand you are called here, the Mad Dog of the Verge."

Devin grinned at him. "You've heard of me, I see." After talking to Dirk, he'd called his boarding party to confirm the absence of prisoners. Then he'd opened up an encrypted call to Kruder.

"You are known to us, yes." Kruder waited patiently for the ten-second round-trip delay to run out.

"And you admit your rank. You're not attempting to pretend that you're just an innocent freighter captain who accidentally jumped into the wrong place?"

Kruder laughed. "Would it work?"

"Absolutely not. We've had plenty of time to get excellent

scans from you now, and before, when we met the other time. And the Earl of Clydebank is ten meters shorter than you."

"We could have had a refit."

"Ships get longer in refits, not shorter. And we could have scans from the real ship, taken a few months ago. Want to guess? But it doesn't matter, we plotted your course. You've been pirating Imperial ships for the last few months."

Kruder cut his microphone and ordered their proper beacon run up, then returned to his call. "I am not a pirate. I am a naval officer, acting on orders of my government, and we have been seizing contraband in an area claimed by the Union of Nations."

"Also claimed by the Empire, and the Confederation, and some other polities."

"That is not my concern. I have my duty."

"Of course you do, of course you do." Devin turned left as something distracted him, and nodded. "A moment, Kapitan. A small matter to attend to." The picture froze—the camera was off, but the channel hadn't been cut.

Kruder looked at Alvarez. "What's going on down there?"

Alvarez put a telescopic-camera output on the main screen. "Pollux has recovered the shuttle they launched that docked with the Hector Dixey. Both ships are maneuvering around that station. But we have a ten second lag, and—oops. There it goes."

An explosion flared white on the station-tanker-freighter monstrosity, silhouetting the Pollux, then the orbital base broke into burning pieces.

"Base is destroyed," Alvarez announced.

"Very well." Kruder's attention returned to his screen. Devin's frozen image resumed motion as the far camera reconnected. "Sorry, Kapitan, a housekeeping matter to attend to. What are your intentions in this system?"

"We are going to recover a citizen of ours held hostage on the Heart's Desire."

"Dirk has one of your people? A Nat? On his ship?"

"Dirk—you know Captain Friedel?"

"Of course. And Dirk is going to allow you to recover this person?"

"That is none of your concern."

"The operations of any vessel in Imperial Space is my concern."

"We do not recognize—"

"Relax, Kapitan." Devin nodded. "You can recover your person with no interference from us. I'll even comm Dirk and order him to hand over this person and have him share course information with you. In fact, I'll send a shuttle and some Marines to see him."

"He and his crew take orders from you?"

"I didn't say he'd listen. I said I'd do what I can, thus the Marines. You have noticed that there is another Imperial frigate in this system?"

"The Union of Nations supports freedom of travel. Even though we claim this area, we respect the right of innocent passage. We have no issue with Imperial ships in our space."

"Innocent passage." Devin said. "Which is not what you said a second ago. We also caught what might be the reflection of a directed communication between you and that frigate.

Kapitan, I'm going to be frank. You've been pirating Imperial ships. You and that frigate both."

"Not pirating—"

"Wrong word, I understand. However, you've been seizing those ships and destroying them or sending them back somewhere. And that frigate, the Castor, is involved with you, either providing cover or collecting supplies. More about that later. For now, we are very concerned about our crews. I'd like some information about them."

Kruder waited for the time lag. "Again, I—"

Devin continued over the response. "We're ignoring your pro-forma protest. But what I am doing is sending a list of ships that have disappeared in this area. Imperial ships, Nat ships, and Confed ships. We haven't seen the ships in weeks or months, and we haven't seen the crews either. I'd like information on their welfare. If you're not able to provide them, I'm going to assume you had them all spaced. Don't bother protesting. I know your crew will back up your denials. But I'm sending you some other information. It includes three Union of Nations ships that disappeared, along with the probable area of their disappearance. I'm also including some footage we got of a ship breaking up in the atmosphere a few weeks back. A freighter. You might recognize it." Devin killed the channel.

Blomberg made a rude gesture at the screen from his station. "Of all the nerve, that Accursed Imperial—"

"Shut up, Blomberg," Kruder said. "You may carry instructions from the Council, but this is my ship. Comm, what are they sending us?"

Tannen scanned her screen. "Lots of data, Kapitan. Lists, reports, a pile of images. Sensor logs, some visuals. It's still coming in."

"Sort it into some sort of order and send it to me. Hans, you have the conn. Don't accept any communications from anyone 'til I've reviewed this data."

"Sir," Tannen broke in. "Pollux is communicating with that freighter, the Heart's Desire."

"Encrypted? Directed?"

"An open channel generally in their direction. And not even encrypted."

"Monitor it and send me the recording."

"And the other frigate, the Castor, is calling us."

"Ignore them for now. Let's see what is going on with this information." Kruder got up from his console and left the bridge.

"I said, Dirk," Devin said, "that I understand that you are being chased by a Nat warship in disguise. We've checked and believe it to be a modified auxiliary cruiser—a former freighter, its beacon says Pinguin. An impressive weapons load if the Intelligence Analysis is correct. But that's neither here nor there. I'm giving you a course that will allow them to rendezvous zero-zero with you, and then you'll transfer their citizen to them. Or more probably, allow them to board you and take him. Or her. Who is it?"

Devin had called the Heart's Desire on an open channel, inquired politely after the crew, chastised Dirk for not being in the core, and brushed away his explanations regarding the problems with his laser.

"Tribune," Lee broke in. "They have no proof that the man they seek, that he's actually a Union of Nations Citizen."

"Do you have proof that he's an Imperial Citizen?" Devin asked.

"Well, no," Dirk said. "But he's a member of my crew. I'm responsible for him."

"And I'm responsible for this part of the Empire, and for not starting a war with the Nats. They're here and they want their man. And then there's that other frigate. You understand my position regarding the Castor?"

Devin had explained that, by the direction of the Chancellor, he was under arrest on suspicion of treason.

"Tribune," Lee said. "This Pinguin, I'm sure that they are the pirate that has been seizing ships."

"So am I. He's admitted it. I've told him he must provide proper information on their crews. All of the crews of all the ships that have disappeared."

"And are you really going to turn yourself over to the Castor? With a warrant from the Chancellor?"

"I'll do what I think best for the Empire. As you should, Commander, Praetorian."

Ana poked his head into the screen. "Hey, your Tribuneship?"

"You again. You're that senior centurion, right?"

"Yes, your Tribuneship. I know this Kruder guy. He and you have a lot in common. He'll do his duty even if it kills him."

"A laudable action, even in an enemy."

"What I mean is, he's pretty unhappy with us. He'll

probably shoot us up. And you won't stop him without firing on him."

"I will do no such thing."

"If he gets his hands on us, he'll kill us. And since he's been pirating Imperial ships, shouldn't you be doing something about that?"

"I will dispatch a squad of Marines onto your ship to oversee the transfer. We have shuttles. We'll send you a course. Stay on the course until you've docked with our shuttle, then surrender to the Nats."

"You want us to surrender?"

"I'll be somewhat busy for the next while," Devin said. "Shuttle will be there shortly."

Dirk shook his head. "I won't do it."

Devin shrugged. "You say you've got weapons. Fire them if you want. Just don't be surprised if that Nat ship fires back."

CHAPTER FORTY-SEVEN

"None of them have checked in?" Kruder asked.

"I can't find any records, sir," the comm officer said. Devin's transmission had included lists of missing ships, and videos of wreckage. Kruder started asking questions. He had the bridge staff checking for details that would refute Devin's claim that the Union of Nations crews had been spaced.

Kruder raised his voice. "Find out! Double-check!"

"Sir."

Fusterheim stepped to Kruder's console and brought up the engine status report on the main screen. The Pinguin's engines had restarted without any problems. Now the ship was running a standard course to planetary orbit, cautiously trailing the Heart's Desire, and avoiding the Imperial frigates circling the ice giant.

"Why are you showing me this?" Kruder asked. "I know the engines are running well after your inspection."

Fusterheim leaned closer and lowered his voice. "What is it?"

"Nothing is wrong."

"You never raise your voice on the bridge, ever. You told the comm officer to double-check reports from the War Navy that we received a month ago. What's he supposed to do? Read them again? We won't get any new updates for months."

Kruder stood and addressed the control room. "Continue on this vector. Fusterheim. Come to my cabin."

They climbed down two levels in the freighters hab module. Unlike a warship, there was no captain's room co-located with the control room. Kruder had a cabin the same size as the rest of the officers, and a second as an office. The office had a small arms locker, a safe, and a display screen.

He seated himself at the console and brought up a display. "This is some of the image that Accursed Imperial sent us."

"Which Accursed Imperial? There are two."

"The Mad Dog one. Here." One of the scenes that Devin had sent was the destruction of the broken freighter pieces burning up in the planetary atmosphere. "What do you see?"

"I see something burning up as it re-enters atmosphere." Fusterheim leaned closer to the screen. "That's a hab module. There, that's the front, I can see the internal structure. Must have been a big explosion. It's split into six pieces. No, eight. Can we zoom in?"

"Yes." Kruder expanded the screen.

"That's what's left of a hab module after an explosion. It's got eight rooms on that hab module or would if it was intact. Did any of the Imperial ships we captured…?"

"No." Kruder and Fusterheim were both former merchant crew—they could draw accurate designs of the internals of ships from memory. The Empire constructed hab modules that had six internal bulkheads. Union of Nation Yards construed their sections with eight. "That's one of ours."

"Indeed, Hans. The Mad Dog of the Verge also sent the blowup of this area here."

"Those are bodies, in skinsuits. Lots. Six, seven… then over there… at least twenty."

"Yes. Here's the blowup of the skinsuits." Kruder put another image on the screen. "Look here."

Fusterheim hissed. Imperial skinsuits' neck collars and cuffs were round. Helmets rotated on and snapped onto the suit collar. Union of Nations helmets pushed on, then were clamped tight by a lever on a hinge behind the head. The lever stuck down when closed, but would stick out when open, creating a distinctive pattern behind the head.

The bodies showed Nat-style helmet levers behind them.

"Those were our people. What's going on?"

"I think we found out where our captured crews went."

"Imin. Glad you're back," Devin said.

"Thank you sir."

"The Marines didn't report any problems getting you here."

"Weren't any sir. The crew and I got along well. They left me alone, I left them alone."

"You left them alone?"

"After some initial discussions, sir. Everybody agreed best that I do what I like."

"Discussions?"

"Discussions. Full and frank exchange of views."

"That was it?"

"I beat two people senseless and broke the navigator's arm. After that, we had an understanding."

"I see. Well, we'll have a full briefing later. But this was the pirate base. These people were seizing the ships in concert with the Castor over there. All to further inflame tensions between the Empire and the Confederation, leading to war."

"Got it in one, Tribune. It looks like the Castor did the attacking, along with some Nat-based ship."

"Indeed. Did you get a chance to look at any sensors recently?"

"Yes sir. I see Duke Friedel is back in the system."

"He is."

"I'm wondering how he got here sir. Odd place for him to be."

"He was on his way somewhere else, it seems. And did you see the other ship?"

"The Nat armed merchant cruiser chasing him? Yes sir."

"You mean the innocent freighter that coincidentally arrived after Dirk?"

"That's the one, sir. That's the Nat ship that's been pirating our ships."

"How did you figure that out?"

"Captain of the Hector Dixey had some information on it, sir."

"Imin." Devin sat at his desk. "A few important things that I need confirmed. Were there any prisoners on the Hector Dixey, or on that base?"

"Didn't see any, sir."

"Any facilities for prisoners?"

"Might have been a storeroom that could be locked, but nothing major that could hold big groups."

"Where'd the prisoners from those missing ships go?"

"That's the question, isn't it sir? Most probably spaced."

"Indeed. Right, I'm going back to the bridge, and deal with that. I have a favor to ask."

"Yes sir. What would you like me to do?"

"Well." Devin reddened. "I'm embarrassed to ask."

"Sir?"

"Imin, that was incredibly brave of you, going onto that ship to suss out the pirate base. You'll get an award for that."

"If you say so, sir. I'll put it with the others."

"I figured that. I know you've had this horrible ordeal, and that we're going into battle, and that we'll possibly die—"

"That's every battle with you, sir."

"Indeed. I know we might be looking at the cosmos for our last, but frankly, Imin..."

"Sir?"

"I haven't had a decent meal in a week. I'd kill for some soup." Devin nodded. "With those little crackers you make? Could I have some of that?"

CHAPTER FORTY-EIGHT

"Tribune on the bridge!" Lionel called out as Devin returned to Pollux's bridge.

"As you were, all that," Devin strode in, then stopped. "Sub—dammit. Prefect, you're in my chair."

"Captain's chair, Tribune." Lionel lounged at Devin's station. "This is where the captain sits."

"I'm not—no, you're right. The Emperor has appointed you captain."

"Not exactly. A ship has arrived bearing a warrant purportedly from the Emperor but signed by the Chancellor, appointing me captain. And promoting me."

"I'll miss my chair."

"You can have it back, if you ask nicely." Lionel stood. "Comm, the relay you were setting up earlier. Is it ready?"

The comm officer nodded. "Any time you want it sir."

"Do it now."

The comm officer typed. "You're ship wide sir."

"What's the meaning of this?" Devin said. "What are you broadcasting?"

Lionel stood and waved at the chair next to him. "Tribune Devin, Lord Lyon, I am in receipt of an order from the Castor, signed by the Chancellor, ordering your arrest for treason against the Emperor. What say you?"

Devin glared at the crew. All the officers were looking at him. He glanced up at the intercom repeater to the side of the bridge. It broadcast the tableau ship wide. "I would never commit treason against the Emperor. He's my brother-in-law, for Jove's sake. The father of my nephew."

"What's going on, then?"

"Lionel," Devin said. "Why are you doing this?"

"It's time to make some things official."

"Lionel, he can't touch you. You've done nothing wrong. Not yet. They can get me, but you're following orders. Real orders."

"As if that will protect me." Lionel pointed at the chair. "Well?"

Devin waved at the assembled crew. "Think about the other officers. And the crew. What about them? Don't they have a choice in all this?"

"They're the ones that brought it up. They want to know where you stand. I want to know where you stand."

"I stand with the Empire!"

"Then prove it." Lionel crossed his arms and waited.

Devin stared at each of his officers in turn. They stood stone-faced. None smiled. He blinked tears away for a moment. "Lionel, some days, I wish you hadn't dragged me out of that compartment, all those years ago."

"Some days, I wish I hadn't. Today isn't one of them." He uncrossed his arms. "Devin, it's time. We need to start this thing."

Devin laid his hands on the back of his chair. He'd sat there daily, for months, telling jokes, laughing, hiding in the Verge, avoiding his duty.

That time was up.

Devin sat in his chair. A sigh ran through the bridge officers. Devin felt for a moment that a sigh ran through the whole ship. "Prefect?"

"Tribune?"

"You are relieved. In the name of the Empress, I am assuming command of the Pollux, and all fleet elements in this and adjacent sectors. I declare the Chancellor a rebel, and a pirate, who has conspired with our foreign enemies against the Empire—seized our ships, killed our crews, and committed treason. His orders are annulled, and he must be arrested. This applies to him, and to all that follow him."

This time, he was sure he could hear the cheering from the rest of the ship.

"The Accursed Imperial is back on the comm, Kapitan," the comm officer said over the intercom. Kruder and Fusterheim had been arguing in private in Kruder's office. "Um. The Pollux-based cursed Imperial, that is."

"The arrogant one?"

"Kapitan, to me, it is difficult—"

"Both of them sound like that. Yes. The Mad Dog of the Verge one. What does he want?"

"He congratulates you on a successful mission, says he has dispatched Marines to seize the Heart's Desire, offers an intercept course that will allow you to reclaim our citizen, suggests you seize supplies from the Hector Dixey, promises you free passage back to the Union, if you leave now, and offers you a chance for 'justice for your people,' in his phrase."

Kruder and Fusterheim exchanged glances. "He does, does he? Does he give any more details?"

"He says he will provide them during his discussion, Kapitan."

"Send it here."

"Kapitan, the encryption he insisted on requires..."

"Yes, I forget we are not a real warship. I will come up. Well, Hans, let's see what this Accursed Imperial has to say."

Kruder and Fusterheim arrived on the bridge, and the comm officer made the necessary changes. The round-trip delay was still there but dropping as the Pinguin coasted toward the ice giant. Kruder faced the screen.

"Ah, Korvettenkapitan Kruder," Tribune Devin grimaced. "Figured it out yet?"

"Where are my crew members?" Kruder asked. "I sent officers along with the prisoners to ensure safe passage."

"Well, that's what I was asking you, Captain. Smart money would say they are dead," Devin said. "Killed by that rebellious scum over there, Saxon on the Castor."

"Him? Why not you? You could have killed them?"

"It's possible, I suppose. But we've never met before. I

don't have any of those special comm codes, like the ones you were using with the Castor. And I was asking you what was going on earlier, a more reasonable answer would be that the crew of the Castor killed them? Or let them be killed. Or was part of the killing?"

"What are you saying?"

"Let me spell it out. Rebel elements within the Empire have contrived to increase tensions between us and the Confederation. They want to start a war and take advantage of the confusion. Your government, of course, would welcome a confrontation between their two strongest neighbors, and would cheer things on as we fought each other to a standstill. When our rebels contacted them, your people arranged to send a disguised warship, that's you, the Pinguin, to prey on Imperial and Confederation ships in the border space. We'd blame the Confeds, they'd blame us, and we'd fight."

"Do you have any proof of this?"

"The missing ships are proof themselves. And it makes logical sense. You'd take advantage by scooping up a few border systems, some extra trade, whatever was happening while this was going on. Good for you."

"I asked before, about the crews..."

"Aha. That was the fly in the ointment. Even your government wouldn't be willing to support wholesale slaughter of captured foreigners. For one thing, you have your own freighter crews to be concerned about. And truthfully, I can't see somebody like yourself being a party to that."

"I will not be a party to that. I was not a party to that."

"What I've figured out, based on what my advisers tell

me, is that you'd refuel and re-arm from your captures, but keep the crews. Then, periodically, you'd send them off somewhere. My impression is most of the Confed crews would be just as happy to be dropped on a border planet somewhere on the other side of the Union. No need to kill them, or even threaten them, they'd be ecstatic to get out from under the commissars." Devin waved and a list of ships appeared on the side of the screen. "Here's a list of Confed ships that are missing, along with their crews. Have you seen any of these ships?"

Kruder didn't even look at the list. "What are you accusing me of? I do not have any of their crews. "

"Not saying you did. Now, my people, Imperial crews, no such luck there. They'd want to go back to the Empire. So, you had a deal, you sent them as prisoners on a ship or two for short hops, back to the Empire. To whoever in the Empire was setting this up. Which means the Castor and his friends. You'd have released them into Imperial custody, and your hands would be clean. I'm very interested in those crews. Do you have any of those crews, Kapitan?"

"We have no Imperial prisoners onboard. No prisoners of any sort." Which was true, Kruder had discharged them all back on one of the freighter hulls just before going in for re-fit. Including some of his officers and crew to shepherd them back. I sent them all to their deaths.

"I see. Well, if you sent them back to us, the Empire would do... something with them. Not your problem. But even then, you didn't think they'd kill them all. They made a mistake, though—I'll bet they shot up the returning freighters and didn't bother to check who was onboard. Some of those people were your people."

"This could all be lies made up to trick us!"

"Could be. But it sure fits, doesn't it? And I'll bet the Castor can't tell you where your crews are. And why would I show you that video footage of that ship?"

"These are all interesting accusations, but what does this have to do with me?"

Fusterheim stepped up and whispered in Kruder's ear. Kruder nodded. "And you want what with us?"

"If you have no Imperial prisoners onboard, you are free to leave. I have other more pressing concerns in this system. The Hector Dixey is a pirate, so if you need supplies, get it from them. I don't owe them anything, so feel free to destroy them —I'd have to do that regardless. Now you, you're a problem. Not exactly a warship, not exactly a pirate."

"We carry the flag of the Union of Nations. Attacking us would be an act of war."

"And attacking our commerce isn't? I could destroy you for doing that. I'd prefer a surrender, but we have the other issue. There's another frigate here. A rebel frigate."

"Rebel against whom? You, not us."

"Kapitan. I'll make you a deal. If you don't fire on me, I won't fire on you. You can have your supplies, and your citizen. But you leave the rest of the crew of the Heart's Desire here, and you skedaddle out of the system." Devin saw their brows wrinkle. "Skedaddle means leave quickly. Sorry, uncommon word. You speak Standard well, and I get over-eloquent at times. Take your man and leave, and I'll forget about you for now."

"That's it?"

"Mission accomplished, Kapitan. Your government's goal was, ultimately, to weaken the Empire. And you've done that—a civil war always weakens. But that's our business, not yours. Get out of here, now."

"I could stay if I wished. You would not dare attack a naval vessel of another power."

"First, why stay here? Now that you're exposed, there's nothing here for you now. Second, I'm in open rebellion against my own government and family, what's shooting up a foreign warship going to add to that? Third, one way or another, in a few hours, there will be only one Imperial frigate left in this system. The willingness of either survivor to deal with you then will be very different. Either to hide evidence, or to take revenge against you. Time to go, Kapitan."

Kruder leaned over in his chair. "You are in rebellion against your own government?"

"I am now. Mission accomplished, Kapitan."

"I am told the Empress is your sister. By all reports, you two get along well."

"Reports can be deceiving, Kapitan. We're siblings, yes. But siblings fight, lots of times. Why, when we were younger, I pulled her hair and made fun of her braces. She pushed back. And beat me up with sticks."

"She beat you with sticks?"

"Tough girl, the Empress. You don't want to meet her in

a dark alley. Or even a well-lit alley, for that matter. You going or not?"

"What will you do now?"

"Defeat the traitors. Capture or destroy their ship, the Castor. Destroy the Hector Dixey if it's still here, collect my Marines from the Heart's Desire. Ensure justice is served. I am a fan of justice."

"As am I. What justice are you speaking of?"

"Punish people for their sins, of course. That's justice. But first, I'll have some lunch. My steward has prepared an excellent soup. You say you are in favor of justice?"

"I am."

"How about soup?"

Kruder darted his eyes left to Fusterheim. Fusterheim shrugged. "I enjoy a good soup."

"I thought you might. I find justice and soup are often related. Don't trust a man who doesn't like soup. I sent some soup along with my Marines, to the Heart's Desire's crew."

"I'm sure it will be wonderful."

"Oh, it is, he does this thing with burnt pepper... I could talk about so much, but that takes time. That's the soup part. Are you interested in the justice part as well? We have an encrypted channel here. The Castor can't hear us. Nobody can. Just two ship captains talking about justice. And soup."

"I'm all ears, Tribune. Tell me about justice. And soup."

CHAPTER FORTY-NINE

"Heart's Desire is on course to meet with our shuttle, Prefect," Alvarez said.

"Very well." Lionel had returned to his old station. The captain's chair sat empty for Devin. "Take us to battle stations."

The battle stations alarm bonged. Bridge crew snapped skinsuit cuffs and collars closed, and checked helmets racked close by. The Marine in the back of the bridge locked into her seat and tested her weapon. Lionel monitored the ship.

"If you think you can get it back working in thirty minutes then try," Lionel said to a sensor crew. "Otherwise, leave it. Hello, Tribune."

"Subprefect." Devin strode onto the bridge.

"Prefect, Tribune."

"What, I thought we said—"

"Just because we're in rebellion against the largest Empire in known space is no reason for me to turn down a promotion. I worked hard for that."

"Of course. Prefect. But, um, if we're ignoring orders from the Chancellor, like to arrest people and things, shouldn't we be ignoring promotions as well?"

"Sure, you'd say that, since it's not your promotion, but even murderous treasonous scum can recognize real ability—like mine—when they see it."

"I thought that your promotion was, well, more of a bribe really. Make you a Prefect and you'd arrest me."

"That's insulting."

"I agree, thinking that they can buy your integrity."

"That's not the insulting part. It's thinking they can buy my integrity so cheaply. A Prefect hardly rates more than a Subprefect. Now if they'd made me a Duke and an Admiral, that would be a different story."

Devin turned sideways. "Prefect!"

"See? I told you you'd get used to it. Regardless, I'm not cheap, but I am easy, Tribune. But that's for later. Could we discuss the tactical situation, please? Navigator, put the system on screen."

The navigator blanked the main screen and replaced it with a simple two-dimensional display of local space.

Lionel pointed. "This is us." An elliptical orbit appeared on screen, a dot representing the Pollux sliding down the ellipse, passing close into the planet before circling out. "Standard orbit.

"Where's that station debris?" Devin asked.

The navigator added another icon, almost touching the planet. This one wasn't an orbit, but a line of dots that spiraled into the planet, eventually stopping. "Major pieces below and getting ready to burn up, Tribune." She added another ellipsis with a circling dot, this one overlapping and almost the same shape as the Pollux's. "And here's the Hector Dixey sir."

"Ignore them and ignore the station debris," Devin said. "Where's our shuttle?"

The navigator blanked the debris and the Hector Dixey. She added a circle that departed from the Pollux's orbit when it was farthest away from the planet, then extended it around to circle the planet. The shuttle dot circled the planet in a true circle, while the Pollux weaved closer and farther away on its ellipse.

"Outstanding," Devin said. "Now put our boy Dirk on screen."

A descending spiral orbit appeared. Dirk circled down around the planet four times before settling onto the circle of the shuttle. "I've been talking to them, sir, and I've also been watching their course. He's thrusting right now. If he keeps up what he's planned, he'll come right in on the same plane as the shuttle. And as us."

The energy to change an orbit varied. It took thrust to change the shape of an orbit to make the circle bigger, smaller, or elliptical. It took more thrust to change the plane of the orbit—tilt it in relation to the planet's equator. Freighters didn't have much thrust to spare.

"Outstanding." Devin grinned. "Now, do you have a position and a course for our Nat friend?"

A dot appeared farther out. "He's not in the correct orbital plane sir. He'll have to change his angle with the ecliptic.

Then he has to slow and adjust orbit to rendezvous with Heart's Desire. Complex calculation sir."

"Indeed it is. But the Union of Nations Navy is a professional organization, don't you think so, Prefect?"

"They are, Tribune." Lionel nodded. "They are. Well trained."

"As are our people, of course. Navigator, are you well trained?"

Tannen raised her eyebrows. "I believe I am sir. I trained at the academy initially and had further classes at the war college."

"Of course you did. Navigator, calculate the best course for the Pinguin to take, to effect a zero-zero rendezvous with Dirk."

"Define 'best' sir?"

"Use your professional judgment. The course you would offer to a demanding, yet fair captain of a warship, one who has confidence in your abilities."

Lionel laughed. "Also, give me the name of that captain, so I can serve under them, rather than time serving lickspittles I've had to deal with in the past."

The navigator played with her board. "It will take time sir. And the Pinguin won't have the final course information for the Heart's Desire."

"Assume he has it. We'll wait." Devin lounged in his seat as the navigator busied herself plotting vectors and putting up solutions on the screen.

Lionel opened a private channel. "Why are you putting

the least important items up on the screen? None of those are a threat to us."

"I find it's always best to put the slowest, least maneuverable ships on the screen first. They're so constrained in their ability to maneuver, the rest of us can just avoid them."

"And what makes you think that the Nat—the Pinguin, has Dirk's planned course information."

"I just sent it to him."

"Indeed." Lionel cracked his knuckles. "Going to tell me why?"

"Matters of grand strategy and politics, Prefect. You conn the ship, and I'll handle the rebellion."

"Fine. But we should address the tabbo in the room. Sensors?"

The sensor operator looked up. "Sir?"

"Add those jump limit calculations onto the screen."

The sensor operator played with his screen. "Here you go sir." Two bands of dim red circled the planet. "Inner is the one reported by the sailing directions. But our mass calculations show that the outer one is the real safe jump limit."

The screen now showed two large red bands surrounding the planet. And the Pollux's orbit stayed well inside them, even at the top.

"Which puts us far, far inside the jump limit, and its associated gravity well. Good initiative showing both, Lukas, thank you." Lionel tapped on his own screen. "And here's the one other thing I've been calculating myself. Let me show you."

Another bright red ellipse sprang into view. It was much larger than any of the other circles, and the area near the planet had to shrink down to allow the smaller scale to fit. The dot on that line moved more slowly than the other dots below it, and it always stayed clear of the red jump limit lines. "This thing I've been calculating, Tribune, is the Castor. They are flying high above us, outside of the gravity well and the atmosphere, not to mention the jump limit. Which makes it much more maneuverable, and able to fire down at us any time it wants, and blow the beJove out of us, while we climb up to meet them. What are we going to do about that one?"

"We attack," Devin said. "Attaque, attaque. Toujours, l'attaque!"

***

"I'm just saying, Navy," Ana said, "that maybe diving into a gravity well with a Nat warship chasing us isn't our brightest move."

Dirk adjusted his harness. "He's a Tribune. He's an officer. He's in command of the biggest warship in this sector."

"He's a pompous ass who's going to get us killed."

"Possibly. Lee, have you got the burns for us yet?"

"First few. We need to change the angle to the ecliptic. Best do that out here, simpler calculation during the farthest spiral."

Dirk tapped the intercom. "Everybody strap in and stand by for maneuvers. We'll be doing some hard burns."

Dena spoke up from her stateroom. "Why are we doing hard burns?"

"We're changing our orbital inclination."

"Why are we doing that?"

"We're changing the angle at which we orbit the planet."

"I know what orbital inclination is, you condescending naval twit," Dena said. "I've been on this ship long enough to learn about it. But why are we changing it?"

"To change the angle—"

"I KNOW THAT. BUT WHAT'S WRONG WITH THIS ANGLE?"

"You don't need to yell."

"Yes, I did. You weren't answering my question. We're not landing or anything, we're only zooming around this planet. If we're not landing on the planet, one orbit is as good as another, right?"

"Well, yes, but we need to rendezvous with that shuttle."

"Why aren't they meeting up with us, then? You told me in the Navy, the smaller, more maneuverable craft always conforms to the larger one. They should meet up with us, not us with them."

"I told you that?"

"You did. You told me that the bigger the ship, the harder to maneuver it is, so the more maneuverable does the work. "

"Navy told you that?" Ana said.

"He sure did, Old Man."

"I find it hard to believe he said that to you."

"He was trying to impress me. During the same conversation, he also said I had beautiful eyes, and that he wanted to take my skirt off."

Ana grinned. "Okay, now that I believe. I withdraw my objection."

"Wait, that doesn't make any sense," Lee said.

"I thought so too," Dena said. "No need to take off the skirt, there's plenty to be done with a skirt still on."

Lee laughed. "I meant, friend Dena, that's a good question. Why bother to change our inclination? The shuttle should dock with us."

"Maybe this Tribune guy is just being weird."

Dirk shook his head. "Devin never does anything without a reason. Sometimes Imperial-noble honor of the Empire type reasons, but always a reason."

Scruggs piped up. "I have a question, Centurion."

"What is it?"

"I've got our telescope pointed at that Nat guy like you told me to."

"I didn't tell you to do that."

"Well, it's the standard thing that you tell me, so I've started doing it automatically."

"Commendable initiative, um, Private," Dirk said.

"Thank you, Captain. But that Nat ship is firing its thrusters too. I can see the glow."

"That can't be true," Dirk said. "That far out? I've conned ships into orbits around hundreds of planets, and you never start changing your orbit out that far."

"Unless you want to change inclination with minimal effort," Lee said.

"I guess I'm reading it wrong," Scruggs said. "Can you double-check me?"

"Never mind, Pilot," Lee said. "I see it. Let me put the radar on him."

Dirk, Lee, and Ana worked on their consoles. Each brought

up a variety of courses, added the notes, then displayed their efforts on the screen.

"He's changing his inclination to match ours," Ana said. "We'll all be in the same plane when he's done. Us, him, the shuttle."

"First, I concur," Lee said. "Second, how do you know how to do that calculation? Something they taught you in the army while you were cleaning barracks?"

"Picked it up somewhere. Navy, what say you?"

"I agree he's changing his inclination. And I also agree that not only is he changing it, it looks almost like he'll be on course to match ours when he's done. And I also want to know how you can do that calculation."

"Outstanding."

Dena came up again. "Just so I'm clear. We're going to be doing this change angle thing, so we're in the same plane relative to that shuttle."

"Yes. That's it precisely. You've learned well," Dirk said.

"I'm reading from a screen here. But not only that, the Nat is doing the same thing. He's started before we have, 'cause you haven't fired the thrusters yet, right?"

Dirk, Lee, and Ana exchanged glances.

"Good catch, Nature Girl," Ana said.

"How does he know what we're going to be doing before we do it?"

"Only one answer," Ana said. "Somebody told him. I wonder who, and I wonder why he did that?"

CHAPTER FIFTY

"Prefect, climb out of this gravity well and engage the rebel frigate," Devin ordered.

Lionel glanced from his station. "First, I believe, technically, we're the rebel frigate. He would be the government frigate."

"Illegitimate government frigate."

"Can I call him IGF for short?"

"If you must."

"Thanks. Second, that's your tactical direction? Climb up and shoot?"

"You can refine it somewhat if you want."

"I do want. But perhaps a little more guidance from the commander is in order?"

"Flip the question." Devin played with his screen. "Assume you're Saxon and you see a warship of equal strength climbing up to challenge you. What would you do?"

"My priority would be to maintain the high ground," Lionel said. "Stay outside the jump limit to keep my options open, stay high. Keep maximum maneuverability for amount of thrust spent. Keep the circle I can dodge in with a random walk large enough that you can't target me easily. That part is a judgment call, and it depends on how high my opponent climbs. If you're trying to get away, I keep staying as far out as possible and blow you to bits as you climb up. But if you sweep up, take some shots and then dive back down, I can maneuver down for a better shot. Let's see..."

It took Lionel a minute before he could put a course on the screen. "Here. More elliptical than their current one. If I project our current course, we'll be as close as we'll ever be. But still out of range. That being said, if I was them, I'd wait for us to move first."

"Very well," Devin said. "We move. Bring us up, just outside of range. Barely outside of effective range and fire a few shots. Then repeat. Let's see what they do."

"Helm," Lionel ordered. "Combat power, now."

"Not full power?" Devin asked.

"Not yet."

The Pollux climbed out of the planet's gravity well, peaking the orbit higher.

"Castor is dropping to meet us sir."

"How much thrust are they using?"

"One-G sir."

"Keep climbing. Weapons, as soon as they come into range, open fire. Use your best guess on her course."

Pollux pushed upwards, fighting the planet's gravity the whole way. Her ideal course plot showed her elliptical course elongating until it crossed the Castor's.

"Helm, institute random walk."

Devin rocked to one side. He fell as the main drive cut to half power for a quarter second. The ship yawed right, and the course plot changed again. Castor did the same. But gravity drops as the square of the distance between two bodies. Castor was always 'higher' above the planet than Pollux. Her random walk was always wider.

"Coming into range in fifteen seconds," the weapons officer said.

"Open fire as soon as you have a solution."

"Acceptable confidence range?"

"One percent," Lionel said.

All the heads on the bridge that weren't banging into restraints turned to Lionel. One percent chance of hitting was stupidly low.

"Say again, Prefect?" The weapons officer typed a figure into his comm but held a finger above it.

"You heard me. Fire at one percent."

The weapons officer glanced back. Devin was in his chair, rubbing his chin. He caught the helmsman's look. "Prefect has the ship until I say otherwise. Carry on."

The weapons officer stabbed a finger. "Firing."

Lights flashed. Alarms bonged. Computers calculated the vector between ships, picked a future course point, and added in the upcoming course changes. The random-walk vectors were calculated in advance so they could be incorporated into targeting solutions. That gave a targeting box, and the computers spaced positron beams within it.

The Castor disappeared from the display as red lines

formed around it. All missed. Castor did the same, beams spinning between the two ships.

"No hits. Recharge cycle. Next salvo in five, four—"

"Status change!" the sensor operator interrupted. "Castor is climbing."

"She can do range equations as well as we can." Lionel slammed back into his seat as the random walk fired again. "Helm, climb after her."

"Recalculating," the weapons officer said. "New target in five seconds...firing."

The ship slipped sideways as the thrusters fired, then hung steady for a half second and the next salvo fired.

"Clean miss." The Castor had cut thrust to zero in the instant before the Pollux fired. Every single beam wasted into space hundreds of meters ahead of the target.

"Again."

"She's still climbing sir."

"Follow her up. Weapons, what's your chance?"

"Two point five sir, climbing slowly. Firing. Miss."

Pollux rolled thirty degrees, then corrected.

"They fired. We're hit," the helmsman said. "A thruster line. Computer compensated."

"Not fast enough," Lionel said. "Keep firing."

"Firing in two. One. Fire. All misses."

"Again."

"Recharging. No answer from the enemy. Firing. All misses."

"Tell me we're closer this time."

"Sorry sir. This altitude difference...whoa, imminent failure warning!" The weapons officer grabbed for restraints.

Pollux spun forward, head over tail. "Pitch control inoperative," the helmsman said. "Random-walk efficiency down by thirty percent."

"Engineering says fuel line hit. Working on it."

"Firing," the weapons officer said. "Another miss. Confidence is three percent."

"Push us up there, Helm. We need better confidence. Weapons—"

Devin stirred. "Prefect. Disengage."

Lionel looked sideways. "Disengage?"

"Yes. Take us down."

Lionel made eye contact with Devin and raised his eyebrows. Devin nodded and pointed down.

"Helm," Lionel said. "Pivot and full retro."

The helmsman blinked, then obeyed the order. Everyone hung in their straps as the ship pivoted, then the main drive fired, and the Pollux dropped like a rock.

Another salvo of the Castor wasted itself above the Pollux. The Castor hadn't expected the withdrawal.

"Dropping," the helm said.

The weapons officer kept shooting and kept missing. After fifteen seconds, he spoke. "Computer reports no target percentage greater than point zero one percent."

"Secure firing," Lionel said.

The sensor operator put the engineering report up on the screen. Both hits were minor and would be fixed shortly.

"Standard orbit," Devin said. "Prefect, your analysis of that battle?"

"Might we do this in private, Tribune?"

"Here is fine. Proceed."

Lionel folded his arms. "First, it was a skirmish or an encounter, not a battle. Second, it was inconclusive. There were no grand tactics employed. We were hampered by planetary gravity. Castor used their maneuvering and height advantage to calculate superior hit probabilities. They stayed on the edge of weapons range and kept jabbing away, counting on the probabilities. Essentially, we were both playing a big game of roulette. Thirty-six slots on the wheel. Thirty-three labeled 'miss' one labeled 'hit on Castor' and two labeled 'hit on Pollux.' They liked those odds, so they kept the range as it was, and we kept spinning the wheel."

"Your suggestion at changing those odds?"

"Get closer and shoot faster."

"Can we shoot faster?"

Lionel looked forward. "Weapons?"

"We're already shooting more often than them, sir, and we can't change the recharge cycle. We'll run down the capacitors in time."

"Don't wait for the recharge. Shoot when we're at half," Devin said. "Prefect, re-engage the enemy. Fire at half power."

"I'd like a moment to recalibrate my controls sir," the weapons officer said.

"Please do. Prefect, you may climb when ready."

Lionel had a discussion with the weapons officer. He gave instructions to the helm and navigation officers, and sat back to wait for the ship catching up. Once the bridge staff was otherwise engaged, he opened a private channel to Devin. "Well, Tribune?"

"Well what?"

"What's going on?"

"You know they call me the Mad Dog of the Verge?"

"Everybody knows that. So what?"

"What does a mad dog do? What type of person is he?"

"Crazy. Insane."

"Aggressive? Narrow-minded?"

"Tribune," Lionel said. "You don't have to be a mad dog to be that. I know some perfectly sane ship captains who are like that. You may have met him too. In a mirror."

"This climbing and hovering above us, that's not particularly aggressive."

"No, but it's the right move from their point of view. Why give up an advantage?"

"Why indeed. But climbing at them, that's aggressive."

"Yes. And if you let me, I'll—"

"Be more aggressive. That's what I want. But I want it in stages, that's all. I want him to keep thinking that we're aggressive, and unaware of any other options."

"That will be easy," Lionel said. "Because I don't see what other options we have. Helm, back at 'em. Again."

Dirk and Lee had put the battle on the ship wide screens as they powered into their orbit. Trying to find two warships that weren't broadcasting a beacon would have been hard for even their augmented freighter sensors, but finding two ships that were sending out bursts of high energy particle beams for minutes at a time was much easier.

"The second one didn't go well either," Lee said. "Tribune is retreating again, dropping down."

"I'm sure they got a hit on the Castor," Dirk said. "At least one. Their course shimmied at one point."

"Could have been a random jerk as a thruster stuck."

"That's what I'd say, if they hadn't been in the middle of a battle, Navigator. In a battle, it's bad news."

"Want some other bad news, Navy?" Ana said from his chair.

"Absolutely not," Dirk said.

"Sorry, I don't care. Look at this." Ana put a short image sequence up on the screen. "Count the shots."

"I just told you I didn't want any bad news."

"I just told you I didn't care what you wanted."

"Then why, in Jove's name, Centurion, did you ask?"

Ana hung his head sideways. "That's a good question. I don't care. So why did I ask?"

"It's polite," Lee said.

"I'm not polite. I don't want to be polite. When did I become polite? I must be spending too much time with Scruggs. Hang on, Navy." Ana tapped his screen. "Scruggs? You there?"

"Yes, Centurion," Scruggs said. "How may we help you?"

"No good." Ana frowned. "No good at all. Dena, you there?"

"Go away, Old Man," Dena said. "We're busy."

"Much better. Scruggs, start talking like Dena. That's an order."

"Um, okay, understood, Centurion," Scruggs said.

"No, tell me to buzz off."

"Um, I…"

"Work on it. Dena will teach you." Ana turned to Dirk. "Well? Did you count?"

"Yep." Dirk pursed his lips.

"What's wrong?" Lee asked.

"Start of the last battle, the Pollux was firing sixteen shots a salvo. Dropped in half. Either they're doing something with their computers…"

"Or they lost half their main battery, last battle," Ana said. "Heavy damage. Not good."

CHAPTER FIFTY-ONE

"Tribune, we cannot survive a close encounter with half of our batteries out of action," Lionel said. "That's a huge disadvantage." Their last encounter had resulted in a crippling exchange of fire.

"Does Castor know this?"

"Tribune, of course they do."

"They won't expect it, then. Drive up again and shoot with half batteries."

"And at half power?"

"Yes."

"Tribune." Lionel lowered his voice. "The danger of catastrophic damage by exposing our ship to concentrated enemy fire when we're crippled is substantial. The risk of us getting hit means that our roulette wheel now has twice as many 'Hit on Pollux' as 'Hit on Castor.' We shouldn't take those odds. Engineering says they only need a couple of hours to run new control lines—"

"No." Devin shook his head and punched up the

navigator's screen. It showed the Castor, the Pollux, Heart's Desire, and the Pinguin, with courses extended into the future. "Our shuttle reported in, they're docking now. Things will change shortly."

"They will surely change," Lionel said. "Just not in a good way for us."

"Keep the pressure up. Castor is reacting to us right now. We want to keep it that way. Not for much longer. Not even for an hour. Seventeen more minutes."

"Tribune, if we can't shoot half of our batteries, then we have to get in dangerously close to do any damage to Castor."

"How close? Is there a spot where your theoretical roulette wheel will be equal?"

"Well, yes. But the whole time we're getting in close, they'll be shooting at us. The odds will be in their favor 'til we can hit them with a thrown rock."

"Get in close, then." Devin shrugged. "How hard can that be?"

"How hard can it be? Let's show you." Lionel tapped his intercom. "Engineer, send a rating to the bridge with two rolls of engine room tape. We're going to conduct a demonstration!"

"The shuttle says they're ready to dock, Pilot," Lee said. "I can see them on the screens."

Dirk brought up the four cameras that displayed the shuttle. "I'll do it manually. Ana, can you set up a welcoming committee?"

"One un-welcoming committee coming up." Ana tapped his intercom. "Scruggs, Dena, gun up and meet me at the air lock." He unstrapped and left his chair. Dirk rang the maneuvering alarm, and Ana pulled himself hand over hand down the corridor until he met Dena and Scruggs at the lock. Scruggs carried her second-best shotgun, which matched her slightly threadbare combat coveralls, blackened utility belt and hard boots. Dena was the sexier opposite, with skintight leather pants and shirt, jacket, and a low-slung holster with revolver.

"You realize you'll freeze or boil in that outfit if something happens to our atmo," Ana said.

"You realize that tight leather clothes are almost as good as skinsuits," Dena said. "I've got full ship slippers on under these boots, and this leather jacket was customized to take gloves." She held up her leather clad wrist. Her jeweled wrist bracelet was actually a metal clamp that would take a glove seal.

"I didn't know that," Ana said. "What about a helmet?"

"Have to use an emergency one," Dena said. "But I'm trying to get a bracelet made up that will seal around the collar of the coat."

"You have been paying attention to our lectures," Ana said.

"Scary, isn't it?" The ship rocked slightly, then the air lock light flashed green. The three stood back, hands on holsters, or holding shotguns, but not brandishing them.

The air lock wheel spun, then the door opened into the lock. A uniformed figure stepped out. It was a she, and she was almost Ana's twin—dark combat uniform, heavy boots, utility belt, and bandoleer of equipment across her chest.

Both she and Ana had hard collars with helmet racked behind, hard sealed gloves and boots, and weapons.

"Senior Centurion?" the Marine asked.

"Here, Gunnery Sergeant," Ana said.

Dena's eyes flipped between them. "You two know each other?"

"We know each other's type," Ana said.

"Hmm." Dena inspected the woman more closely. "Hmm. Well, looks like your type wins, Centurion. You've got three pouches on your belt, and the sergeant—"

"Gunnery sergeant," the Marine interrupted.

"Sorry, the gunnery sergeant only has two pouches. You win by a pouch."

The gunnery sergeant shook her head. "The centurion is not a Marine, therefore he needs extra space to store a spare pair of his frilly panties, for when he soils them."

Dena laughed. Ana smiled. Scruggs looked appalled.

Ana extended his hand. "You've got packages for us."

"Yes." The gunnery sergeant turned back and called into the air lock. "Bring up those two boxes."

"What are they?"

"One is a communicator. It has a special encryption package installed. The Tribune's steward briefed us before we left. The Tribune has left you instructions here."

Dirk nodded. "What's in the other?"

"Soup."

"Soup?"

"Soup."

"What are we going to do with a soup?"

"You're supposed to give it to a Nat captain if he boards your ship. Which I'm told could happen shortly, if you don't follow instructions."

"Aren't you supposed to stay and stop that from happening?" Ana asked.

"I have no orders to that effect. Once I've delivered my packages, we're to return to the shuttle and await the Pollux. They'll pick us up after they win the battle."

"About winning the battle," Ana said. "They appear to be stuck in a gravity well."

"Yes. So?"

"They're losing."

"The Tribune will win. He always does."

"How's he going to do that?"

"I don't know. Nobody knows. Nobody ever knows how he does it." The gunnery sergeant shrugged. "That's why he always wins."

"Prefect," Devin gasped. "Are you trying to kill me?"

The Pollux climbed at full power. Not combat power, or regular power, but as much thrust as the engines could give without exploding.

The helmsman's hands hovered over a big red button on his console labeled 'emergency stop.' The slider that controlled the dead man switch had been locked into place with big bands of pink engine room tape. If he passed out, the ship would keep accelerating unless engineering shut down the engines.

The whole bridge crew was locked into their chairs,

grunting as they tapped screens. More than half of the screens had flashing red or yellow lights.

Lionel grunted. "Not trying, but if it happens, it's a beneficial side effect. Serves you right."

More red lights flashed on screens. "Castor is firing," the weapons officer said.

Devin burped. "I'm going to vomit."

"Don't do that, you'll choke to death. Weapons, return fire."

The weapons officer sweated and gasped as he tapped his buttons. "No target. Castor continues to retreat."

"No target? Are they staying out of range?"

"Prefect, they're in range, but our computer is having trouble compensating for the acceleration."

Lionel slammed sideways. The Pollux rocked as they took a hit. "Their computer seems to be working fine. Do they have a better one than us?"

"I think the inputs aren't reflecting the excess speed, so we're using the wrong targeting model."

"Take manual control and start firing. Best guess."

The weapons officer slammed his console. "Firing."

The Pollux's working weapons spat positrons beams. Castor continued to retreat, unscathed.

The bridge lights flickered, then died. Emergency lights came on. Consoles continued to display the battle. The ship rocked again, and acceleration dropped to half.

"Status?" Lionel yelled.

"Weapons online. Main drive online, but half power. No answer from engineering or damage control."

"Get the speed up."

"Unable." The helmsman played with buttons. "Thrust controls not responding."

"Castor is retreating, range opening," the weapons officer said. "We're—I have a target. Firing."

Devin ignored the chatter around him. He looked at his own private screen. "Come on, Dirk. Do your duty."

The Castor and Pollux powered up and away from the planet. They'd drifted from their original orbits. Now they were higher, slower, and had changed their angle to the planetary equator.

Devin extended his course plot. Two other lines crossed close to his in the next few minutes. The Heart's Desire, and the pursuing Pinguin. Neither would touch, or even come that close.

But they would come into weapons range.

"No, I am not going to die saving an Imperial Tribune," Ana said. "It's not a great idea. And I don't like him. And I'm not entirely fond of the Empire, for that matter."

"Senior Centurion," Dirk said. "I can't believe I'm saying this, but I have my orders. That communicator has encryption codes, and as soon as I loaded them up, here was this course info that we needed to make this work, and orders to engage."

"First, when did you ever follow orders properly? Second, who's the enemy, because, isn't the Tribune a rebel of sorts, and third, even if he wasn't, why should we get killed for him?"

"Exactly," Dena chimed in over the radio. "Why should we

get killed for him? Or by him. There's plenty of other people in this system who are happy to kill us. That Nat ship captain, he sounded unhappy, and even if he doesn't want to kill us, his officer guy sure did. And I don't think that other Imperial ship—the Casper or whatever—likes us. Don't they hate us too? Why not just leave?"

"They may not like us," Ana said. "But they currently have no particular reason to kill us, so I'm against giving them one."

"How are we giving them one?" Dena asked.

"Nature Girl, you understand that we're in a space battle right now, don't you?"

"Sort of. I'm a bit confused. What's with this up/down and gravity well thing you keep talking about? First, we have to change the angle for no reason. Dirk just fired the thrusters, and then the main engines. I know enough that that's important."

"The spatial vectors..." Dirk paused. "I mean, how to."

"Nature Girl," Ana said. "We're running up a rocky canyon on a very steep hill. That's the gravity well. The hill slows you down. The canyon walls on either side are close to you, so you can't dodge more than a few feet to each side. You're throwing rocks at a person above you, but the canyon gets both wider and flatter as you run up. So the person above always finds it easier to climb, and has more space to dodge in. And they're throwing rocks back at you. That's the Castor and Pollux. Pollux is climbing up, and Castor is dropping rocks on them."

"But where are we in all this?"

"Standing up top and waiting 'til the upper person runs by, then we trip them," Ana said.

"Oh. That could be fun. And we're kind of on the Tribune's side. We should help him."

"I'm against it," Ana said. "I don't think—"

Scruggs cut in. "You're all going about this the wrong way. Centurion?"

"What is it, Private?"

"You've blown up tanks, and trucks, and, I don't know. Boats?"

"Sure. Hundreds."

"Planes?"

"Lots of planes. I destroyed a blimp once. Outstanding shot, if I do say so myself."

"What's a blimp—no, never mind. You've destroyed tanks, trucks, cars, boats, planes and blimps."

"Yep."

"Don't you want to add an Imperial frigate to that list?"

CHAPTER FIFTY-TWO

"Range is dropping," Lukas, the sensor operator said. "But slowly. Their acceleration advantage is reduced."

"Dropped, or they're faking it?" Lionel asked.

"Unclear."

"Increase thrust."

"Unable. Controls not responding."

"What's engineering say?"

"Unknown. They're not responding to comms."

"Send a runner. And stop starting words with 'un'."

"Understood—sorry, Prefect."

"Weapons?"

"Targeting as best we can, Prefect. I list two hits. One of them hit a weapons mount, I'm sure of it. Their fire is down. If we could get better anticipation of maneuvers, I could improve."

"Do what you can. Wait." Lionel checked his screen. "No response from engineering, and you can't add thrust. Can you cut thrust? Cut thrust by ten percent."

The helmsman tapped his console. Then again. Then he typed and hit enter. "Prefect, no response to any thrust commands. The helm is not responding." He typed another command. "Thrusters are no longer under my control. Checking other helm controls."

Devin looked up from the screen he was perusing. "So we're not under command?"

Lionel shook his head. "We're under command. I'm right here, you're right here. Command away."

"Fine," Devin said. "We're under command, but not under control, then."

Lionel nodded. "Helm?"

"I'm not driving sir. The displays are working, everything reports normal, but the systems aren't taking controls from me."

Lionel nodded. "Some of the valves are disconnected, or not providing feedback. Doesn't matter, we're—gaahh."

The thrust maxed out again. Everyone on the bridge slammed into their seats as the engines revved up to max. People screamed and cursed as hands and arms slammed back into seats.

"Get a runner.... Whoa." Lionel slammed sideways and the Pollux swirled in a circle, spinning forward. One of the yaw thrusters must have malfunctioned. We're spinning like a top. No runners in this. "Weapons, keep firing. Everybody else hang on."

"Frigates are engaging again, Kapitan," Kruder's sensor operator said.

Kruder slapped his gloves onto the magnetic holders next

to his chair. After speaking at length with Devin, he'd put the Pinguin at battle stations. He was overhauling Dirk and crew, but the two frigates' running battle was blazing along behind him. He was worried that they might decide he was a target.

"Very well. Are we in range of their weapons yet?"

"Soon, Kapitan. Four minutes, twenty-one seconds. Perhaps four seconds less, with the correct course."

"So soon?"

"They are engaging at longer ranges than we were led to expect, Kapitan. Our warbook says that Accursed Empire lasers are ineffective at those ranges, but they apparently disagree."

"Are they damaging each other?"

"Yes, Kapitan. Pollux has maneuvering damage. Castor had vented atmosphere and debris. But, Kapitan, there is something curious about their weapons. We can't see laser blooms at all. No visual indicators."

Kruder looked at Fusterheim. "Hans? What do you think?"

"Could be those new positron guns we've been hearing of. I've never seen one in action, and I'm told we can't detect them visually. Unless they hit us."

"Sensors, how did you determine engagement range?"

"We're assuming that they're in range at minimum distance between them, and we've got a maximum based on the damage to Castor we saw. But the maximum could be farther. We added ten percent, but that's just a guess."

"How does it compare to us?"

"Much farther, Kapitan. Our lasers are much shorter ranged."

"Watch those Imperials and record your data. This will

be of great interest to the intelligence directorate. Helm, put our course on screen." Kruder tapped his fingers. "If they continue on these courses, when they overhaul us, we will be in range of their weapons, but they will not be in range of ours. Can you take us out of the calculated range of both of them?"

The helm officer shook her head. "I have already checked, Kapitan. If we wish to board the Accursed Freighter, and if it keeps its course, we will have to pass within the range window of at least one of the frigates. We can't escape them if they don't want us to. They will have no problem keeping us inside their weapons range if they so desire. We can dodge one, or the other, but not both."

"I see." Kruder turned his head to Fusterheim and raised an eyebrow. Fusterheim jerked his chin at Blomberg, sitting in the second row, then nodded once.

Kruder nodded back. "Hans, suggestions?"

"Keep our course to close that freighter and remove the high value prisoner. But no need to give two Accursed Imperials the opportunity to shoot at us. The Pollux was not aware of our operations and has been the least accommodating so far. Change course, take us away from the Pollux, and let the Castor overfly us."

"As the first officer said, Helm." Kruder straightened. "Everybody be wary. I do not trust these Imperials. All weapons ready for deployment. But do not decamouflage yet."

Dirk ran through the laser checklist. "Capacitors charged, Engineer?"

"Ninety-six percent."

"Navigator, radar on?"

"Wide-scanning radar is on. We've got approximate courses to the combatants." Lee tapped her screen. "I'm updating the courses as we're running, but we're—"

"Just update the one to the Castor—"

"Hey, kids!" Dena yelled into the intercom. "Scruggs and I are watching the old man's screens. Tribune's ship just went ballooy!"

"What in the name of Jove does ballooy mean!" Dirk yelled.

Ana put a picture from the telescope onto the main screen. "Target-2 is spinning like a top."

"Went ballooy, like I said."

"He's still firing, though," Ana said. "Navy, are you going to give us a shot, or not?"

"If I can," Dirk said. "We've got weapons powered up, a course to the target, all I need is the targeting radar turned on."

Ana reached above him and flicked a toggle switch. The lights dimmed, then went out. "Targeting radar on."

Dena spoke over the intercom. "The screens are off. And the microwave died."

Gavin came over the intercom. "Power usage just spiked two hundred percent. What did you do?"

"Turned on the targeting radar." Ana snapped his fingers. "High-powered radar. Engineer, didn't you check the power draw of this thing before they installed it?"

"No, Old Man, when the illegal technicians jury rigged our stolen radar system onto our rogue ship at the secret pirate shipyard, I didn't check the power rating. I promise to do it next time."

"It's not stolen," Dirk said. "We paid for it."

"You mean you paid for it," Dena said, "when you had to go with Miss 'come to my room so you can see my big laser'."

"That's more a guy's line, Nature Girl," Ana said.

"Had a similar effect in this case. Are these lights ever going to come back on?"

"Soon," Dirk said.

"No," Gavin said. "Everything is going to that radar. Life support has switched to batteries. Which we don't want, because the capacitors are wired into the battery system, so the capacitors also draw from the batteries. They'll kill life support."

"Turn 'em all off," Ana said. "We don't need life support for a few minutes. How long 'til we can fire at these twerps?"

"Our optimal firing window opens in two minutes, two seconds, and closes in eleven minutes, thirty-three seconds," Dirk said.

"That's a long window."

"They're going to overfly us, so they'll be in range for a long time."

"Well, if we're going to shoot, we need radar."

Dirk slapped his console. "Engineer, do it. Shut everything down."

"Turning off life support."

"Right," Dirk flexed his fingers. "Ana, prepare to fire."

"Navy," Ana said. "It fires automatically if you sweep the

ship's nose over the target, remember. Your girlfriend's people set it up that way. Pivot us over the target and the laser fires."

"Right. Lee, you have a course?"

Lee nodded. "On your screen, Pilot."

Dirk grasped the helm controls. "Plus four point five x, two hundred sixty-three Y, and twenty-two Z. Hold on everyone, maneuvering."

Dirk cut thrust to zero. The Heart's Desire floated. He pushed the control stick up slightly, pivoted to the right, and stabbed at the pedals. The ship rolled, pivoted more, and yawed all together. Ana put a display up on the screen. A line extended from Heart's Desire's bow and passed by the two fighting frigates. The line swept across, touched the Castor, and continued.

"Too high on the Y-axis, Pilot," Lee said.

Dirk grabbed the controls and pivoted down and reversed the clockwise spin. The line swept back and nearly touched the Castor.

The targeting radars pulsed from the bow of the ship. Like the Heart's Desire, the Castor and Pollux orbited prograde to the planet. Heart's Desire's orbit was higher, travelling slower, and Dirk had rotated the ship so it orbited stern first, making the radar scan behind and below. The targeting radar focused narrowly but some bled to the sides. A detector on the Castor picked up the radio energy crossing from the side and didn't like it. It overrode the random walk and shoved the Castor fifty meters higher.

With no target on the radar, the Heart's Desire didn't fire. A clean miss.

"Another hit on the Castor, Tribune. Another turret, I'm sure of it. Their response is down sixty percent." The weapons officer had to yell. Most of the comm links were down. The helm was being operated by engineering. The bridge still had weapons control of the remaining four positron guns, and the link to the firing computers was intact.

Lights flashed on screens. "Hit on us. Lost another radar." The sensor operator checked another screen. "Strike that, two radars."

"Another hit! Castor is venting atmo."

"Range is decreasing. Castor is not climbing."

Devin looked at Lionel. "Why not climbing? Damage?"

Lionel shook his head. "Impatience. They want this over with. Up until now, they've been careful not to hit our propulsion, but it's a knife fight now. You've really irritated them, Tribune. Then again, that's what you do."

"Irritate people?"

"You certainly irritate me."

The main screen changed to display a course plot. "Two new targets coming into range. Heart's Desire and the Pinguin. Pinguin is pursuing Heart's Desire."

"What's Dirk doing?"

"Spinning."

"Spinning?"

"No substantial course change. Just pivoting on his axis. Pinguin is maneuvering." The navigator changed the screen display. "We're going to overfly both of them in fifty seconds. Pinguin is moving away from us and closing Castor's track."

"The Heart's Desire is doing those spinning maneuvers again, Kapitan," Kruder's helmsman reported.

"Why are they pivoting so much?" Fusterheim said. "They don't have weapon batteries."

"Not that we know of," Kruder said. "Not out of the factory. But they were at Casarubrum for a reason."

"The Accursed Imperials are closing," the sensor operator said. "We estimate that we're in range of Castor's weapons now. Pollux will pass below us. Another thirty seconds and we'll be in range of the Castor with our weapons. Given their speed and vectors, we'll be in mutual range for perhaps seventy seconds. They'll range us for another minute 'til they pass over the horizon."

"Very well." Kruder nodded.

"We'll be in weapons range of the Heart's Desire starting in twenty seconds."

"When will we lose it? The range to Heart's Desire, that is."

The sensor operator shook her head. "Never. We can chase them down now, no matter what they do. In fact, they're doing that spinning thing again."

"Target dodged away," Lee reported.

"How are they doing that? How can they see us?"

"They can see our targeting radar," Ana said. "They might not know what it is, but they can be sure it's not good. Try again. Faster this time."

"Push your faster up your—"

"Shut up and pilot." Ana flicked the switch off. All the lights came back on.

Gavin came up on the intercom. "What's happening now?"

"Pilot's too slow," Ana said. "I'll let him sneak up on them, and then I'll fire."

"Good idea."

"It's my idea. Of course it's a good idea. Lee, give him the course again."

Lee repeated a different XYZ offset, and Dirk again manipulated the controls, swinging the nose to point at the Castor.

"Navigator," Ana said. "Is there a way to narrow that radar beam? Cut it to a quarter of the size, cut down the bleed so it's harder to see?"

Lee nodded and swiped through screens."

"Centurion," Dirk said. "I'm going to aim in front and let him fly into it. As soon as I say, hit the radar."

Ana put his hand on the switch. Dirk pivoted the ship. Lee updated the screen.

The range line swept right, then lifted on the display, then turned green as it hit the right plane. Offsets in the XYZ axis displayed on the main screen. The flashing dot that was the Castor pulsed left, then intersected the line.

"Now!" Dirk yelled.

Ana flipped the switch. All the lights went out again. Nothing else happened. The laser didn't fire.

Dirk cursed.

Lee ran her screens. "Again, too high on the Y axis. Pilot, you should—"

Ana smacked Dirk on the back of the head. Dirk snapped forward and hit the pitch controls. The ship jerked down.

Castor's upward climb crossed the beam. The targeting radar pulse reflected to the Heart's Desire. The radar activated the firing computer in the control room. The firing computer accounted for the time for the beam to reach the target, and the inertia of the Heart's Desire. It aimed at the spot it thought the Castor would be when the beam fired, assuming all these variables were correct. It sent this to the laser power controllers.

The power controllers were located on the laser itself, under the ship. They started a timer in picoseconds, and considered what else would affect the shot. The only remaining variable was what type of motion the Castor would make during the time these calculations took.

The controller chips specialized in combat maneuvers. They took location and course information, and vector history. The algorithm made two guesses. A ship likely dodges in a different direction than before, and ships in gravity wells tend to dodge 'down' because they get more distance for their thrust. It added the two values, applied the correction, and fired.

Bright lights flashed on every screen and camera that showed anything outside of the ships. The hull shook. Static electricity arced through the air. Ana yelled as electricity surged through his hands. Dirk jerked in his seat. Lee shook. Electricity arced between the consoles and the hull plates. Plastic burned and melted, and foul smoke filled the air. The inside lights died and there was an almighty CRACK, and the ship jerked sideways. Every piece of electric-powered equipment died. The control room darkened, not even emergency lights. Smoke filled the air. The fans stopped. The ship sat quietly, heat and stink wafting around in the dark.

"Outstanding," Ana said. "Did we hit them?"

CHAPTER FIFTY-THREE

As a tactical exercise, it was an interesting problem, Kruder thought.

The Heart's Desire had achieved orbit around the ice giant, orbiting stern first.

Pinguin was chasing behind them, on a lower orbit. She would pass below Heart's Desire. But a pivot and minor action of her main drive would drop her into the same orbit as Heart's Desire—close enough that she could launch a shuttle and board. Her acceleration advantage was such that there was no way Heart's Desire could escape her. Dirk could try to ram the Union of Nations Auxiliary Cruiser, at which point Kruder's unmasked lasers would melt her into steam. Heart's Desire was doomed to boarding.

Pollux and Castor were racing along behind the two ships, shooting at each other. Their orbits changed as they climbed, ducked, dodged, weaved, and generally made a nuisance of themselves. Just as Heart's Desire couldn't escape the velocity advantage of Pinguin, Pinguin and Heart's Desire couldn't escape the pursuing warships.

Of course, neither Castor nor Pollux had any shots to spare for the other two ships.

Yet.

"Heart's Desire fired a laser!" Kruder's weapons officer said. "At us."

"At us?" Kruder said. "They fired at us?"

"In our direction."

"They're attacking us?" Fusterheim asked. "Kapitan, we must respond."

"Did they hit?"

"No sir. Passed by. Perhaps they were really targeting the Castor."

"Why would they fire at the Castor?"

"Status change," the sensor operator announced. "Castor is rolling. Looks like they're unmasking their batteries to prepare to fire at us!"

"It's a trap!" Fusterheim yelled. "They've suckered us in. Kapitan, we must flee."

"Decamouflage. All stations stand by to engage."

Blomberg spoke. "Kapitan, I remind you, orders from the Council—"

"Shut up. The Council is not here, and they would not trade a spy for a warship. Target the Castor. All batteries fire when you bear."

The Pinguin yawed sideways, slewing around to point most of her weapons at the oncoming frigate. The sensor lashed out, decided that the Castor was stuck until she finished her roll, figured out a course, and passed it to all the weapons.

At Kruder's command, the weapons officer shifted the main batteries to computer control and turned on the automatic sequencing.

The Pinguin's lasers would fire in a staggered broadside, as the targeting computer directed. Like the Heart's Desire, it ran a target calculation, based on vector, distance, target capabilities, and likelihood of a vector change. Then it pointed each laser at a slightly different part of space and prepared to let loose. Even at this close range, it was unlikely that there would be any hits. Space is big, ships move, and even a minor change in course would have the ship move out of the danger zone.

Heart's Desire had hit the Castor with Dirk's wild, sweeping shot. Damage was limited, only a few control lines, but it was damage.

A sub-routine in Castor's computer woke up screaming. A ship previously ignored because it was listed as unarmed and harmless, was now not only armed, but in range closing fast and hard. And hitting with lasers. The main computer recalculated its threat matrix, and Heart's Desire now climbed to the top of the most list. Castor re-oriented to engage and destroy the now dangerous ship. Castor's computer rolled the whole ship and skewed it to target the maximum remaining broadside. It checked the Heart's Desire course history and detected limited ability to maneuver or dodge. Castor's computer decided to hold fire to align the most possible weapons at the best possible range and distance. It calculated the possible firing cone of the weapons detected on Heart's Desire and maneuvered away from it.

The Castor's main engine paused, the thrusters fired, the ship yawed, the main engines fired again. Castor moved into optimal position to destroy Heart's Desire with one salvo.

Which was why, from Kapitan Kruder's point of view, his opponent suddenly turned his most vulnerable side toward him, yawed, and flew directly into the path of his first broadside.

"Hits! Multiple hits!" Pinguin's sensor operator yelled. "Again."

"Good work!" Kruder clapped his hands in excitement. "Well done!"

"Firing! Hits again. Severe damage to Castor."

"How many of the broadside hit?"

"All of the forward lasers!"

"Repeat that."

"They all hit, Kapitan. Every single forward laser. And again! We're shredding them!"

"Good job." Kruder clapped his hands again. "How many hits?"

"Hitting again. We're pounding them. No response!"

The sensor operator interrupted. "Castor is not maneuvering. Neither thrusters nor main drive."

"We got both?"

"She's on a ballistic course, Kapitan. We see power, and there are radar emissions, but no maneuvering."

The helmsman placed his hands over the controls. "Close for a better shot, Kapitan?"

"Where are the other ships?" Fusterheim asked. "The other frigate?"

"Pollux is maneuvering!" The sensor operator's hands flew. "Climbing. Base course points at us. Her thrust is down, but she can still catch us."

"Kapitan!" Blomberg grinned. "Kapitan. We can destroy both of these cursed Imperials, and nobody will know."

"Except that freighter."

"We will destroy them too!"

"Before or after we take off the prisoner?"

Blomberg's face fell. "I forgot about him, Kapitan."

"Kapitan," Fusterheim said. "I have run the calculations. If we leave now, we can beat the Pollux to the jump limit, even with her thrust advantage. But we must go now."

"Kapitan," Blomberg responded. "We need to capture that spy. And we can take—"

"No, youngster, we can't," Fusterheim said. "That was luck. They were damaged, and they weren't ready for us." And just hope he doesn't ask why they turned toward us then. "We must do our duty, Kapitan."

"Duty?"

"We have recordings of two brand new Imperial units in combat, and recordings of their range and acceleration profiles. This is valuable information, and it should go back to the War Navy. If we stay, we risk not only destruction, but the loss of extremely valuable intelligence." Fusterheim turned so that Kruder couldn't see him and winked.

Kruder grimaced. "Our duty is clear. Helm, bring us around. We're withdrawing. Flank speed for home."

Blomberg turned. "Kapitan, we cannot leave the spy."

"We must."

"The Council demands—"

"The Council is not here. And if they were, they would agree that this information is worth a single spy who has already escaped."

"Are you betting your career on that, Kapitan?"

"I already have. Carry on, Helm."

Blomberg stood, stepped over the helm, and covered the helmsman's hands. "Stop. Kapitan, I cannot allow this. In the name of the Council, I am assuming command of this vessel, and ordering us to follow that spy."

"Mutiny, Leutnant? Here? In the face of the enemy?"

"I know my duty, Kapitan."

"You know the penalty for this!"

"We will not—"

The helmsman stood, spun Blomberg sideways, then punched him in the jaw.

Blomberg thudded to the deck.

Fusterheim stepped up. "He really does have a glass jaw. Helm, you heard the Kapitan. Carry on."

"Hans, call engineering and get us extra power. We need to get away from the Pollux."

"Of course, Kapitan. And I will call medical for young Blomberg here?"

"Yes, of course. Of course." Kruder leaned sideways and looked at the leutnant, passed out cold on the deck. "Call medical. But talk to engineering first."

"Status change!" Pollux's sensor operator yelled. The

bridge radio channels were still not working, but engineering had corrected the uncontrolled spin. "The Nat is firing on the Castor. Has fired. And again. Several salvos."

The Pollux had been spinning around the sky. Engineering had cut power to the broken thrusters. Maneuvering was affected, but at least possible.

Devin snarled.

"And again." The sensor operator put a damage display on the main screen. "Castor is venting atmosphere. Heavy damage. She's lost all acceleration."

"Weapons, target her positrons," Lionel ordered. "Get her weapons."

"Castor is not maneuvering. Dead on a ballistic. Not rolling either."

"Confirm that?"

"Her main drive is not firing. No evidence of thrusters."

"Check fire," Lionel ordered. "Helm, can we get in a blind spot protected from her weapons?"

"Yes sir, but that Nat is climbing. Climbing more. Looks like he's heading for the jump limit, Prefect. Should I chase him?"

Lionel hesitated, then looked at Devin. "Tribune?"

Devin shook his head. "Let the Nat go for now. He hasn't fired at us. Yet. Secure the Castor first. Communications, get me that Nat on the radio."

Lionel maneuvered the Pollux behind and above the Castor, hiding from any functioning weapons. The Castor's orbit now drooped into the atmosphere. Something would have to be done about that soon. Engineering wanted to cut power further to repair Pollux's thrusters and put some crew on the hull to fix control runs. They figured an hour, and they'd have maneuvering control back to the bridge, and perhaps half of the weapons up. Castor continued to drop, not firing.

Devin got Kruder of the Pinguin online after some back and forth between the comm officers on both ships.

"Tribune."

"Korvettenkapitan."

"How may I help you?"

"You fired on an Imperial warship."

"I was fired on first by an Imperial flagged naval auxiliary."

"Huh? A what?"

"The other warship."

"What other warship?"

"The Heart's Desire. She fired on us as we closed to retrieve our citizen. A retrieval that you authorized."

"The Heart's Desire fired on you."

"Yes."

"Hit you?"

"No. Hit the Castor in error, we believe."

"Wait." Devin shook his head. "Dirk fired at you but missed and hit the Castor?"

"Yes, then the Castor deployed to assist her in attacking us. We defended ourselves, of course, as was our right."

Devin looked up to see Lionel and the sensor operator playing back the battle. The sensor operator did one of those 'ohhhh-that's-what-that-was' nods.

"You're saying that the Castor was getting ready to attack you?"

"Yes. We have videos of her maneuvers after her consort's ineffective strike. I will say that such incompetence as was shown there would not be allowed in the Union of Nations War Navy but is perhaps typical of those who work with you in your Accursed Empire."

"I'll speak firmly to her Kapitan. I mean Capitan, Captain. I'll talk to Dirk."

"As well you should. You suggested earlier that we leave this system. We are doing so. I was unable to retrieve our citizen because of the dangers of the ongoing hostilities between your two units here. But I reserve the right to return and collect him at any time."

"Tell you what, Kapitan. I'll talk to the crew of the Heart's Desire. Any of them want to go live in the Union, I'll put them on the first liner I find, under guard. In your case, you are ordered out of Imperial Territory, effective immediately."

"We leave of our own accord. You cannot force us."

"Think you can take us?"

"We have just disabled one of your frigates. Another should be no bother."

Devin laughed. After a moment, so did Kruder.

"Til next time, Kapitan."

"Indeed." Kruder smiled, then very carefully dropped one eye in a wink to Devin.

Devin grinned and winked back, then cut the connection. He took a deep breath, then another, then looked up at Lionel, conferring with the helmsman again. "Prefect. Status?"

"We can fly and fight," Lionel said. "But not well. Castor

is in trouble, orbit is decaying. We need to get some people over there."

"Will we be allowed to make repairs?"

"We're in contact with a couple different groups over there. There's some dispute about who is in control. I don't think she will be doing any repairs until we get a team on-board. We're arranging to rendezvous now, and the Marines and repair parties will be standing by."

"Carry on." Devin snapped his fingers. "Dirk. Where's the Heart's Desire?"

Lionel shrugged. He looked at the sensor operator, who shrugged as well, then typed into his console. Ten seconds later, a picture popped up on the main screen.

"Doesn't look that damaged," Devin said.

"Nope," Lionel agreed. "But looks like they're missing a container on the bottom. Like something fell off."

"Hope it wasn't important," Devin said.

CHAPTER FIFTY-FOUR

"Catch, Rocky." Scruggs bounced the ball off the compartment wall onto the overhead. Rocky the whippet, now an experienced low-gravity chaser, pushed off from the corner, backwards. The ball bounced down from the overhead, right into the jaws of a spinning Rocky. He rolled onto his back and bounced himself off the far deck and back onto Scruggs's lap.

"Well done, dog." Ana ruffled his hair. "Outstanding spatial awareness. Great recovery."

"That dog is talented for sure," Dena said. "His three-D skills are amazing. Just like this soup." The crew had gathered to finish off the last of the soup Tribune Devin had sent over.

"That Imin guy is an incredible cook," Gavin said.

Scruggs spooned some into her mouth. "Is Gerhart Sorge really your name, Gavin?"

"Is Scruggs really your name?"

"No. I made it up."

"So did I. It's a historical reference. I read a story once

about a guy with that name. I liked the story, so that's what I used."

"Gavin isn't his name either," Ana said. "Great soup."

"I'll bet Anastasios isn't your name." Gavin picked up his bowl and licked the rim.

"It is. One of them."

"One of them?" Scruggs copied Gavin. "What are the others?"

"Mind your own business, and none of your concern. In Greek, of course, Private."

"And Lee's full name is…"

"Michaelson," Dena said. "Lee Michaelson. It's in the crew list. Is that your real name as well?"

Lee shook her head and took the bowl waiting for her. "Not relevant."

"Am I the only one who uses my real name?" Dena asked. "The only honest person here?"

"As far as honesty goes, you stole your way onto this ship and started a war." Ana spooned the last of the soup. "And as far as names go, nobody outside of Rockpit cares what you're called."

"Rockhaul. What happens next, Lee?"

"Pilot's helping those Marines undock. Tribune Devin said they should take the special communicator back with them, and I gave them all those Nat software coding modules to take back. I think he can make use of them."

"We could have sold them to somebody," Gavin said. "Coding modules are worth money."

"He could have blasted us out of space," Lee said. "No consequences for him, just another missing freighter."

Lee glared at Gavin. Gavin glared back.

"Says the Imperial rebel," Gavin said.

"Says the foreign spy," Lee said.

"I love it when the family eats together, makes me all warm inside," Ana said. "But to answer your question, Pirate Princess, once Navy and the Tribune guy finish yelling at each other, we're probably continuing back into the core to investigate for him. And get that laser fixed."

"Why will they yell at each other?"

"Dirk didn't do what the Tribune said, so the Tribune will have to assert his authority over Dirk. Dirk helped save his butt, so the Tribune will have to apologize."

"More alpha male posturing."

"Yep." Ana dropped his spoon. "Did I just agree that Navy is an alpha male? What's in this soup?"

BONG BONG BONG. "General quarters. General quarters." The alarm rang through the whole ship for five seconds then cut off.

"Who put that setting on his board? Gavin? Can you fix that?"

"I think I need to fix that burning set of capacitors on the ventral surface first. That laser stuff, you remember?"

"Sorry, that was me," Dena said. "I had the sensor screen up, and he said to leave it there, he wanted to look at something."

"You go see what he wants." Ana grabbed Rocky's ball. "The rest of us are going to play fetch."

"No need." Dirk had come back from the bridge. "Just finished talking to the Tribune."

"And he fired you as captain, and Princess Dena is in charge now?" Ana asked.

Dena giggled. "Fun! I can get a new wardrobe. What does a pirate captain wear?"

"You'll have to pilot the ship and dock it. Think you can do that?"

"I don't think I have the skills, Centurion. I'm not so good in three dimensions yet."

Ana rubbed Rocky's hair. "Let Rocky help. He's good with three dimensions. He can bounce around like nobody's business. He'd make a great pilot."

"True." Dena nodded. "He's got all the characteristics of a pilot. Tongue hanging out, drooling on every woman in sight, humps your leg. Hard to tell him and Dirk apart most of the time."

"I have thumbs," Dirk said. "Lets me operate the controls."

"If we ever get Rocky cybernetic limbs, you're out of a job."

"Til that day..." Dirk plopped himself down on his chair. "Tribune and I had a full and frank discussion. We're forgiven for taking so long getting a laser and not heading into the core right away. Mostly because he wants a closer look at that software Lee gave him. We're to head into the core and do some spying for him. Proper spying this time."

"No more spying," Ana said.

"He gave me more banking codes, Centurion," Dirk said.

"What are we waiting for then? Let's get spying. Does he want super spy here?" Ana jerked his fingers at Gavin.

"I talked him out of it."

"Really?" Gavin said. "Why?"

"We need an engineer. You're a good one. When we have problems, you help us out. I don't want to lose that. You're getting paid. Do you want to go somewhere else?"

"Nope." Gavin shook his head. "Staying here is easier, now that I don't have to hide so much of my past. Besides, I kind of like you all."

"Awww. Let's all hug," Ana said. "Just give me a minute to get my hand on my wallet."

"What's he going to do?" Lee asked.

"Not sure. He said for us to carry on, and gave me some rendezvous sites, and some new codes. He's got a rebellion to plan now."

"Why didn't you tell me?" Lionel yelled. He and Devin were in the Tribune's cabin after Devin had signed off from Dirk. Devin was sorting different calibers of small arm ammunition on his desk.

"Tell you what?"

"That you had arranged for Dirk to fake fire at the Pinguin, and have Kruder blast the Castor?"

"That was an accident. Circumstance." Devin held up a cartridge "At least as far as you know. Is this a rifle bullet?"

"Jove's testicles. No, it wasn't. It was a setup. And that's a cartridge, not a bullet."

"If it was, and I'm not admitting it. It was a neat setup, wasn't it?"

"Why didn't you tell me?"

"Assuming that your suspicion is correct, which I am not

confirming. First, I didn't want the knowledge of what was going to happen, or could happen, to cloud your tactical judgment. You had to be fully invested in the fight, your reactions had to be genuine. Otherwise, Castor wouldn't have been so focused on you. They would have suspected a trap. Second, Pinguin is technically an enemy ship. We might lose, and if we lost, I didn't want there to be any blowback on the crew, or you, or Dirk, or anybody else. Who knows what would come out in interrogation afterward?"

"You almost got us killed because you wanted genuine reactions? That's why you didn't tell us?"

Devin rolled the cartridge between his fingers. "Are you sure this isn't a bullet?"

"The bullet is the metal thing inside. That's a bullet, the propellant, and the primer. It's called a cartridge."

Devin typed on his desk and started paging through screens. "No. I didn't tell you anything then, and I'm not telling you anything now, because I promised on my honor as an Imperial noble that anything Kruder and I discussed wouldn't go any farther. Same with Dirk. That's why I didn't tell anybody anything. I promised. I do what I promise."

Lionel walked to the sideboard and poured himself a drink.

"Help yourself to my liquor, Prefect."

"I checked. It's technically the captain's cabin. Which made the contents my liquor. Or did, for a little while. You can have it back after this drink."

"I pay for it."

"Pay more." Lionel swallowed. "Your taste in booze is dropping."

"All we could buy out here." Devin brought up pictures of ammunition. He held the cartridge up next to the screen and paged through. "But don't worry. Engineering says both us and the Castor will be jump ready shortly. I'm taking us back to rendezvous with whatever units we can find, repair the battle damage."

"And you'll buy better booze?"

"First, we'll fix the ships. Second, there're a few pirate contacts that Imin and Dirk provided information on. We'll have those taken care of. Third, Dirk's ship is in reasonable shape, and I'm sending some information with Lee coreward. They're going to sound out the local governors and see who will be on what side, and get some intelligence of fleet movements." Devin sat the cartridge on his desk and tapped his screen. "If we're going to rebel, we're going to do it in style." The screen bonged. Devin swung it around to face Lionel.

"Order accepted. Cued for transmission," Lionel read. "Oh good, now that we have a steady supply of rifle bullets, we're ready to take on the greatest empire in known space."

"They're called cartridges, not bullets, Prefect." Devin grinned. The intercom beeped. "Yes?"

"Tribune," Trevor said. "Engineering reports both ships jump ready now. We can go back to Fawkes. And we have tentative courses laid in coreward from there."

"Very well, let me know when we clear the jump limit."

"Already done sir. We can go anytime."

"Stand by." Devin clicked the intercom off and faced Lionel. "Well?"

Lionel raised his glass. "The Empire!"

Devin toasted him. "The Empire." He clicked the intercom back on. "Jump."

Get a Free Ebook

Thanks for reading. I hope you enjoyed it. Word-of-mouth reviews are critical to independent authors. Please consider leaving a review on Amazon or Goodreads or wherever you purchased this book.

If you'd like to be notified of future releases, please join my mailing list. I send a few updates a year, and if you subscribe you get a free ebook copy of Sigma Draconis IV, a short novella in the Jake Stewart universe. You can also follow me on Amazon, or follow me on BookBub.

Join my mailing list here:
https://BookHip.com/JTHTJK
Andrew Moriarty

ABOUT THE AUTHOR

Andrew Moriarty has been reading science fiction his whole life, and he always wondered about the stories he read. How did they ever pay the mortgage for that spaceship? Why doesn't it ever need to be refueled? What would happen if it broke, but the parts were backordered for weeks? And why doesn't anybody ever have to charge sales tax? Despairing on finding the answers to these questions, he decided to write a book about how spaceships would function in the real world. Ships need fuel, fuel costs money, and the accountants run everything.

He was born in Canada, and has lived in Toronto, Vancouver, Los Angeles, Germany, Park City, and Maastricht. Previously he worked as a telephone newspaper subscriptions salesman, a pizza delivery driver, a wedding disc jockey, and a technology trainer. Unfortunately, he also spent a great deal of time in the IT industry, designing networks and configuring routers and switches. Along the way, he picked up an ex-spy with a predilection for French Champagne, and a whippet with a murderous possessiveness for tennis balls. They live together in Brooklyn.

Please buy his books. Tennis balls are expensive.

57

BOOKS BY ANDREW MORIARTY

Adventures of a Jump Space Accountant

1. Trans Galactic Insurance
2. Orbital Claims Adjustor
3. Third Moon Chemicals
4. A Corporate Coup
5. The Jump Ship.

6 The Military Advisor
7 Revolt in the Palace
Decline and Fall of the Galactic Empire

1. Imperial Deserter
2. Imperial Smuggler
3. Imperial Mercenary.
4. Imperial Hijacker
5. Imperial Privateer

www.ingramcontent.com/pod-product-compliance
Lightning Source LLC
Chambersburg PA
CBHW061533190726
48289CB00004B/1030